TRAIN HOPPERS – THREE

REBELS & SAINTS

CATCHING FREEDOM

LENA GIBSON

Black Rose Writing | Texas

This is a work of fiction. Names, characters, businesses, places, events, and incidents are either the products of the author's imagination or used in a fictitious manner. Any resemblance to actual persons, living or dead, or actual events is purely coincidental.

ISBN: 978-1-68513-587-4
LIBRARY OF CONGRESS CONTROL NUMBER: 2024948422
PUBLISHED BY BLACK ROSE WRITING
www.blackrosewriting.com

Printed in the United States of America
Suggested Retail Price (SRP) $24.95

Rebels and Saints is printed in Minion Pro

*As a planet-friendly publisher, Black Rose Writing does its best to eliminate unnecessary waste to reduce paper usage and energy costs, while never compromising the reading experience. As a result, the final word count vs. page count may not meet common expectations.

For my mom.

Praise for Rebels & Saints

"Multiple story lines are skillfully intertwined into a complex tale of survival. Gibson will have you rooting for each of her characters to survive the coming fight. Like *Star Wars* and *Lord of the Rings*, the *Train Hoppers* trilogy is the tale of ordinary people doing extraordinary things under dire circumstances to bring freedom from tyranny. Don't pass on this trilogy."
–Gary Gerlacher, author of the *AJ Docker series*

"Fitting Conclusion to an Enthralling Dystopian Series! I'd been waiting anxiously for the conclusion to this engaging series, and it did not disappoint. Gibson does a masterful job of pulling several disparate story lines together, weaving the tales of several characters into a spell-binding chronicle of a not-so-distant future."
–Bill Schweitzer, author of *Doves in A Tempest*

"The future of the West will be decided in a clash between the evil Greencorps and the ragtag Rebels...get a running start, leap for a handle, and pull yourself aboard for the epic conclusion of the *Train Hopper* trilogy."
–Cam Torrens, award-winning author of *Stable, False Summit,* and *Scorched*

"In this final book of her trilogy, Lena Gibson excels once again, creating another thrilling train-hopping adventure in the rebels' fight against GreenCorps. With a few new engaging characters added to the mix, this is a heart-palpitating journey across Western America in the year 2195 when my favorite group of freedom fighters struggle to reinstate democracy. Ms. Gibson is a skilled writer, creating characters I will miss terribly and a storyline that kept me on the edge of my seat. This is a must-read series!"
–A.J. McCarthy, author of the *Charlie and Sim mystery series*

"Good things come in threes, and *Rebels and Saints*, the final volume in Lena Gibson's Train Hoppers series, is a good thing. Gibson's talent for crafting believable characters and world-building is unmatched. Everything comes to a head in this final showdown between good and evil."
–Karen K. Brees, author of *The WWII Adventures of MI6 Agent Katrin Nissen*

"Lena Gibson does it again! The story of Elsa and Walker comes to a close in this edge-of-your-seat finale where bravery and sacrifice are wisely woven into the fabric of the tale."
–Michele Amitrani, author of the *Omnilogos Singularity* series

CATCHING FREEDOM

CHAPTER 1: ELSA

The broken, snow-capped dome of Mount St. Helens jutted upward, dominating Elsa's view. She stared into the distance, away from the waiting train leaving Canada soon. The river across from the train station had swollen from the fall rains while gray skies with shifting clouds loomed above. The trees on the hillside were a riot of color, yellow, orange, and brown, mixed with the varied green landscape. There was so much living green compared to SoCal, even now as the season changed.

She swallowed, clenched her jaw, and stepped aside as a small group of travelers bustled toward the well-kept train platform. She should be getting on that train. But waiting for her injuries to heal and the Canadians to replicate the key's electronics, which were old technology, would keep her here longer than planned. She hated being helpless and on the sidelines. The injuries she could work around, but waiting for the creation of duplicate keys was beyond her control. It made sense for her to be the one to wait.

Bright LED lights and a series of screens lined the station, so unlike home. News played on a loop, while departure and arrival schedules flashed between advertisements for a hundred unfamiliar places. Portland seemed like something from the future, instead of stuck in the crumbling past. That's what came from being a modern city and out from under GreenCorps' rule. Perhaps some other time Elsa could enjoy the benefits of the Canadian city, but right now so many lives depended on breaking the corporation's monopoly on food and water. She couldn't stay and didn't want to become too attached.

Last week, she'd handed over the original bunker key to the Canadian prime minister. The stately older woman had assured Elsa that their government would handle collecting and growing the seeds from the Doomsday seed bunkers from Corvallis and Pullman. They had resources that Elsa and the rebels didn't. Her original mission was complete, but she wanted to bring GreenCorps to its knees. She now considered herself a rebel.

Elsa glanced at Tatsuda with his backpack slung over his shoulder and bit the inside of her lip, determined not to fret. "Have you got everything?" She'd asked twice already, but the words jumped out of her mouth on their own accord. He would think she was acting like a mother hen again.

Walker's handsome face broke into a crooked grin. "She can't help herself." He squeezed her arm to accompany his gentle teasing. He knew her so well.

"We've got it." Tatsuda stepped forward to give Elsa a hug. When had he gotten taller than her? "You don't have to worry. I can take care of myself. I lived on my own for six years before we even met. Remember?"

With his bunker clothes and the new purchases from Portland, the young man barely resembled the scrawny youth who had joined her and Walker in Reno last spring. It was more than the haircut, clean clothes, and broader shoulders. Tatsuda projected confidence and now looked like the fifteen or sixteen-year-old that he was. He must have grown almost a foot in the six months she'd known him. He no longer looked like a street waif.

"It's not just yourself anymore." Elsa let out a long breath.

"I'll be fine too," said Ginger from beside him.

"You're the sensible one. It's not you I worry about," said Elsa, shooting the girl a quick smile. "And I appreciate that you promised to send updates when you can."

As expected, when Tatsuda volunteered for this job, Ginger followed within a second.

Ginger McCoy had dyed her flame-colored hair an inconspicuous shade of brown and had extra henna dye in her bag so she could keep the roots from giving her away. It was dangerous to send her to SoCal, but it was a move that the GreenCorps elite, including her father and brother, shouldn't see coming. They expected Ginger to stay out of GreenCorps territory now that she'd gotten away. They underestimated her grit. As someone who'd grown up with luxury, ample food, and water, they wouldn't expect her to head to a hell hole like SoCal where she'd be in danger of starving. She could hide right under their noses. Brilliant.

With few other options, that was the plan.

"This is a big ask," Elsa said. "The Heap isn't like other places."

"We know," said Tatsuda with a pointed stare. "But you've briefed us. Hide our coin. Find Avery and the girls. Help get them out of SoCal. We'll pay attention to curfew and follow the rules. We'll make sure your family has food and water. Nobody will look at us twice." His tone was somewhere between exasperated and patient.

"Try and keep your theft to a minimum." Elsa couldn't help repeating that part. Tatsuda could slip a tablecloth from the table during dinner, then lift dessert and the cutlery if nobody was paying attention. But, it only took one moment of bad luck to get caught and face harsh penalties, like deportation south. That would help no one.

She narrowed her eyes as Tatsuda shifted his stance, his eyes flicking toward the open door of the train. She sighed. "What have you taken since we left the house?" Best to be specific and send him off clean.

He blushed and emptied his pockets, passing two watches and a wallet to her waiting hand. "Just checking that I still can. You never know when pick-pocketing will come in handy."

Elsa would turn the contraband into the train station *"Lost and Found"* before she and Walker headed home. Someone might claim the missing items. She massaged the ever-present headache by her jaw and temple, trying not to let on how much it ached. Walker's quick eyes followed her movement. No fooling him.

Walker gave Tatsuda and Ginger hugs. "You two get going. For once, you get to ride a train with seats and a roof over your heads. Enjoy."

"It won't be as fun as hopping," said Tatsuda, "Even if it's less dangerous." His subdued manner made having a ticket and riding with passengers seem boring.

"There'll be plenty of other chances," said Ginger. "We're switching trains in Sacramento. We'll get to hop then." She patted his hand and some of the sparkle returned to his hazel eyes.

Thrill-seekers. Both of them. Walker was no better, and if Elsa was being honest, she was also jealous of their trip.

Tatsuda and Ginger would hop from Sacramento to Long Beach. They planned to ride the first leg of the journey in the open, even if they used false names, then hop a train to SoCal, sneak into town, and find Elsa's sister. If Jaxon McCoy had been telling the truth, he'd thrown his wife and children out, to be at the mercy of GreenCorps and the Heap—a generational work camp with harsh conditions at the best of times. For an unemployed single mom with two small children, prospects of getting by on their own were poor.

Elsa hoped Jaxon had been lying, as he'd seemed to care for Avery before the latest mess and his quarrel with Elsa escalated with his brother's death. But, based on his drama in court two weeks ago, he'd seemed unhinged. His claim had carried the ring of truth.

She couldn't help worrying about conditions in SoCal. There'd been a clampdown on the water supply since the spring. Times were tougher than ever.

Before Elsa had fled, she'd stockpiled water tokens and hidden her renewed Heap recovery license in a safe location that Avery would know to look since they'd often hidden valuable finds when younger.

Those things could be sold, but the proceeds wouldn't last more than a month for her sister's small family.

Avery couldn't work while tending her children, who were two and four, so she couldn't return to scavenging the Heap, even if so inclined. Which she wasn't. Avery had sworn never to work in that filth again. She'd always hated scavenging and been too claustrophobic to work the tunnels. There was no way she could handle the sector on her own, and it would be tough to find a partner she trusted. Or anyone who would take a chance on Jaxon's castoff wife.

Elsa took a deep breath. Her family needed help and with her concussion, broken ribs, and a price still on her head, she couldn't go home. Instead, she was sending Tatsuda. His resourcefulness and ability to keep a low profile would be invaluable. Ginger wanted to meet her sister-in-law and her nieces. Plus, Tatsuda was her best friend, and they were inseparable.

Tatsuda took Ginger's hand, and they left, climbing the stairs into the train's passenger car at the front. He waved from the top stair and disappeared within.

"I wish I could go," said Elsa. "My injuries aren't that serious."

Walker draped one muscular arm around her and kissed her temple. "Follow the doctor's instructions. We're going back soon enough. We'll do our part when you stop getting headaches and your ribs have healed. By then, we should have the special keys."

She couldn't leave just yet, as Jaxon would have left people watching for her to leave Portland. Even though he'd been banned from Western Canada, he would have spread enough money around when he was here, that someone would report her departure. She met Walker's warm gray eyes, grateful that he'd be with her when she traveled back.

Down the line, the freight cars crashed as they inched away from the station. Elsa watched it head south, the engine gaining speed as it headed toward GreenCorps territory, leaving Canada and the refuge they'd found three weeks ago.

Elsa waved, wishing good luck to Tatsuda and Ginger. They would need it. The only fond memories of SoCal she had were about her family. It would have been impossible to return without expecting to see Granny at every turn. Tears pricked behind her eyes and she willed them away. Regret still lingered that Granny had died shortly after Elsa had fled, and she'd never gotten to say goodbye to the feisty old lady who'd raised her.

Elsa's throat remained tight as they walked back to the house allotted for the length of their stay in Portland. Mason and Caitlyn were still here, though they'd be leaving later this week. They were headed back to join the rebel leader, Elsa's great-uncle, who was Caitlyn's friend and Mason's father. Staying behind chaffed, but Elsa wouldn't be sidelined for long. She was ready to help take the fight to GreenCorps and end their monopoly.

CHAPTER 2: JANNA

If Janna ever saw her damn brother again, Wade would wish he'd never been born. Horrid as it was being shipped to Texas and being a whore, the worst part was her asshole brother had sold her into this life of drudgery. She stared out through her dirt-streaked bedroom window at the perpetual smoke-gray skies of San Antonio. She'd never thought she'd find somewhere grimier and harder than SoCal, but this place was hell. Even inside, the greasy air carried an acrid taste—like burnt rubber and heavy fossil fuel smoke.

Turning from the window, Janna flopped on her bed and stared at the cracked ceiling, watching an enormous spider scurry from one corner to another and then disappear into a gaping hole. She shivered at the thought of its furry legs scuttling across her skin. Dealing with drunk, groping men was easier than dealing with huge crawling bugs at night. She snatched a ripped sock, wadded it into a ball, and stuffed it into the crevice. While she couldn't keep all the critters out, it might help. She sighed. Who was she kidding? Insects were the least of her problems.

Wade had come to her last spring, saying he'd found her a new job and he'd worked out the details. She'd been so excited. It wasn't working a fish farm, which she'd hoped for, but had known deep down that dream hadn't been realistic, but he'd made the job sound like an opportunity—so much better than her former work sifting beach refuse that washed ashore. She'd believed him, packed a duffel for her out-of-town job, and followed him to the train station, thrilled with the prospect of escaping SoCal and the nowhere life her family had fallen into when her dad had lost his railway job three years ago.

Though it had only been five months, she felt like a different person than the one she'd been back on the beaches of SoCal. That gullible young woman had known nothing about life. These days, she was more realistic. For many, unless you were one of the lucky ones, making a living was a dead end with a bleak future. You worked, you slept, you died. She wasn't sure how much longer she could take that kind of nothing existence. Shouldn't there be a point to living?

She closed her eyes and took a deep breath. It was hard to face another day at her job. Only the hope that one day she would escape kept her from giving in to the drugs some of the other girls did or from taking her own life. She wouldn't let Wade win. Once more, she leaned back onto the lumpy mattress, wishing she was anywhere else. With ten minutes left before her shift, her mind drifted and memories of her brother's betrayal came flooding back.

Loaded onto the train car like cargo, Janna shivered, though she should've been hot, pressed into the crowd. The stench made her gag—sweat, urine, and shit with an undertone of terror. Though it was only late April, the stifling heat of SoCal made the air pungent in the confined space. Traveling third class, she had low expectations, but a seat would be nice. Where were the benches? Confused, she twisted, about to ask her brother a question, but Wade had disappeared. She turned and shoved her way toward the opening, fighting the steady current of incoming passengers.

When she tried to step outside, a uniformed GreenCorps soldier barred her way.

"Not so fast, missy. Once you're on board, you don't get off until we reach our destination."

"Where's the train going?" An uneasy feeling crept over her as she stood and scanned the people milling about the train station. Maybe she should have asked Wade more about her new job. The guards must have heard the fear in her voice as they shifted, blocking the doorway more fully. Why hadn't her brother stayed to say goodbye? He must have gotten distracted by his fellow soldiers. He should still be nearby. There must be some mistake.

She leaned forward. The guard on the left flailed toward her with his gun, and she stepped out of the doorway and back inside, fighting a wave of panic.

She lifted onto her tiptoes and angled herself against the faded sun-baked metal of the boxcar, peering out from the dim interior through a jagged gap in the wall near the door hinge. She inhaled the scant fresh air and peered outside, still searching for Wade. A burly guy in a GreenCorps uniform shouldn't be that hard to spot. He was taller and broader than most and had that damn ugly beard that made him look like an ogre.

There was nothing of interest to see and still no sign of her brother. Anxiety rose to choke her. The familiar sight of a group of a dozen scruffy men, most wearing the woven plastic shirts and ponchos of SoCal, marched into sight. Their chains jingled as they walked, taking small steps with their ankles hobbled. Deportees. Prisoners and thieves. They were men who'd broken the law and were being sent to work camps even harsher than SoCal. Places like Texas.

Their escort in black and green didn't include anyone she recognized. An uneasy feeling trickled down her spine as the prisoners loaded into the same train car where she stood at the edge. They filed into the shadows at the front. This had to be wrong.

"Wade," she screamed out the door, hoping he would materialize and save her from this nightmare. "Wade." There was no answer, and panic lent a fluttery sound to her voice. "Excuse me," she said to one of the guards. "I was wondering…"

Before she finished speaking, he sighed and half-turned in her direction. "The bucket's at the front. You should have used the facilities before you loaded."

Her cheeks burned and her voice caught. "That's the thing. I'm not supposed to be here. My brother organized work for me out-of-town. I think putting me into this car has been a mistake." She squeezed her fist, her nails biting into her palm.

The other guard watched the last of the grubby prisoners filing in, but let out a loud guffaw. "We heard your brother sold you south, honey. Get outta the way. We've got to load this lot and hit the rails."

It couldn't be true.

"Wade," she yelled again. There was no response.

Off balance, Janna stumbled, bumping into several other passengers before she regained her footing. She looked toward the bright spring sky outlined by the doorway. One woman beside her stared vacantly, kiting no doubt. Another glared. Janna tucked her bag closer to her side and tried not to cry or scream. She was a grown woman, and she struggled to keep her emotions in check.

Wade wouldn't have sold her—she was his sister. Would he? With a sinking feeling, she swallowed. For enough coin, or to curry favor with his superiors, he might. A sea of red swam before her eyes and a stabbing pain knifed through her skull as she became incapacitated by her fury. No wonder her fucking brother was gone. The coward. Could she get off the train? Maybe if she rushed the entrance.

Maybe it wasn't too late.

She'd just made up her mind to try again when the guards stepped away. With a scraping sound, the metal door closed, blocking off most of the outside light—also her hope of escape. From down the line, several other doors closed with a screech of metal on metal. Several minutes passed while she waited for something more to happen, her heart hopping in her chest, unable to settle.

Her chest tightened as the train lurched and inched forward. Several loud crashes followed and Janna grabbed onto the nearest wall to stay upright. Perhaps she could find someone to listen to her story when the train reached its destination. Maybe they would make an exception and send her on her way.

There must be lots of places better than SoCal. Perhaps she could find her own work. Something better than sifting the beach for plastic nurdles. There was only one reason she'd have been sold south, though, and she wasn't a whore. She'd find something decent to do for a living. She latched onto that shred of hope and clutched it close. Without it, she would despair.

That first afternoon, the soldiers tossed several dozen oatmeal bars inside, causing a wild scramble. They opened the sliding boxcar door wide enough to pass a bucket of water inside. Janna joined the throng as they passed the bucket from person to person. She gulped her share, even though the liquid must be full of germs. At least it was water. In SoCal, they'd learned not to examine water too closely. If it was wet, it was good. If you didn't have water, you died in a matter of days.

Staking her claim once more, she rode with her back to the wall, sitting on the floor. She glanced around, breathing the stuffy air through her mouth. Even doing that, there was no avoiding the stench. A few of the women sniffled and cried while one had a nasty racking cough, but there wasn't much talk over the grinding roar of the train. Janna would have to let this play out, no matter how scared she was.

She avoided moving for as long as possible, but after several hours, the need to relieve herself became urgent. She stretched her muscles before threading her way to the front and headed toward the reek of the sloshing bathroom bucket—now partway full. One of the chained men sat on the floor next to it. He wiggled his eyebrows when he caught her gaze and raked her from head to toe with a leer—taking far longer than necessary. His eyes remained on her while she undid her pants and slid them down. She shifted her shirt to maintain a modicum of dignity, but hovering over the bucket was awkward.

Janna's cheeks burned, and she stared in the opposite direction, pretending she was alone and that this journey wasn't degrading.

She'd waited so long that her bladder ached. The intense relief with the pressure release was almost pleasurable. Without covering chatter, the sound of her urinating seemed magnified. Privacy would have been nice. Even animals shouldn't be treated this way. Fumbling with her waistband, she straightened her dirty clothes, adjusted the strap of her duffel, and held her head high. Afterward, she retreated to a different section of the car, hoping to find another crack in the wall where she could breathe outside air.

Janna wasn't quick enough to snag a processed food bar the first day—or the second. She chose water. Her stomach gurgled for hours before settling into an aching knot of persistent hunger. When she stood, her head spun. It was easier to just sit and drift. Had the rest of her family known of the plan? Unlikely. She'd always been close to her parents. Her family hadn't been well off, but at least they'd shared what little they had. Except for Wade. He'd moved out three years ago when he'd been recruited by GreenCorps. Here, she had nothing.

She sank onto the filthy flooring by her chosen section of wall to pass the time and to reduce the swaying motion of the train that bothered her empty stomach. Her butt became numb and her clothing sticky with sweat, but moving took too much energy.

By the second day, her parched lips were dry and cracking, and she lived in a constant state of thirst. It hurt to swallow. She kept to herself, saving strength by sitting or leaning when possible in the limited space. At least with nothing to eat and so little to drink, she didn't need the bathroom bucket more than once a day. Even then, she endeavored to use it as seldom as possible. The creep maintained the same position each time. His staring when she relieved herself made her skin crawl.

For three days, the train headed east, stopping only to load other cars with more downtrodden people, many in chains. She wasn't a criminal and didn't have debts, but nobody listened when she approached the guards. Her fear and frustration grew as fast as the miles from home stretched farther. Should she rush the door the next time it opened and try to escape? The soldiers might shoot her, but she wouldn't have to face what awaited her at the end of the line. She couldn't take much more.

Janna stumbled off the train at the end of the third day, reeking and faint from hunger, desperate for food and water. They shoved the women into communal showers, gave them shapeless gray smocks to wear, and transported them to the auction block. She and three other dazed young women were sold to a mid-level pleasure house in San Antonio. The only way to eat was to screw whoever the owner said to screw.

Her first day in the whore house she wrote to her parents. It took weeks, but her parents wrote back, replying to her desperate plea for help. They couldn't afford to buy her freedom. While that hurt, it was even worse knowing that Elsa's Granny had been injured and the women next door had been forced to stop scavenging the Heap. Elsa had picked herself up and taken a job slinging drinks at Ginny's, the most notorious whorehouse in SoCal. She was a survivor. Reading between the lines, Janna's parents must hope she could do the same.

Janna was on her own.

She asked herself the same question every day since. "What would Elsa do to stay alive?" That's how she made it. Her friend was tough as nails and a fighter. Janna would try to be the same. She walled off her feelings, smashing her anger into a tight, contained ball, and dealt with life as it was now.

From that day on, Janna slipped into her new role as a pleasure house whore—followed orders and stayed out of trouble. The patrons might have sex with her body, but her mind drifted elsewhere. She didn't even cry anymore. She imagined herself married and living anywhere else. Some days it even worked. She had a few regular clients, rough railroad workers who were decent enough, just lonely. If she stayed off the drugs that pleasure house girls were known for, she might save up enough someday to pay her own way free. In five to ten years.

Until then, she'd do what Elsa did and survive.

The ruckus and increased activity of a train arriving down the block at the station brought her back to the present.

Life wasn't like one of Elsa's black market novels or like her Granny's stories. There was no one to rescue Janna. She'd lost her virtue and her pride, and nobody, except her family, knew or cared where she'd gone. She swallowed and closed her eyes to keep the angry tears at bay, needing to smother her raw feelings. Best to be hard.

As she got up, Janna smoothed her dark hair, applied some flaming red lipstick, adjusted her boobs to better display her wares, and headed downstairs. Time for work.

Chapter 3: Tatsuda

Tatsuda and Ginger slipped off the passenger car of the train, after an uneventful trip down the coast from Portland, and strolled into Sacramento. Nobody paid attention to them—just what he preferred. The view during the trip had been more interesting than he expected along the rocky shore filled with awe-inspiring forests. He'd never imagined trees so gigantic he couldn't see the top branches or so wide that several people holding hands couldn't have circled their width.

Sacramento had the usual mishmash of buildings built from repurposed brick, most of them belonging to GreenCorps. Besides the train station, their logo marked all food, hardware, and supply stores. No mistaking—this was another corporation town. Until Portland and Salt Lake City, which had independent stores, bakeries, and a variety of family-run businesses, Tatsuda had thought that was how everyone lived. Now, the GreenCorps monopoly stood out and he understood why the rebels thought it wrong.

This town was quiet, except along the strip of bars and brothels, where voices and music spilled onto the street as the evening business picked up. Tatsuda hadn't traveled this way last spring, and he scanned the seared brown hills above the station with interest, glad they'd arrived while there was still daylight. For all the risk, one thing he enjoyed about hopping was seeing new places. The land here was dry, like in Idaho, and different than Portland by the rivers, where greenery lined the water's edges.

The next train to SoCal was tomorrow morning, so they had time to wander. Wanted posters with Elsa's face still plastered every GreenCorps storefront. A reward of twenty gold coins was almost beyond imagination. Ten had been enough to jumpstart his search from Denver last spring. Still, almost as soon as he'd met Elsa and Walker, he'd decided he would never turn her over to the authorities to collect the reward. There were things more important than coin. Six months ago, he never would have believed he would have changed so much.

"Elsa wasn't exaggerating," said Ginger, probably noticing his gaze. She kept her voice to a murmur. "The posters are still everywhere. There's still a few left for me, too." She nodded to the poor likeness with fire-red hair. "It's a good thing she didn't come home. They'd spot her in a second, in a sleepy place like this. How long is the train ride to Long Beach?"

"Twelve hours. Walker told me where to camp outside town and the best place to hide to hop the train outside the station. He said Sacramento is pretty easy. It leaves at dawn, so we'll have to get up early."

"So, anything we want, we should get now," she said, looking at the storefronts. "I'd forgotten how quiet things are without cars and buses on the busy streets, like Portland." She'd liked the modern city, and many of its conveniences. One day, they'd even traveled through the city by bus.

Similar to most places in the West, at least in the GreenCorps-controlled lands connected by train, regular people traveled on foot or by pedal cab. He'd seen bicycles a few times in bigger cities, such as Salt Lake, Vegas, and Denver. Here, there seemed to be nothing but walking and the trains.

Tatsuda and Ginger didn't stay in town long, as they didn't need to buy anything else for their stay in SoCal. Before twilight, they hiked to the campsite Walker had recommended. It was above the station in the rolling valleys and hills, but not so close they would need to be on constant watch for security. They should be able to relax. Of course, there could be other hoppers around. Tatsuda had been on the wrong end of a few interactions in the past, but he wasn't alone this time and he no longer looked younger than his age. Hopefully, he seemed tough enough to keep predatory travelers at bay. If there was a possibility of trouble, they could hide.

He didn't make a fire. Instead, they ate a quick dinner from their packaged food, spread their sleeping bags, and he climbed in. Sleeping on the ground didn't faze him. He could fall asleep anywhere, but Ginger hadn't always lived rough. She'd grown up in a mansion. He smiled as she slid in next to him, her sleeping bag rustling as she settled. No complaints from her about conditions. She chose to see life as an adventure, one of the things he liked about her most—her positive attitude.

He relaxed, enjoying the peace away from the bustle of the cities, especially when he got to share it with his best friend. He listened to the breeze in the whispering grasses and the chirping sound of nighttime crickets. Once, he might have been disturbed by the mysterious sounds of nature, but Walker had taught him to identify the unfamiliar noises. Overhead, the night sky seemed huge, an inky dome with a sprinkling of white stars.

Tatsuda hadn't always noticed things like that, but Elsa had changed that. She'd grown up in Long Beach where it was dreary and ugly—so covered in smog she'd seldom seen the stars. Now she always took the time to admire them, often staying up later than everyone except Walker to stargaze. She said that everywhere she'd been since leaving SoCal seemed beautiful by comparison, but that the night sky was her favorite.

"What if Jaxon was lying and this is a trap?" Ginger kept her voice hushed.

Though quiet, her voice had seemed to come out of nowhere, startling Tatsuda. "Elsa thought he seemed unhinged enough to be telling the truth." He whispered in return.

"That's true. I'd never seen him rant like that. He was practically foaming at the mouth. He really hates Elsa."

"If it looks like Avery still lives in the fancy house on the hill, we'll lie low and catch the first train out." They shouldn't have much trouble evading the GreenCorps soldiers again.

"What if Avery doesn't trust us?"

That was Ginger's worry? If Avery had been abandoned, or left to fend for herself with no job and two small children, she'd probably be thrilled to have help. Even sent by her sister, the outlaw.

"I've got Elsa's note," said Tatsuda. "And she said her sister is the practical type."

"Did you read it?" Ginger's voice seemed curious, not judgmental.

He shrugged, though she probably couldn't see it in the darkness. "Elsa didn't seal it."

Ginger's voice changed, amusement leaking into her tone. "She knew you'd read it, anyway."

"True." The silence stretched while he waited for her to ask about the contents. She wouldn't be able to help herself. He'd give it a minute. Two at most.

"Do you have siblings?" Ginger's voice lowered, and she breathed deep.

One of her brothers was dead, and the other was a vindictive ass with a personal vendetta against Elsa. Ginger had chosen to stay with them over returning home with her brother. She wouldn't be welcome home now.

"No." He'd told her ages ago about being kicked out and being burdensome to his alcoholic parents by the time he was nine. If he had younger siblings, he'd be surprised. His parents had seemed intent on drinking themselves to death. He seldom spared them a thought. They weren't worth it and he'd gotten along okay without them.

"I think Elsa loves her sister. She was really worried. If Avery didn't go back to their old shack, how will we find her?"

"We'll find her." That part didn't worry Tatsuda. Someone in Long Beach would know where Avery was. Everyone would know who she was. Marrying Jaxon McCoy would have made her well-known, if only because of how rare it was to marry so far above her station. Some of those struggling to survive might even be pleased to see her knocked down.

"I wonder why Avery married someone mean, like Jaxon. How could my brother do that to his children? Just toss them onto the street like garbage." Ginger's sleeping bag rustled again as she flipped over.

Tatsuda shrugged again. Ginger worried about the hungry little girls. To distract his friend, he answered her unspoken question from a few minutes earlier. "Want me to tell you what the note said?"

"Yes, please."

"Dear Sister,

Though our uncle passed along the sad news about Granny's death, I can't come home right now. I'm sending my friends with my letter. One is your sister-in-law, and she's excited to meet you and the girls. She could be another sister for you. I think you'll like each other. Please trust them to help you—they're a resourceful pair. I'm hoping you will consider moving near our uncle now that you are on your own.

Take care of each other. Hope to see you in a few months.

—Your loving sister."

Tatsuda turned to face Ginger. Six months ago, he wouldn't have been able to snoop, not without her reading lessons. He was proud he'd learned so quickly.

Ginger's breath caught. "Elsa said that? She called me a sister?"

"She did. We're Elsa's family too. We're all any of us have, other than Avery and her little girls." He understood the awe in her voice. When he'd first realized he had a true family he could count on, he'd felt that way, too.

"I still can't believe I have nieces. I'm so excited to meet them," said Ginger. "When I was younger, I used to pretend I had little sisters to entertain in my tower room. I wanted to read with them and have tea and cookies." She glanced at him, her eyes shimmering in the pale starlight. "It helped to pass the time."

She must have been lonely on her own. Tatsuda yawned. He was tired, but he didn't mind Ginger talking. He might fall asleep anyway. Her voice was soothing.

"Jace was sweet to me when he was young. I don't know what I can do to help the girls, but I'll think of something." There was determination in her quiet voice.

"You'll be a wonderful aunt," he said. "We should get some sleep. I'll wake you when it's time to go. Okay?"

"Thanks for letting me tag along," she said.

He groped for her hand and squeezed it. "I'm glad you're here." His jaw creaked when he yawned again. He closed his eyes and let himself drift into peaceful sleep.

* * *

Tatsuda's eyes popped open and his muscles tensed. It was pitch black, so he listened for what had alerted him to a change in his surroundings, tilting his head first one way and then the other. He'd always been a light sleeper. Surprises were almost always unpleasant.

Voices.

Hushed voices on the path from below, coming toward their campsite. A faint glow of a portable lantern bobbed on the hillside. It became brighter as they moved closer. He covered Ginger's mouth lightly with a cupped hand and whispered. "Wake up. We've got company."

Her eyes fluttered open, and she nodded. Sliding from her sleeping bag as he did the same, taking care to make as little noise as possible. They rolled their bedding and stuffed it into their packs while the approaching voices grew louder. He made out three distinct, deep tones.

The men headed their way might be nothing serious, but he wasn't willing to take that chance. Even fellow hoppers or vagabonds could be trouble. Motioning to Ginger to follow, Tatsuda slid into the deeper shadows behind the massive rocks by the trailhead. They could slip away down the path if necessary or stay and listen to determine if the newcomers were dangerous.

"I don't know why we have to patrol up here. We haven't seen anyone out here in months. Nobody's dumb enough to hop trains to SoCal anymore. Even to Sacramento. There's nothing in this nowhere town." The disgruntled voice carried in the still night.

"Stop grumbling. McCoy's orders. He's convinced his bitch sister-in-law will be headed home soon."

There was a low, mocking laugh from another of the men, and Tatsuda recognized the last speaker's voice as he continued. "He dangled the perfect bait. She'll go home. That do-gooder won't be able to help herself."

Ginger stiffened beside him. She must recognize who this was, too. They'd run across this prize asshole twice before. Not only was Wade one of her brother Jaxon's men, born and raised in SoCal, but he'd attacked Ginger in Pocatello. That was the night Tatsuda had intervened and brought her to meet the others. She'd been with them ever since.

He averted his eyes from the light so he didn't ruin his night vision, trusting his other senses to alert him if the immediate danger increased.

"See," another said. "There's nobody here. No fire in the pit. No warm ashes. McCoy's wasting our time. As usual. He doesn't think straight where his sister-in-law is concerned."

Tatsuda and Ginger had gotten lucky. They'd eaten their dinner without a fire. He held his breath—while they remained rooted like trees. He pressed his hip against the cold stone to keep steady, his arm steadying Ginger beside him. She remained tense, but he admired her ability to deal with her fear.

"How much longer are we waiting in Sacramento?" said the first speaker. "There's nothing to do except drink."

Wade answered. "A few weeks. Maybe a month. If Elsa hasn't come through by that time, we'll probably get new orders. Let's go."

"Yeah. I want to head into town. I'd like someone to warm me up. There's a chill in the air tonight."

"Lead the way," said Wade. "I'm off tomorrow too and could do with a drink."

"More like six or eight," said one of the others as they left the clearing, passing the far side of the rocks where Tatsuda and Ginger hid.

The men tromped down the hill, their conversation fading and becoming indistinct.

Tatsuda kept his hand on Ginger's arm until it seemed safe for them to move.

She exhaled, blowing out the air in her cheeks. "That was close. That Wade makes my skin crawl. I don't dwell, but when I think about what almost happened in Pocatello, I feel sick. I don't think I'll be able to go back to sleep tonight."

"Me either. Let's settle in down by the train. Walker recommended the bushes and tall grass outside the trainyard at the far end. Let's try there. We've got time to adjust the plan if something below has changed."

They grabbed their packs and trudged down the path, alert for Wade and his fellow recruits, but the men were long gone—their pale light no longer evident. As Tatsuda and Ginger neared the train station, he slowed their pace and stepped with care. Security had been heightened since the troops had been waiting for Elsa. The bulls would patrol this area as a matter of course; the trick was to be outside, past the station. He and Ginger would hop the train when it was already moving but not yet up to speed. Getting off in SoCal unseen might be harder, and leaving still more difficult.

Best not to worry yet about getting out of SoCal—it might be tricky getting the young children on the train. He would make a plan after he met Avery and her little girls.

Chapter 4: Clark

Clark tugged off his sweaty, dust-covered work shirt to catch the last rays of warm sunshine on his tanned skin, tossing it to the ground at the end of the row. Pausing, he scanned the almost bare field. One more row would finish this section. This late in autumn, such a warm day was a bonus, and he wanted to enjoy every minute. Soon, he would be stuck indoors too much—with not enough to occupy his mind or body. Winter would be cold and at this elevation, just around the corner. Last year, there had been snow in late October and it would be several yards deep by December.

He surveyed the fields around the Saints' settlement up Ogden Canyon. They'd almost finished harvesting the second crop of carrots and peas. Last week, they'd finished collecting the potatoes and squash. Let the frost come. The Saints were ready.

Halfway to the end of the row, he stretched his weary back muscles. Stooping for hours to pull carrots and pick peas was back-breaking work, but familiar after having spent most of his twenty-five years on the family farm. Clark took a long pull on his canteen, relishing the cool water in his parched throat. He took a second to marvel at the variety of the food here. He'd grown up in Utah, where seeds were available on the black market in Salt Lake City—cheaper than seeds sold by GreenCorps. They were still terminator seeds—viable for only a single crop. Fields like these were a major investment.

Until his time away, Clark had taken food for granted, and after seeing so many starving people arrive from the South, he recognized he'd been lucky. While Clark sometimes missed his family's more modest farm, there was too much work there for one person now that his parents and brothers had passed on. It had also been too isolated, and he'd been beyond lonely. He'd left three years ago, choosing this out-of-the-way community in which to live.

Last fall, he'd heard that his sister-in-law Caitlyn had taken up residence on the Dawson farm at the mouth of the canyon, but this summer she'd gone on the run—one step ahead of GreenCorps. If she escaped her current trouble, she was welcome to the family farm. He didn't plan to return.

It wasn't the first time his thoughts had strayed to Caitlyn and his brother, Mat. They'd all been close years ago and if he allowed himself, he missed them like an integral piece of himself, like an arm or a leg.

While Clark believed in their cause—freeing the people from GreenCorps tyranny—he'd never been a rebel. His oldest brother Mat had joked throughout their youth, calling Clark "a lover, not a fighter." There was truth to that. There'd been a time he'd considered fighting with words, perhaps writing for the rebel underground movement, but he'd never shown his writing to anyone except Mat. Besides, Clark preferred the quiet life of neutrality with the Saints to the more dangerous lifestyle that had taken both his brothers too young. Violence wasn't for him.

Thoughts of the rebels and what he'd lost were upsetting, and Clark struggled to get back into his rhythm—to regain the pleasant feeling of growing food with his own hands through hard work and sweat. While the rebels had a noble cause, they'd taken everything he loved. His middle brother, John, had turned to drugs to numb himself from the pain of what he'd seen. His father had died doing a secret job, while his oldest brother, Mat, had gotten involved with rescue missions that were too dangerous, and he'd paid the ultimate price.

Clark pulled another section of carrots, shaking off the dirt, and adding the vegetables to his heavy bucket, tops and all. There were plenty of animals in the Saints' barns who ate the leafy greens.

When the last rays of sunshine disappeared over the mountains, leaving an evening shadow on the fields cast from the nearby mountains, he called it for the day. Enough. Looking around, he was alone in the fields—the others having knocked off an hour earlier. He had no one to miss him or cook his dinner, so he took his meals at the community tables in the church buildings, as did many of the single Saints or anyone living in the communal bunkhouses without their own houses. He collected his belongings, left his loaded bucket with the others in one of the storage sheds for processing in the morning, and headed toward the main settlement.

He washed up at the cleaning station outside, the cool water sluicing off the dirt as he scrubbed the soil from under his nails with the handy brush by the sink. Inside, he grabbed a plate, loading it with a baked potato, fresh greens, and slices of roast pork. The Saints seldom ate the processed food bars so common in corporation towns. He shuffled toward a quiet table in his usual corner and set his plate down.

"Clark?" A woman's astonished voice caused him to turn, his tongue tied in knots.

"Clark. It is you," said Caitlyn, as if conjured by his earlier thoughts.

Why would she be here among the Saints? She'd come through a few months ago, in secret, but by the time he'd found out, she was long gone. However unlikely, his sister-in-law stood in front of his table, loaded plate in hand and her startling blue eyes wide. He remained standing, a rush of emotion sweeping through him. He blinked a few times. She looked terrific, as usual—like an Amazon of legend.

"Give me a hug." She set her plate down and rounded the end of the table before he'd uttered a word.

She grabbed him and squeezed, looking him right in the eye. He always forgot how tall she was. "You look the same," she said. "What's it been, three years?"

"Four," he said, his voice scratchy from disuse. He swallowed to clear his throat. "You're the same too. Far too pretty to have married my ugly brother." He said things like this to her, but it was true. She still looked perfect.

She laughed, her blue eyes sparkling with mirth as she nudged his shoulder with her hand. "It's been too long, anyway. I'd heard you'd joined the Saints but didn't know you were so close to home."

"Have you left the rebels then?" he whispered, scanning the room for eavesdroppers.

Caitlyn shook her head, keeping her voice low too. "I took a break for almost a year, but now I'm deeper than ever. We're on our way to meet with Grady tomorrow." She glanced over her shoulder, her face becoming more serious. "I hope it isn't awkward, but I've met someone new." Her smile faded, perhaps worried about how he'd take that news.

His stomach dropped. She couldn't mourn Mat forever. Of course, someone like Caitlyn wouldn't stay single for long. Clark wouldn't have stood a chance. He should be happy for her.

It must be hard to move on and not feel guilty. He wouldn't add to it.

Clark peered over her shoulder, toward the kitchen. A tall slim man dressed in faded jeans, with a battered cowboy hat, and pistols on both hips, stood talking with Brother Campbell. In this peaceful community, his guns labeled him as an outsider. The Saints believed in standing apart from the conflict that plagued the West. Something about the stranger's stance seemed familiar, but Clark couldn't place him until the man turned in their direction.

"Mason." The name burst from Clark and he left Caitlyn, trotting across the room.

His oldest brother's best friend's face creased in a pleased smile.

"What do we have here?" said Mason. "Another Dawson, as I live and breathe. I wondered where you'd gone." He pulled Clark into another hug.

Clark tried not to stiffen up. Two hugs in one day. This was more than anyone had touched him in years.

"It was pretty empty on the farm after my parents passed." Clark shrugged. "I thought I might enjoy the quiet life in the mountains." He looked at the worn floorboards as he struggled to regain his equilibrium. He seldom spoke about his former life.

Mason probably hadn't had an easy time the last few years, either. He would have seen a lot of action in Texas, the last place Clark had heard Mason had been sent by Grady. There was too much death everywhere.

"I was sorry to hear about your folks." Mason had been like an extra older brother, having grown up on the neighboring farm with his mother. He and Mat had been inseparable.

Clark returned his gaze to his old friend.

"They were decent people." Sympathy showed on Mason's weathered face.

Clark swallowed. He still got an egg-sized lump in his throat thinking of his parents. John's overdose had hit them hard. Then, his father had been asked to help the rebels with a special, one-night job. It had been a disaster. He'd been there one day, gone the next. His mom had died of a broken heart, outliving him by less than a month. Clark was just glad they'd been spared the news of Mat's death. Now, almost two years later, only Clark remained from all the Dawsons. He imagined walls of ice, keeping the pain at bay.

"So, you and Caitlyn." Clark forced a smile to show his approval. They were a match that made sense.

Mason's eyes softened more than Clark had seen in all the years he'd known the man. The rebel had it bad. "Yeah." Mason rubbed the back of his neck. "We met again this summer. We were sweethearts in Denver when I was sixteen."

"Caitlyn was your Angel? The girl you left behind? That's unreal. That's an amazing coincidence," said Clark. Mason had phenomenal taste. There wasn't anyone in Clark's life that he longed to run into like that. He'd always been shy. Other than Caitlyn, he didn't talk to women if he could help it. He never had. He never seemed able to string words together in their presence, constantly tripping over his tongue.

"What brings you two up the canyon?" said Clark as he and Mason returned to Caitlyn and dinner.

She lifted an eyebrow from where she sat, eating. She tossed the length of her blonde braid over her shoulder. "You two caught up now?"

Clark narrowed his eyes. "What does that mean?"

She chortled, a sound that carried in the dining hall over the scrape of knives and forks on plates and the usual buzz of conversation. "You two are the least chatty people I know. What did you say in one minute?"

Her tone lowered as she imitated a man's voice. "You good?"

"Yeah, me too." She cocked her head to the side, her lips twitching as she spoke both sides of her made-up conversation.

An unexpected, slow smile spread across Clark's face. It had been too long since he'd been with family. "Something like that, though Mace told me quite a bit about you in the old days."

To his delight, her cheeks blossomed with pink. "Oh, he did, did he?" She turned to Mason and gave him a direct stare.

Mason kissed her temple and sat down beside her with his plate.

Clark sat to resume his dinner. "Are you here recruiting?" His food turned to ashes in his mouth awaiting their answer. Would they pressure him to join the rebels—something he couldn't do? Would they think him a coward? He shifted his focus to his pork as he sliced off another bite.

"We're here to collect my cat from Sister Hope. We left her here a couple of months ago. I'm going to take her back to the city," said Caitlyn. "Then we're off to Texas. Grady is sending us there for a while."

"I heard you were back at the farm and left in a hurry back in August." Clark hadn't realized Sister Hope's cat belonged to Caitlyn. Of course, he hadn't asked.

Caitlyn glanced at Mason before answering. She leaned in and lowered her voice, though there was no one in earshot. "We aren't just here for something so frivolous as just getting my cat. We delivered seeds to Brother Campbell and the Saints elders. There are lots more to come."

"Seeds?" He whispered back, feeling his forehead bunch. How was that a big deal?

"We met someone who found access to seed bunkers from before the Collapse. She found a long-lost key, and we helped her escape to Canada with GreenCorps hot on our trail. The Canadians are working with the rebels now. We're going to take down GreenCorps, once and for all."

Despite his promise to stay out of the fight, Clark was interested. "How will seeds topple their empire?"

"The seeds from before the Collapse are different. The plants yield seeds for new crops so people can grow more on their own. When we break their monopoly on food, people won't have to worry so much about subsistence. They'll have time to fight for what's right. We've been working with our friend Elsa, as well as Grady, to spread the word. It's a powder keg out there. Us rebels are just the ones to light it."

"Some people have a lot to lose if that goes sideways. Won't they just fill the workcamps again?" He didn't have much and couldn't get involved. He'd rather stay here, out of the way. "The Saints will be fine up here. GreenCorps mostly leaves us alone." Clark bit his tongue before he said more. Mason and Caitlyn would never be convinced. They'd chosen lives filled with danger.

"Not everyone is as fortunate as the Saints or the people of Utah. You'll see. The rebellion is starting for real, and we're a part of it." Her blue eyes shone.

Clark wished he could believe it would work, though even up here in the canyon, they'd heard of Elsa Lee. Few people had gotten away from GreenCorps and won. The price on her head ensured she was already a legend. Made sense Caitlyn and Mason were her friend.

Throughout dinner, they regaled him with stories of their adventures. They'd been inside a seed bunker deep underground and hopped trains across the country and into Canada. They kept him entertained and hanging on their words until his face split with jaw-creaking yawns. Exhausted, Clark stood and said goodnight, as he'd been up since dawn. When he headed to bed, so did they, holding hands as they strolled to the guest bunkhouse at midnight.

The words from their conversation persisted when he lay in his bunk trying to unwind—looping through his brain. Caitlyn and Mason seemed so sure they were going to bring change at last. Maybe someday, if they won, this could be a land of freedom and peace for everyone, not just the Saints. Right now, that seemed distant.

Instead of being pleased that GreenCorps' monopoly might break, Clark worried about the future. If the rebel plans didn't work, Caitlyn and Mason might get injured or die. His blood turned to ice water in his veins. The rebellion could take them, too. More people he cared about, dead for Grady's cause, and those that remained would still be under GreenCorps' thumb.

Clark tossed and turned, waking again in the early morning hours. He slipped out of his bunk and hurried to the fields and sorting sheds at first light, choosing to skip breakfast and goodbyes. It would be easier that way. Right? He wasn't so sure when Caitlyn and Mason rode away and he hadn't said farewell. His chest tightened. He hoped they didn't take his absence personally and that they would stay safe. He'd like to see them again someday.

Clark turned back to his task, shoving them from his mind. Cutting himself off was for the best. It didn't hurt so much when you were left alone. After all, he'd already lost just about everyone he loved. He couldn't take any more loss.

CHAPTER 5: MASON

Mason and Caitlyn finished their hearty breakfast of smoked bacon and fresh eggs, planning to hit the road. He stared around the Saints' dining hall, watching for Clark. He glanced at Caitlyn, who shook her head before they carried their plates to the bin beside the kitchen.

"Thanks for breakfast," Mason said to one of the kitchen staff.

The food was another reason he enjoyed being back in Utah, rather than traveling for the rebels. Their stay with the Saints had been brief, but it was always a welcome respite. The ride down the red rock canyon would take several hours before they would emerge onto the bench land where scattered farms ran parallel to the mountains. From there, it would be another full day's travel to Salt Lake City. Mason would take every precaution to arrive in the city without running afoul of GreenCorps.

He glanced at Caitlyn, who stood beside their waiting horses. They would pass her farm today. Should he suggest they stop there overnight? There would be some risk in staying—who knew if the place was being watched—but it would allow them to arrive in Salt Lake when it was busy tomorrow. They had a better chance of slipping in unnoticed than if they pushed on and arrived late at night. After the eleven o'clock curfew, the streets would be bare while an increasing number of soldiers patrolled.

Mason double-checked the straps on his tack before swinging onto his horse and settling into the saddle. He nudged the mare forward, and they headed for the canyon trail. Two days ago, when they'd disembarked from the train, he'd been pleased to find his horse in one of Grady's stables in Salt Lake as promised.

The Saints had delivered her to Grady, no questions asked when he, Caitlyn, Tatsuda, Walker, and Elsa had fled Caitlyn's farm and arrived at the Saints' settlement for an afternoon in August. His mare was steady, reliable, and well-trained. She'd been key to escaping several missions in Texas over the years. He'd disliked leaving her two months earlier, but he'd chosen to follow Caitlyn into the mountains on a trail too narrow and precarious for a horse, even his sure-footed mare. After a couple of hot meals and a nap, they'd trekked deeper into the mountains to avoid pursuit as they headed north.

As he rode, Mason's body automatically shifted into rhythm with the horse's motion, and his mind drifted back to last night's visit. It hadn't been as easy to see Clark Dawson as he'd let it seem. Mason had never pictured the fun-loving scamp he'd grown up with as the serious, aloof young man he and Caitlyn had spent the evening with. The initial exclamation of Mason's name from across the busy communal dining hall had been one of the few sparks of interest and sign of the old Clark all night. The rest of the time, he'd been reserved to the point of disinterest. What had happened to him? Mason's instincts told him that something more than Mathew's death had caused this much change.

At least Clark hadn't seemed to have a problem seeing Mason and Caitlyn as a couple. If anyone had the right to be upset, it could've been Mat's younger brother. Instead, Clark accepted their relationship with grace. Maybe he'd seen that they were both content and was genuinely happy for them.

Mason's thoughts remained stuck on Clark and his changed demeanor. Mason hadn't always been in a positive place, either. Hell, Caitlyn had changed Mason's life as much as Elsa and her mission with the seeds. A warm feeling filled his chest. He couldn't remember the last time he'd been content before their reunion. His gaze rested on Caitlyn riding just ahead, her cat peeking out of the backpack from time to time by lifting the top flap on the pack with its head.

Who cared so much about a tabby cat that they would trek two days into the mountains to retrieve one? His Caitlyn, that's who. She had a soft spot for children and animals. Hard as nails with a heart of gold. It had worked out that they'd been tasked to deliver seed packets, sent from the Canadian bunkers to Brother Campbell and the Saints' Elders. The northern bunkers had access to different seeds than the ones in GreenCorps territory. The Saints could be the first to grow the new crops with viable seeds they could collect and plant next year.

They rode down the mountain trail, toward the city, where they'd been asked to meet with Grady at rebel headquarters. The rebel leader said he had a plan about where he'd like to send them next, but Caitlyn had insisted on dealing with the seeds and collecting her cat first. Mittens could catch city mice while they campaigned.

Mason ran through scenarios for conversations with Grady, his estranged father. It was odd that Caitlyn and his father were close, friends even, when he barely knew the man as anything except the leader. Maybe with Caitlyn's help, Mason and his father could improve their relationship.

He kept a sharp eye on the windy trail below as they rode. They passed the dam and descended the steeper section of the canyon— water gurgling in the creek nearby as it flowed around the tumbled rocks. Near the water, bare shrubs had discarded their leaves, littering the ground with brown and yellow. Though the mid-day sun was bright, the shade of the canyon kept the ride pleasant. Mason remained quiet, deep in thought, the motion of the horse peaceful.

Though safer in Utah than most places, he and Caitlyn needed to watch for GreenCorps soldiers. While the Wanted posters were vague and the likenesses general, there was always a chance he and Caitlyn would be recognized. They weren't worth more than a gold coin each, but Mason would hate to be sloppy and get caught. Best to stay alert and out of trouble.

Traitors and informants were rare in Utah compared to the other western lands controlled by GreenCorps, but they popped up even here. People desperate for food could hardly be blamed. At least GreenCorps struggled in Utah. Between the rebels and the Saints, the corporation was unpopular.

After Caitlyn and Mason left the high walls of the canyon, the wide open plains stretched ahead of them dotted with sparse golden grass. The sway from the breeze fanned the tops in rippling waves, and a tumbleweed rolled across their trail. He scanned the open expanse. Lumps that Elsa said contained the remnants of buildings from long ago dotted the landscape, spreading toward the horizon. With so many mounds, this area must have been a city at one time. Now it was sparsely populated, with scattered farms like the one where he'd been raised.

The farther from the mountains they traveled, the more alert Mason became, often turning to check the trail behind. As a lifelong rebel, the twitchy sensation was an occupational hazard.

Their shadows lengthened behind them before they reached Caitlyn's farm in late afternoon. Mason glanced upward. Dark clouds scudded across the sky, traveling fast from the north. Maybe a windstorm or hailstorm was on the way. He turned his attention to the Dawson farm. The garden had been harvested, probably by the Saints or by Caitlyn's distant neighbors. Nobody would have left the food crop to go to waste; he didn't blame them. The chicken coop and animal pens were empty, the animals collected by the same friendly people.

Hopefully, the soldiers had left the locked root cellar below the house intact. Though she'd only been gone for two months, the farmyard wore an air of neglect without the roaming chickens or comfortable animal sounds from the pigpen and corrals. Nearing the cluster of buildings, he clicked his tongue in disapproval. Someone had smashed the windows of Caitlyn's house. GreenCorps soldiers were likely responsible for the destruction the night of the raid. At least, they'd considered the tinder-dry conditions in August and hadn't set fire to the buildings.

Mason had joined Elsa's group at the Dawson place for less than a week in August. Before that, he'd been living out of his saddlebags for as long as he could recall, but Caitlyn had occupied the farm for a year. Perhaps she could collect warmer clothes since the cold weather approached. They should at least inspect the damage. He'd hate for the upcoming storm or winter winds and snow to destroy her cozy house.

"You need anything from inside?" He tossed his head toward the house nestled below the row of barren fall trees, their branches whipping back and forth in the gusts of wind. Shelter from the storm sounded good too.

"I'd better not," she said, turning to look at him as she dropped back to ride at his side. "The Saints collected my animals so I have little to worry about. I brought everything important with me." Her eyes flicked to the holes in the windows and back to the trail toward the city.

"There's a storm ahead and we don't know if we'll be back before winter." He cast another glance skyward. "Let's board up the holes, at least." He could have the job done in under an hour, provided she had wood in the barn. "It won't take us long and best to be done before snow flies."

She shot him a grateful smile, dismounted, and guided her horse to the corral beside the horse shed while Mason followed, casting an eye on the deserted farmyard. It didn't appear as though anyone had been left posted here to watch for their return. Or if they'd been here, they were now long gone.

Mason removed the saddles and lugged them over to sit near the front wall of the house, under the roof's overhang, in case the ominous clouds brought rain.

"We could stay the night." She filled the trough with three buckets of water she pumped from the nearby well. He grabbed an armful of hay from the barn and filled the feed boxes for the horses. She was thinking along the same lines he had been when they rode up.

"You just want a bed tonight. You've gotten soft." He winked so she wouldn't think he meant it. His girl was tough and could sleep on the ground as well as he could. She'd said little, but she'd worried about her place when they'd been on the road. She might feel better if they inspected the damage and righted what they could.

She swatted his shoulder, turned the horses loose, and closed the gate, dragging it across the dry ground. Both animals dunked their velvety noses to drink, then headed to their stalls to eat and take shelter.

The brisk breeze ruffled the wisps of Caitlyn's hair that had escaped from her braid as she scanned her home, her eyes lingering here and there.

"Let's stay. Just tonight." She swung her pack off her shoulders and let the cat out of her pack. Mittens wound around Caitlyn's ankles, once in each direction, then ambled toward the barn, as if making her daily rounds. There would be unsuspecting mice in the barn for her dinner.

Following the cat, Mason headed for the barn to collect a hammer, nails, and pieces of wood. With the materials in hand, he and Caitlyn inspected the inside of her house. In his youth, he'd been here daily, but he'd only been inside a few times since it belonged to her. To his critical eye, it appeared almost undisturbed—other than the wind whistling through the jagged holes in the windows, and a bird that erupted out of the kitchen window with their entrance. Someone had knocked over the furniture, but it wasn't broken or splintered. Most of her remaining belongings seemed dirty but undamaged. The soldiers must have been in a hurry, trying to apprehend Elsa instead of their usual wanton destruction.

He gave the interior another lingering look and nodded. It wouldn't take much to make it comfortable. A flattened stack of dry firewood rested beside the woodstove. Perfect for cozy fall evenings.

Underneath a round braided rug, the trap door for the root cellar that doubled as a storm cellar remained hidden.

Mason flipped up the floor covering, lifted the ring, and creaked the trapdoor open, peering into the darkness—it smelled musty and like the earth. A cold draft of air hit his skin as he leaned farther. Jars of food still lined the tall shelves. If they returned for the winter, they had a solid base of provisions that she'd put aside with Elsa and Walker's assistance. This could work.

Caitlyn grabbed a broom from behind the door and swept the fine orange dirt, broken glass, and scattered leaves from the concrete floor while he covered the first of the broken windows. She glanced up at the first sounds of pounding nails but kept cleaning. The main kitchen window that overlooked the farmyard was gone, and several others in the living area had broken panes, but all but one bedroom window was intact.

The repairs were quick and before long, he finished with the front room and headed for the minor repairs in Caitlyn's bedroom where she was straightening the quilt she'd replaced after shaking out the dust.

"When this is all done, you ever think of settling down?" He'd love a place like this someday, but only if Caitlyn was willing to live there again. Maybe it would be too weird, since once she'd lived here with Mat—at least between rebel assignments.

"I miss the animals. I miss waking up in a proper bed every day." She shot him a look that went straight to his groin.

They'd been together less than two months and the heat between them hadn't cooled. All she had to do was smile, and he was ready to make love again. Last night's accommodations in the Saints' bunkhouse had been designed for solo travelers, not couples. Nor had they been alone.

"Would you consider farming here again?" He waited a beat for her to answer. It should be too soon to think of marriage, but that's where his mind went whenever he thought of the future. He'd spent too much of his life yearning for Caitlyn. He wanted to make things official, sooner rather than later. "We could make a life here." The words slipped out before he considered them. She might think he was rushing things or giving up on the rebels. They had no idea if they would live through the next campaign. Their lives were dangerous.

"Are you asking to live on my farm with me?" Her eyes twinkled, her smile growing as she ducked her head as if to hide her amusement.

Damn. He tried to clear his face of any expression that might give away how much her question meant.

She tugged on her braid and raised an eyebrow, waiting for his response.

"Would that be strange? Since this was Mat's home." He stared straight ahead, holding a board to the last gaping hole and adjusting its position. Maybe they could get some glass in town, at least for the front window.

"Mason, if we live through the next year or two, I'll insist on returning. This is my home. The one I see in my dreams. I hate seeing it broken and empty. There's been too much sadness here, and the place deserves some happiness." She reached out and rested her hand on his arm, stopping him from swinging the hammer.

He looked down as heat surged through him.

"The question is… would you give up your days of wandering?"

He turned and gazed into her cornflower blue eyes, drowning as usual. He struggled to keep his face expressionless and his voice even. "To be with you? In a heartbeat."

She licked her lower lip and met his gaze. "Mason, will you marry me?"

He smiled, his feelings infusing his reply with a stronger accent than usual. "Yes, Darlin'. There's nothing I'd like better."

"Then it's settled," she said. "We can take care of that in Salt Lake. I've learned that life is short. No waiting for someday for the things you want."

He tugged her in for a long kiss, figuring actions would speak louder than words.

* * *

Mason stood out of the way on the cobblestones while Caitlyn pounded twice on the green door in the alley. He glanced around. The nearby market square was busy packing up for the day; nobody seemed to pay them the least bit of attention, but you could never be too careful. He watched but didn't find anyone out of the ordinary showing interest in their presence. Though they were inconspicuous, he spotted two of Grady's guys and nodded to a young woman stationed outside on watch. They were always careful near the rebel headquarters.

From inside, footsteps approached. The door was yanked open, revealing Darren's smiling, craggy face. Grady's right-hand man swung Caitlyn up in a bear hug before he shook Mason's hand and slapped him on the back.

"I heard you two were still together. You're a lucky man."

Caitlyn snorted as they stepped past him and into the shadowed hall lined with dusty shelves, spare jackets, and assorted junk.

"The boss man expected you several days ago. When your train arrived." Darren's grin revealed a hole where his front bottom tooth should be. "C'mon, he's upstairs."

"We had business up the canyon and stayed a night with the Saints, where we visited with Clark Dawson. We didn't know he'd be there. On the way back, we took care of repairs at Caitlyn's." He didn't have to justify their time, but knowing he'd be seeing Grady was one of the few things that made Mason nervous.

While the man was his father, Grady hadn't raised Mason, instead sending covert money to his mother. She'd died when Mason was sixteen. He'd hopped a train and been beaten outside Denver. Teenage Caitlyn had nursed him back to health. When he'd returned to Utah, he'd lived with the Dawsons for a year before he and Mat had joined the rebels.

"Come in. Have a drink. I'll get Grady." Darren turned for the bar and living quarters.

Caitlyn and Mason strode down the dim hall toward the bar that was headquarters for the rebels.

The bartender nodded when Darren called, "Get them drinks. On the house. Plus a beer for me." He trotted up the narrow wooden staircase at the back of the windowless room.

From above, his muffled voice said, "They're here."

"Cold beer, please." Caitlyn's eyes lit up as the man opened a chiller and took out a frosted mug.

The bartender filled it from a tap, the beer foaming at the top, and set it on the counter.

Mason watched, lips twitching, as she tipped back a long draught, set it down, and sighed.

"I'll take a shot of whisky." He drummed his fingers on the scarred wood of the polished bar.

"Double?" said the slim young man behind the counter.

Mason shook his head. Best to have a clear head to deal with Grady.

They carried their drinks to a round wooden table and sat. He and Caitlyn didn't have long to wait. Darren and Grady came downstairs right away.

Caitlyn jumped up and hugged Grady. Then Grady turned his steely blue eyes on Mason, who met his father's eyes with a nod.

"I thought you two might stop by after you got off the train a few days ago. Instead, you collected your horse, borrowed another, and left town for four days." Grady pulled out a chair across from Mason and sat.

Darren scraped another chair across the floor and sat beside Grady at the next table.

"Things went well in Canada. I understand Elsa has been keeping you up to date." Mason continued at Grady's nod. "We took a batch of seeds to the Saints for them to try out. From bunkers up north in their country. They should be reproducing seeds. Tree and nuts, hops, and berries that supposedly like warm weather. There's more water for growing up the canyon."

"I also wanted to collect my cat from the Saints before she stopped being mine," said Caitlyn. "Traveling up the canyon in the dead of winter can be hazardous."

Grady looked around. "And?"

Caitlyn laughed. "She stayed at the farm. She can look after herself for a month or two, living off mice in the barn. The Saints paid me for my stock, so I've got money for supplies. I plan to be home for the worst of the winter." She raised an eyebrow. "Unless you're sending us somewhere warm."

Leaving Mittens at the farm had been Caitlyn's assurance to herself that she'd return soon.

"I've planned a series of raids along the route from El Paso to San Antonio this fall. I want to disrupt the fire-fighting work camps and set the unwilling laborers free. Maybe some of them will join us. Reports say conditions down there are more brutal than ever and over-crowded." He grimaced. "I got another letter from Walker, smuggled in by rebels who work for the railroad. Elsa's headaches are slow to leave. They're going to stay in Portland a little longer and join us before spring, so we won't wait for them. I want to try sending our troops by train, as Walker suggested, just on a smaller scale. You two will lead a group of a dozen rebels and hit towns all over Texas. If you're up for it." Grady leaned back.

Caitlyn nodded, and Mason squeezed her hand under the table. They'd agreed to go where Grady sent them, as long as it was together.

"Walker's convinced his train-hopping plan will revolutionize our raids." Grady looked at them both while he spoke. He shoved his hair back from his forehead and Mason glimpsed the edge of the wine-colored birthmark shaped like an ax on Grady's forehead.

Caitlyn nodded and turned to Mason. "A few quick raids to try hopping with a group, back to Utah for the winter, and step up the scale of the skirmishes when Walker and Elsa arrive."

"When should we leave?" said Mason, shooting his whisky. Its fire burned his throat, and the heat settled in his stomach. Not quite liquid courage, but he liked the feeling. Still, one was enough. He met Grady's pale eyes, that supposedly matched his own.

"How does tomorrow sound?" said Grady, leaning forward in his chair. "We can have the guys ready to be briefed in an hour. Have some dinner while I send out the messengers. You leave at dawn."

Mason met Caitlyn's gaze, and she nodded.

Tomorrow, they would head back into the action.

"Want to come to a wedding after we get some dinner?" Caitlyn grinned.

CHAPTER 6: TATSUDA

Tatsuda checked the track ahead as the train slowed, running through Walker's instructions in his head. He'd hopped several trains, but he didn't have Walker's experience. There weren't many people Tatsuda trusted to observe with as much detail as him, but Walker's account would be solid.

This early in the morning, the town existed in that expectant hush before the busy hum of regular working hours. Other than the train's motion, there was little movement in the pale morning light—everything appeared faded. Most people were probably either still sleeping or getting ready for work in their homes. GreenCorps never slept. They would have railroad security working at all hours.

Tatsuda wrinkled his nose. The stench of the Heap was no joke. He glanced over his shoulder and grinned. Ginger was trying to strap on her backpack with one hand while plugging her nose with the other.

He laughed. "We'll get used to the smell. Elsa lived here for twenty years and hadn't realized how horrible it was until she left and breathed actual clean air." Tatsuda shouted over the crashing sounds as the train slowed. Their train car bounced off the ones in front, jolting them against the side of the covered porch where they stood wide-legged, braced for further impacts.

Right on cue, the train came to a shuddering stop with their covered hopper outside the train yard. They should be able to avoid the bulls posted as security near the station. He turned and scrambled down the cold steel ladder, landing on the balls of his toes in the crunchy gravel below. He crouched, ready to run.

Ginger dropped behind him—making more noise. He cocked his head toward the station building two hundred yards up the track. Nothing. Other arrival sounds masked their slight sound. He checked on Ginger while removing his earplugs and shoving them in his pocket for next time. He searched the shadows for any sign of movement or oncoming light if their landing had attracted bulls. It remained silent. No outcry. They probably thought no one would ever want to sneak into SoCal.

He sprinted for the bushes behind the long station building, where they scrambled into the second alley behind the row of brothels and bars. They dashed around a corner and into another, darker alley where the buildings crowded closer together. Easy so far. He puffed out his chest. He'd gotten them into SoCal unscathed.

They continued down the pungent alley for the length of a dozen buildings, disturbing a couple of scruffy rats and a scrawny coyote rummaging in a trash can. Nobody from inside paid attention to their quiet footfalls. Behind the second to last building, he located the loose board on the outer wall by counting from the end back toward where they'd stopped—Walker's temporary hideaway. They stepped through the fence into the darkness of the half-fallen shack Walker had built on the other side.

Tatsuda lit a nub of candle from his pocket and held it up to examine the hidden space. The crumbling shack smelled moldy and damp from the bare earthen floor, but it looked unoccupied with a smattering of fine dust on the wooden crates stacked to make a table with single crate seats on either side. Spider webs caught at his face when he took a step forward. There was just enough floor space at either end for them to stow their packs and spread out their sleeping bags—if they chose to sleep here.

Walker must have slept curled up or diagonally. He was too tall to have slept across the end or to have stood upright. He probably hadn't spent much time in the dank room. Tatsuda glanced at Ginger. Though she remained quiet, she stared at their surroundings as if ready to bolt. This place must be quite the shock.

"We shouldn't have to sleep here more than a night or two," said Tatsuda. "Maybe not at all."

Ginger swallowed. "Let's go look for Elsa's neighborhood and her sister."

"Did you get enough sleep on the train?" Even in the yellow candlelight, she looked paler than usual. It would suck if Ginger got sick.

She shrugged. "For now. Do you think we'll find Avery today?"

"You know Elsa's old place won't be much better than this. It'll still be an old shack. Bigger and drier, but it also might have a dirt floor. She said it was a constant battle to keep the place from falling down. Without her there to make repairs, it could be in worse condition." He didn't want Ginger to be shocked when they found Avery's home. Best to lower her expectations.

"I'll take my chances," said Ginger as a brown furry spider crawled across the floor between them. She winced and covered her eyes. "I'm not keen to sleep with the local wildlife. Nobody's been here for months. This hut is their territory."

He'd forgotten her particular fear of bugs and snakes, something she hadn't been used to dealing with in her previous mansion lifestyle. She never complained about heat, cold, lack of food or water, just the occasional creature.

"Let's go." Tatsuda peered both ways down the quiet alley and ensured they were alone. He took her hand and stepped over the lower bar of the fence and outside the hidey-hole. He swung the board back into position and they headed out. Back half a block and left, they exited onto the main dusty street. Through the haze and the distance, a few crumbled concrete buildings stood as monuments to the distant past. From the pronounced lean of the one farthest left, its walls could fall at any time.

Elsa had tried to give directions to Granny's house and Avery, but because he and Ginger hadn't been to SoCal, her landmarks meant nothing. Rather than committing everything to paper before their travels, she'd suggested they ask for directions at one specific GreenCorps store because Vic and Martha, who ran the place, should be helpful. They worked for the corporation, but they'd been in Long Beach for a long time and had known Elsa's family for years. If Avery was back in the old neighborhood, she would shop at their store.

They headed for the main square and the shops. It looked much the same as all the other corporation towns Tatsuda had passed through. Except grayer and bleaker. He'd seen nothing with color since they'd left the train, other than a few faded, ash-covered bushes parallel to the tracks. There were no parks, green spaces, or trees, except a few leafless barren ones on the hillside by the mansions where the rich lived. Like all GreenCorps towns, the faded lettering was the same on the repurposed brick buildings and the inhabitants had the same hollow-eyed hungry look.

Tatsuda wouldn't have thrived as a pickpocket in SoCal.

He and Ginger passed half a dozen women with gray-looking skin and a dozen children, ranging in age from about six to thirteen. The workers trudged toward the Heap in their funny plastic clothes, carrying buckets, trowels, and several long poles. Many were younger than ten or twelve. Elsa had told him she'd worked full-time at the Heap since she was ten, helping her great-grandmother scavenge from pre-Collapse trash. It was horrible to see even by the standards of his own childhood.

In Canada, hell, even in Utah, kids this age would be in school. Before Ginger, that wasn't something he would have noticed. Her gaze followed the group of scrawny children until they were lost from sight. He cleared his throat and grimaced. The air left a disgusting film in his mouth and throat. He took a swig of water. At least they'd been sent with coin for food and water. Hopefully, they wouldn't have to stay long. Find Avery and get out.

He and Ginger strolled past the bars and brothels, which were closed for the morning—including Ginny's, the pleasure house where Elsa and Walker had worked.

Tatsuda identified the store they'd been sent to find by the name "*Vic's General Store*," even though it looked identical to the others. It was the last store across the square by the cracked and pitted road heading to the enormous mound of trash in the distance that dominated the scrapyards surrounding the town—a steaming mountain of garbage and treasure made from remnants of life long ago. Even in Denver, he'd heard of the Heap.

Tatsuda squared his shoulders and opened the door, which rang a bell above as he entered. He strode briskly to the counter while Ginger stared at the jumbled clutter for sale on shelves. Some of it had probably been unearthed in the Heap. Closer to the door were stacks of canned food and shelves with GreenCorps processed food. At the back, a small chiller hummed. Behind the counter, a balding man with glasses and a round face turned in their direction with a friendly look.

Tatsuda smiled. "Are you Vic?" He spoke with confidence, wanting to be treated as an adult, not a pesky kid. It was all about attitude and approach.

The man nodded with a pleasant, if practiced, smile. "Yes. I haven't seen you two before." He scanned them with an assessing eye, his gaze taking in their clothes that screamed "not from here."

Behind Vic was a bulletin board with Wanted posters, including ones for Mason, Caitlyn, Walker, Ginger, Elsa, and himself. The hair on the back of Tatsuda's neck rose, and he calmed his racing heart. Only Elsa was recognizable.

Tatsuda didn't allow his eyes to linger, instead maintaining the shopkeeper's gaze. No need to draw any extra attention. Asking about her would be dangerous enough.

"We just arrived today and we're looking for our cousins. We were told they shop here. I haven't met either of them before, but my older sister sent me to find this branch of our family when we heard Granny passed. I'm not sure our cousins still live in Long Beach, but we took a chance."

"You've come to the right place," said Vic, his chest puffing up. "I know everyone in town. Who're you looking for?"

"Avery and Elsa Lee," said Tatsuda.

Vic frowned and his eyes narrowed. He pointed to the poster on his left. "There's Elsa. She's not here."

Ginger gasped. "Oh my! We had no idea. What about her sister?"

This was where it might get tricky. Tatsuda willed Vic not to look at any of the other pictures too carefully. Ginger's description didn't match with her dyed hair and his own didn't match his growth spurt or haircut. Still, the posters on the wall gave him hives.

"You mean Avery McCoy? That's her married name."

Tatsuda nodded. He couldn't say Elsa had sent them. She'd said Vic couldn't keep a secret to save his life—friendly and helpful, but a blabbermouth.

The man leaned in and lowered his voice. "Can you believe her fancy-pants rich scumbag husband kicked her and her two little girls out of their grand house?" He shook his head, his lips clamped together. "Her Granny barely in her grave and with the poor woman as big as a house. What kind of man does that?"

Vic was clearly talking about the correct Avery, even if Tatsuda didn't understand everything the man said. Scumbag sounded like Jaxon McCoy alright. He hoped the shopkeeper was telling the truth and had made no connections that would link them to Elsa's whereabouts.

"We'd heard she got married," said Tatsuda with a nod.

Vic slapped the counter. "Avery was in here yesterday."

"Do you know where she's staying if she isn't at her fancy house anymore?" said Tatsuda.

"Her Granny's place," said Vic. He frowned. "You don't know where that is, do you?"

Tatsuda shook his head.

"I'll write directions," said the shopkeeper. "You read?"

Tatsuda shook his head. He did, but he preferred saying no. Sometimes people slipped up or were careless with information if they underestimated him. They needed to be going soon.

Ginger came up behind him and smiled her sweetest smile for Vic. "I can read. I'll help with the directions."

"You a cousin too?" said Vic.

"I am," said Ginger. "I've heard one of her girls favors me."

Vic gave her a closer look. "Damn. The oldest is your spitting image, except for her red hair." He grabbed a pre-cut sheet of brown paper wrap from under the counter and a pencil from behind his ear.

Tatsuda moved further right, pulling Vic's attention in that direction, away from the Wanted posters. The red hair comment had him back on edge.

Vic sketched several streets and a few rectangular buildings, marking one with an X. "This is us." He marked a second X a few streets over, drew a large oval, and labeled it *The Heap*. "Not all the streets are marked, but Avery lives on Bayberry between Beach and Ocean. You'll have to ask which house when you get close. Should be some old-timers around at this time of day, ones who don't work. I know the area, not the house numbers."

"Thank you, sir," said Ginger. "We appreciate your assistance."

The bell over the door jingled as customers entered, one wearing a black and green GreenCorps uniform, followed by an aging strawberry blonde in a low-cut dress.

"Captain. Ginny. How can I help you today?" Vic turned away from Tatsuda and Ginger, sliding the paper toward them as his attention shifted.

He'd forgotten them for paying customers. That was fine. Elsa's former employer and a GreenCorps captain. Great. It was time to continue their search. Tatsuda folded the map and he and Ginger slunk away, leaving the store.

He blew out a deep breath once they'd put some distance between themselves and the captain. Tatsuda angled the map to check their orientation before leaving the main square. "I think I saw Bayberry on the way here." He turned right and reversed their path.

Bayberry Street turned out to be little more than a cracked and pitted lane, the edges lined with fragments of plastic bags fluttering in the morning breeze. It wound into a neighborhood made of falling-down shacks of varying sizes. Most were constructed of a mix of wood, cinderblocks, and rusted metal sheets. Many had cracked solar panels on the roof and all had "Property of GreenCorps" stamped water meters on the side of the building.

The rough signs for Beach and Ocean Avenue were both misspelled as Beech and Oshun Avs, but this was probably the right area. Tatsuda looked for someone they could ask about Avery. A balding, older man with gray teeth sat on the bottom stairs of a house on the left. His back was turned to them as he spoke to someone inside the house.

Tatsuda halted and waited for him to finish his conversation. It was a fine line to walk. They needed to look and seem unconcerned about the danger of walking into enemy territory, but his nerves were on a razor's edge. He needed to find Avery's place and get off the street for a few minutes. He took a step closer, even if he was intruding.

The man stopped mid-sentence and stared.

"Excuse me," said Ginger, stepping forward. "We're looking for our cousin, Avery. We heard she was back at Granny's place, but we aren't sure which street because we haven't been here before."

The man's eyes narrowed and his gaze swept them head to toe, perhaps taking in their foreign clothes and solid boots. "You're new in town. What business do you have with Avery?" He knew her alright and was acting protective.

Tatsuda and Ginger must be close to her place.

"Her sister sent us," said Tatsuda, taking a gamble.

That earned a sharp nod. "About time," said the old man, rubbing his hand across his fringe of gray hair. "Those are good girls. They were friends with my Janna. I'm glad Elsa's sent someone." He stood up and moved closer. "We would've helped Avery out, but times are tough. Elsa must have stockpiled tokens before she skipped town, but they won't last long. I take it she's done okay out there?"

Tatsuda nodded, maintaining eye contact but saying nothing. Friendly or not, he wasn't sharing anything else about Elsa with a stranger. Not to anyone except Avery.

The older man held his gaze and nodded. Perhaps deciding to help. He waved toward the house across the street. "That one. Aki Lee and I were neighbors for forty years. Hard to believe she's gone."

"Thanks," said Tatsuda. Feeling the old man's eyes still fixed on his back, Tatsuda climbed the six cinder block stairs, noting the bottom one was loose. He knocked on the door, the sound louder than he intended.

The door opened a crack and a soft voice said, "Yes?"

"I'm Tatsuda and this is Ginger. Are you Avery?"

"I am." The door didn't budge.

"Your sister sent us. She heard what Jaxon did. We have a note." Tatsuda kept his voice pitched low.

Ginger passed the envelope through the open slit in the doorway.

Pale, slim fingers grabbed the paper, and the door closed.

Tatsuda and Ginger waited on the porch for Avery to read the contents.

He felt a growing target on his back as they stood. They couldn't be more conspicuous with their outsider clothes and clean skin. He wished this conversation could take place inside. Out of reflex, he searched the area without turning his head while he chatted with Ginger. "I don't see anyone watching us, other than the helpful neighbor. No Jaxon or Wade. I don't think they have anyone watching the house. At least not right now."

A pair of old women with leathery skin and fluffy white hair shuffled past on the broken street. They wore faded gray plastic ponchos and cracked boots covered in duct tape that seemed to be the SoCal uniform. One nudged the other, perhaps noting Tatsuda and Ginger on Avery's doorstep. He hated standing out.

While he appreciated Avery's caution, he willed her to read faster.

Two minutes passed, and Tatsuda shifted his feet, feeling more anxious by the moment. The neighbor man returned to his stairs and resumed his previous conversation. His gaze flicked back to them several times while they waited.

At last, Avery's door cracked open, the hinges squeaking. The gap widened to reveal a heavily pregnant young woman with long dark hair, a slim face, and pale skin. Warm chocolate brown eyes dominated her serious face. She resembled Elsa, but softer, with fewer angles and less attitude. Avery would have been called the sweet sister.

Crushing disappointment raced through him, making it hard to stand straight. She looked like she was going to have another baby any day. This was going to be much more complicated than anticipated. Wasn't everything?

"Come in," Avery said, looking at each of them. Her gaze lingered on Ginger. "Let's talk inside." She stepped back, allowing them to slide past her into the main room. It was a kitchen with a bunk on one side. A lamp burned on the table and light filtered through a thick sheet of plastic over one window. The place might be run down, but it was clean and tidy. The floor was made of concrete and polished smooth in the high-traffic areas.

Two little girls sat at a table eating oatmeal, one strapped into a worn wooden highchair. The older one had fire-red hair that matched Ginger's natural color. Their eyes were wide and at first, they didn't speak.

"How can you be my sister-in-law?" Avery said to Ginger. "Did Elsa get married?"

"She and Walker are happy and together," Tatsuda said. "They may as well be married, but a better introduction would be, this is Ginger McCoy, recently of Denver."

"Jaxon didn't mention he had a sister," said Avery, her eyes sparkling with unshed tears. "Welcome." She stepped forward and hugged them. "My girls are Rose and Charlotte, after Jaxon's mother and mine."

"I had no idea Jaxon ever thought of Mama," said Ginger, her eyes also suspiciously moist. She'd mentioned she didn't remember her mother, who'd died during childbirth.

The littlest girl looked feisty, like a miniature Elsa, with yellow hawk eyes and dark curls. She banged her spoon on her tray, demanding attention. "Who's here? Who's she?" She pointed the spoon at Ginger and glared.

"That one is Charlie, for short." Avery sighed, a flash of exasperation in that breath. She turned to her girls. "This is Aunt... Geri and..." her voice trailed off. "And Aunt Elsa's friend." She raised an eyebrow. He shrugged. Any new name would do. "Sam. They're family."

Tatsuda gave a slight nod, appreciating both being included and her caution in not telling the children their real names. "We were going to take you on a train to Salt Lake City soon, but I'm not sure you can hop a train." He waved a hand. "In your condition." He wanted to slump in defeat. Elsa had given him this mission, and he didn't want to let her down, but there was no way they could leave.

Avery gave a rueful laugh. "No kidding. I'm stuck here until I have the baby. Any plans for how to hop a train with a rookie, a newborn, and two small children?"

* * *

E,

T and I have arrived safely. Your sister and her girls send their love. Our trip went as planned, but our departure will be more difficult than expected. Your sister is expecting another child in the next few weeks, which will make immediate travel impossible. T and I will keep you posted and take care of everyone until the spring.

You weren't exaggerating. The price of water here is outrageous. Worse than my time in Pocatello. Though expensive, we took your advice and sold the sector license and now have coin to stretch for several months' worth of necessities. It eases our minds, though we hope to leave as soon as A is able.

Next week I'm starting reading lessons for the neighborhood kids. Several parents have agreed as they see it as free babysitting. It will allow a few more moms to work and bring in extra coin for their families, and give me something constructive to do for the children. If they learn to read, it will open up another universe. That's probably why your Granny taught you and your sister, and maybe it's why Jace taught me.

You should see little Charlie. Your sister calls her a spitfire and says she's just like you—same eyes and attitude. Even with three of us taking turns, she runs us ragged, and she's only just two. Everything is "why?"

We'll figure out a way to meet with your uncle in the city before the spring, even if we aren't yet sure how or when. We're taking care of everyone. See you there.

Don't worry,

G and T

CHAPTER 7: JANNA

Janna woke to the smell of smoke. She bolted upright from her bed in the darkness of her room, wincing at the sudden movement that jarred her sore muscles. She yawned as she swung her bare feet to the wooden floor to investigate. The acrid smell was much stronger than the persistent background smell of San Antonio. Even the air seemed hot. Something close was burning.

She peeked outside and stepped back, her hand over her mouth, her heart racing. Scattered orange glows illuminated half the block in the dawn light—flames instead of washed-out gray lit the sky. In the distance, someone rang the city fire bell—the clanging insistent.

From street level, came an ear-splitting scream, several shouts, and a general commotion, unusual for early morning. Two gunshots further shattered the silence, followed by a loud clamor of voices on the neighboring street. Trembling and short of breath, she dressed, shoving her feet into her more practical shoes. She snatched her travel bag and stuffed her change of clothes, book, and canteen inside. A quick glance around the room showed nothing else important. Time to get out.

Janna had no idea what had caused the fire, but perhaps she could use the distraction to escape. In all the confusion, she might make her way to the train station. She would hop a train anywhere. She refused to live the rest of her life as a whore.

Last night was excruciating. She glanced down at the livid bruises and bracelets of scuffed and bloody skin circling her wrists. The final customer, well after midnight, had tied her to the bed and used her hard. It had been impossible to send her mind elsewhere. After all these months, she was used to some rough treatment—a sad fact that surprised her—but the pain and humiliation were too much to take. She'd tossed and turned until the wee hours. She'd even contemplated taking her life to end this misery.

Hands shaking, Janna slung her bag across her chest and over her shoulder, headed toward the door, and stopped. Though she'd acted fast, furling waves of thick charcoal-gray smoke now wafted in from underneath the door, spreading like fog up the wall and flowing into the room. Too late to take the stairs. She coughed and glanced at the ceiling, where the dark smoke pooled and cascaded outward.

She gingerly touched the doorknob with one finger. It was blistering hot. She'd have to chance the window and the roof. Ducking lower, she grabbed the sheets from her bed, yanked them off, and shoved them against the bottom of the door to buy an extra minute. She coughed again and opened the reluctant window. It jammed and inched upward less than a foot. With the window open, a roaring sound burst from the back of the building, flames shooting into the air. Her shirt clung to her, sweat dripping everywhere.

She yanked on the window, trying to force the wedged piece farther up, but it wouldn't budge. Adrenaline coursing through her veins, she pushed again. It only gave an inch. Panicking, she shoved the window upward in the frame, scraping it to its maximum height in quick, short bursts. Would she fit? Glancing right, her next door neighbor, Muriel, climbed onto the roof. She nodded in Janna's direction and helped two other women in night dresses climb out of the same room.

Those two had come from across the hall where the rooms must be engulfed in flames by now. Their eyes were wide and their faces streaked with soot and tears. It might be too late for the others.

Janna gulped a deep breath of the smoky air and wormed through the narrow opening, slithering onto the slate-covered roof. From this vantage, brilliant flames leaped like hellish dancers in billowing cloaks of black smoke, licking her building, the one next door, and the one after that. All the way down the block on both sides of the street, the fire crackled and raged.

Even outside, the air quality was scorching and horrible. She hacked as the thick smoke tickled and burnt her throat; her chest ached while her eyes watered and stung. She covered her mouth and nose with her arm. How long until the roof was ablaze on this side? A minute? Two?

"The rebels have come," shouted one of the younger women next door, pointing toward the train station. "They've set the town on fire."

"That wasn't the rebels," said Muriel with a scornful glance at the younger woman. "The bastards that own us would rather we burn than go free."

Janna glanced their way. Muriel probably spoke the truth. The rebels wouldn't set fire to the buildings with innocent people inside. Would they? Improbable. Were they really here? Hope surged within her chest. Based on the snippets of gossip she'd gleaned over the last few weeks, the rebels had been hard at work further west, rescuing deportees and sending them home. Maybe they were here, even if the fire wasn't their fault.

That's when Janna spotted her owner, Jarrold. He and several of the building owners and GreenCorps proprietors from fellow drinking establishments stood in the middle of a vacant lot across the street. They clumped together, their arms crossed, watching the spreading flames—ignoring the chaos and cries for help. She took a moment to get a better look. The owners wore bandanas over their faces. They'd been prepared for the fire. They weren't doing anything to save the buildings. No water, no buckets, and no fire brigade. Muriel was right.

Those bastards.

Sparks danced in the air as chunks of cinder rained down all around. One burned the back of her hand. Snatching her hand to her chest, she sucked in a breath, scooted to the brink of the roof, and carefully sat on the warm tiles. Her feet dangled as she leaned forward, gripping the edge. The bottom dropped out of her stomach. The distance to the ground looked too far to jump, even at the lowest point, but she wasn't about to stay here and burn. When it came down to it, she still valued her life.

She wiped her clammy hands, turned over, and wiggled over the edge, reducing the amount left to drop. Her sweaty fingers slipped on the hard surface. But, she caught the last seam with her fingernails. Taking a deep breath, she let go and jumped. Better to break something than to burn to death. She braced for impact.

Fiery pain shot through her right ankle as she landed. She fell to her knees, scuffing her hands on the rough brick. One palm bled, with bright red droplets, and the other stung with road rash. Her whole body screamed in agony, but she ignored it.

She was out.

She looked up, noting the other women still standing on the roof, looking down, their mouths in astonished O's.

No one moved to follow her example. Fools. They could stick around to be rescued, but she was tired of waiting for help. Not anymore. If she wanted to survive, she had to take care of herself. She checked over her shoulder. The proprietors standing near the corner hadn't noticed her yet, or if they had, they didn't care. What was the value of one more whore? Not much.

Despite her opinion of their indecision, she couldn't leave the others to burn without giving them a chance. She spun and checked beside the building. A heavy wooden ladder lay on the ground. Janna dragged it several yards and leaned it against the edge of the roof. That would have to be enough. She whirled and headed down the street.

Muriel cupped her hand to her mouth. "Thanks."

Janna didn't dare yell or call attention to herself or the ladder, and checked that Jarrold was still busy doing nothing as she jogged in the other direction. She shuddered. Not waiting to see if the others descended, she focused on her escape. She didn't have friends, and she'd already done what she could. They needed to take care of themselves.

She limped toward the train station. She'd only gone a block when a tall woman with a long blonde braid materialized from the orangish-gray haze as though summoned. The woman beckoned for Janna to come with an insistent wave.

"This way. Hurry." The blonde turned and faded from sight.

Ignoring the shooting pains in her ankle, Janna followed. She kept her mouth covered to smother another coughing fit as she ran in a hobbling gait.

The woman continued toward the train station where a group of two dozen men in the ragged and soot-covered clothes of deported firefighters stood huddled next to the station building. A lanky man with cleaner clothes and a battered hat arrived, bringing two dozen whores from other pleasure houses. Two were women from SoCal who'd arrived on the same train as Janna. Though the women acknowledged each other with a nod, nobody spoke. Perhaps they were all in shock.

Most newcomers wore their nightclothes, and many had escaped wearing only socks on their feet. Janna looked down at her split boots—her left toe stuck out of a hole. Did these count as shoes? Maybe not, but they were better than bare feet. The man in the hat nodded at the blonde and maintained eye contact for several seconds. The two had a silent interaction that made Janna think they were together—not just working side-by-side.

"That's all from your side of town?" the man in the hat said to the blonde woman as he drew closer. "They fired the bunkhouse. At least two dozen men didn't get out. GreenCorps has a lot to answer for. As usual." His fists were clenched.

The blonde nodded. "The fucking brothel owners lit their buildings on fire, too. They'd rather lose their businesses than be seen helping us." She spat on the ground. "Almost like they had it planned in case we showed up."

Muriel had been correct.

Janna glanced back toward the flickering light of the menacing fire. No sign of her neighbor or Jarrold. Not yet. There was also no sign of the GreenCorps forces from the garrison or train security. But that wouldn't last. A train stood on the second track. A pair of young men appeared from the shadows and one signaled to the rebels with an exaggerated, over-the-head wave. Perhaps they had something to do with the missing bulls.

"Load the gondolas," said the blonde, pointing to the train cars that resembled boxcars that had been chopped in half, the tops open to the wintery sky. "They're empty and easiest to load and unload."

Another group of grimy deportees arrived from deeper in town, a crowd of thirty or more. Janna didn't know if she trusted the rebels, but going with them was better than staying here. Her eyes still burning from the smoke, she followed the group loading onto the flat box-like cars the blonde indicated. A dozen people scrambled up the metal ladder, one by one, as a line formed behind them. The line moved to the next car as well.

A huge whoosh sounded behind them, the flames towering several stories in height as the fire took off with a gust of wind. Sparks danced through the air, disappearing into the morning sky. The haze was so thick, most of San Antonio had disappeared. One of the closest buildings collapsed, the bricks cascading the ground as the beams and contents burnt.

The train lurched forward, inching further along the track while several crashes farther ahead showed movement. Anyone from a corporation town knew what that meant.

The train had better not leave without her. She was leaving.

Janna's heart raced, and she scurried to the last car, no longer in line.

"Time to go," yelled the man in the hat. "Everyone up a ladder. Get on the train, it's moving out. Anywhere you can climb." His voice carried over the sounds of confusion as everyone crowded closer to the tracks, scrambling for a ride.

Janna grabbed the ladder near the rear of the train car and hauled herself up, climbing awkwardly. At the top, she straddled the side and looked back. A few others had followed her mad dash, most aiming for the closer cars. She wasn't the only one determined to get away.

"Keep going. Drop in so we can use the ladder too." The blonde was right behind her.

Janna turned and landed in the box of the train car with a metallic thud. Her injured ankle rolled again and she let out an involuntary moan, catching her lip in her teeth. She limped out of the way, sliding on loose gravel on the bottom as the train picked up speed. Holding the chilled edge of the car, she hopped to the front and sat, leaning her back against the cold steel. Nothing would be comfortable, but at least she'd escaped that awful place. The throbbing in her ankle matched the rhythm of the fast-turning wheels.

The blonde woman helped six others climb into their gondola. Each of the passengers had smoke-streaked faces. Like Janna, their reddened eyes watered from the smoke and everyone looked dazed and confused. She hoped she didn't look as stunned and weak as they did.

"I'm a medic. Let me check that ankle," said the blonde. "I'll put something on that burn on your hand too." Her words were almost lost in the clamor of the accelerating train. She crouched in front of Janna and picked up the sore foot. She bent it carefully in each direction, stopping when Janna whimpered. "Not broken. Just sprained." With no wasted motion, the medic grabbed a kit from her bag, elevated the ankle using her knee as a prop, and wrapped it, winding a bandage around and around.

Janna's ankle no longer moved and it hurt less. "Thanks."

The medic got out a jar of white paste and smeared some on the back of Janna's hand. The heat of her burn lessened immediately and she let out a breath.

As the train gathered speed, heading north, the sun peeked over the horizon in the east.

"Was the fire intentional?" Janna addressed her question to the blonde in charge.

"Not from our side. No matter how GreenCorps might spin this," the woman said, slumping down, her back against the metal wall of the train car. "I'm Caitlyn, by the way."

"Janna. Where are we headed?" She shouted to be heard over the deafening train.

"Salt Lake City via Denver." Caitlyn cupped her mouth to direct the words into Janna's ear.

"Denver?" Why the hell would they go through Denver, where GreenCorps headquarters was located? Some of this thought must have shown in her expression.

"We've arranged for the train to stop before entering the city. We'll hike around town and get on a different train after it leaves Denver station. Anyone who wants to stay near there can leave on their own." Caitlyn caught her breath.

Janna hadn't seen a map, but both Denver and Salt Lake City seemed far. It had taken three hellish days in a boxcar to get to San Antonio from SoCal. She hoped this second ride wouldn't also be a nightmare. She glanced skyward. They'd left the fire behind, but the overcast sky gave few clues to the brisk November weather.

"How long will we be on the train?" Janna shouted her question.

Several other women turned their heads to hear the answer.

"Twenty-one hours to Denver. We'll be on foot for six hours between hiking and waiting for a new train. Twelve more onboard to Salt Lake. Then two days to safety."

One of the barefoot women sitting nearby burst into tears and another gathered her into a hug. Janna sympathized with their feelings, but crying wasn't her style. She'd been near the end of her rope, too. However, after what she'd been through the last six months, she could endure the chilly discomfort of a few days on the train—especially if freedom lay at the other end.

"We've got food and water onboard," said Caitlyn. "My husband should be along soon with something for everyone to eat."

"The man in the battered hat?" said Janna, remembering the intense look the two had exchanged, as if checking to see if the other was unharmed.

Caitlyn smiled, the skin crinkling near the corner of her eyes. "That's my Mason." She leaned back. "Try to get some rest. We're safe for now. Lots of time to worry about getting off and back on near Denver."

CHAPTER 8: MASON

Mason took a long drink from his canteen and wiped the grime of sweat and smoke from his face with a damp handkerchief. That was as close to a wash as he'd get for a few more days. He was looking forward to heading back to the farm for a rest and a peaceful, ordinary life once they got off this train and finished the job, at least for the winter.

He'd been on the road for too long, looking over his shoulder for longer than he cared to admit. Fifteen years—his entire adult life. Spring would bring more campaigning and another push all too soon. He might be only thirty-two, but from the way his bones ached in the morning, he was getting too old for this lifestyle.

He slung eight additional canteens filled with water across his body, nodded to one of the experienced rebels sitting with this lot of rescued prisoners, and headed toward the rearmost train cars. Though the driver had been paid off, appearances had to be kept up. Security would report that hoppers had scaled the final cars. Mason climbed the back and glanced down before sliding to the thick metal frame by the joint on the rear of the car. The blurred ground rushed underneath. One misstep and he was done. He swallowed. One quick step over the knuckle, then he'd be safe.

He averted his gaze to prevent dizziness before leaping to the next car, which he scaled, then dropping inside to join the next group. He handed out water and kept going, landing in the next car, distributing canteens. After ensuring everyone would have a share, he continued. His team had spread out between the occupied train cars and were distributing food bars and blankets. He scanned the group one more time, shaking his head. Many of the refugees were woefully unequipped for the weather or the journey. There'd been no time to warn them to pack.

On the move again, this morning's raid played through his mind as he moved toward the next car. What a shit show. The rebels had been overconfident because the first three raids had gone off as planned. They'd freed over a hundred laborers and whores in each town and shipped them out of Texas. Of course, GreenCorps expected them in San Antonio—it had been the next big town in Texas that hadn't already been hit.

The local corporate garrison had been ready, setting fire to the helpless as soon as the rebels made a move. They'd been lucky to escape from town, but he felt sure that the blame for the destruction would be placed on the rebels. There could be all kinds of reprisals for ordinary citizens there—if any remained. That might play into rebel hands… or damage their cause. It could go either way.

Mason dropped off more water, still musing over recent events before he jumped the knuckle joining the next two train cars. A month ago, he and Caitlyn had left their horses behind in Salt Lake City and hopped the trains with a dozen volunteers, showing them the ropes.

Because they'd started in Salt Lake, Grady used the bulls on his payroll to turn a blind eye to their first attempt at hopping trains. Mason had insisted on running the operation like they had to hide, dash, and jump, but it had been comforting to know that barring a flagrant problem, the rookies would get on board.

After that, they'd been circumspect and hid like experienced hoppers, making sure not to be seen or caught. They couldn't let

GreenCorps know the scale of the operation and foreshadow what might happen in the spring.

The next few weeks had gone without a hitch as he and Caitlyn trained the rebels to use the trains proficiently. GreenCorps was so huge, they weren't used to mass movements of people except under their authority. Each region was beholden to the corporation, but many local leaders didn't like to admit failure or confess they were having problems with the rebels—hoping to handle things on their own. Once they did, GreenCorps took control from afar. That failure to communicate worked in the rebel's favor, they just needed to take advantage.

A lot of regular people tried not to fall afoul of the corporation but weren't on either side, they just wanted to do their job and get paid. That's who the rebels needed to persuade to join the fight.

When the rebels arrived somewhere new in Texas, they dispersed into town, with a plan for the coordinated time to strike, less than half an hour before a departing train. The key was to wait until the last minute. Until today, it had worked like a charm. Mason had to hand it to Walker and his experience. Train hopping for raids and rescues worked well. Even on a small scale, their success had been an accomplishment.

Until today, which hadn't been a total failure, but had mixed results. No deaths for his people, even if they'd brought fewer people than usual out of servitude. Better than nothing. Hell, the problem today might play into the rebels' hands if GreenCorps declared a victory and believed the rebels had given in and fled. In the past, a setback like this might have been enough to make them go to ground.

In the spring, the rebels would ensure their raids were more random to guarantee GreenCorps couldn't predict where the rebels would strike. Walker and Elsa would be back in the game, and this original group of a dozen rebel train hoppers would be ready to lead teams, at least in pairs. They could hit multiple locations simultaneously or back-to-back, giving GreenCorps a massive headache.

Mason jumped from car to car, dropping off a canteen or two to each group until he reached Caitlyn in the last gondola. He sat beside her and kissed his bride. She smelled of smoke and sweat, but beneath that, was his angel—his long-lost love and he savored the strawberry taste of her full lips. He still couldn't believe this gorgeous woman had married him. He felt like the luckiest man alive.

She leaned against him with a sigh and he pulled her closer, tugging the collar of his jacket higher. He tucked a frozen hand into his armpit while Caitlyn wriggled closer, probably seeking heat in this arctic airflow. The weather had changed two days ago, and he didn't think he'd been warm since. She hadn't distributed the blankets yet. She must be exhausted.

"After this, no matter what Grady wants, it's time to go home for the winter. Let GreenCorps sweat, not knowing when and where we'll strike next."

"Agreed." He nodded to the smoke-streaked young woman who sat on Caitlyn's other side. She'd been the first of those from San Antonio to assess the train's movement and take it upon herself to board a new car without prompting. She was sharper than many they'd rescued. Not everyone could keep their wits when facing their fear. Her ankle had been wrapped with his wife's expertise. He leaned forward to introduce himself. "Mason."

"Janna." Her voice was weary as she slumped against the train, swaying slightly with the car's motion. "I want to stay with the rebels. I can't go home."

That was probably the case for many onboard.

Caitlyn nodded and patted Janna's leg. "We'll settle you in with the Saints for the winter. Come spring, if you still want to join us, send word."

The young woman flinched at Caitlyn's casual touch. He and his wife exchanged glances. This girl might take longer to warm up than some.

Janna shrugged. "Why would you lot be interested in me?"

"You're tough and have a cool head." Caitlyn was quick to answer.

Janna raised her eyebrows pointedly, as if skeptical about his wife's words.

Caitlyn said, "You're dressed, have shoes, and packed a bag. The ladder. I can tell you're resourceful and smart. We need people like you." She leaned forward, unzipped her pack, and tossed blankets to the groups nearby, keeping one on her lap. She sighed, slumped back, and closed her eyes, just for a few seconds.

They hadn't slept much last night.

Caitlyn spread a wool blanket over the two of them. Mason tucked the excess under their legs on the edge and leaned in. All around the car, the people gathered in clumps to share body heat. Nobody moved to join them or talk to Janna, nor did she join the others. She seemed to be alone.

"Scoot this way," said Caitlyn to Janna.

The girl complied, moving closer, though not touching Caitlyn. His wife reached across and tucked in the blanket's edge, ignoring the second wince. She would have noticed. She'd probably chosen not to react. Knowing his Caitlyn, Janna would be her next project.

With winter fast approaching, the chill was more intense than usual. Too bad they didn't have more blankets. At least they'd started their trip in the morning with most of the day ahead of them. Mason draped his arm around Caitlyn, careful not to bump the new girl. Tonight would be a cold one, even with shared body heat.

The train rushed onward. They had left the smoke of San Antonio behind and the sky brightened, a pale, wintery light blue as daylight broke.

"Think we'll have snow overnight?" Caitlyn spoke into his ear, her warm breath for him alone.

His body reacted and he shifted, finding her hand beneath the blanket and lacing his fingers together with hers as they both relaxed.

"Snow in November in the mountains? I'd say so." Mason leaned back next to his wife, determined to doze while they had a chance. There'd be time enough to worry about Denver and the frigid weather tonight.

* * *

Mason woke after a few hours sleep, sitting in the dark beside Caitlyn. They'd spent a day and part of the night onboard. His eyes adjusted and he inhaled. The freezing air smelled like snow. It was a complication, but not unforeseen, and couldn't be helped. He'd gone through the gondolas to spread the word about what to expect for the disembarking last evening while there'd still been light. He had to trust everyone would be ready when the train halted—he wasn't jumping between cars in the dark.

Sliding to his left and out of the warm cocoon of blankets, he tucked his share around Caitlyn as he stood, the icy wind making his tired bones ache. She could sleep a little longer.

It was pitch black on either side of the racing train, with only the pale half-moon near the horizon peeking through the clouds. It was the kind of night when the world seemed hushed. A snowflake landed on his cheek, cold and wet. Then another. Good.

He glanced at the timepiece Grady had entrusted to him, tilting its face to catch the scant light. Should be less than ten minutes until there was an "unexpected" obstruction on the tracks. Elsa remembered reading about how an electromagnet could disrupt the rails on which the trains ran. Grady had bought several devices from his Canadian contacts and they worked like a charm—halting the trains long enough between stations for quick-footed rebels to board or dash away.

Mason's breath plumed white in the icy air as he ran through the upcoming scheme one more time. If things went according to plan, the rebels and their charges would slip off and melt away into the night. No one from GreenCorps should be the wiser, even if they'd done this three times previously in different locations. It wasn't unheard of for trains to stop in the winter, often to clear deep snow or ice from the tracks. GreenCorps shouldn't suspect tampering—not yet. Security would swarm the train when it reached Denver a few hours before dawn, but there would be no sign the rebels had ever been onboard.

On the three previous trips, Mason and Caitlyn had handed off the rescued at this point before they'd hiked into Denver and hopped trains south to start over, meeting with their team at an agreed-upon location four days later. Today, they would travel with the refugees to the next hidden trackside location to hop the train to Salt Lake. Security would greet them on arrival in Salt Lake, but many were rebel sympathizers—the search wouldn't be as diligent as in other cities.

Many of the refugees would stay in Salt Lake, while some without family, would be taken to the Saints, who, while unwilling to fight, welcomed those who needed a fresh start. No questions asked. Once the newcomers settled in Utah, he and Caitlyn would collect the horses and head home.

Mason moved through the gondola, waking the passengers with a light touch on the shoulder. They'd gone over the instructions last night. He woke Caitlyn and Janna last. Up ahead, the train cars jolted—a hard screeching sound filled the air. The crash of slack action was stronger than usual with the emergency stop system, causing the train to grind along the rails with a shower of sparks. The shrill sounds penetrated through the ear protection, making his teeth ache.

He'd arranged for everyone to disembark to the right and make for the bluffs. A waiting rebel team would meet this group and help them fade into the foothills. They hoped to evade the search that might ensue after the empty train arrived in Denver. Had railroad officials in Denver gotten into trouble over the absences? He hoped so. Anything to disrupt the GreenCorps system and throw them off balance.

As soon as Mason felt the final motion lurch to a stop, he climbed over the frigid metal back of the train and helped the others from this car disembark. Caitlyn came last, and he steadied her when she landed on the ground. He squeezed her gloved hand before letting go. The snow crunched underfoot as they walked, seeming loud in the silence but still dominated by a faint hissing from the stationary train. He looked ahead to the front of the train, where its bright light still shone on the tracks amidst the falling snow.

The snow coming down grew thicker by the minute, swirling in the gusts of wind, which would make for a cold, wet hike. Those without shoes had wrapped their feet in rags or strips from the blankets. Until Salt Lake, it would have to do. He glanced skyward and hoped the flurry continued. By daybreak, their footprints and their trail should be covered.

He slipped away from the groups, heading for the rocks, paralleling the train to make sure there was nothing else of concern. He stuck to the edge of the tracks where the snow had been swept clear by the motion of the train so he could remain quiet.

Light pooled near the engine. Two engineers were already on the ground with a lantern, while a third remained onboard, leaning out the door and peering ahead. From the concealing darkness, Mason kept low and listened.

"Nothing on the track now. Some kind of glitch, I guess," said the engineer on the right.

"Yeah. Something's up with the rails. This is the third time we've had to stop on my run in the last month. All some kind of unexplained disruption. We stop, there's nothing. We continue," said the engineer on the left.

"You think it's the rebels?"

"More power to them. Lucky we don't have an exact schedule and don't need to account for minor delays." The second man laughed.

"I'm not logging this one unless we can't continue. Anyone have a problem with that?" The original speaker seemed in charge.

From inside the cab, the third engineer called, "As long as I'm paid for driving, it doesn't matter to me. Let's try again." His deep voice was closer than the other two and carried in the quiet night. The signal for the waiting rebels to turn off the device.

Mason peered at the men—memorizing the features in their shadowed faces by yellow lantern light. It might be handy to contact a few rebel sympathizers next spring. If they hadn't already been brought on board. Grady had spoken with many railroad men and some were already part of his network, even if they worked for GreenCorps. The problem was, many railroad men lived better than the average person—steady wages and privileges. Few would openly support the rebel cause or risk that lifestyle.

Grady's reach extended throughout the West in the lower classes, but when the time came, they'd need everyone. Getting more railroad workers involved would be crucial.

The engineers trudged back to their door and hauled themselves back into the engine, stomping off the snow on a platform before returning to their enclosed compartment

"Nothing on the tracks. Let's go." The door slammed; the rest of their words lost.

Slowly the train accelerated, the usual crashes accompanying the movement. The wheels turned slowly at first, then faster. Mason used the din of the departing train to mask his noise as his boots broke through the crust atop the snow. He jogged after the group from the train, feeling an ache in his lungs from running in the cold air. This was going to be another long night.

GREENCORPS ANNOUNCEMENT:

After the heinous burning of San Antonio by the radical rebels and their illegal use of the railroad to remove property stolen from the business leaders of Texas, GreenCorps has enacted several measures to curb rebel activity. Details below.

—Malcolm McCoy, President and CEO of GreenCorps

Effective immediately:
All railroad workers, including security, linemen, laborers, and onboard personnel, including drivers, will take a fifty percent pay cut. No exceptions.

Beware:
Rebel sympathizers could be among us anywhere. Report anything unusual.

Rewards:
For any relevant information about rebel movement.

Chapter 9: Clark

Clark woke with a pounding heart, covered in a sheen of sweat, his sheets tangled and stuck to him. Fuck. Another bloody nightmare. He forced his shoulders to relax into the cold, damp bedsheets and took deep breaths, forcing himself to exhale. Night after night, it was the same thing. His mind flashed to the last image, seared into his brain—himself plummeting off a cliff, with no one the wiser as he disappeared into a yawning pit of darkness. Even awake, the sense of utter loneliness clung to him like static.

He swung his feet out of bed, his stomach churning as he reached for his icy clothes, draped over the trunk at the head of his bed. The bunkhouse was quiet this early in the morning, but he wouldn't go back to sleep. He may as well get up. A quick check of the others showed everyone still sleeping in their bunks. All twelve beds, besides his, were occupied right now, but Clark hadn't met the new men on the upper bunks—they'd arrived last night.

His upstairs bunkmate turned over with a snort, muttering as he rolled. Clark froze, waiting for him to go back to sleep. He didn't want to bother anyone or talk to them while still dealing with the nightmare aftermath. When it seemed the sleeper hadn't been disturbed, Clark shoved his feet into his boots. Accompanied by the deep, even breathing and a couple of sets of snores from around the room, Clark finished his preparations. He grabbed his notebook, jacket, hat, and gloves before slipping into the wintery dawn.

The slow breeze carrying freezing particles of snow nipped at his cheeks as he zipped his jacket higher and yanked his beanie lower to cover his ears. There'd been several inches of fresh powder overnight—the snowbanks were already two feet deep beside the trail and it was only early November. Last winter, the snowdrifts had been taller than his height of just over six feet. This year would probably be much the same. Though he'd grown up in Utah, the snow was extreme here in the mountains compared to the lowlands where he'd been raised. Sometimes those minor differences still surprised him.

He finished adjusting his outerwear and headed to the dining room in search of caffeine. On his third step, his feet shot out from under him, and through fancy windmilling action and a miracle, he avoided a fall. He continued, placing his feet carefully after the first near slip. The ground was slick with a layer of ice beneath the new snow. His were the first tracks from this side of the settlement, though several sets preceded him into the dining area. Probably the cooks and a few insomniacs who may have already come and gone.

Stomping his feet and pushing inside, Clark strode to the communal urn and filled a mug of steaming yaupon tea. He added a generous spoonful of honey and a dollop of milk. He didn't need food yet, so this should do the trick. With his notebook in hand, he headed toward his usual quiet corner, where he could sit and write. He needed something to do to occupy his mind since he couldn't do chores for a couple of hours—outdoor work happened after seven a.m.

He would write for an hour or two, like most mornings, then shovel snow. Maybe they'd need extra hands on the firewood crew later. The best way to get to sleep tonight would be to exhaust his body. Sometimes it worked.

He hadn't paid attention until he was almost at the table, but to his surprise, a young woman with shoulder-length brown hair sat in his customary seat near the end of one of the long tables. He didn't recognize her—she must be new. For the last month, the rebels had sent groups of people to the Saints in larger numbers than any previous time he could recall. They might be related to the action Mason and Caitlyn had been involved with. Until now, he hadn't paid attention to the influx of newcomers.

Clark glanced around the dining hall. It was busier than he expected before six a.m. Several parents with small children were scattered around the room, most near the kitchen and the food. He could sit in a different section, or he could sit near his usual place, just a table over. He clenched his jaw, deciding not to be driven from his preferred area because it was occupied. This was the optimal corner—close to the warmth of the kitchen, close to overhead lights, away from foot traffic, and the chilly draft by the door. Still, he hesitated. The young woman might think he was being friendly for the wrong reasons.

Making up his mind, he didn't hesitate long. With the feeling of free-falling into darkness still fresh in his mind, he slid onto the bench at the far end of the table beside his favorite one. The young woman didn't look up from her book. He took a satisfactory drink of his piping hot tea, flipped the pages of his notebook to where he'd left off yesterday, and wrote.

This morning, the words came easily, and his pen flowed across the page. He was writing an original story about a young man on a quest to slay a dragon, alternating between his point of view and the dragon's. Clark had gotten the idea from a battered fantasy hardcover he'd found in the library that dated back before the Collapse, almost two hundred years earlier.

Today he was writing as the dragon and was midway through the story. He'd scrawled it by hand in his notebook, and it was unlikely that anyone else would ever read it. He wrote for himself. When the stories bubbled up inside him, this was how he got them out of his system. He immersed himself in the dragon's world and lost track of everything around him.

"Can I move here?" The new girl stood beside his table, tapping her toe.

The jarring words startled him into looking up into a pair of unreadable, flat brown eyes. He stared. The clink of plates and cutlery was louder than expected in the background. How had he not noticed the room become so full? He must have been writing for longer than usual—perhaps hours.

"Well. Can I?" Her grouchy tone grated on his nerves. Couldn't she see he'd rather be alone?

"What's wrong with where you were?" His reply sounded rude, but he didn't feel like backing down or sharing his space. He couldn't believe he'd spoken to her, but her tone had lit a fire in him that superseded his discomfort. Several newcomers now shared his table at the far end, and he hadn't noticed their arrival. They'd left a bubble surrounding his end, like no-man's-land.

Clark glanced at her previous table, where an old couple and two of his bunkmates sat, while a couple with four children were settling. He wiggled his tight jaw. She'd moved to be polite and make room for the family to sit together. He was an ass.

He nodded and rose to his feet, his chair scraping against the wooden floor. Overwhelmed by that familiar fear; he managed to mumble a few words her way. "The table's yours. I'm going to shovel snow." He avoided further eye contact and gathered his notebook and pencil, shoving them into his deep coat pocket. He grabbed his empty mug to deposit with the other dirty dishes on his way out.

The young woman glared and sat without another word. He dropped off his mug and snagged a couple of slices of fruit loaf as he left, wending his way through the busy breakfast area filled with people. Several tables were filled with faces he didn't recognize. And two familiar faces. Shit. He'd avoided them last night when they'd arrived with a new batch of refugees, but Caitlyn and Mason were still here. He'd heard they'd gotten married since he'd seen them last. His throat tightened. He should be polite.

Clark nodded in recognition, but his feet kept moving. He almost made it to the door before a hand grabbed him by the collar and stopped him in his tracks. He shrugged the hold away and whirled around, expecting to yell at Mason. Instead, it was Caitlyn and his protest died on his lips. His cheeks burned.

"Clark. I have a favor to ask." Her deep blue eyes bored into him; her mouth set in firmer lines than usual.

"I have snow to shovel," he said, nodding toward the door.

"I won't detain you long." A crease appeared between her brows and she took a step closer. "Are you doing okay?"

He waved off her concern. "Yep. Fine. I just didn't sleep well last night."

Her frown persisted. "Look, Clark, if you ever want to talk…"

"Nope. I'm good," he interrupted. "I just have places to be. What's the favor?" His gaze flicked to the door before returning to Caitlyn.

She pursed her lips. "Mason and I won't return until spring and are headed down to the farm." She tugged on her braid. "Do you want to join us? It's still your place, too."

Clark sensed that wasn't the original favor. "Nope, I'm fine here. It's alright. Is there something you want from me? No offense, but I'm not into living with a couple of newlyweds." His words came out sharper than intended. Emotional stuff affected him more than it should. To remove the sting, he attempted a smile, though, from the way his muscles stretched, it might be more like a grimace.

Caitlyn's eyes opened wider, and she rested her hand on his arm. Even through his thick jacket, her touch was like a scorch. "I didn't think you'd be upset that Mason and I got married, even if it was quick. You seemed okay about us last month." She opened her mouth to continue, but he cut her off with a scowl.

Clark stepped back. Her hand dropped to her side, her frown remaining.

"I'm fine with it. It's great that you're happy. Mason's a decent guy and he deserves to be with someone like you. I'm not mad. I'm busy." The hurt in her eyes from his rebuff stabbed his chest like a knife to his heart. Damn. He couldn't say anything right. Caitlyn was one of his favorite people.

He rubbed his hand over his face, reminded that he hadn't shaved this morning. "I'm sorry. I must be more tired and grouchy than I realized. What can I do for you?" He widened his stance, bracing for impact.

She shot him a pointed look that said she didn't believe his excuse. "There's someone from the last group we brought in from Texas. She's pretty tough and we got along, but I hadn't realized until we were on the road that she isn't friendly with the others. I think she must have had an even more difficult time than most. She pulled away from all offers of friendship on our trip here. I suspect she doesn't think she needs anyone, and I fear she's going to isolate herself. That isn't how anyone should get a fresh start. She's here, waiting for spring to join the rebels." Caitlyn's eyes bored into his.

If she thought he might join up in the spring too, she was mistaken. He wasn't planning to fight. Ever. That's why he'd chosen life among the Saints.

"What has that got to do with me?" Clark swallowed. He had a feeling he knew where this was going. The image of the girl with the hard eyes sitting alone in his corner flashed through his mind. Her wary question about the table. Deep down, he'd recognized something like a gut punch. Like him, she'd been damaged and wanted to be left alone.

"I'd like you to check in on her. Her name's Janna." Caitlyn's next words confirmed his suspicion. "She's the one who moved to your table and spoke to you. Please."

Clark nodded. "I'll try." He turned for the door, only to spin around. Fighting tears, his throat thick. He lunged forward and hugged Caitlyn, squeezing her tight before letting go. "Congratulations," he whispered. "Give my love to Mason and stay safe."

Before she could respond, or he could acknowledge the confusion and pity in her eyes, he bolted for outdoors. Around a corner and out of sight, he stopped, gasping for air, tears pricking behind his eyes. He leaned against the back of the building, tapping his head against the wall. He covered his face with his hands. What the hell was wrong with him?

His mind slipped back, memories cascading one by one until they landed on a specific afternoon many years ago.

Caitlyn and Mat had been newly married, and they'd snuck into the barn to be alone, not realizing that he'd been there, writing in the loft in a swath of dusty sunshine.

Clark's cheeks flamed. He wanted to escape the barn, to leave it to his brother and his bride, but he couldn't slip down the ladder without giving away his presence.

Positioned in the loft, he focused his thoughts on his writing and became so engrossed, he forgot about Mat and Caitlyn below and his inability to speak to girls.

"How long have you been here?" Caitlyn's face was level with his knees where she stood on the ladder.

He flinched, his pencil flying from his hand and landing in the drifts of scattered loose hay while his heart stuttered and lurched like a dying creature.

Her cheeks flushed pink as, startled, he met her eyes. Speechless, he froze and couldn't answer. He bit his lip and his eyes filled with tears. His fair skin was aflame, burning everywhere. He swallowed, trying to speak, but no words came.

"I'm sorry Clark. We embarrassed you, didn't we?" Her forthright blue eyes met his anguished ones. "We should have checked the loft. Are you often up here writing?"

He nodded, still unable to find his voice. He closed his notebook and dropped his gaze to the weathered boards of the loft floor.

"It's not fair of us to drive you from your special place. From now on, Mat and I'll pack a picnic or go for a hike to find private time. I'm sorry we invaded your space. This is your home, too. Besides, we're off soon. Back to the rebels." Her calm words struck just the right note as he appreciated the direct approach. Caitlyn wasn't terrifying. She seemed like a perfect match for his fun-loving older brother. Why couldn't he find someone like that, someone so much less confusing than the local girls?

"Thank you," he whispered.

His fear of Caitlyn disappeared like smoke.

Clark shook his head, clearing his thoughts and returning to the present. That summer day had been a long time ago. Back before his mom's illness had taken root.

He caught his breath and regained control of his emotions, sucking in the wintery air. He headed for the toolshed, where he grabbed a snow shovel from the rack. A few of the main walkways had a partially cleared track down the middle, but he'd widen them and do the outer paths.

He attacked the fresh snow, tossing each shovelful well back from the trail. He went over each section a second time, chipping up thick chunks of ice until he came to the path below. Working up a sweat, he cleared the ice from the rest of the walkways in the settlement. Mindless busy work suited him these days.

Chapter 10: Tatsuda

Tatsuda strode through the streets of SoCal, headed back to Avery's broken-down house where they'd been staying the last several weeks. He clutched a roll with a dozen water tokens in his hand as his eyes scanned both sides of the lane ahead. Better to hold his wealth than leave it in a pocket where the plastic coins might clatter or show. No reason to make himself a mark. Though he was the strongest and most fit in their new household, he was no match for the bullies and gangs that preyed on the unwary.

Long Beach was filled with the desperate. Living in this environment would do that to you as there was insufficient food or water for most and opportunities to do something with your life were rare. Even thieves wouldn't find much here unless they were bold and strong. Twice this week he'd run footraces to give someone bigger the slip. He'd grown the last several months, though his growth spurt hadn't slowed him down. He was still quick. Scouting the streets as soon as he'd moved into Elsa's old neighborhood had also paid off. The twisty roads and neglected buildings provided excellent hiding places, with many out-of-the-way nooks.

This time, as he walked home, nothing pricked his intuition, telling him he was in danger, so he slowed, watching to see if anyone matched his pace before he turned onto their street. Nobody did. He seemed to be in the clear. He nodded to the helpful neighbor across the street. Tatsuda had been shocked to discover the older man was Wade's father. They were so different.

Arriving at the shack, he used the key Avery had given him and slipped inside.

Ginger looked up from the table where she sat with Rose and Charlie. Her eyes were wide. "Thank goodness you're back. You need to go for the medic. It's time."

A deep groan came from behind the curtain that separated the main living room from the room where Avery and her girls slept. Without a word, Tatsuda turned and ran up the street for the medic. There wasn't anything else he could do to help. Marcus had come by twice this week to check on Avery and wouldn't be surprised to see Tatsuda. He hoped Marcus was home as he'd said that because this was Avery's third child, delivery might happen fast. As worried as he was, it was also exciting. The baby was coming. They'd been waiting for this.

* * *

The race for the medic might have seemed urgent, but it was still nine hours later when the new baby arrived—another little girl that Avery named Aki after her Granny, who'd died earlier this year. Tatsuda glanced around the shack, hard to believe there were now six of them sharing this limited space. Still, it had been kind of Avery to share her home.

Marcus emerged from Avery's room and washed his hand in the basin with water from the gray water pump. He'd done that at least a dozen times.

"Avery is resting. The baby is healthy and a decent size." He addressed both Tatsuda and Ginger. He held his hand up just before Ginger spoke. "Because the baby got stuck and delivery was tough, Avery has several dozen stitches. She's going to be very uncomfortable for several weeks. You two are going to have to take care of her and her girls." His dark eyes met their gaze in turn. "She'll need a lot of help, and she shouldn't do much standing or walking for at least a week. Even then, she's going to be sore. See that she doesn't overdo it."

Tatsuda shared a glance with Ginger. So much for leaving right away, with the newborn in a swaddled bundle. His heart sank. They'd already stayed here longer than expected. Winters in Salt Lake might be harsher than in SoCal, but they would have been safer. Besides, Grady was expecting them. Caitlyn had promised to set up a place for Avery and her family to stay for the colder months.

Tatsuda swallowed his disappointment. They'd have to make the best of this situation.

* * *

Tatsuda and Ginger took turns changing and walking with the baby, who never seemed to sleep at night. His hearing had always been sharp, so Tatsuda was almost always the first to leap from the platform bed in the kitchen to pace the confines of the tiny house with Aki after she'd nursed. He'd change her then walk. Six paces forward. Six paces back. Over and over. The first night, the baby had howled for hours, waking both little girls, who'd also cried at being woken in the night. What a nightmare.

Baby Aki seemed to sense that he was safe, though, and now she seemed to trust him. After the first quick cry to wake him, Tatsuda would wait for her to feed, take her from her mom, burp her as Avery had shown him, and then walk with a certain bounce until she fell asleep. Her already chubby little hands, often curled around one of his fingers, melted his heart. He'd never been close to a baby before and found her fascinating, at least when she didn't stink. Still, he took care of diapers too when necessary.

He left the daytime feedings to Avery while Ginger took charge of Rose and Charlie, keeping them entertained for hours. She'd brought thick, colored waxy sticks called crayons and a special book with picture outlines for the girls to fill in. Rose took pride in staying in the lines and using colors that made sense. Charlie's were vibrant scribbles of whatever color she chose. Yesterday, her favorite was sky blue. Today, it was tomato red. His mouth watered thinking of the delicious food they'd had on Caitlyn's farm, including tomatoes. The bland oat bars they lived on had grown monotonous.

Ginger had also brought three small books from Portland. They were printed on glossy pieces of cardboard that she read to the girls every day. They would both crowd into her lap and plead for, "One more story." She'd also taught the girls an alphabet song and showed Rose how to write the letters of her name. Not only was Ginger patient, she was a natural teacher.

Tatsuda couldn't believe how happy Ginger seemed caring for the girls. She smiled all day, even cooped up in the little house for hours, and answered Charlie's countless questions with extreme patience. Both girls had taken to her, calling her Auntie Geri. The first time Rose had called her that, Ginger's eyes had glistened and she'd shot him a look like she couldn't believe her incredible luck.

Yesterday, Avery had stayed out of bed for almost an hour, twice—the first time since the baby had arrived two weeks ago. The new mom was still sore, and struggling to do her part around the house, but she was trying. He didn't know how she would have gotten by on her own. She seemed to realize this as well and thanked them often.

On the surface, she and Elsa looked like sisters, though Avery had soft brown eyes, instead of piercing yellow ones like Elsa, but she was patient and kind instead of fiery. Avery was nice, but he missed Elsa more than he'd expected. She didn't let him get away with much, and he appreciated she cared enough to give him a hard time. He'd taken her SoCal warning seriously. It wasn't like he was going to stop lifting things forever, though he'd been on his best behavior here—no matter how hard his fingers itched in the stores. He wouldn't steal from people with nothing, and he wasn't taking stupid risks.

When Aki fell asleep again, Tatsuda slipped into Avery's crowded room. The sun was coming up and he could just make out the shapes of Rose, Charlie, and Avery sprawled in the bed together—the two little girls curled together like kittens. Tatsuda tucked the baby into her nest of blankets beside the bed and ducked back through the curtain.

He plugged the water meter with the last water tokens and set water on the stove to boil for herbal tea and hot water for oatmeal. Drinking the water hot helped to cut the morning chill. He would head into the trading post later this morning to trade for additional tokens. The others stayed inside or in the neighborhood while he took care of errands. Elsa had sent them with coin, and with the sale of the license, they were okay, even if they might be stuck here for a while. He was capable of getting more coin if the need became dire, so he traded for only a week's worth of water tokens at a time.

It took four tokens for enough water for their group every day—three for the adults and one for the children combined. A whole winter's worth would be expensive. He'd resigned himself to them being here for at least several more weeks, maybe even months. He frowned, hoping the price didn't increase more.

After their breakfast, with extra dried fruit for the little girls, and vitamins purchased from the medic for Avery, Tatsuda strolled toward the shops. Though the stores were essentially the same, with identical GreenCorps prices, he favored Vic's Trading Post simply because Vic and Martha were pleasant people. He understood Elsa's preference. Plus, Vic was a gossip and often slipped choice bits of information into the conversation.

Tatsuda had almost reached the town square when the sound of a disturbance reached him. He stepped into a shadowed doorway to assess the situation. From the thumping noises and guttural groans, it sounded like someone was getting beat up. He wanted no part of that.

"I'm sorry. I'm sorry," someone said between ragged breaths. "I didn't know Daisy was your favorite. You haven't been around."

"Well, I'm back in town for a while. Stay the fuck away from her." Wade's deep voice carried across the square.

Tatsuda flinched. This asshole again. He needed to let Ginger know to be on her guard, especially if she went out walking. She should re-dye her hair again too. Just in case. Her roots had just started to show and the semi-permanent color had faded. Not that any of the others went out alone, as they were always tending children. Wade wouldn't recognize him, so Tatsuda was about to carry on with his errand when the next words froze his blood.

"How long do we have to stay in this cesspool?" said someone near Wade.

"Since Elsa didn't come through Sacramento, or she slipped past us, we're going to do the next best thing. We're going to make an example of her sister. We'll put out word that she's been deported. Elsa will find out and come. I give it two weeks. Tops."

"Why wait until then? We're here. We could arrest the sister today. For real, not just some story." The voices came closer.

Tatsuda stopped breathing, intent on hearing Wade's reply.

"With all those raids to free the whores in Texas, the towns down there need a new batch. After that mess in Boise, they will collect the whores from places like this, where they can't fight back. We've been ordered to do a round-up next week, starting here. We'll grab Avery then. She's living across the street from my folks, so we can scoop her up anytime. Once she's in jail, someone will pass on the news. Hell, maybe those chatty shopkeepers will spread the word." He cleared his throat and made a spitting sound. "But Elsa will be too late to save her sister." The ass sounded smug.

"What about her kids? Aren't they really young? What a pain."

"McCoy doesn't want the brats, but there'll be some rich couple in Denver who can't have kids. There's a market for orphans that young, no matter where they're from. Even heapster trash."

Tatsuda clenched his fists. No way was this going to happen. None of them would allow the children to be taken and sold. They'd have to kill him first. And Avery. And Ginger.

He remained frozen until the soldiers passed, heading toward the garrison beside the train station. How would he and Ginger sneak the others out of town? His gut churned. They had less than a week to figure it out.

Mulling over options, he continued to Vic's and bought five days' worth of food—they could save some to travel—and three days of water tokens. Before he returned home to break the despicable news about Wade and GreenCorps' plans, he checked the train schedule and the hidden rebel drop box behind the station in case there was a letter. Nothing.

The train they needed left in two days. He didn't stay near the station for long, fading into the shadowy alleys as soon as he discovered the necessary information. They would just avoid Wade until the train left. Two days gave them time to plan and gather what they'd need. Somehow, they were leaving.

Hopping the regular way with Charlie, Rose, and the baby would never work. Hell, Avery probably wasn't strong enough to get on a moving train on her own either—especially with stitches. Maybe if she was healthy, but she still had trouble walking without pain. Running and jumping onto an accelerating train would be almost impossible.

Tatsuda would come back tonight and snoop around by the tracks, pick the perfect place to hide, and leave a quick note for Elsa in the alley drop box. Perhaps there would be another option he hadn't figured out. At last, he turned for home. Avery and Ginger might have ideas he hadn't considered.

Back at the house, he glanced across the street to Wade's parents' place. Did they know their son was back in town? How likely was he to visit?

* * *

November 4, 2195

E,

You have a new niece, named after your great-grandmother. We've also run into another complication getting out of town, but T has a plan and we hope to see you soon. Your "friend" from across the street is back and plans to deport your family. We won't let it happen and will leave, even if it's complicated. See you at your uncle's place.

G and T

CHAPTER 11: JANNA

Janna examined the crowded dining hall, scanning for an empty table. Caitlyn and Mason had left for their farm, and Janna wasn't sure where to eat. They'd been the only people since she'd left SoCal that she'd interacted with by choice. Today their absence left her feeling odd and on edge, and like drawing inward again. Despite the warmth inside, she zipped her jacket all the way to her chin and ducked her head. Maybe it was best they'd left so soon. They'd been kind and understanding, but she didn't like feeling like she needed anyone.

She took a deep breath. Today would be her first workday with the Saints, starting in a couple of hours—washing dishes. Cleaning plates and scrubbing pots weren't glamorous, but in exchange for food and a place to stay, she didn't mind pitching in to do her share—a vast improvement over Texas. Nobody here seemed to judge her for her past or ask what she'd done to survive.

Maybe everyone had similar stories—an idea that brought little comfort, even if it might someday. For now, she was still too angry and hurt.

She hesitated a minute longer, hoping someone would leave and a place would become free. No such luck. There were people throughout the room and few scattered places where she could sit to eat in peace. Many diners were no longer eating, just socializing before heading out to work. She didn't want to have to sit and talk.

Her breakfast tray wobbled while she considered her options.

Families, chatty saints, her fellow refugees, or that writer. She seldom saw him except at meals and he seemed to prefer quiet too. The last two days, she'd noticed he sat alone. Like her, he often came early and late, maybe to avoid the crowd. Or perhaps his job kept him busy until later. Not that she knew how he spent his time. Nor did she care. It was none of her business.

Making up her mind, Janna ducked her face, a curtain of her dark hair screening her from the sides, and walked toward the corner he preferred. Based on his previous behavior, he'd probably leave her to her desired solitude. She didn't need friends at the settlement, or anywhere else, for that matter. She could take care of herself, but sitting next to someone without talking wasn't being needy.

The Saints settlement was a temporary stop, just a place to stay until spring and the rebel campaign resumed. Then, not only would she get revenge for what GreenCorps had done to her, but she could be useful.

She checked the slim, dark-haired man writing in a store-bought notebook, instead of rough homemade pages, with a surreptitious glance. Janna held her breath and stopped next to the table. She sat on the opposite end of the same bench, placing her tray without making noise. She peeked to her left. He remained engrossed in his scribbling and didn't look up or acknowledge her presence. She slowly exhaled. Perfect.

Janna picked up her fork and ate the first several bites on her plate before taking out the book she'd brought. Reading at the table had become customary in Texas. Here, she at least had access to books from the library, instead of just the one from her travel bag, bought on the SoCal black market almost two years ago.

Several minutes later, the writer looked up, his pale blue eyes widening a fraction as he registered her presence for the first time. She tried to gauge his reaction without being obvious, pretending to be engrossed in the borrowed book, though in reality, she'd reread the same page multiple times. She still didn't know what the story was about. Her cheeks warmed. Why did he keep staring?

"What?" She said, turning toward him, irritated into speaking. "Any reason I can't sit at this otherwise empty table? You don't own it." She lifted her chin, daring him to argue.

He shook his head, drank some of what must by now be tepid tea, and returned his gaze to what he'd been writing. Several minutes passed as his pencil flew across his page while she went back to eating. The ripping sound as he removed a page startled her. He didn't so much as glance in her direction again before he stood. He hovered over the table where she was finishing her hash browns and scrambled eggs, but he didn't speak.

Since leaving San Antonio, Janna had become a slow eater, savoring every bite of scrumptious food. It had been years, if ever, since she'd eaten this well. Her dad's old railroad job had been enough to buy the odd luxury, but here actual food was available every day— unlike SoCal and Texas, it was free. Well, she was expected to help with community chores and pitch in, but that was nothing. Nobody would touch her unless she allowed it. She hadn't imagined anywhere like this. Why couldn't more people grow their own food and be free of GreenCorps with their strict regulations and high prices?

The silence stretched and the back of her neck prickled, not with danger but with a flustered feeling. She knew it was the writer without even looking. What did he want?

"What?" She met his startling pale blue eyes again. Icy blue with darker rings around the outside edges. He held out the page he'd torn from his notebook. When she'd taken it, he left without speaking. She watched as he dropped off his dishes and continued toward the door. His silence hadn't been threatening, just awkward.

She glanced down at the paper in her hand.

Janna,

I'm not much of a talker either, but if you have questions or need a listener, you know where to find me. Same table tonight for dinner? 8? I prefer to eat late.

-Clark

How the hell did he know her name? The thought threw her off balance and a thousand questions flooded her mind—her curiosity roused by his odd behavior. Why hadn't he spoken? It was refreshing not to have to make small talk. His silence was a gift. Maybe he had a throat injury and couldn't speak well. She remembered the scratchy quality of his voice at their first encounter when he'd been surprised into words. Perhaps he was a refugee too and had been traumatized. If so, where had he come from? Also, what did he write in his notebook? Her list went on, his unexpected note making her want to discover the answers.

She didn't like not knowing or blindly accepting everything. Without knowledge, she had no power or control. She was done with believing everyone at face value without learning what was behind someone's intentions.

Janna scanned the dining room, but Clark was gone. She finished eating, closed her book, shoved it into her satchel, and stood. She had an idea. Caitlyn had introduced her to Sister Hope in the library when they'd arrived. The soft-spoken woman had seemed kind. After Janna's first shift washing dishes, she resolved to find Sister Hope and ask how to get paper and a pencil. Then, she'd write back to this Clark. Two could play this game. Maybe he didn't speak, but she might still get some answers.

* * *

That night, Janna stood outside the dining hall, watching pairs and groups of laughing and chatting people exit, heading home or to shared cabins. The others from the train had paired off—some as couples, others as friends. She hadn't been able to join their groups as they told their own stories of their life before now. She didn't know what was stopping her, but she couldn't bring herself to socialize. Nobody had wanted to be working for GreenCorps in Texas and the rebels had saved them all from a bleak life, but the words for Wade's betrayal were too raw to speak aloud. If she spoke about what he'd done, she might scream.

In a matter of days, she'd become the only isolated newcomer—which is what she wanted. Right? Her heart felt heavy as she stared at the double doors. Why couldn't she enter? What was she waiting for? Her nose grew cold in the crisp air as she delayed. If she arrived at the table at the appointed time, was she admitting that she wanted someone to talk to? Was she planning to write a note in return? Ridiculous.

Had Clark simply been polite because she'd sat near him twice? Or he felt sorry for her? Feeling silly, she blinked back tears. The tough girl act was just that, an act; no matter how hard she tried to be like Elsa, she wasn't. Janna ached all the time and was hungry for connection, but she wasn't sure how to make one anymore. After cutting herself off from others to survive, it had become ingrained. What if it was permanent?

She swallowed. Maybe he wanted what many men wanted from women, which wasn't happening. She was nobody to Clark. Janna would have to remain on guard. She took a breath and briefly closed her eyes. That wasn't the vibe she'd gotten. Still, she was done with sex. If he could be a friend, that might be nice—but in twenty-two years, she'd only made two, Elsa and Avery. Maybe Caitlyn could be a friend too, though she wasn't here and was also so intimidating.

Janna shifted her feet, which ached from the cold. Damn. She needed to decide—dinner or leave. Her stomach gurgled. She wanted to eat. Maybe there would be more meat and vegetables. Delicious food would be worth the discomfort of forcing herself to meet Clark.

Screwing up her courage, she stepped toward the entrance. It must be well after eight. Perhaps even half past. What if he'd gone? Then, she might have the table to herself. Her feet moved again, and she opened the door. Purposefully avoiding looking at the table where Clark might be sitting, she grabbed a tray and dished up a plate of hot, delicious food. The delectable smell of roast meat made the risk worthwhile. Turning, she took a deep breath and checked. He was there, eating. Alone.

His notebook sat on the table beside him, but he wasn't writing. His pale blue eyes watched her, his expression unreadable. Her cheeks flamed and her steps faltered, but she forced herself to continue. Reaching the table, she sat a foot closer to him than before, but far enough away that she wasn't crowding him.

Clark said nothing, but picked up his pencil and scrawled something, before sliding the sheet of paper toward her. She shifted a couple of inches closer, reached out, and pulled it so she could read what he'd written. She still refused to look straight at him.

"I didn't think you were coming."

Her hands shook as she took her own pencil from her pocket. She swallowed. With shaky lettering, she wrote a reply.

"I wasn't sure either. I stood outside for ages." She nudged it toward him and ate a bite of creamy mashed potatoes covered with brown gravy. They melted in her mouth. Something about feeling full and fed allowed her to relax. At least a little.

His long arm slid the page in his direction and he wrote again before angling the paper so she could read. *"That must have been cold."*

She met his eyes and shrugged.

He raised an eyebrow and wrote. *"What made you change your mind?"*

"How did you know my name?"

He smiled. Then frowned, as though surprised that he'd smiled. *"Curiosity then."*

She mirrored his previous expression and quirked her eyebrow in return, waiting.

"Caitlyn."

Upon seeing the blonde woman's name, his interest now made sense. He was checking in with her for a friend. She wasn't sure how she felt about that. Janna chewed on her lower lip and drew the paper within reach.

"She directed me to the train when the rebels liberated some of us in Texas. I rode with her and Mason. How do you know her? I don't think she was ever a Saint." Janna nudged the paper toward Clark and held her breath, waiting for an answer.

He stared into the distance for a moment before he wrote, perhaps formulating his thoughts. She appreciated he didn't rush and seemed thoughtful. While he contemplated what to write, she ate. The crispy meat was phenomenal. Janna hadn't ever had anything so delicious. She almost felt stronger, braver, after eating it. She glanced over to where Clark wrote, his arm covering his words until he was ready to share.

At last, he shoved the paper toward her.

"Caitlyn's first husband was one of my brothers. Mathew. He was Mason's best friend and, like them, he was a rebel. Seventeen months ago, soldiers killed him outside Dallas."

Seventeen months was a precise amount of time. Most people would have called it a year and a half or almost two years. That loss felt like one of the corner pieces of the Clark puzzle.

"How?" Her question startled both of them when she spoke aloud. The words hung in the air over them like a cloud.

Like she'd broken a spell, the gulf between them widened and his expression became distant. He swung his legs over the bench and stood, gathering his things.

The bottom dropped out of her stomach. She tugged on his long sleeve, startling them both. A fluttery panic filled her chest. He was leaving.

"I'm sorry." She scribbled, tapping the paper with her pencil so he would read. *"Please stay. You can ask me questions. Anything."*

He stared at her—those pale eyes unnerving as though they could see inside her. He might be deciding what to do, but he was impossible to read. She underlined the world, Please. Her stupid lower lip trembled. Why did this conversation matter?

Clark returned to his seat, sitting a little closer than before. She held her breath as he flipped the paper over. His hand shook when he wrote.

"Where were you before Texas?"

Leaning toward him, they didn't have to move the paper for her to write. *"I grew up in SoCal."*

"Were you a criminal?"

She shook her head. Everybody who found out she was from SoCal asked that. Clark wrote so much faster than she did, but she was scared to speak aloud again.

"My dad worked for the railroad, but wouldn't take bribes from someone important in the corporation who wanted him to turn a blind eye. Probably one of the McCoy brothers. He got fired. We stayed in Long Beach but were dirt poor. Now my brother works for GreenCorps."

"Shouldn't that have been protection?" Clark's gaze met hers. Up close, his icy eyes were just as unfathomable.

Reading his question, Janna understood his impulse from a minute earlier. She wanted to bolt. Instead, she wrote the words she'd only admitted to herself.

"My brother sold me. Turned me into a whore."

As soon as she wrote the words, her vision blurred. She covered her face with her hands. Great gulping sobs burst from her, and her entire body shook. Though mortified at her outburst, she couldn't stop.

To her surprise, Clark slid closer and wrapped his arms around her while she cried. She rested her head on his shoulder and he turned so she was wedged against his chest. It took several minutes, or almost forever, for her to compose herself. Her cheeks heated and she couldn't look up. She'd bawled like a silly baby.

"I'm sorry," she whispered.

"You're safe now." His voice was barely audible. If she hadn't been so close, she wouldn't have heard. There must be a lot more to his story than his brother dying.

She leaned into him a few seconds longer. With a deep breath, she pulled back, immediately missing his scent, which was clean like soap, with a hint of something spicy. Somehow, he made her feel safer than she'd felt in a long time.

"Finish your dinner. May I walk you back to your cabin afterward? I'll wait. It's cold and dark out. I wouldn't want you to slip or get lost."

"Thank you." She wiped her eyes. She had no idea what any of this meant, but crying had been a release. Maybe she and Clark could be friends. It would be nice to know someone, since she'd be here for the next four to six months, depending on winter conditions. They might be cut off in the canyon until March or April. For the first time since that first day when Wade had tricked her and abandoned her on the train, she admitted she wasn't just angry with her brother. He was a monster and she wanted him to pay.

Chapter 12: Tatsuda and Clark

Tatsuda stole out into the chilly night, slinking through the winding neighborhood as he made his way toward the rich houses on the hill. Even this far south, the November air had a bite at this late hour. With Wade in town, he, Ginger, and Avery had discussed the escape plan and agreed they needed to leave. Avery needed things from her old house to travel with the children, and she'd sent him with a mental list.

Last summer, Jaxon had given her only ten minutes to gather her belongings before soldiers would remove her from the house. She'd collected a few essential clothes and toys, and left before anyone got physical.

Avery had returned once when her ex-husband was out of town, hoping to collect a few more supplies, but he'd changed the locks. She said the place had looked deserted, but because it was in the wealthy neighborhood, the streets were well-lit and patrolled by security. Her former neighbors and so-called friends were no help—unwilling to speak to her, even those she previously had spent time with.

Tatsuda snorted and shook his head. They'd treated her like poverty was contagious.

Avery hadn't dared to break a window to get inside or known how to pick a lock. He didn't share the same concerns. This was better. If she'd taken things for the children right away, Jaxon would have guessed it had been her and probably had her arrested or deported. He was that kind of asshole. Now it wouldn't matter, they'd be gone.

Since that first attempt, Avery had stayed away from her old neighborhood. She also wouldn't risk being out after curfew, leaving her small children without someone to care for them. Before he and Ginger had arrived, she'd been alone.

Tatsuda didn't care about security measures, or minor inconveniences like locks. They weren't the problem. He put on a confident front for the group, but security patrols would be difficult to bypass because rich people were obsessed with protecting their stuff. He would need a good bit of luck to get in and out with no one the wiser.

Even more difficult would be moving through the town at night. The gangs of thieves were relentless and skilled at spotting people hiding in the shadows. How would he move the entire group through town? He was stealthy, but Avery and her children? The baby? One cry and their escape would be over.

He slid into the shadows along the buildings on the right-hand side of the street. In this workers' neighborhood, it was easy. The gangs tended to make more noise than he did, so they weren't difficult to avoid. Until he spotted a lone lookout, causing him to backtrack. It wasn't as simple as he'd hoped. He ducked down a different street as he wound his way toward the bluff overlooking Long Beach.

He paused at the edge of the town, scoping out the route ahead. The road seemed too well-lit as it swooped across the slope, and too exposed without greenery or shrubs on the sides, just flattened grass and tangled junk. So, Tatsuda tramped through the dusty grass and bushes beyond the pools of pale yellow light. He stumbled once, on hidden roots, but caught himself before he fell.

At the top, a single paved street with eight houses on the same side overlooked the dismal town and the Heap below. Four additional houses sat on the far side. Clusters of moths fluttered around the streetlights, making the lights look like they flickered. The lamp posts were positioned at regular intervals. The hilltop neighborhood was serene; not even the distant sounds of bars and brothels below marred the peace, and he almost felt like he was in a different world.

Remaining in the shadows, he scanned the area until he finally spotted the security guards. It looked like two men worked here, one posted at either end of the street. He waited to determine their patrol pattern. Every ten minutes, they switched positions to the other side, passing in the middle. Jaxon's house was the third from the far end. Tatsuda slid into the rear of the houses and crossed from yard to yard without a sound. Avery said three of the houses had dogs, but they should be in at night.

Tatsuda halted a few times as he caught sight of movement within the occupied homes through the glass windows. It wasn't so late that everyone inside was sleeping, and he would hate for a chance sighting to ruin his mission. His heart rate increased, but he wasn't worried about being caught, it was the thrill. He'd missed this. His fingers tingled, anticipating his gathering.

He reached the appropriate house and sidled up to the back door. He placed his ear against the chilly metal door and listened. While the interior looked dark, that didn't mean it was empty. Jaxon might have a new girlfriend, allowed friends to stay inside, or hired a housekeeper to maintain the place when he was out of town. It was even possible Jaxon would be here. Tatsuda hadn't been able to keep tabs on all arrivals by train and they'd passed the deadline Wade had mentioned outside Sacramento.

With several minutes of quiet from inside, Tatsuda set to work with his pick and shearing wrench, the faint scratching seeming louder in the dark than during the day. Still, no security out front would hear the minute noise. His most stressful moment came just as he popped the lock with a click while the security guards passed the house next door.

"Clear."

"Yeah. Still quiet as a funeral." Their voices carried in the still night, so they seemed closer than expected.

He gave them another minute or two to pass beyond the front of the house before he continued. He eased the back door open and slid inside, dropping a pebble into the doorway to prevent it from fully closing. It would appear closed at a glance, but wasn't. If he had to leave in a hurry, it was best to ensure the door wouldn't be latched. In that situation, every second mattered.

Faint light came from the streetlights outside and he let his eyes adjust to the near-dark conditions before he moved farther into the house.

He'd asked Avery about the layout and the probable location for the items he was hunting for, so his stay would be brief. She wanted baby items she'd stored when Rose and Charlotte outgrew them, plus a few special items the girls missed. Those should be on the main floor. He gathered the most important items first and slipped them into his bag, always keeping his ear cocked for movement from within the house. Something told him he wasn't alone—though it was just a hunch. The air seemed lived in, and the building wasn't cold enough to be empty. Nobody would heat an unoccupied house.

If it was deserted now, they could soon return.

He collected the baby bottles, manual pump, extra travel diapers, and another blanket for each of the girls, ones Avery had crocheted with store-bought yarn. That the girls had so little at their house when this house was filled with luxuries set his teeth on edge. Under the stairs, he located the hall closet with stored winter clothing. He eased its door open without noise. Checking over his shoulder, he tugged the window curtains closed before flicking on a small closet light.

Tatsuda located jackets for Avery and the girls, taking a second to admire the thick fabric and solid make. These looked new and must've come from Denver, Canada, or the East—definitely not scavenged from the Heap. Nothing like what most families had. He'd never had a winter coat until they found the bunker last fall. Turning off the pale light, he bundled everything into his backpack before moving on. The last item had been stored upstairs and Avery had said only to try for it if the house was empty. He hesitated. It was one of the most important things on her list. She'd stressed how useful a sling would be.

He set the loaded backpack outside by the house where he could grab it if he had to leave in a hurry and returned inside. He had gone no more than a few steps, when there was a thud overhead, the upper floor creaked. Tatsuda froze in mid step, caught in the doorway between the kitchen and the open area by the front door. He backed into the deeper shadows of the kitchen and waited, holding his breath. There was no movement on the stairs, so he stayed—listening, every muscle coiled. Upstairs, a toilet flushed, and the footsteps returned to what should be one of the bedrooms.

He waited until the upstairs door closed with a faint thud before he resumed.

The house wasn't deserted, but he also didn't want to return without the baby sling. They could rig something if they had to, but Avery had an actual baby sling with proper support that someone could wear when they hopped the train. Something rich people had. For their escape, it meant without one, whoever held the baby would only have one arm for climbing the train ladder. Proper equipment was worth the risk, especially when the other options were poor, even at short notice. They were leaving tonight.

Tatsuda retraced his steps to the base of the stairs. Taking a slow, deep breath, he started up. On each step, he placed his foot near the wall at the edge and imagined himself as light. Avery had said the stairs were solid and didn't creak, but he couldn't trust her to remember every tiny sound. He doubted she'd snuck around her house in the dark when the smallest sounds carried and seemed magnified.

He reached the top. The upper hallway seemed darker, the air heavier.

He advanced, passing the first door on the left. That had been Rose's room. He needed the next one. If it was occupied, he was ready to flee.

Stretching out his hand, he was about to turn the knob, when someone squeaked across the hall—a woman. Then there was a giggle and a murmur from a deeper voice. Then, a sharp intake of breath. Not the room he needed, but he grimaced. That was the master bedroom. Tatsuda doubted Jaxon would let guests sleep there. Though Tatsuda hadn't seen Jaxon McCoy in town, there wasn't much doubt that he was home and entertaining female companionship.

The quiet sounds from next door increased in volume and tempo.

Tatsuda would need to be fast. He couldn't risk being caught upstairs in the hall—trapped without a way out. Or nabbed anywhere in the house, for that matter. Wade might not recognize him, but Jaxon would. He'd seen them all in broad daylight more than once. Tatsuda twisted the door handle and slipped into Charlie's room. He was in luck; someone had left the blinds open, and he used the nearby streetlights to navigate.

He tiptoed across the floor. Once the wooden floor creaked. He stopped and shifted his weight, waiting for a response, his ears straining to pick up a change from across the hall. Nothing. Staying away from the window, he inched the closet open. The door folded toward him, whispering across the carpet. He held his breath. Still nothing.

That quiet sound shouldn't carry across the hall, but the sense he needed to hurry grew stronger.

With his heart pounding so hard he was afraid Jaxon or his guest might hear, Tatsuda widened the opening and felt for the baby sling on the middle shelf. For a second, he didn't feel anything where Avery had said she'd left it. He groped around in the dim light. No luck.

Tatsuda took a deeper breath and tried the next shelf down. Still nothing. He glanced over his shoulder as the sex moans and grunts increased further. He was almost out of time. With a last grab on the shelf above the first one, his hand met soft, stretchy fabric. He tugged an object out and held a strangely shaped cloth lump with straps and plastic clips. It didn't look like anything, but it must be what Avery had described. He gathered the straps together so they wouldn't clatter and closed the closet. Best not to leave a trace he'd been here—even if they were leaving town. Without obvious clues, Jaxon should be none the wiser.

Across the hall, Jaxon let out a deep moan and a final yell.

Time to go.

Tatsuda slid out, closing the door behind him. Like the thief he used to be, he slipped back down the stairs without sound. He made it as far as the kitchen before Jaxon's heavy tread moved across the floor. With his heart still thundering, Tatsuda slid out the back door, removed the pebble, and left, tugging the door closed before releasing the handle with a gentle turn. He scooped up the backpack, jammed the sling inside, and crouched at the edge of the backyard. He was out of the house, but not in the clear. Not yet.

He'd lost track of time and needed to figure out where security was on their route. He listened. The street in front of the house remained quiet. The guards must be elsewhere, but he needed to be sure. This was all for nothing if he got caught by GreenCorps on the way home. They wouldn't care what he'd stolen; they'd send him to Texas for sure. He slowed his breathing. Without his heart pounding so hard, the silence deepened and pressed into him.

He waited to move until the light upstairs flicked off in the bathroom. Then, he hopped the fence to the next yard, moving from one to another until he reached the end of the street. He peeked around the edge of the first house on the street. The original guard was back in position.

Tatsuda crouched in the shadows. He waited until security once more marched down the street, then Tatsuda scurried on silent feet to the road. As he had on the way up, he avoided the obvious route and traversed the darker hillside to make his way to the train station.

He had one more quick errand before returning home for an hour or two of sleep.

* * *

Tatsuda felt conspicuous as he, Ginger, and Avery exited the dark shack, each carrying a sleeping bundle with a child. The frosty air nipped their noses and cheeks while their breath plumed white in the air. This was the coldest night yet. Avery had the baby, Ginger held a drowsy Charlie, and Tatsuda had volunteered to carry the heaviest burden. He carried most of the new gear stuffed into his backpack on top of his belongings, and Rose, who at four, seemed like a bag of rocks in his arms. Adjusting her weight, he glanced up and down the street, sweat already dripping down his back and forehead. He stepped onto the crumbled asphalt of the road, the others following.

Wade's parents' house remained dark and silent.

This wasn't like his earlier jaunt or any other nighttime roaming. The others were relying on him now more than ever. The responsibility of their safety weighed on him as they snuck through the night. He doubted Avery had broken curfew before. This late, with the bars and brothels long closed—their patrons having stumbled home—fewer gangs would be around than hours ago with pickings slim. He'd gambled on that as part of the reason to leave at this desperate hour. Plus, the train leaving at dawn was an express. They'd only have to climb aboard once and hide as it slowed through Sacramento and Reno, but it would continue on to Salt Lake City.

Tatsuda's shoulder blades twitched as the silent group moved toward the station. Though early, anyone could be watching from inside any of the small houses. Most people wouldn't care, but informants could be anywhere.

He jumped twice at small noises, but both times it was just raccoons pawing through alley trash, their masked faces glancing upward as the group passed. One hissed and stood its ground, glaring as it held a chunk of dried bread between its paws. When they reached the town square, Tatsuda darted across the street, awkwardly carrying his load, hoping the motion didn't jar Rose awake. Once across the well-lit section, he whistled a low sound he'd demonstrated at home as the "all clear" signal.

He held his breath until both Avery and Ginger reached his side. Charlie moaned. Tatsuda's eyes met Ginger's, and she tucked the little girl's thumb back into her mouth. Charlie sucked noisily for half a dozen pulls before her mouth became slack. They wouldn't be able to keep the kids asleep much longer, especially with all the running and jouncing.

A few more twists and turns in dark alleys before they came to the trickiest part.

Tatsuda stopped behind the train station. He reached down and touched the stolen key in his pocket. He'd scouted the train on the way back from Jaxon's and made a hard decision. The train had a middle engine sleeper car, and he'd nicked the master key from the station office. In the few hours since, he'd gambled on nobody noticing that it had gone missing. Since hopping a train the usual way, sling or no sling, would be challenging, the enclosed car should be more accessible and provide more safety.

Staying in a line, he led everyone past the length of the train, into the darkness up the tracks beyond town. This time of year, they still had another couple of hours before sunrise, but a hint of the morning sky lightened the horizon with a pale band in the east. The gravel crunched softly under Ginger and Avery's feet, but that couldn't be helped. Twice he stopped and held his breath as bulls called out to each other behind them. Their patrol seemed heavy, but standard.

Somehow, Tatsuda's group reached the front of the train and crossed to the far side, away from the station. They moved near the edge of the bushes along the fence line, back toward the middle engine. Their best bet was to get on from the side opposite the station. He swallowed. This had better work.

They remained in a tight bunch until they came to the second looming engine hugging the track. He'd done this one other time in Reno. Memories of his bravado about stealing the key and getting onboard with Elsa and an injured Walker flashed through his mind. That trip had cemented their relationship as friends. He looked at the metal door above. He couldn't climb while carrying Rose.

Tatsuda crouched down at the side of the track and set her feet on the ground while he held her. She clung to him, whimpered, and then her eyes popped open.

"We're having an adventure and going on a train," he whispered.

She looked around with enormous eyes. Her lower lip trembled. "With Mommy, my sisters, and Auntie Geri?" Her voice echoed in the darkness.

He nodded. "All of us. Can you be a big girl and stay super quiet?" He rested his icy finger against his lips.

She nodded. Avery reached out a hand and took her oldest daughter's tiny hand in her own. Avery's lips clamped together in a firm line. She might be in pain or had ripped her stitches while running across town. He hoped she would be okay. Not only would Elsa kill him if her sister got hurt, but he liked Avery.

Tatsuda scampered up the ladder, unlocked the side door, and held it wide. He tossed his bags into the interior, climbed back down, and went to help with the kids. From the station, came thumping feet on the platform and booming voices. Must be a shift change and workers arriving, their voices and boots causing a commotion. He looked both ways again and strained to listen to the words being said. Still no extra alarm. They'd almost reached the moment of truth. He held out his arms and pointed up. Avery guided Rose to the base of the ladder.

He showed the four-year-old how to climb, moving her arms with her and helping her to step. With her short limbs, she was slow, but one step at a time, she boarded the train. He climbed behind her to make sure she didn't fall. He returned to the ground, took Avery's burdens, other than the sleeping baby in the sling, and carried them inside.

Rose sat on the floor. "I'm guarding the packs." Her voice was a loud whisper that made him wince. A quick glance out the window showed no change to security.

He put a finger to his mouth and whispered. "Good girl. Your mom is next."

At the top of the ladder, he helped Avery aboard.

At the station, the sound of voices grew louder. Maybe workers doing a final check before the train departed. They were cutting it close.

Sweat dripped down his forehead. Tatsuda wiped his damp palms and took Charlie from where she'd slept, her head on Ginger's shoulder. The little girl cried, a long piercing tired wail.

Shit. He held his breath. The sound carried in the muffled silence of dawn.

Boots pounded the crunchy gravel as bulls raced up the track toward them.

"What's that noise?" said someone.

Tatsuda motioned to the ladder, and Ginger scrambled up. At the top, she lay down and reached for Charlie. He climbed the cold steel ladder as best he could, the crying child in front of him—louder and more unhappy with each passing second.

"Check the other side," said someone on the opposite side of the train. They must be only a couple of cars back.

Gravel crunched as men approached, their lanterns swaying.

From the top, Ginger grabbed the struggling Charlie and disappeared into the car. The door wouldn't lock from the inside. Remaining outside, Tatsuda swung it closed. Charlie's screams faded. Then, stopped. Good. The car must be insulated, but for that level of quiet, Avery must have silenced her daughter—at least for now. He needed to keep them from being found.

Tatsuda locked the door and swung onto the side of the train. Gripping the grooves and seams in the metal, he passed the empty cab, and inched onto the front of the engine. He hung above the ground, hoping the searchers didn't glance upward.

"There's nobody here."

"Check the bushes. Hoppers don't make it this far very often, but we're supposed to check everything. McCoy's fed up waiting for that Elsa. He thinks she might have snuck into town under our noses and is hiding somewhere."

"Think of the reward if we're the ones to bring her to justice."

Tatsuda dropped lightly onto the knuckle of the train and hopped to the car in front of the second engine. Though it was a covered hopper—Walker's favorite type of car to ride on—the porch at the back was too exposed for an inspection. He scooted up the pole at the back and lifted himself onto the cold metal roof. He lay spread-eagle, facing the engine and back toward the station and security. His heart drummed triple-time while he fought to catch his breath.

Lights and voices continued around, up and down both sides of the train. They beat the bushes and peered into the hoppers, front and back. Checking everywhere.

He held his breath when someone climbed the engine ladder and tried the door. He prayed the others kept little Charlie silent. She'd probably think this was a grand adventure once she was properly awake.

"Nobody here. Still locked."

"I could have sworn I heard a baby crying." The voices were closer than before.

"Must have been carried on the wind from the neighborhood. Somebody's kid with a nightmare. Forget about it."

The voices dropped, as two men stopped just below his perch. Railroad workers, not soldiers like those he'd overhead a few days ago. Their voices were hushed.

"I'm sick of this high-alert shit. If it wasn't for that reward, I'd say more power to that Elsa girl. Jace McCoy beat her, and she still managed to hop a train out of town. He says she stole something, but Vic says she asked about a metal tube at least a month before Jace McCoy came to town. She didn't steal from GreenCorps, even if that's what they claim the reward is for. That girl's a survivor. I hope she makes it."

"I'm sick of this bullshit, too. On half wages, no less. The rebels free a bunch of people in Texas and all of us railroad workers get blamed. It isn't fair. How am I supposed to feed my family?"

Tatsuda's heart soared. If some of the best-paid citizens were complaining, the rebel plan was working. They needed everyone on board to defeat GreenCorps.

The frost-covered metal of the roof stole his heat, but he remained motionless.

He couldn't hear anything else of interest and the searchers returned to their standard patrol as others finished loading the boxcars in the rear section. Tatsuda didn't dare climb down or join the others. He regretted tossing his bag inside with the others, but it wasn't safe to retrieve his belongings. He would get hungry, but he'd have to go without food for the duration of the trip. At least he had his canteen.

Once the train was moving, he would slide down to the covered porch to ride. It would be less exposed and warmer than up top where he was now. He'd explained the beds and bedding inside the engine to Ginger, and he hoped she was getting everyone settled. This would be a long ride—more than twenty-four hours before they would arrive in Salt Lake.

Waiting for the train to leave, he drifted off to sleep; he could use a brief nap.

Tatsuda woke to the crashing sounds of slack action adjusting as the train cars banged into each other. Finally, the train was departing, heading toward the rising sun. Once the train was at full speed and away from town, he slid down the pole and tucked himself into the riding porch. He wrapped his arms around his knees, tugged his collar higher, curled up, and went back to sleep, his arm a pillow.

* * *

Alone in the dark, Clark fumbled for a candle beside his bed. With a practiced strike, he struck a match and lit the wick, throwing soft light into his bunk. He sat up and unfolded the pieces of paper with the written mealtime exchange between himself and Janna. Each day, he tucked them into the back of his notebook, taking them out to reread when he couldn't sleep.

Janna: *Why don't you speak? Were you injured?*
Clark: *I speak. But I can't seem to speak to women. Just Caitlyn, who is family. There wasn't an injury or a specific event that started it. I just get anxious and it feels like my throat closes.*
Janna: *Do I make you nervous?*
Clark: *All the time.*

Even here in the dark, his ears burned. He couldn't believe he'd admitted that to her.

Janna: *Where are you from?*
Clark: *I grew up in Utah, on the farm where Mason and Caitlyn live now. It isn't far, just at the mouth of the canyon below. We interacted with the Saints more than many, but traveled to Salt Lake City twice a year for supplies and news.*

Janna: *What was it like growing up on a farm?*
Clark: *My brothers and I had a lot of chores and helped with everything we could. We'd scrape together every coin we could afford to buy a piglet in the spring and black-market seeds for our garden. We couldn't grow much because it was so hot and dry, but we always had a few greens and tomatoes from the garden. Between that and the chickens we raised, we were luckier than most.*

He remembered pausing here, wondering if he should dredge up her own painful past.

Clark: *What was SoCal like?*
Janna: *Bleak and gray, but for a long time it was okay. We got by. When my father first lost his job, the neighbors helped out. Especially the Lees, across the road. Nobody had much, but they liked my dad's*

integrity and how he stood up to GreenCorps, even if it meant he lost his job.

Wade joining GreenCorps was like a slap to our father's face. It went against what he believed. My brother was always a bully. It suited him to be with the worst bully of all.

Clark had never met the man, but despised her brother. He couldn't imagine betraying his family that way. He clenched his hand into a fist.

Janna: *How did you end up at the Saints settlement?*

Clark: *My parents and my brothers died. Nothing kept me tied to the family farm, so I dismissed the farm hands and hit the road. I traveled for about a year before making my way here. Life is simple and peaceful here among the Saints.*

That wasn't the full story, but it was a piece of the truth. Sometimes, he felt like he was avoiding real life. Hiding.

Janna: *What do you write about in your notebook?*

Clark: *It will sound frivolous. I write stories. Just silly things I make up in my head, things with adventure and romance.*

Janna: *How did you become a writer?*

Clark: *It was actually because of Mat. I used to follow him around the farm when I was a kid. I probably drove him nuts telling him stories I made up. One day, on one of his first visits home after he joined the rebels, he brought me a notebook. He told me to fill it with my stories and he'd bring me another next time. He wanted to take my stories with him when he traveled. Mat said he'd missed them. In the beginning, I wrote for my brother. Now I write for myself.*

CHAPTER 13: ELSA AND CLARK

Elsa paced the confines of the living room, her fists clenched so hard they ached. Despite everything she'd done to protect them, her sister and her nieces were in danger. Bile rose in her throat at the idea of them being sold. Jaxon was scum. Worse than scum. This was reprehensible. She shouldn't be surprised at the latest horrific news. He'd done so many things that were unforgivable.

"He's gone too far this time. I need to get back and let him have it. He has to know he can't get away with this." Her jaw and molars ached.

"Sweetheart, it's too late. No matter how fast we are, whatever has happened in SoCal, has happened," said Walker from where he stood in their bedroom by the window, the view of the river behind him. "They must have left by now. Jaxon wanted you to rush there months ago, but we knew it was a trap. You trusted Tatsuda and Ginger to take care of everything. You have to believe that they did." His voice was soothing, but she wasn't ready to be calm. Her anger still ripped through her with white heat. She wanted to hit something.

Elsa flattened the crumpled scrap of paper that someone had slipped under their door this evening. She reread Ginger's tiny note. It said little, just that Wade was back in SoCal with his disgusting plan and they had to leave. It was dated ten days ago. How on earth would Avery and everyone hop a train? Elsa's jaw ached, the pain reminding her to unclench.

She was now healthy enough to travel, even if the doctors disapproved. The main reason they were still here was waiting for the government to reproduce the electronics in the bunker key so she could take several copies to the rebels and the Canadians could keep their own. She'd been warned it would take time. She wasn't used to government bureaucracy. Action was more her style.

"Time to pack," she said, glancing at Walker, hauling her dresser drawer open. "Don't worry. I'm not racing to SoCal, but if everyone goes to Salt Lake City, we can join them there. I need to be sure they're okay. Not knowing is killing me."

"I'd like to meet your sister," said Walker, "but we don't have to hurry. Grady said he'd take care of her and the girls whenever they arrived. He'll keep Tatsuda and Ginger out of trouble, too. If he needs help, he has connections throughout the West and all over Utah. They won't starve to death without you." He crossed the room and pulled her into an embrace. His solid muscles and his reliable presence helped her control her panic. "Breathe." His voice was calming. "Call that number they gave you. Maybe the keys can be delivered right away, if you say we have to leave."

She exhaled. He was right, but not knowing how things had turned out was excruciating. She hated when events were out of her control. There were so many ways things in SoCal could have gone awry. Tatsuda was competent, but this may have been too much, even for him. GreenCorps wouldn't hesitate to punish him—especially if he was identified.

"I know. Avery isn't a child, but caring for three small children as a single mom must be challenging. I'm sure Ginger and Tatsuda mean well and will help, but they're still young and inexperienced." Her voice still carried her frustration. She took another deep breath, feeling some of her tension leave as though Walker absorbed her stress through their hug.

"You have an appointment tomorrow," said Walker. "Let's hear what the doctor has to say and collect the keys. Then, we'll make travel plans."

* * *

"Your concussion symptoms are gone," announced the doctor. The words Elsa had been dying to hear for two months. "You've been eager to travel, and I appreciate you waiting until I gave you the 'all clear.'" The Portland doctor glanced at Walker, who sat on a chair across the examination room, his long legs tucked as far underneath as they would fit. "Anything else was risking a serious relapse."

Elsa stifled a grin, not only pleased to pass her health check but at the sight of Walker cramming himself into the tiny seat and tucking himself out of the way. He looked like an adult attempting to fit into child furniture. That, combined with the assurances that the duplicate bunker keys would be delivered this afternoon, had her in a pleasant mood.

As they strolled along the smooth sidewalk back toward the house where they'd been staying, Elsa ran through the list of what she had left to finish before they departed. There wasn't much; she'd been ready to travel on short notice. At long last, she could help the rebels and her family.

Ginger's terse notes, while appreciated, had only increased Elsa's anxiety. They should have heard from Grady too, but his communication had been infrequent. Perhaps letters or news had been delayed because of the winter weather.

She and Walker stopped at the train station and checked the departure schedule. Here in Canada, the schedule was set and trains ran on time, unlike GreenCorps trains that left when they were ready. Which was often the reason they'd had to wait hours ahead of time, in case of a sudden change. There was a southbound train tomorrow. It should be a standard one with a passenger car for diplomats and business people as well as freight cars. After waiting for the keys for so long, it figured that at the last minute, everything was done, no problem, and they'd have to hurry to catch a train early tomorrow. About damn time.

She looked around the city, taking in the modern cars, the stores, and the restaurants that almost seemed ordinary after their months in the Canadian city. Returning to GreenCorps territory and all the people scraping to get by would be a shock, but at least it would be familiar.

While she finished packing and straightening the house, Elsa's pulse quickened. If all went well, she and Walker would join the rebels in Salt Lake City in less than two days. She was looking forward to seeing their friends again.

They'd received a quick note from Caitlyn and Mason shortly after their return in October. The two of them had gotten married. The news of their small wedding ceremony wasn't surprising, as they had waited half a lifetime to be together. It made sense they wanted to make things official. Caitlyn and Mason's second brief note said that they'd returned to the Dawson farm for the winter. The location was remote enough that they must not worry about GreenCorps returning.

Elsa glanced at Walker. Maybe they would get married one day too. She didn't see how it would change much. They were together and planned to stay with each other, but he would like it. Right now, her priority was her family and the rebellion. Of course, Walker was also family—something no ceremony would change.

Walker's only other family was his previous travel companion that he'd called his brother. Hayden had betrayed them, first stealing the tube with the bunker key, then shoving Walker down a cliff. Later, Elsa and Caitlyn had saved him from Jaxon McCoy and Hayden had repaid them by revealing their location to GreenCorps. Elsa and everyone from the farm had barely escaped the soldiers in a midnight raid.

Sometimes Walker fretted about what happened to Hayden, but even if they returned to Salt Lake, near where he'd last been seen, there was no guarantee they'd find him. He could be anywhere, or perhaps dead of his drug addiction.

With thoughts of family still on her mind, Elsa hoped she could spend time with her sister before the spring campaign. She checked the small inside pocket of her backpack, pleased with the addition of half a dozen keys to her gear. The Canadians had, at long last, been able to duplicate the electronics in the key to the Doomsday seed bunkers.

With assistance from their northern allies, Grady promised to send teams to the bunkers to retrieve another selection of seeds to share. She and Walker would lead one team, Mason and Caitlyn another, and Grady would find someone else for the third bunker. The Canadians would distribute the seeds from the Pullman and Corvallis bunkers, sending shipments south into GreenCorps territory for the rebels.

Caitlyn had already taken seed samples for the Saints to grow in the spring and another shipment would follow, with most of the seeds to be distributed for free, using Utah's black market and the Canadian contacts. They would supply people under GreenCorps' nose. For once, the new crop of plants would reproduce on their own. These viable seeds could be grown in most backyards and small gardens. Growing everything would take a generation or two, but this would be a start.

Large crops of grain and potatoes would be harder to hide this year, but if they wrested control of everyday life away from GreenCorps, they could grow sustainable crops far into the future.

GreenCorps probably wouldn't notice the extra food supply at first. They were used to potted tomatoes and miniature backyard gardens. People would have to be discreet with the seeds and not flaunt their new riches, but as early as this summer, some people might feel less strain to feed their families. The idea filled Elsa with warmth. This would make a real difference.

The hope was that each subsequent year, more people would have access to viable seeds, and then spread the wealth. Water was a separate issue, but one they would tackle if the rebels gained control of the trains. Water supplies existed, GreenCorps just regulated the supply as a form of control where it was limited. Her mind flashed to the fenced water reservoir in Idaho. There might be dozens of places with ample water to share. There were also nicer areas to live than SoCal and Texas. She pictured the open, uninhabited lands in northern California and Nevada. There was so much space. Maybe one day, people could move and spread out to reclaim more arable land.

Additional teams of rebels and Saints planned to plant young trees in safe locations throughout the West. Trees would take years to grow and develop, decades for some to produce fruit and nuts to supplement their diets, but the sooner the trees were planted, the sooner they might provide food.

Walker had suggested Boise as another possible place to distribute seeds. He had participated in an uprising there two months earlier that GreenCorps had been unable to quell completely. From all reports, Boise was now under martial law. It would be one of the first places Grady would want liberated. With the groundwork Walker had laid last year, the town was ripe for full-scale rebellion. Either that or Boise would be reduced to rubble, and everyone's spirit would be crushed. She hoped it was the former, and that the townspeople were ready for action.

Elsa took a deep breath and let it out slowly. She shouldn't get carried away. There was so much left to be done, and she still needed to get home.

Walker's original Boise contact, a medic named Kurt, and his teenage daughter Cora had supposedly fled toward Utah, so they wouldn't be able to use him to assess the current situation. Perhaps they would run into them again when they reached Salt Lake. With Kurt's medical training, he'd be valuable when the rebels went to war.

"Are there things about Portland you'll miss?" Walker zipped his full pack and leaned it against the wall.

"Beds," said Elsa. "Clean water. The food." They'd been spoiled by the wealth. Part of her felt guilty for staying so long and living a life of luxury when back home, people still worked themselves to the bone for food and water. She shoved the last of her belongings into her pack. She looked around the room where she and Walker had stayed for the last two months.

There was nothing else she needed. She'd gotten to Canada and handed over the bunker key. Her original mission was complete. Instead of that making her feel empty, she felt capable and satisfied. Elsa squared her shoulders. She'd accomplished what she'd set out to do last spring and changed her life for the better. She glanced at Walker. He was an integral part of that success, as were Ginger, Tatsuda, Mason, and Caitlyn.

A flutter filled Elsa's stomach as they slipped out into the city after dark—one last stroll through town before their train. Their best chance to leave unobserved was at night. Though they'd been unmolested for months, now that they were leaving, Elsa felt imaginary eyes at every turn—a habit on the road. She and Walker wouldn't be riding a passenger car the way Ginger and Tatsuda had. They would hop from the start, assuming that Jaxon would have paid watchers at the station. He would want to know if and when they left Portland. She would rather keep him and GreenCorps guessing.

When they reached the perimeter fence around the station, Walker and Elsa circled the buildings, following a route parallel to the tracks outside town. They walked south several hundred yards until the station lights became distant specks of white light. They would hop the train before it was up to full speed, but after it had left the station. Here in Portland, the air was chilly, though lacking the bite of more interior towns, as it was moderated by the ocean. Thanks to the bunkers, at least she and Walker had decent gear.

They lay low, crouched in the dark, cold seeping into her bones as they waited for the train's scheduled departure, while Elsa's mind drifted back to their earlier trips. This was how she and Walker had started—hiding trackside, waiting to hop a train in the last hours before dawn. A rush of warmth filled her. After the last nine months, she couldn't imagine her life without him. As if reading her thoughts from the glance in his direction, he shot her a lopsided grin.

When the slack action crashes started in the trainyard, Walker bounced to his feet and stretched, his eyes gleaming in the faint moonlight. She, too, stood and loosened her muscles, particularly her legs and shoulders.

"We're headed home," he whispered, his voice quivering with excitement.

"I hope we get to see everyone again," she said. As usual, Walker's train-hopping enthusiasm was contagious and her heart rate increased, warming her body despite the winter chill. They were heading back into danger and the unknown.

They remained in the shadows until the first engine passed—the train speeding up as it headed south. It hauled three passenger cars, a dozen loaded boxcars, the second engine, and a fleet of covered hoppers filled with goods and resources purchased by GreenCorps. She and Walker aimed for the second half of the train, letting the first half pass before they started jogging, Walker in the lead.

Elsa glanced down, careful of her footing on the uneven ground. Though she'd done this several times, she never forgot the danger involved in hopping. This far from the station, the train was almost too fast for her to count the spokes on the wheels, especially in the low light conditions. Her chest constricted and she focused on breathing. They were cutting it close and needed to get on. This was the second to last car. Much faster and it would be too dangerous.

In her head, she played Walker's mantra. *Hand, hand, step, hop.* When one of the final covered hoppers came alongside, he scrambled up the ladder. She inhaled. Time to follow.

With an extra burst of speed, she grabbed the ladder with first one hand, and then the other. She stepped, hopped, and hauled herself aboard. The fear of missing the train dissipated as they clambered over the top of the ladder and swung onto the covered porch to ride. Once seated, she stuffed in her earplugs, muffling the unpleasant roar of the train. Walker covered their legs and fronts with a tarp, and she leaned into him, sharing his warmth as they headed back toward GreenCorps and the life they wanted to change.

* * *

Clark bolted upright in bed, his heart racing and the taste of bile in his mouth. He'd had a disturbing dream again, not unlike the reality of his mother's tragic death, but in his dream, he'd stepped off the cliff to bring about his end. He took several calming breaths, lit his candle, and took out the last couple of pages of conversation between himself and Janna. Reading these interactions made him feel less lonely. They were proof that he wasn't alone after all.

Clark: *How old are you?*
Janna: *Twenty-two. How about you?*
Clark: *Twenty-five. Hard to believe that's it. Sometimes I feel a lot older.*
Janna: *I bet you were the youngest in your family too, weren't you? Both your brothers were older.*
Clark: *Why do you say that?*
Janna: *It sounds like you looked up to your brothers. What happened to your middle brother? If it's too painful, you don't have to answer.*
Clark: *He got mixed up with the wrong crowd. He got addicted to drugs and overdosed. My parents took it hard. Trying to help him is how Mat and Caitlyn met. She was a medic in Denver before she married Mat and joined the rebels.*

Clark seldom spoke about John and his death, though he noticed he'd shared several things with Janna that surprised him. Something about her invited confidence, or perhaps it was writing instead of speaking that allowed him to be so open. He flipped the page, feeling his skin heat in the dim light as he continued to read.

Clark: *What's your favorite color? If we're friends, I feel like I should know.*

Janna: *Purple, like the mountains at sunset or like the flowers that grew along the railroad tracks in Texas. SoCal didn't have flowers like that. We were lucky to have scraggly weeds. Yours?*
Clark: *Blue like the morning sky on a cloudless summer day.*
Janna: *Like your eyes. That's a nice color.*

CHAPTER 14: TATSUDA AND CLARK

Tatsuda sat up from his nest-like bed on the covered hopper as the train neared Salt Lake City. At last. He flexed his cramped muscles in the winter air, trying to regain circulation in his limbs. The cold had leached into his bones, but curling up had preserved enough heat that he'd survived. He'd slept most of the more than twenty-four hours the express trip had taken from Long Beach to Salt Lake. He'd barely moved as the train slowed, but not stopped, in both Sacramento and Reno, tucked as far back into the shadows as possible so he wouldn't be spotted. Tatsuda couldn't wait to get off now and stretch.

He watched the brilliant morning light as it peeked over the mountains in the east with a blaze of soft orange. There wasn't enough daylight yet to call it morning, but it would be soon. Getting off the train would be tricky, to say the least. His thoughts flew to the others riding in the protected cabin behind. He smiled with satisfaction. They'd gotten to travel in relative luxury with a roof and supplies. Still, they'd need help to get out and away.

Tatsuda couldn't wait for this trip to end. He'd worried about the others, and was ravenous. He sneezed, hoping it wouldn't be long until he found a place to get warm and eat a hot meal. On cue, his empty stomach rumbled. He'd never been so glad to have his canteen strapped to him as when he'd hidden on the roof of the train car back in SoCal. He was lucky he hadn't also been without water and that it wasn't cold enough to freeze overnight or he would have had to worry about frostbite.

Tatsuda glanced toward the second engine behind his covered hopper. There'd been no noise or sightings of Ginger, Avery, and the kids since they'd left. They might have been concerned about him, but he hadn't been caught and, despite his hunger, he'd been okay. He'd gone without food longer than this—back before he'd become a proficient thief. Those days now seemed a lifetime ago.

When the locomotive slowed and the lurching increased, he braced himself, holding the uprights with his gloved hands until the train ground to a screeching halt. He needed to be off as fast as possible to help the others disembark and avoid getting caught. Despite his protective clothing, the ice-cold ladder stung his hands as he climbed down. He jumped the last few feet, landing lightly in a few inches of snow. He grimaced. They were going to leave tracks and there was no way to hide them. They'd just have to be fast and get somewhere safe without delay. To come all this way and be nicked by security would be devastating.

He jogged beside the second engine, his breath pluming white. He glanced up and down the line to get the lay of the land. There were two more stationary trains on his left, several sets of empty tracks, and a third train parked on his right. Behind that, was the station. At least they had decent cover, even if he couldn't predict where the workers should be positioned. He spun, searching for signs of security or laborers unloading the other trains.

To his surprise, there was nobody in sight, though Salt Lake Station was usually a hive of activity. He scrambled up the engine ladder and knocked on the door. The sound echoing in the quiet morning. Best to warn the others inside before unlocking it with his stolen key. When he opened the door, the others stood ready, bundled into their jackets and their bags packed.

Ginger threw herself into his arms. "We worried you might have been caught or left behind." She pulled back almost immediately, picked up his pack, and handed it to him with a relieved smile.

He shook his head. "I'm good. We've got to hurry." He met Avery's glistening eyes. She'd better not cry now. They weren't safe yet. Plus, if she cried, her girls probably would too. He put on his backpack, tightening the straps.

Avery nudged Rose and Charlie forward. "You girls go with Sam. He and Geri will help you down the tall ladder." Dark circles ringed Avery's eyes and her face was chalky.

He narrowed his eyes, about to ask how she felt when Ginger and Avery exchanged a glance. She must be struggling and didn't want to scare the kids.

The children took a step forward and looked at him with wide eyes. Charlie came to him first—brave little girl.

"Turn around," he whispered, and he helped her climb down the ladder. She was so slow, as she stretched between rungs with her short arms and legs, but she squirmed and fussed if he did more than guide. He held his breath, scanning along the train as they descended. Quiet and slow would do. For now.

Ginger followed as soon as there was space, with Rose in front of her, also taking forever to climb down. Last of all, came Avery with the baby in the sling.

When everyone had reached the ground, Tatsuda took one last glance around to check they were still unobserved, before clambering back up the ladder, locking the door, and dropping down. "Let's go." He kept his voice to a whisper. Sound carried easily in the still morning air. Though thankful, he was surprised someone hadn't noticed their small troop. They'd taken too long getting off the train, but so far, they were still in luck.

Staying between the train and the empty tracks on their right and the next train, they scurried. He scooped Charlie into his arms, telling her with a finger against his lips to remain quiet. She rested her finger on his mouth, as if reminding him to do the same. They moved in single file, stepping on an existing narrow track, trying not to slip on the crunchy snow and uneven lumps of ice. His shoulder blades twitched. With each step, he expected GreenCorps railroad workers to appear.

He winced with every loud step, but there was no alternative. At least on the path, they wouldn't leave too many new footprints. Tatsuda still couldn't believe how quiet the morning was. Where were the railroad workers? They should be loading and unloading the trains in this busy depot, but his ears picked up no sign of activity. It was making him twitchy as goosebumps rose on his skin. Something didn't seem right, and his sense of unease increased.

They slunk past the station, crouching at the low points to stay behind the final train. They were almost out of the train yard when a heavy-set railroad worker emerged from between two cars of the parked train. He landed nearby with a thud.

Tatsuda's heart rate soared, the blood pounding in his ears, while it was all he could do not to flee.

For a moment, Tatsuda and the man stared at one another. Then, the man lunged. Tatsuda dodged with Charlie, but the man scooped up Rose, who kicked and wailed when he grabbed her. Ginger grabbed the man's arm and tugged as he turned away, still holding the child. He clamped his big hand over Rose's mouth as she struggled, cutting off her cries.

"You can't be here," he said with a hiss. He twisted and shook off Ginger.

His words were menacing, but his tone sounded worried. Whose side was he on?

Avery gasped as the man took off running along the snow-packed trail between the trains, headed for the front of the southbound train. Tatsuda shared a panicked glance with the others. They had to get Rose back without making noise and drawing additional GreenCorps security. They chased the railroad man as he rounded the last train car, leading them toward a low outbuilding separate from the main station. Some kind of shed?

The man removed a jingling keyring from his overcoat pocket. Looking around, he took a deep breath, unlocked the door, and threw it wide. "Get in there—all of you. Don't argue. I'll be back when I can."

The room beyond was dark. Tatsuda didn't know what to expect. The man hadn't called out to others, so it might be okay, but who steals a child? The man's motives remained unclear.

Ginger's lip trembled, but she raised her chin and darted inside, holding out her arms to Rose as she passed the stranger. Rose jumped and put her head down on Ginger's shoulder, wrapping her arms tight. Tears overflowed from Avery's eyes as she followed. She must have been terrified for her daughter, and she looked too out of breath for such a short sprint.

Tatsuda waited to be the last to enter. His gaze flicked down the tracks again, concerned about the almost deserted station. Though his feet still itched to bolt, he restrained himself. He wouldn't leave the others, and Charlie was wound around him like an octopus from one of Ginger's children's books; he could barely move. With a stare for the man at the door, Tatsuda shrugged and trudged into the dark opening.

Once they were inside, the door clanged shut, and a key turned with a click, locking them in. The man's footsteps crunched, fading as he strode away, leaving them captive and alone. How long until he returned? Was this a trap? Or was he helping and, if so, why would a railwayman help them? They worked for GreenCorps.

At first, the darkness inside seemed total, but soon, his eyes adjusted. Light seeped in around the door, illuminating a charcoal gray panel to their left along the wall. Tatsuda groped toward it and located a switch, which he flicked upward. A long overhead strip of pale white light turned on, emitting a low buzzing sound that filled the small dingy room.

Tatsuda had been picked up in Salt Lake before by the bulls. This shed wasn't where they'd taken him last time. There were no other prisoners, no cells, and no guards. Was this trackside location where they kept people for deportation? Or for questioning? His blood ran cold.

"This is new," he said, trying to be positive and not contribute to everyone's palpable fear. "Last time they caught me, they took me to the main building." He tried not to let his fear into his voice. Panic would help no one. There was a lop-sided aluminum table with four ancient-looking frame chairs, and a padded bench with shiny armrests on either end.

"You were caught before? You didn't mention that," said Ginger as she set Rose down on the long seat.

He shrugged. "It was deliberate. I wanted information about Walker's brother. Besides, I wasn't there long. Walker pretended to be an asshole farmer and collected me."

"Mommy, I'm hungry." Charlie's lower lip quivered. This must all be overwhelming for the girls. Rose looked just as upset. They needed a snack.

Tatsuda set Charlie down next to her sister and rummaged in his backpack.

"Any idea what's happening?" Avery's voice shook and her complexion seemed paler than usual, though it may have been the odd overhead light strips.

Beads of sweat dotted her forehead. She'd done too much.

Avery rested her hand on the wall beside her. "I feel faint." Her knees trembled.

"Nope. But, breakfast sounds good." Tatsuda grabbed several oat bars and pulled them out. Maybe they all needed to eat. He opened one packet, and split the bar in half, giving part to Charlie and the other to Rose. He tossed another bar to Ginger and held one out for Avery. She took it with shaky hands. He tipped his canteen and held it for the little girls to have a drink.

Only then, did he rip open a package for himself, and take a huge bite of the tasteless GreenCorps nutrient bar. "Eat first and then we can get caught up about our train ride." He turned to speak to Avery, his food in hand.

She hadn't moved from her position by the wall. Nor had she taken a bite.

Her eyes rolled back, and she wobbled, her knees collapsing.

Tatsuda dropped everything and caught Avery just before she hit the concrete floor. He awkwardly unclipped the baby's sling and passed the still-sleeping bundle to Ginger. His hands shook. That had been close.

She placed the baby next to Rose. "Your turn to watch the baby for a minute."

Rose nodded and rested her little hand on her sleeping baby sister, a crease between her tiny eyebrows as she stared at her mom laying on the floor, her head cradled in Tatsuda's arms.

Ginger helped him to lift Avery to the padded bench where he placed her between her daughters. She slumped toward Rose. Seconds later, she moaned. Tatsuda exhaled. She was regaining consciousness. What would he do if she passed out again? Something must be really wrong. She needed a medic. His eyes scanned the walls. Still no way out.

Avery's eyelids fluttered, and she regained consciousness. "What happened?"

"You fainted," he said. "Stay there." Tatsuda gave her food and water, then picked up his fallen breakfast. He wouldn't let food go to waste just because it had been on the floor for a few minutes. He dusted it off and ate it, washing the dry bar down with a couple of swallows from his canteen.

Tatsuda and Ginger finished eating and inspected the cold room thoroughly. No windows, no other doors. There were no mystery seams or loose sections. No way out. They returned to waiting and worrying about Avery's deteriorating condition, the time ticking by at a crawl.

When the jangle of keys signaled someone's return, they jumped to their feet, positioning themselves between the door and the wan Avery who sat with her children. When the door opened, a gigantic man with a wild beard and a familiar grin thrust his head inside the door. The stocky workman stood at his shoulder.

"What have we caught here?" The tall man said with a hearty laugh. "Not what we expected when we took control of the station. Bonus gifts and a pleasant surprise."

Tatsuda let out most of the air he'd been holding in. "It's alright everyone."

"What makes you think that?" said Avery, pushing herself to her feet. Her legs still wobbled, even if she was trying to appear strong. This was more than hunger.

"This is Darren. He's Grady's right-hand man." Tatsuda gathered their packs. "Let's get out of here."

The man laughed again. "Kid, I see you're still only one step ahead of trouble." He shook his head. "But somehow you land on your feet. If the man who found you hadn't been with us, your arrival could have gone badly." He stepped farther inside. "Introduce me to your friends." His eyes fixed on Avery. He nodded and said, "You must be Elsa's sister. Nice to finally meet you."

"This is Ginger and you're right, that's Avery. Her girls are Rose, Charlie, and little Aki." Tatsuda pointed to each. "If you don't mind, maybe we could go somewhere else for a proper meal? We've had enough oatmeal and nutrient bars in the last six weeks to last a lifetime. You chew them, but you're never full." He glanced at Avery. "We need a medic, too. I think Avery might have ripped her stitches climbing ladders and running for the train. The doctor said to take it easy, but we needed to leave town quick."

She gave him a quiet nod. For her to agree, she must be in a lot of pain. Like Elsa, Avery had an inner strength that had gotten her this far.

Darren clapped Tatsuda on the back, making him stumble with its force. "You did great getting everyone here. We'll help take care of things now. I remember something else about you. You're the kid who thinks with his stomach." He nodded. "Grab your gear and the children. I've got a ride out back to take you to Grady. He's been waiting for you for weeks." He scooped Avery into his arms as if she was light as a feather. "We'll take care of you and your young'uns. Don't you worry."

Her eyes rolled back in her head as she lost consciousness again.

With Avery cradled against Darren's chest, they headed toward the wagon.

* * *

Alone in the dark, Clark took out his favorite reading material again while he waited for the lingering effects of his nightmare to fade. Reading Janna's words was the closest he could bring his friend at this time of night.

Clark: *Does your family know where you are?*

Janna: *Last they heard, I was in Texas. My parents couldn't afford to help. My brother is dead to me.*

Clark: *Caitlyn and Mason are my only family. I hadn't seen either of them in years, but when they came through last October, we re-established contact.*

He had a feeling that they wouldn't forget he was here. They'd make a point to keep in touch, a fact that made guilt surge through him. He'd never tried to maintain contact with either of them. Mat would have expected more. Clark would have to do better.

Clark: *Are you going to tell your parents you are free?*

Janna: *I don't think so.*

Clark: *Why not?*

Janna: *I don't want Wade to find out and look for me or to force me to do anything else. If I avoid him, he can't hurt me.*

What about you? Why didn't you tell anyone where you were before Caitlyn and Mason showed up and found you?

Clark: *I didn't know how to contact them. With the rebels, they moved around a lot.*

Janna: *That sounds like you're avoiding the real answer. Didn't you want to see them?*

She was right. Of course, he wanted to see them, but afterward, when he was alone again, seeing Caitlyn and Mason only made it harder. The world became lonelier.

Clark: *Do you want your own family someday?*

Janna. *I haven't given it much thought. I suppose.*

Clark. *I used to want a wife and kids.*

Janna: *What changed?*

Clark: *I'm a coward.*

Janna: *Why do you think you're a coward?*

Clark: *Because I can't fight. I'd rather stay here. Both my brothers joined the rebels and look where it got them. Dead. Plus, I made a promise.*

Janna: *To whom? Sit back down. Don't go. I'm sorry. You don't have to answer that one. I take it back.*

That night he'd almost stormed out of the dining hall, his anxiety getting the better of him. Instead, they'd been quiet for several minutes before he'd asked his own question.

Clark: *If you could go anywhere, where would it be?*

Janna: *Anywhere with the rebels. I want to be part of breaking GreenCorps. I want to free people who were sold like I was. I think everyone deserves another chance at happiness. You?*

Clark: *Here. I have time to write when I want. Plus, the Saints let me be.*

CHAPTER 15: ELSA

The first leg of their train journey went well, but Elsa couldn't relax and her rest was fitful, even after nightfall. She spent a lot of time staring at the dark countryside as it rushed past. She leaned into Walker's shoulder, huddled together for warmth. The train ride was chilly this time of year, though they'd come prepared with warm clothing. The hours seemed endless as her busy thoughts swirled while she chewed the inside of her cheek raw. She'd chosen this journey, but what they had left to accomplish would be difficult. Was she misguided to think they had a shot to wrest control away from GreenCorps?

Her thoughts were about more than that, including the incessant buzz about the deportation order for her sister, which cast a desperate feel to her return. She reminded herself half a dozen times she had to trust Tatsuda.

As the train slowed coming into Boise, she and Walker gathered their backpacks and folded the tarp in preparation to slip off and hide for a few hours until the train resumed. Here in Boise, there would be crates of goods to be unloaded and stored potatoes to load to ship south. She looked around at the wintery town. The quiet neighborhoods below the tracks didn't look much different than before, other than the bare trees and deep snow.

The status of the trains and the garrison here were unknown. GreenCorps had probably clamped down in ruthless fashion after the round-up incident when they'd come through a few months earlier. The townspeople had tipped a train car in that skirmish and had fought back, rescuing the young women from GreenCorps.

Elsa nibbled at her lip, thinking of all the ways it might be challenging to resume their journey. Would they be able to hop back on? She glanced at Walker, who didn't seem concerned. He had all kinds of hopper tricks. She should take her cues from him. She rotated her neck and shoulders, inhaled, then exhaled in an attempt to loosen her tense muscles.

The train decelerated, and they stood by the ladder to disembark, but she couldn't shake a nagging feeling that something was about to go wrong. It differed from her usual instincts, more of a paranoid concern. Returning home couldn't be this easy. Where was Jaxon? Might he be waiting outside the station or with security? She banished the unpleasant thought, but scanned both sides of the track, her palms sweating.

Walker checked both the right and left sides as the train slowed. He cupped his hand and yelled into her ear to be heard above the noise. "Lots of security out there." He cracked his neck in either direction and rotated it, then swung his arms to limber up. He checked his laces and the straps on their packs, causing her to follow suit. Nothing was loose. "We head forward this time. We'll be off railroad property quicker that way. If we can head into the hills. Unless anyone who might see us, knows it's us, they might not think we're worth the effort to chase." He grinned his crooked grin.

Was he just saying this to appease her? Keep her calm? It wasn't working.

When the train stopped, they scrambled down the ladder, landing in six inches of crunchy snow. They scurried toward the front of the train, toward the path to the hillside campsite. At first, the route was clear. Then, to her surprise, the passenger cars emptied their loads, sending close to two dozen men into their path. With so many strangers around, her heart stuttered. On previous occasions, they had always taken a path toward the back of the train and the paying passengers unloaded later. Had something happened?

Walker and Elsa dropped to a walk, trying to navigate through the cluster of people while trying not to be conspicuous. At the same time, she watched for clues.

Her heart raced as she followed Walker, keeping him no more than an arm's length ahead. She tugged her cap lower, keeping her head down, and remained hidden behind him. All it would take would be one person to recognize them, and Jaxon would find out they'd returned. Even though she hadn't been in the Boise station, Elsa was certain her poster was still plastered on every wall. The feeling made the hair on her nape rise and uncertainty made her chest tighten.

"I paid for a through fare to Salt Lake City," said one of the better-dressed passengers on the right. "Why are we taking our suitcases when we unload? We're supposed to continue in a couple of hours." His voice carried as he planted his feet, turning toward a uniformed railroad official stepping off the front car, blocking her path.

The bull working GreenCorps security, looked her full in the face. She could have sworn there was a glint of recognition in his eyes. Then he turned to the curious passenger.

Elsa ducked her head and stepped to the left, further slowed by people listening, her heart pounding. Why hadn't the man said something? Security should have cared about her. Yelled for help. Grabbed her. Anything. Was this type of stop normal or a serious concern? Walker kept moving while she paused for information.

"This is a scheduled stop, sir, but with the amount of snow ahead on the tracks, we're staying here at least twenty-four hours while they clear the track. There was an avalanche just around the corner outside town and the railway line is buried in several feet of ice and debris." Elsa carried on. The man raised his voice. "Don't anyone worry. Your accommodations for the night in a Boise hotel are courtesy of GreenCorps."

Elsa's fist clenched as she kept her head down and her face averted while she walked faster. Getting back on board might be more challenging than anticipated, especially as railroad time was not always exact. At least twenty-four hours could mean waiting near the track all day tomorrow and into the evening. What a hassle. Also, far too dangerous.

She sped up, trying to match Walker's longer strides as he continued weaving through the final passengers. Though security guided everyone to cross in front of the now stationary train, it was also Elsa and Walker's best chance to slip away from the others. Even if their departure from the other passengers risked discovery.

They went with the flow of the crowd and just before the next set of tracks, they angled toward the three other parked trains. Ensuring nobody was watching, they hopped near the knuckle between two cars and hustled into the narrow gap between the next two trains. She took a breath. All the while, Elsa expected to be asked where they were going, but behind them, remained silent.

Her heart remained lodged in her throat as they sprinted down the track another hundred yards, where the track curved along the hillside. There, they lost sight of the delayed trains and the milling people. Still no sign of GreenCorps.

"We can't stay here," Elsa's words came between gasps. The cold air affected her breathing. She glanced back, but it seemed no one had followed. "It's stopped at least overnight."

Walker nodded as they dropped to a walk. "Let's head for the campsite in the mountains so we can have a fire. The first section will be steep, but at least we can get out of the way."

"We don't have shelter," she said, glancing upward where ominous dark clouds loomed overhead. "This stop was only supposed to be for a few hours." They hadn't planned for an overnight in the cold temperatures, especially at a higher elevation. "More flurries are on the way." At least it might not be far below freezing due to the cloud cover. Clear weather was the most frigid. Still, a night out might be uncomfortable, especially if there was wind.

"Stick with me," said Walker with another crooked grin. "The tarp doubles as a tent. Remember what I made on the way to Lake Tahoe and the cabin? Plus, I can keep you warm." He waggled his eyebrows.

Once her cheeks would have warmed at his last remark, now she just smiled. She remembered. She'd been sick and he'd taken care of her. That week was when she'd fallen for him.

They scrambled up the steep hillside, their breathing ragged, and a dull ache in her chest from the extended exertion in the rising altitude and cold. Even once they'd left the lower foothills, the occasional set of bootprints crossed their narrow path.

"Do you think these are fresh tracks? They look new to me?" The idea of confronting strangers out here made her nervous. They were just as likely to be soldiers as not.

"New today. Hunters, probably," said Walker. "Those are deer tracks they're following."

Despite the logical conclusion, Elsa remained on edge as they headed deeper into the mountains.

They'd almost reached their old campsite perched on the mountainside when a brawny, bearded man stepped into the path from behind a thick pine. He wore the clothes of a civilian, but that didn't mean he wasn't dangerous. Elsa's heart lurched as she ground to a halt. Her hand dropped to the hilt of her knife while she searched for clues about his intentions.

"Well, if it isn't my midnight thief and his innocent-though-she's-been-found-guilty girlfriend," said the stranger.

Elsa's hope of remaining anonymous plummeted.

* * *

"Kurt," said Walker, forging past the frozen Elsa. He shook the other man's hand.

Her stress level dropped at the warm greeting, but her gut told her something important was about to happen.

"You remember my story about the medic in Boise?" Walker said, resting his hand on her arm.

She nodded. The former rebel with the dog and the daughter that Wade had tried to take on his round-up. "Elsa." She stuck out her mittened hand to shake Kurt's.

"Walker didn't tell me how beautiful you are," said Kurt, his dark eyes intent. "No wonder he had to catch that train last fall. Your picture doesn't do you justice." He winked.

Elsa's cheeks flamed. Compliments made her uncomfortable, but he was just being friendly. "GreenCorps isn't known for their accuracy. I also don't think Wanted posters are intended to be flattering." Her words came out sharper than she intended. She'd try to tone it down. She smoothed the muscles in her face to reduce her scowl.

"We didn't expect to see you in this part of the country anymore," said Walker. "I thought you and your daughter were leaving for Utah."

"We have our own small rebel camp on the mountain. Grady just doesn't know about us. A bunch of us fled Boise, planning to hop a train when the situation cooled." Kurt shook his head. "Instead, GreenCorps tripled the garrison and clamped down tight. So, we stayed. We keep out of sight and steal garrison supplies as needed. Cora's adjusted to life outside town better than expected." His eyes shone. He must be proud of his daughter for being adaptable.

"I was hoping we might run into you in Utah. Big changes coming with the spring campaign." Walker said, flashing Kurt a smile.

Walker had mentioned the medic used to work with the rebels before his daughter had been born. He must feel safe in telling Kurt about the spring. They could always use solid allies.

"I'd love to hear more about that," said Kurt in his deep voice. "Come on into camp and you can talk to the group. They're suspicious of newcomers, but I'll vouch for you." He turned to continue up the path.

"No offense," said Elsa. "Maybe I'll stay here." She didn't want everyone to see her face. No telling who might want the reward. It was bad enough someone in town had seen her.

Kurt turned, his brow furrowed before he continued in a deep growl. "You're a hero to these people. You stuck it to GreenCorps and evaded capture for almost a year, throwing in your lot with the rebels. You give us hope we can do the same. Please join us for dinner. I promise that among us, you'll be safe." His dark eyes met hers. "No matter what the group decides about the spring, the least we can do is provide a hot meal for some weary travelers."

Elsa glanced at Walker.

He took her hand and squeezed. "Kurt's no liar. We'll be okay." Walker had solid judgment, and she trusted him with her life. She'd take the chance.

She nodded and followed Kurt, Walker falling in behind, until they reached the bench of land around the next corner where they'd camped in September. Close to a hundred men and women were scattered along the edge of the forest and in the clearing. Some worked in front of new log shelters of pale-yellowish wood. Others were occupied—cooking, butchering a deer, and chopping firewood. Still more people sat on logs eating around one of the three large crackling fires. Busy camp sounds filled the air along with the pervasive scent of smoke.

"Why haven't the authorities found you?" said Walker, indicating the expanded campsite. "This isn't low profile."

"They know we're here." Satisfaction filled Kurt's deep voice. "They just can't catch us unaware. We have guards at all hours. Even at night. GreenCorps has lost three dozen soldiers to our zero. We're in a holding pattern until the weather breaks. They probably hope we'll starve over the winter, but there's not much chance of that. We get by. Come spring, we'll relocate."

"I have some ideas," said Walker, scanning the camp. "Grady will be thrilled to hear about your group. How would you feel about setting up a new base of operations next spring near Pocatello or Idaho Falls?"

Chapter 16: Clark

Clark tried not to stare at the door to the community dining hall while he waited for Janna to appear. Around him, children laughed and plates clinked over a background buzz of conversation. Every time someone entered the room, he sat straighter, hoping it was her, only to slump again when it wasn't. She'd been prickly as a cactus the whole six weeks he'd known her, but they continued to eat most meals together, writing their back-and-forth conversations on sheets of paper. The times she hadn't come, the long table had seemed empty—despite the uniqueness of their silent conversations, the room seemed more vibrant and alive when she was there.

Through their notes, he'd shared more with her than anyone since Mathew's death. He swallowed, trying not to feel disappointed. Maybe she was busy.

She might still be in the library, getting another book. She might even read more than he did and had often stayed to speak with the librarian, Sister Hope. Maybe he shouldn't expect anything from Janna. He reminded himself that she would leave in the spring, but he kept seeking her out. She was here for at least the winter. It would be months before she would leave to join the rebels—if she didn't enjoy living in peace too much. While he hoped she'd change her mind, he didn't expect her to. Unlike him, she was brave.

He kept telling himself that he would talk to her, woman or not. Clark would like to use his voice, but he couldn't utter a word when faced with her unfathomable brown eyes. He was foolish and a coward. This was yet more proof.

He wrote his first and most important question while he waited, erasing it three times before he was satisfied with the wording. It shouldn't be this difficult to speak to a friend, but his anxiety escalated with each revision. He wiped his damp palms on his pants under the table and closed his eyes, letting the regular sounds of the dining room wash over him—concentrating on blending the voices, the clink of cutlery on dishes, the scrape of benches and chairs, and laughter. It would be okay.

Clark concentrated on his breathing and blew out a whoosh of air. He inhaled the scents of fresh baked bread and savory venison stew—tonight's offering for dinner. The ordinary sounds and smells grounded him. He could do this. Not for Caitlyn, but because he wanted to. He was sick of being alone and had Janna to thank.

When at last she entered the dining hall, she made a beeline toward him, or at least toward the table where they always sat. He covered his question with his arm as she gave a quick nod in his direction, passing him to collect dinner from the kitchen. She glanced back toward the door and scowled. He scanned the room, but nothing seemed unusual. What was the reason for her displeasure?

He stared at his written question and took a deep breath.

"Will you go to the holiday festival with me on Friday night?" The words looked ridiculous on the paper. He should just ask. Out loud. His throat constricted, and his breathing grew tight. He had a feeling she'd refuse, but he didn't want to go on his own. In crowds, he felt lonelier than ever. Maybe he should rethink this and spend the evening reading or writing. It's what he would have done if she wasn't here. It's how he'd spent mid-winter the last three years. He gazed skyward, as if searching for courage in the off-white stucco ceiling— no such luck.

Even if he and Janna wrote instead of speaking, she was the closest thing he had to a friend in the settlement. He hadn't meant for that to happen. He'd just planned to keep an eye on her for Caitlyn. Before he knew what had happened, Janna became the first thing he thought of each morning when he opened his eyes and the last thing on his mind at night before he fell asleep. She was a kindred spirit, one he'd never expected to find. Someone as bookish and lonely as he was.

Clark wanted to know more of her story—her dark eyes hinted at so much more than what she wrote or said—but she must not be ready to tell it. Like him, she didn't trust easily and had left her old life behind. He didn't know most of the gruesome details, except what her brother had done. She didn't have anywhere else to go. Also, like him. He wouldn't think about when she left in the spring. It was months away. Anything could happen between now and then.

He flipped over his paper as she settled on the bench beside him. She raised an eyebrow and looked pointedly at his closed notebook.

She produced a stubby pencil and a fresh sheet of homemade paper from her pocket, unfolded it, and wrote, *"No writing today?"*

He shook his head. *"The story's done."*

"Can I read it?" Her question made his heart stutter to a stop.

What if she hated what he'd written? He hadn't intended it for an audience, just for himself. Mat was the only one he'd ever shown his notebooks.

Her cheeks flushed when he hesitated. *"Am I overstepping? I'm sorry. It might be private. I should have thought."* She set her pencil down, looked at the wooden table, and picked up her fork before diving into her dinner. She ate several slow scoops of stew before the tension left her shoulders. What was bothering her? Had someone tried to touch her? Because of her time in Texas, she didn't like anyone trying to get her attention that way.

Clark shouldn't be surprised Janna had asked to read his story. She read everything else she could get her hands on. Sweat dripped inside his shirt, which now stuck to him. The thought of her reading his original story was as terrifying as asking her to the winter festival.

Which he also hadn't done. He took a deep breath and flipped his paper over to expose his burning question. He slid it across the table to rest beside her plate, keeping his gaze on the wooden table.

She read his inquiry while he stopped breathing. She took forever to glance up—still, she didn't answer. Her silence was killing him. Was she figuring out how to decline?

To his surprise, she wrote on her page without looking in his direction. *"What happens at the winter festival? I've never been to one."* She bit her lip.

"SoCal didn't have winter festivals?" He frowned. From what he'd heard, that was consistent with that hell hole. However, it was still hard to believe there hadn't been some kind of celebration. They were pretty common.

"NO." Her letters were harder and more jagged than usual—standing out like a scar carved into the thick paper.

His hand shook as he added to his page. He'd heard nothing positive about SoCal or Texas and now he could kick himself for reminding her of things she'd missed. GreenCorps ruled there, more ruthlessly than most places, discouraging travel and keeping everyone under their thumb. No wonder she wouldn't return home.

"At the winter festival, the Saints make hot chocolate and cookies and sell crafts at tables—things they've made, built, carved, sewn, and crocheted. They roast nuts and pop corn. Often there is music and a special dinner." More than ever, he wanted her to say "yes," and share this experience. It wouldn't make up for all the ones she'd missed, but a fresh start in life should include opportunities and new traditions.

"Why me?" she wrote. *"Don't you have other friends you'd rather hang out with?"* She should know the answer to that by now.

He raised his eyebrow and shook his head. *"I don't have other friends."*

"Caitlyn? Mason?" She wrote.

"They're family. They don't count."

"The festival is the day after tomorrow?"

Clark nodded while his heart thumped. Was it too much to ask for a friend?

Her eyes narrowed while she continued to chew. "Okay," she said at last. She so seldom spoke aloud it made his heart skip to hear its sound. She frowned when she returned to eating. Something was still on her mind. Should he press for information? Maybe not right now. She would explain when she was ready. Hopefully.

Janna showed trust in him by saying yes. He should return the favor. With shaking hands, he slid his notebook toward her and shrugged. He fumbled with his pencil before he wrote. *"Please bring it back when you're done."* His dinner churned inside his stomach. Though fantasy, his writing was personal, his creative outlet for his feelings.

Janna rewarded him with a breathtaking, sweet smile—the first sign of genuine pleasure she'd shown since her arrival. *"Thank you."*

* * *

The Saints' Winter Festival was in full swing when Clark and Janna arrived. The main event and craft fair were held inside the brick church building where Clark had seldom been. Though he'd joined the Saints, he didn't attend their church very often. Janna stopped inside the door and inhaled. He detected the fragrant aroma of the Christmas tree, overlaid with rich chocolate and buttered popcorn. He'd need treats first.

He picked up two brown paper bags filled with popcorn and passed one to Janna. She smiled in thanks. Volunteers had packaged several dozen bags for the guests. Snagging a few white fluffy kernels, he stuffed them into his mouth, savoring their buttery taste. He'd only had popcorn a couple of times. Corn was a challenging crop to acquire seeds for as the plants needed multiple rows to pollinate well and few could afford that many seeds. The Saints were the exception.

They planted extensive fields of the crop. Next spring, they'd have different varieties to try, courtesy of Caitlyn's friend Elsa, the one all over the Wanted posters.

At the back of the room, an eight-foot-tall potted fir tree sat, decorated with a multitude of handcrafted ornaments made of cloth, wood, wool, and shiny trinkets. Many of the ornaments were examples of those for sale at the various craft tables. He led her past the hot chocolate table next, picking up two full mugs. He took Janna to the side, out of the flow of traffic of the other celebrants.

Clark wanted to say, "We can't go anywhere else until you try this. It will blow your mind." But he didn't speak, and writing here without a flat surface would be too awkward. She'd have to understand through actions. He blew on his drink and inhaled the scent. He sipped his creamy hot chocolate, all the while watching Janna, dying to see her reaction. If she thought potatoes were unbelievable, this would rock her world on its foundations.

Janna blew at the steam and took her first cautious sip. Her eyelids fluttered. "Oh my. It's like heaven." She took another, larger sip.

Clark grinned. Hot chocolate was a special treat the elders brought in just for the Winter festival and solstice parties. It was worth the anxiety of coming—and the asking—just for the beverage. Last year and the previous one, he'd stopped by just for a cup of chocolate before returning to his room to read.

They wandered the tables, often stopping to admire the wares. Janna sometimes picked up a scarf or socks or a piece of jewelry to examine more closely. Clark paid attention to what she liked, but she didn't buy anything. The coins in his pocket grew heavier, feeling almost hot against his leg. The more he looked, the more he wanted to buy her something. He wanted her to remember this mid-winter as something special. She lingered the longest over a table covered in handmade sweaters.

One had bands of color, starting with red at the top, then running through the rainbow, each with a swath of color, ending with violet at the bottom. She stroked the soft wool, then turned, her expression one of longing. She bit her lip and shook her head. He guessed she wanted it, but was likely saving her limited coins. He recognized the expression of self-denial.

Behind her back, he motioned to the older lady behind the table to save it. He held up coins for her to see. She smiled and tapped her index finger beside her nose, showing that she understood. Mrs. Rodgers would save it for him and he could give it to Janna as a present. Until he'd seen her stroking the handmade sweaters, he hadn't thought about her clothing or lack of personal belongings. Nobody here had much, but she had even less.

The Saints took care of outfitting the refugees with a few basics, and she'd mentioned she'd worn boots and packed her bag when she left SoCal. Leaving Texas one step ahead of a burning building hadn't given her more than a few seconds to throw things together, so she had little to wear that she would have chosen and nothing pretty. Her clothes mostly fit and were functional, but he hadn't seen her with anything colorful or warm. This would be both. She would have made a few coins working the kitchen, but not many. Knowing she would have one nice thing after tomorrow, made him feel warm inside, satisfied.

Clark and Janna continued their wander through the tables. He was content to watch the way her eyes lit up with new discoveries, and he bought nothing else. After completing a full circuit of the room, they swung by the front table for a second hot chocolate before ending their evening. Somehow, two hours had passed—the time had flown.

With frost biting at their warm glow, he walked her back to the cabin where she stayed with seven other single young women, several of whom the rebels had rescued. None of her bunkmates were back yet, but Janna didn't seem to mind. After they nodded goodnight, he hastened back to the bustle of the winter festival to pay for the sweater. Mrs. Rodgers wrapped it in crinkly leftover paper and gave it to him with a wink. Tomorrow was Christmas Eve. He'd give it to Janna over breakfast on Christmas day.

Everything about his life was better with a friend like her. Every day was more fun with something to look forward to. Then reality crashed over him and stained the evening with a hint of bittersweet. Times like this couldn't continue because Janna wasn't staying. Come spring, she was leaving and joining the rebels. He'd have to enjoy their remaining days because this feeling wouldn't last.

Chapter 17: Elsa

Elsa and Walker monitored the train action daily from above Boise. They'd tried to return every other day, but the trains had stopped running four times due to heavy snow, and activity from the garrison had remained busy. They hid at the edge of the treeline with binoculars, watching the activity at the station below. With milling soldiers, it remained impossible to approach the station for more up-to-date news or the schedule. She tried not to worry about when they would get back on and leave for Salt Lake, but it was challenging.

For the entire two weeks of their detour in the camp with Kurt's people, Elsa lived with a persistent knot in her stomach. She came to terms with not knowing what had happened with Tatsuda, Ginger, and Avery with her girls—for the most part. She became frustrated with no news from Grady, although to be fair, they had no way to communicate with him and explain where they'd gone. But there was no alternative.

This morning, a northbound train arrived, the first to get through in weeks. Excitement fluttered in Elsa's stomach. At last, they might continue their journey. She and Walker crept down the slippery mountainside and approached the station with more success than on their previous attempts, using the new arrival as a distraction.

In that time, three more trains arrived and departed. At least they were running again, though security at the station seemed surprisingly lax. There seemed to be more railroad workers than soldiers. This change left her feeling uneasy, as she didn't understand the reason.

When Elsa and Walker took positions along the southbound track, they passed several other ragged hoppers waiting for trains, which Walker said was uncommon for this time of year. Many found places to live and work during the winter. From the other travelers, they picked up odd rumors about trouble for GreenCorps that sounded encouraging for the rebels, but Elsa didn't know what to make of them. She hoped they were true.

She and Walker let the others hop trains first, waiting for the one to their destination, and boarded in their usual fashion—at the back and without company. They preferred not to travel too close to strangers, probably a holdover from when Walker and Hayden were young, though it was just as important now. All it would take was one person to recognize her and they'd have trouble.

She glanced across to Walker as they prepared to disembark from the train in Salt Lake after their chilly ten-hour ride. His hair had grown in the weeks they'd stayed in the mountains and he hadn't shaved, citing the cold and lack of hot water. His beard took some getting used to, and she looked forward to returning to civilization so he could shave. She missed seeing his bare face. Did she look as ragged as he did? Living rough after their time in Portland had been shocking for a day, but they had both returned to the old familiarity of making do with less.

Taking a breath, as the train came to a rest in the Salt Lake City depot, they leaped off, prepared to sprint for cover as usual, but the trainyard seemed deserted.

Several stationary trains sat on the tracks, but there were no workers in sight. Maybe the snowfall had played havoc with their schedule, too. They slowed their pace and proceeded with caution, her nerves on edge and her muscles tense.

Without workers or passengers waiting, the platform seemed too quiet. Elsa and Walker maintained their vigilance and took their time picking their way through the snow-covered station, heading for the tall chain-link fence around the perimeter. The icy wind whipped their hair and faces, making Elsa long to find shelter. Still, no one accosted them. They climbed over the fence without incident, while her unease grew.

Something odd was going on. Where was everyone? Even the other hoppers had disappeared without a trace. Unless they'd avoided Salt Lake City. Maybe they knew something she and Walker didn't, since they'd been without information for three weeks.

"Where is everyone? Any idea what's going on?" said Elsa, keeping to a whisper.

Walker shrugged his broad shoulders. "We're almost there. Grady can fill us in." His voice was low, but calm. Unlike her, he almost always remained unruffled.

They headed deeper into town, bound for rebel headquarters. This late in the winter, daylight had almost vanished by the time they strode through the quiet town. The market square was deserted for the season, but some had cleared the walkways of snow. Straying from the path would mean wading through knee-deep banks of gray snow.

Almost too excited to speak, Elsa's stomach fluttered. She could hardly wait to discover if those she cared about were safe. Reaching the green door in the alley near the market, Walker pounded twice on the door in the standard pattern while her heart rate soared. Less than a minute later, Darren, Grady's large right-hand man, flung open the painted door. He was the only person she'd met bigger than Walker, and he filled the entrance.

"Look who finally graced us with their presence." Darren grinned and pumped Walker's hand before he lifted Elsa into a giant bear hug, her feet dangling in mid-air. She stiffened at first, not used to hugs from anyone except Walker or Tatsuda, but she wasn't offended, and soon relaxed. That was just Darren's way. Friendly. He balanced the cool and thoughtful Grady, who'd often been called reserved.

"Did Tatsuda and Ginger make it here with Avery and the kids?" Elsa blurted, not willing to wait any longer.

Darren's pleasant smile broadened. "Everyone made it. They're safe. They've been here a month and your sister has healed, though the medic ordered her to take it easy a little longer. We've been looking after her and her little ones." His face softened.

An immense weight lifted for Elsa. From his reaction, he must like children. Headquarters didn't seem like it would have seen many kids, at least not recently.

Walker said, "That's the news we needed." He squeezed Elsa's forearm, and his gray eyes twinkled. "You needn't have worried. Knew Tatsuda would get everyone here safely."

"I know." She smiled again.

Darren motioned them through the doorway. "Let's get you two inside, out of the weather. Looks like another cold snap is setting in. Bloody sick of the cold. Dinner should be ready soon and we've got a room ready for you upstairs. This is the fullest the building has been in years." He winked.

They followed him through a dim, cluttered storage room to the bar beyond, the temperature increasing the deeper inside they walked. Though a drinking establishment, Grady owned the building and lived here. He kept the downstairs warm and the interior cozy.

Elsa sniffed at the aroma of roast meat and spices, and her stomach growled in response. She could eat after their long day on low rations. Grady sat at his usual round table, papers strewn across its surface. He looked up at their arrival, and a faint smile twitched at the corner of his mouth—like Mason. Seeing Grady again now, after becoming friends with his son, the resemblance was uncanny. Everyone who spent time with both of them must know, even if Grady had never acknowledged Mason that way—unless that had changed.

"I'm glad you two arrived. We knew you'd left Portland because that message got through, but we hadn't heard anything since. Everything okay?" He stood and wandered toward them; his eyes shrewd in their assessment. In this light, his ax-shaped birthmark stood out bolder than ever against his winter-pale skin. A far cry from his tanned complexion in the summer.

Before Elsa could answer, Tatsuda thundered down the wooden stairs at the back and ran across the room. He picked Elsa up in a bone-crushing hug. "You're here. Don't be mad, but Grady has had me working, lifting papers from the railroad offices. He's taken over most of the railroad and GreenCorps doesn't even know. It's the best con."

She loved that his first words were honest and excited. She hoped he never changed, even when he grew up. His enthusiasm was infectious most of the time. His confession also explained the change in activity and atmosphere at the station. The trains were still running in some capacity, or GreenCorps would have been alerted, but snow closures and extreme weather were excellent cover for the intermittent trains. Trust Grady to have taken advantage of the situation. She looked forward to hearing the details. She flicked a glance at Grady, who shrugged, his expression neutral. He wasn't fooling her. This was huge. Still, she could hear his account later, after she saw everyone.

"It's terrific to see you too," she said as Walker also hugged Tatsuda and ruffled his cropped hair. "Thank you for keeping Avery and the girls safe, and away from the long arm of the McCoys." She glanced around. "Where are they? It's been too long since I've seen them." Her heart squeezed. She'd missed too much. Even when they'd all lived in SoCal, she hadn't seen them enough, thanks to Jaxon.

"Rose and Charlie are out shopping with Ginger. They ate early, and she took them for a walk to get them out from underfoot." He glanced at a clock on the wall. "Though they should be back soon. That Charlie needs stuff to do, or she gets fussy about being cooped up." He laughed. "At least in Utah it's safe for them to go out, at least for quick trips." Tatsuda's eyes sobered. "Avery's upstairs, asleep. She's okay now, but it was kinda rough having the baby. Then she ripped her stitches when we left SoCal. She wasn't well most of the trip and freaked me out at the end when she collapsed."

"You have to tell me everything about SoCal and how you got everyone out," said Elsa, her eyes drinking in Tatsuda. His Wanted poster was unlikely to be a problem anymore, as it described him as a long-haired kid. He was nearly grown, having shot up even more since his departure in October, and she wasn't used to looking up to make eye contact. All the responsibilities appeared to suit him. She squeezed him in an extra hug, fighting tears.

"Yes, the notes were very short," said Walker, joining their conversation. He held a hot drink in each hand and passed a mug to Elsa.

She took it with a grateful smile and wrapped her chilly hands around its heat before taking a sip of the slightly bitter liquid. Some kind of tea.

Tatsuda tugged on his too-short sleeves. "The messages couldn't give specific details because they were passed along by at least three strangers between us each time," he said. "Railroad workers, we think. Turns out a lot of them are on our side now." He grinned. "Thanks to the GreenCorps blanket punishment of all the railroad workers since November. Many people crossed over from sympathizer to performing acts of rebellion. Living without food and proper wages seems a crime now." He paused. "What happened to you? We expected you ages ago."

"I know," said Elsa, "We got delayed in Portland waiting on the duplicate keys, then the train stopped in Boise because of heavy snowfall and we hid out in the mountains with some outlaws. We've had no word since you said you were leaving SoCal."

Grady's interest returned as his steely blue eyes locked onto Elsa's. His mouth opened, but just before he spoke, Avery came downstairs with light footsteps. Her skin was paler than Elsa had ever seen, though she was as lovely as always. As Elsa ran to her, with her peripheral vision, she noticed Darren sit up straighter and smooth the front of his shirt. Did he have a thing for her sister? That might be interesting. Avery could use a kind man instead of a monster in her life.

Avery's slim frame was thinner since Elsa had seen her last spring, but the warmth in her smile still lit up the room. Elsa squeezed her in an embrace. She'd missed her sister.

She turned toward the door as Ginger and Avery's girls came in. They were all aglow with health and from the cold. Elsa gave her nieces quick hugs while Avery reminded them who she was. They didn't seem impressed, but Elsa was reminded of how important it was for them to grow up in a free world. Rose, Charlie, and little Aki would have opportunities Elsa had missed. It only strengthened her considerable resolve.

"I'll put them to bed and let you stay with your sister," said Ginger to Avery, smiling at Elsa before taking the little girls upstairs.

Soon after their reunion, one of Grady's staff emerged from the kitchen and announced that dinner was ready. Grady collected his papers into a thick stack and set them on the end of the bar.

"Be my guest," he said, motioning them to take a bowl of stew and chunks of bread and pick a table. "We have a lot to discuss, but food before business."

After they'd finished their meal and her stomach was full, Elsa and Walker updated Grady and Darren on the situation in Boise. They agreed that Kurt and the others on the mountain could use official rebel support, as they were another valuable resource.

"I'll draft a letter and send it to them with half a dozen volunteers to set up a clear line of communication." Grady wrote a note on a long to-do list. "Maybe we should send one of the bunker keys along with our rebels to help."

Elsa smiled. "Already done. The Aberdeen bunkers aren't too far from their location."

"I'll send someone to bring in Mason and Caitlyn next week. It's almost March," said Grady. "They should be here for the final planning before we scatter for different assignments."

"I have a question." Avery had sat quietly through the meal and news, listening without speaking, until now. Everyone gave her their full attention and her cheeks turned pink, probably from the intense gazes turned her way. "I understand that your mission is to break GreenCorps and distribute seeds and food. You've taken control of the railroad, swayed many of the workers to your cause, and promised to send water to SoCal and Texas, or anywhere else lacking. But." She paused and they hung on her words. "If you take down GreenCorps, who or what will replace them?"

Darren's craggy face split into a wide smile. "That's a smart question and not one many people have asked. Our man Grady has been organizing a system for the people to vote. We want to have an election, like in the old days. We expect the people will vote him in as the new president of West America. We wanted to connect the name to the country that was here before the Collapse."

"You're all leaving here, for several months," said Avery, staring at the tabletop. "Where will the girls and I go?" She looked up and continued before anyone answered. "I don't want to stay here without family, and it's too much to ask any of you to stay. Everyone else is necessary. I'm not."

Elsa chewed on her inner cheek. She hadn't thought that far in advance. Maybe Avery and the children could live on Caitlyn's farm? It might be safe, but her sister knew nothing about farming or gardening, and out there she'd be isolated. That wasn't the answer.

She looked at Walker. He shrugged, and they turned to Grady. Perhaps he had a suggestion.

Avery continued. "I'm grateful to have spent time here, but this city isn't for me on my own, especially if it might be dangerous. GreenCorps knows your headquarters and support base is in Utah. What if they strike back? I don't think I should stay here for that reason as well. I don't want to put the kids at risk and on the campaign. We'd be liabilities."

"You'll be safe in Salt Lake," said Darren. "They've never taken it yet."

Grady pursed his lips, tapping them with his finger—probably thinking. "GreenCorps has never had a powerful presence in Salt Lake

City, which is how the Saints and I prefer it. I don't think it will be a problem, but I see your point."

"I can drop you off with the Saints. They'd keep you and the little ones safe." Darren's suggestion was unexpected, but Elsa liked the idea. She'd only spent a few hours in the Saints settlement up the canyon last year, but they'd impressed her with their self-sufficiency and their peaceful community. Avery would fit in well.

"Who are the Saints?" said Avery, turning to the former mountain man.

"They have communities in the mountains, here in Utah—up the canyons. They have their own water and grow their own food. We've sent some of the viable seeds to them already for crops in the spring," said Grady. "Mostly garden vegetables and crops to mix with their usual stuff, plus the first seeds Elsa brought for fruit trees.

"I think I'd like living there," said Avery, turning thoughtful eyes on Darren. "Thank you. I appreciate your thoughtfulness."

He blushed at the compliment and cleared his throat before continuing. "We'll pass near Caitlyn's farm and I'll send a message through one of their neighbors to get them here. I'll carry on with Avery and her kids. Two birds, one stone. We'll travel by horse-drawn sled while there's still plenty of snowpack. I can be back in five days, round trip. Mason, Caitlyn, and I should arrive here close to the same time."

CHAPTER 18: JANNA

Janna stared out the frost-edged glass of the second-floor library, and with her fingernail, she scraped away a larger patch of the thick ice crystals. With a hole to peer through, she had a decent vantage, allowing her to see over the six and seven-foot snowbanks that lined the paths through the Saints' settlement in the dark blue-gray light. If she hadn't experienced it, she never would have believed that snow this deep existed. It hadn't snowed in SoCal during her lifetime.

Here, the deep drifts and piles insulated the buildings from the cold, keeping them toasty warm inside. Still, she was sick of winter, cold, and being stuck inside. How much longer until spring? Time spent here waiting for warmer weather and to be part of the action dragged. Though eager to be on her way, Clark had made this place more than just something to be endured.

At least she was no longer freezing all the time, unlike the early days of her stay in the mountains. Today she wore her favorite sweater, the one Clark had given to her for the winter solstice. Janna frowned despite the pleasure the thought gave her. She hadn't had the coin then to buy a gift in return. She hadn't been here long enough and was saving for necessities for the spring, like boots that weren't full of holes or falling apart.

At the time, she'd felt bad, but Clark hadn't seemed to care that he hadn't gotten a present. Luckily, under Sister Hope's guidance, she'd made him a birthday present for tomorrow. He'd let the date slip awhile ago, and she'd filed the information away. A small smile about Clark and their connection replaced her frown.

Janna needed to pay attention inside, not outside. Sister Hope was waiting to show her how to finish her project.

The kind older woman had taught Janna how to make paper from pulp consisting of old paper, bits of wood, husks, and other plant fibers saved for that purpose. They'd mashed it into a thick paste, flattened it onto a screen, and let it dry. Yesterday they'd cut the stiff chunk into sheet-sized pieces and she'd sewn them together on one edge. Today they planned to attach the creamy sheets to the fabric-covered front and back pieces of thick cardboard.

The notebook should look great when they were finished and she could hardly wait to give it to Clark at breakfast. She was proud of learning a new skill and happy she could reciprocate his thoughtful gesture.

She looked down at the rainbow bands of color on her sweater, running her fingers over the soft wool. Being even shouldn't matter, but she'd feel better once she'd given him something special in return. If it hadn't been for their friendship, this winter would have been lonely and miserable.

Janna looked back at the new notebook pieces on the table. She had loved Clark's writing and was looking forward to reading his current story. He'd worked hard on it since the New Year and would soon be out of paper—this story was longer. So, finishing her project now was perfect timing. What she'd made wasn't like the thin paper notebooks brought in from back East, but it would be serviceable. He'd fill it with his vivid imagination—that's what would make it the most incredible—what he would create to fill inside. The idea of making Clark happy filled her with warmth. Growing up poor, she'd seldom had an opportunity to do something kind like this for anyone else.

Movement outside the frosted window caught her eye.

"Someone new arrived in front of the hall." She turned back to the librarian, knowing this wasn't an everyday occurrence in winter. They hadn't seen anyone from outside the community for a couple of months. Not since her arrival with Mason and Caitlyn last October. Her heart rate increased. There might be word from the rebels about their upcoming campaign.

"In this weather? That's brave. Or foolhardy," said Sister Hope with a slight frown marring her gentle features. She smoothed her gray-streaked brown hair and joined Janna at the window overlooking the main trail into the settlement. "That's Darren. One of Grady's top men. Nobody we need to be concerned about, though perhaps he's brought important news of the rebellion. Why they keep us informed, I don't know. We just want to be left in peace."

Janna let out a breath she'd been holding.

Sister Hope continued, the crease between her brows deepening. "I don't recognize the woman from the sled or the children. I don't think Darren has a family, though I could be mistaken. Or, perhaps he's brought someone in trouble. He's done that before." She paused. "I should see if I can be of assistance." She turned. "Why don't you come with me? I'll show you how to attach the covers after dinner."

Janna fidgeted with her zipper as she put on her jacket. She thrust her hands back into her crocheted mittens, her mind whirling. Darren was with the rebels. Maybe he'd come to recruit early or needed help. This might be the chance she was waiting for, even if it was only the end of February. She swallowed. While anxious to get things rolling, it was still unexpected. In her head, she'd had another month of waiting.

She followed Sister Hope through the open-air snow tunnels to the dining hall where visitors were often welcomed. They missed the official greeting by Brother Campbell, the leader of the community, but not much else. Janna's eyes strayed to her usual table, but it was still empty. Disappointment zinged through her, though she hadn't expected Clark to have arrived yet. Their regular dinner time was in about an hour. She'd been here for over four months and he still didn't speak aloud, but he would miss her when she left. Probably. They'd never talked about the future. She'd miss him, too. She shifted her feet. Clark's possible reaction wasn't a reason for her to stay.

Shifting her attention to the newcomers, Janna stared wide-eyed in recognition. Her vision grew blurry and her hands shook. The woman from the sled was Avery Lee, carrying a tiny bundled-up baby. The little girls beside her were Rose and Charlotte—the younger one a dead ringer for a mini Elsa.

Janna and her neighbors had been close growing up, but since Avery's marriage, Janna had seen little of her in SoCal—she and Avery had lived in different worlds—but Elsa had given Janna the odd Avery update after a visit up the hill. Janna had been jealous of Avery's grand house and rich husband, or had been until she'd heard how her friend had been treated. There must have been a major shift in Avery and Jaxon's relationship since Avery was here now, with a known rebel officer.

For a few seconds, Janna hesitated, time slowing while her brain caught up, allowing this piece of her old life to click into place with her new one. Then activity resumed at a normal speed.

"Avery." She rushed forward to hug her old friend. Emotion choked her voice, giving it a strained quality. "What are you doing here? This is the last place in the world I'd expect to see you." Avery smelled of something sweet and fresh air.

"Janna! I should say the same about you," said Avery, her dark eyes shining. "I can't believe you're here on a mountain in Utah with the Saints." Her voice lowered, her smile fading. "I heard what Wade did from your parents—that must have been awful." Avery's sympathetic dark eyes glistened with unshed tears. "They said you were in Texas." Her words kept coming, and Janna didn't know what to address.

"You're one of the women Caitlyn and Mason brought out of Texas last fall," said Darren, turning his attention to Janna. The bulky man seemed huge next to petite Avery, and his stance seemed protective as he angled his shoulder in front of Avery. "Looks like being with the Saints agrees with you." He glanced at the others eating at the nearby tables and the half-filled room. "The food must be excellent, as always." He rubbed his hands together.

"You know Caitlyn and Mason too?" Janna blurted.

"I've learned this is a small world," said Avery with a gentle laugh. "I just heard about them a few days ago. They're close friends with Elsa."

Darren gave a hearty laugh, one that had heads turning throughout the room. "We all know Caitlyn and Mason. I've worked with them for years. Separate and together."

"Do you ever hear from Elsa?" said Janna, turning back to Avery. Had Elsa fallen prey to those at Ginny's brothel? The idea made her stomach churn. The whole time Janna had been in Texas, she'd worried for her friend. Had she also been forced to become a whore?

"I'm thankful every day that Elsa escaped SoCal when she did. Her fate could have been just like yours." Avery squeezed Janna's hand.

Janna's body tensed at the second reference to her time in Texas. She'd do anything to forget those months.

Darren's bushy eyebrows rose to meet his black and green striped knit beanie. "You know our Elsa?" His toothy grin slipped and his voice dropped. He checked around for anyone who might be listening to their conversation. "That's a much larger coincidence than a refugee knowing the rebels who've been doing most of our recent raids." He stared at Janna, his eyes drilling into her.

The room grew several degrees colder.

"Janna grew up in SoCal in the house across the street," said Avery. She patted Darren's arm, as though soothing a menacing guard dog. "Elsa, Janna, and I were all friends." She shifted her weight and looked down at her round-eyed girls watching the people drifting past with plates of food. "We should get everyone fed so I can put the girls to bed. It's been a long couple of days." Her gentle smile for her girls showed how much she cared—they were lucky.

"Oh, of course," said Janna, turning to leave. She could take a hint.

"No. You stay," said Avery, reaching out to grab Janna's sleeve. "There's so much to tell you. It's wonderful to see you here. I can't believe you're free. That's the best surprise." Her eyes seemed sincere. Avery might be quiet and kept a lot of her thoughts to herself, but she'd always told the truth.

So Janna stayed and claimed her regular table, throwing her jacket on the bench to save a place for Clark. She didn't grab food yet, deciding to wait for him so they could eat together, as usual.

Once seated with plates of food, between feeding her children and stealing a few bites for herself, Avery explained how Jaxon had thrown her out last fall, ending their marriage. She didn't seem distraught as she spoke, her hands gesturing like they always had. Her story about Elsa hopping a train last spring with a hopper named Walker was riveting. Elsa had been having adventures. Her friend had also evaded GreenCorps despite a huge reward being offered for her capture and had been sent on a special mission for Grady to Canada. The seeds the entire community had been buzzing about for months were also because of Elsa. The entire story was almost too much to believe.

Elsa had only recently returned to Utah. It sounded like she was vital to the rebellion, making Janna more anxious than ever to join them.

"What about you?" said Janna. "I guess you can't fight much because you've got your girls to think about." She couldn't disguise the longing to get involved from her voice.

Avery laughed. "I'm not important like Elsa, but Grady and the rebels have taken care of us all winter, and not just because we're related, though it was nice to find more family."

"More family?" said Janna. Had she missed a key piece of information?

"Once upon a time, Granny Lee was a rebel leader, even if Elsa and I had no idea. Grady knew her when he was a child—she was his aunt. Can you believe *the* Ryan Grady is our great-uncle? Or maybe some kind of cousin. I didn't pay attention to the details, something about my grandmother marrying his father's twin brother, which makes his son Mason our kin."

Mason was Grady's son? He'd left that part out of the introduction. Maybe it wasn't important to him, or he didn't want to be judged based on who his father was. "You're right. it is a small world," said Janna, feeling hollow. If only she could find more family. Sometimes she felt very alone. "I heard about Granny's death. I'm sorry." She gazed down at little Aki, sleeping in Avery's arms. At least Granny had a namesake and would live on through the girls.

Janna's throat tightened. The old lady had been a key part of her best childhood memories. Despite her gruff manner, Granny had been generous, a wonderful storyteller, and an excellent reading instructor. Most of the Heap kids weren't so lucky.

Avery nodded and brushed a stray tear from her cheek. "It's okay. Granny was well over a hundred when she passed. It was her time and I'm glad she came to live with me for the last couple of months. I got to spend time with her again and take care of her when she needed help. She did so much for us when we were young. I can't imagine where Elsa and I would have been without her. She took us in, no questions asked, even if we were two more mouths to feed." She glanced down at the baby, her lashes wet.

In SoCal, a selfless act like that wasn't always a given, family or not.

Avery and Janna chatted more while the girls ate under their mom's quiet supervision. The adults recounted their favorite stories about Granny Lee and shared some of the choice bits the acid-tongued old lady had said, until Rose yawned with a loud, creaking sound. A second and third followed in quick succession. Her sister's eyes were drooping.

"I need to get my girls to bed," said Avery with a soft chuckle. "It's been a long couple of days traveling. Darren took excellent care of us, but we're exhausted." Her eyes scanned the busy dining hall, probably for the mountain man's form, but he'd been gone awhile. Much longer than it should take to help himself to a second plate of food.

Janna checked the clock on the wall above the door. She'd expected Clark some time ago. He must be running late or staying away because of Avery and the others. She tried not to be worried by his absence. Maybe he'd just been giving them space to catch up. Her stomach growled. If she couldn't track him down, she'd come back soon and eat on her own. "Good night. It was wonderful to see you again, and I hope you enjoy staying with the Saints. They're wonderful, kind people." Janna smiled as she stood to leave.

Just then, Darren rejoined them with a wide grin. He set a heaping plate on the table and shoveled in a giant forkful of mashed potatoes. Making appreciative sounds, he closed his eyes. After another bite, he turned to Avery. "Sister Hope said to tell you she will be here any minute to take you to your cabin. She's got a place organized and you can settle in. You only have to share with one other single mom and her four-year-old." He grinned down at the drooping Rose and Charlie. "I'll say goodbye tonight as I'm off first thing in the morning."

Janna should join the rebels now.

"I want to go with you," she blurted.

A wounded sound, part gasp, part cry, caught her attention and her gaze shifted past Darren's massive shoulder to Clark's ashen face. He dropped his tray with a crash and fled. Nobody spoke until he'd dashed into the night.

What had she done? She should have told him in private before stating her intention to leave early. His look had been pure pain and not what she'd intended.

"You sure about that?" said Darren, his attention straying to the still-swinging door. "I think someone might like you to stay." He gestured to the door with his fork.

Janna lifted her chin, trying to project confidence, though Clark's anguished eyes had struck like a dagger to her heart. She would need to make that right. He never should have found out that way that she was leaving. "Yes. I'm positive. I didn't get rescued to sit in the mountains and let the revolution happen without me. It's all aboard.

I'm ready to do something. Anything that's needed." Despite her words, her voice came out strained and she couldn't banish the image of Clark's dismay.

He'd always known that she would leave come spring. He couldn't have thought she'd remain here much longer. A month tops. Just because she was leaving didn't mean they couldn't be friends, even if the idea of not seeing Clark every day made her stomach hurt.

"Breakfast's at six," said Darren, his intense gaze meeting hers. "Then we hit the trail no later than six-thirty. Dress warm. It'll be cold and dark and we'll be breaking a trail through fresh snow on the way down." He laughed, his mood changing once more. "At least tomorrow will be downhill. We'll be two days on the road to Salt Lake." He scooped another enormous bite of potatoes, his eyes straying to the place where Clark had stood. "If you're sure."

Feeling her cheeks flame, Janna nodded, then turned to Avery. "I'm so glad you made it here. You'll be safe with the Saints." Over Darren's shoulder, Sister Hope approached, so Janna rushed her final words. "You'll like it here, but you'll have to excuse me. I have to pack, though first, there's someone I need to talk to." She rushed into the night to find Clark.

* * *

At first, Janna couldn't find Clark anywhere. She stood outside shivering in the frosty night air as she spun in a circle, trying to decide where else to search; she should have grabbed her jacket before she'd chased after him. Where could he have gone? Most communal buildings had closed for the night and he hadn't fled to his cabin, because she'd checked there first. She wracked her brain, staring at the glow from inside the windows of the dining hall.

At some point, it had started to snow again, large flakes drifting down from above, muffling the ordinary evening sounds. In the distance, the scraping of a snow shovel on the stone-lined paths made her snap her head in that direction. Who would shovel at this time of night instead of eating or relaxing?

The answer streaked like lightning across a stormy sky. Clark.

She followed the sound through the twisty snowbank-lined paths. When she found him, she stopped eight feet away and waited for his attention to shift from the ground to her. She tapped her toe. He didn't look in her direction. Had he noticed her presence, or was he ignoring her? She waited, her teeth chattering, her bare hands shoved into the pockets of her cargo pants. Her hair was drenched, soaked with melted snowflakes; an icy rivulet trickled down inside her collar. She wanted to talk to him now and head back inside for food and where it was warm. Maybe he would come and they could talk.

She crossed her arms and shivered. "Clark." She grabbed a handful of snow and threw it into his path.

At last, he looked up with a hectic flush to his normally pale cheeks, affected by more than just the cold. He turned and walked in the opposite direction, still scraping new-fallen snow.

"Please. You're my friend. Don't make this harder." Her voice turned to pleading. "I can't be someone who sits on the fringes and does nothing. That's how too many people live. To defeat GreenCorps, there can't be any more bystanders. Everyone needs to pick a side and fight for what they believe."

He glanced toward her, then met her eyes. His pale blue eyes were scarlet-rimmed and swam with unshed tears.

She moved closer and took the snow shovel from his hand. He didn't resist. Tossing the shovel to the side, she hugged him, squeezing hard. His body shook like a leaf and remained as stiff as a tree. Who'd made him so desperate and so scared? His reaction wasn't all about her departure. It couldn't be. There must be more to his story; he was scarred inside. She rested her head against his shoulder and his arms pulled her in tight. They fit together as though they'd done this many times.

He took several deep breaths and his body relaxed infinitesimally. She waited another several heartbeats before speaking.

"Come with us Clark." She kept her voice quiet, but her plea wouldn't matter. Still, she had to ask, even if she didn't expect him to change his mind.

"I can't." He pulled away, twisting his tortured face away. His voice was so quiet she almost could have imagined it. He took a deep breath and his expression became distant as he took several steps back. Why couldn't he fight for anything? The Saints. Her.

"That's on you." A red haze descended as she snatched the shovel off the icy ground and threw it back at him. "Then, just keep shoveling the damn snow and avoiding the real world."

He caught it with a stunned expression that soon turned to hurt—perhaps noticing her anger. Later, that might matter. Now, she didn't care. Why wouldn't he even consider joining the rebels?

"You're the one who has to live with your choices." She spun on her heels and stalked away, mindful not to slip.

* * *

Janna woke in the still dark morning to discover a folded sheet of paper had been slid under her door. Hopping out of bed onto the chilly floor, she snatched it off the floor and returned to bed to read. She angled it toward the dim light of the lamp on the crate beside her bunk where her packed bag sat.

Janna,
I can't say goodbye. I've said it to too many people who've never returned. Just. Don't. Die. I'll miss you.
—Clark

She folded the brief note and shoved it into her bag with her few possessions. It hurt that he hadn't come to say goodbye in person, but she wasn't surprised. She hated the way they'd left things, but couldn't regret her decision to leave with Darren. Maybe she should find Clark to talk. After reading his note, it seemed he'd already forgiven her anger and that some of his fear was worry for her. He also wouldn't thank her for forcing a goodbye. Besides, she didn't have extra time; she needed to get moving if she wanted to have time to eat without being left behind.

Janna closed her eyes, exhaled, and got dressed.

She took a last look around the bunkhouse where her roommates still slept. There was nothing to show she'd ever stayed here. Everything she owned was on her back. She rubbed her bleary eyes and headed for the door with Clark's birthday present in hand. She'd leave it on their table, with one last note. Janna had been up late finishing the notebook and packing, but she wasn't going to miss this opportunity to be part of the rebellion.

* * *

Dear Clark,

Thank you for being concerned about my safety, and I'm sorry I frightened you. I wanted to let you know that when the campaign is done, I'd like to come back. Meeting you has been the best thing to happen to me in a long time. I'll miss you.

Think of me when you write and find peace.

Take care,

— Janna

CHAPTER 19: MASON

Mason adjusted the girth strap on his saddle and glanced over at Caitlyn, where she was making final preparations before they left the farm—for who knows how long this time. She stopped packing and her gaze swept the deserted farmyard and the snow-covered mountains to the east, her eyes filled with longing. He would miss this place, too.

The day before yesterday, a message had arrived with a summons from Grady, requesting their attendance at an important meeting in the city—meaning their quiet interlude was over. Darren had sent one of the neighbor's children with the note as he'd passed nearby. Seeing Darren would have been enjoyable, but he'd taken a different route into the canyon because he was traveling by sled. He'd written that he was taking Elsa's sister and her children to live with the Saints—where they'd be safe.

"Grady must hope to apply pressure soon. Earlier than expected." Caitlyn's deep blue eyes caught his own. "I wish he'd mentioned what happened with Elsa and Walker. I would appreciate knowing if they're back yet. We haven't heard anything since they were waiting on the keys in Portland."

Mason smiled at his wife. "You know he couldn't mention her by name. Not in writing. GreenCorps still wants her almost as much as they want Grady. But you're right. They could have found a way. Maybe there's no news."

Caitlyn tugged on her braid before mounting her horse. "I know, though it'll be nice to reconnect."

"Are you sorry we wintered out here on our own?" He certainly wasn't. It had given him a hint of the peaceful life they could enjoy in the future, and he'd loved every minute. Hard work, cold, and isolation were nothing when you were with someone you loved.

"Of course not." She smiled—the special one that was just for him—and stole his breath. "It's just that we've been cut off most of the winter, and Grady's note didn't say enough. I could've used news or an update on our friends."

Mason had missed their company more than he'd expected. "We'll find out soon enough." He winked as he mounted his steady mare. He would have to leave her in Salt Lake City again when he traveled by train, but it would only be temporary. One day, hopefully soon, they could live on the farm. This was the first home he'd looked forward to having since he was sixteen and his mother had died.

"How long do you think we'll be gone this time?" Caitlyn once more stared at the puffy white lumps that made up the chicken coop, barn, and house. She blinked several times. His wife was going to miss their solitude and her home.

He'd picked that much up from what she hadn't said. They'd only spent three months living here, and a part of her longed to sit out this next campaign, to grow her own food and get new animals to raise. She'd enjoyed the farming life. In his heart, he believed she'd done enough already and wished he could tell her to sit this one out. However, her presence was indispensable. Everyone was needed, especially those with medical training. Having her along could be the difference between life and death if someone was injured.

With a last look around the deserted farmyard, he clucked to his horse. Caitlyn mounted, the stirrup creaking under her foot, and they headed out. Neither of them looked back as they kicked the horses into a trot and aimed toward Salt Lake City. Mittens would have to hold down the farm for the summer on her own.

* * *

Mason and Caitlyn prepared to jump off the train just before it slowed, coming into SoCal's Riverside. The last ten days since leaving the farm had been a blur of organization, planning sessions, and assignments. As planned, they'd left their horses in Salt Lake and hopped trains, as had their friends. Though focused on rebel business, it had been a reunion of sorts, with Elsa, Walker, Tatsuda, Ginger, Janna, and themselves present.

Mason patted his front pocket, checking he still had the copied bunker key. Elsa had brought the duplicates and he and Caitlyn had been entrusted with one. He was going to see the inside of a seed bunker at last; he'd missed out in Aberdeen last summer, electing to stay above ground. McCoy and GreenCorps had been hot on their trail, and Mason hadn't wanted to be trapped inside, deep underground. Instead, he and Caitlyn had worked on getting the others out and he stood by that decision.

He still wasn't wild about the idea of going so far below ground, but it was a trade-off worth his minor discomfort. They needed the seeds and would bring out boots, clothes, and extra backpacks to outfit the many refugees who still had so few belongings. The gear and supplies wouldn't last long, but were an added bonus. Later, teams would be sent to bring up books from the libraries. The bunkers not only contained seeds for the future, they would provide a link to the past, one that GreenCorps had done their best to stamp out by controlling the knowledge and rewriting history.

Mason double-checked his backpack balance, ensuring he'd tucked in the straps, and made sure his bootlaces were tied. He gave Caitlyn a quick once-over. As usual, nothing was out of place. He sometimes forgot that she was the more experienced hopper.

The war council in Salt Lake had gone much as expected, with Grady handing out orders and splitting the rebel commanders into several groups. He'd kept the couples together, and he'd assigned the new girl, Janna, to stay with himself and Darren. That she'd grown up with Elsa had been a surprise, each thrilled to see one another. They'd both been through a lot to escape SoCal, and here he was arriving in Riverside, the place they'd worked so hard to get away from.

The biggest shock had been leaving Tatsuda and Ginger behind to run headquarters and act as a communication hub. Grady was putting a lot of trust in the youngsters. It was probably the safest job, but everyone's would be difficult. Trying to achieve economic, social, and political change all at once was a big ask for the people of the West.

Mason leaned over the edge of the hopper, checking the tracks, and replayed the words in his head from Walker's train hopping workshop for the new rebel hoppers as the train banged and crashed as it decelerated. He winced, even with earplugs in. Without them, the bashing created a din that echoed and would give him a headache. He and Caitlyn had attended the talk as a refresher, though Walker had run them through a short version in Portland before they'd returned to Utah.

After their missions last fall, and thinking about how to save precious seconds, Mason had asked about jumping off a moving train. That idea was dangerous enough that Walker recommended against doing it—ever. That and hopping a knuckle, where two trains joined. If a train was moving, the joint was unstable and dangerous, shifting back and forth with the motion of the train. That would be a painful way to die, crushed or caught and dragged underneath the wheels.

Hopping trains in rebel-controlled land and stations was easy, or at least less dangerous than before. Jumping off into strict GreenCorps areas would be more challenging, even if the rebels now controlled the railroad. Security in a work camp like SoCal or strangled corporation towns like those in Texas would still be tight. Though most railway workers had joined Grady's side after the GreenCorps' wage cuts, they would have to keep up appearances and maintain a minimum level of outward security. Meaning, the rebels would still have to scramble down and run, scattering until it was safe to reconvene away from the station. The longer they could operate without GreenCorps learning the truth about the railroad, the better for the rebel cause.

Mason surveyed the bleak landscape. He'd never been to SoCal. So far, he was unimpressed—what a gray shit hole. No wonder Elsa had always wanted to escape. He ran through the plan in his mind. He gripped the rail near the top of the ladder because Caitlyn waited to swing over the side first.

In a few minutes, they would leave the train yard to search for the ruins of the California University site at Riverside. According to Elsa's memory of the maps found with the original key, they needed to move east. He hoped the university buildings, now rubble, would be obvious, so his team wouldn't have to search for too long.

Every hour that passed out in the open, was more time for GreenCorps to figure out what was happening and follow. There wouldn't be a lot of cover near the station in Riverside, with the scrapyards and junk heaps, though neither Elsa nor Walker had firsthand experience here. If the bunker site had been compromised, Mason needed to let Grady know from Riverside station. A flutter filled his stomach at the imminent prospect of action.

Every bunker location could already have a contingent of soldiers stationed there, waiting—like what had happened in Aberdeen. That was another reason for coordinating their seed retrievals early in the season. As far as the rebels could determine, GreenCorps still considered last fall a victory, having shoved the rebels back onto their heels after the fire in San Antonio.

The corporation hoped to capture Elsa and her key, but any bunker key would do now. Not that they should know about the duplicates. The rebel teams had been told to guard their key at all costs. Tatsuda had recommended swallowing it if caught. Mason patted the key. No way he was swallowing a chunk of metal. Best to avoid capture.

The train jolted to a halt and Caitlyn was the first down the ladder, landing with a soft thud on the hard-packed ground, sending up a fine poof of gray dust. She waited at the bottom, waving the airborne cloud away from her face. Around them, rebel hoppers jumped from several cars up the line. When it appeared all the pairs had disembarked, Mason motioned them toward the rear of the train. They'd agreed beforehand to get off on the side farthest from the station, so the rebels spied each other with ease.

He and Caitlyn led the others, crouching as they ran. They reached the bushes without incident, followed a tunnel through the thick brambles to the fence, then climbed up and over. Leaving the trainyard, the rebels gathered in a cluster, awaiting their orders.

"Stay together. Single file along the path," said Mason. "Once we get past the town, we're hiking due east, approximately three miles." If the terrain remained flat and the trail unobstructed, it shouldn't take more than an hour to reach the university grounds they needed to search. "Remember when we get there, we're looking for a stone hut that seems intact and has a metal door jamb inscribed with a leaf. Move out." He shared a glance with Caitlyn. Together they led the group, but she often let him give the orders. They made an excellent team.

The troop of a dozen rebels fell in line. He and Caitlyn had a whole new crew this time, as the men and women they'd worked with last fall now led their own groups with a sheet of random numbers that matched dates for their raids on GreenCorps towns. Some were to free people, others for food supplies and water. Others had been sent to Texas and the north; they'd all stay on the move. He wasn't sure when and where the others would strike. Each group had a unique set of dates and targets to make it challenging for GreenCorps to predict patterns or set up ambushes.

This spring, because the rebels controlled the railroad, they could check in with railroad workers who would be in contact with Tatsuda via the train station phones.

Mason glanced back, noting the three extra tanker cars of water attached to this train. Elsa had been forceful in making sure additional water was sent everywhere it was scarce. She'd grown up scraping out a living to buy expensive water tokens. Delivering water was a small thing, but he understood its importance. Elsa hadn't lost sight of what mattered.

After they found the bunker, the rebels had one more assignment in Riverside. Then, they needed to make the short trip up the line to Long Beach, Elsa's hometown. In both places, their job was to mark a patch of ground for an airdrop from their Canadian allies.

Airplanes overhead would be new and stand out, but it was worth a try as the planes would be far overhead. If the drops were successful, the locals could continue to receive food from their allies. GreenCorps would catch on in time, but every crate of food would help people and he hoped enough would make it into the hands of the starving to make a difference.

The Canadians would drop the first shipment before dawn tomorrow and another in Long Beach three days from now. His rebels should have enough time between collecting from the bunker and the food drop. Based on the train schedule, it might be tight.

Delivering food and water was Mason's favorite part of the campaign. Each corporation town along the coast and into Texas would receive help. Part of Mason and Caitlyn's job would be to mark the drop sites and distribute food to the locals. They needed to advertise by word of mouth without GreenCorps becoming the wiser. They would also ensure the inhabitants knew about the rebels and learned what an election was—a chance to express their opinion by voting. No matter how hard GreenCorps tried to suppress this news, it had to get out. These missions were their chance to promote the rebel cause.

His troop gave the town itself a wide berth, hiking north until they were into the rolling hills to avoid being seen from the station and the town while they walked. On the way, Mason scouted for potential drop sites and chose three worth considering, ones out of sight from the town, but not so far that the townspeople wouldn't monitor them for subsequent drops once discovered.

At last, he found one with a distinctive landmark—a gnarled oak tree. This time of year, it was bare of leaves, but it was memorable, especially in an area where trees were few. The surrounding land was flat and accessible.

"Hold up. Drink time." He took a long pull on his canteen, letting the refreshing water slide down his dusty throat. They planned to ration their water for the days they were here, each person bringing two jugs so they didn't have to purchase GreenCorps water. "What do you think?" He indicated the crooked tree with his chin. "You can't see Riverside, but it isn't too far for the townsfolk to walk."

"For the drop?" Caitlyn scanned the area again, her gaze assessing the location. "It's good."

Mason nodded. "I like it." He and Caitlyn marked the site with glint tape tied on stakes, which they pounded into the ground in a circle beyond the tree to give the planes a target. Three of the others stood watch while they worked. It didn't look like much when they finished, but the special tape and been brought by Elsa from Canada and she'd assured him that those overhead in the planes would wear special equipment called night-vision googles that would enable them to find the drop zone even without lights.

Trekking to the university ruins took longer than expected, but by mid-morning they'd reached the site. Though only March, the scorching sun beat down as the morning progressed. There was more ground to cover than expected and little shade or cover among the ruins. He wiped the sweat dripping down his face.

The team spread out in pairs to wander the mounds and chunks of rock and brick that littered the area. Some buildings were partially intact, with chunks of brick wall, though the roofs had long since collapsed. Most structures had been destroyed either during the Collapse, or since. A tangle of low weeds and brambles choked much of the crispy land and searching was thirsty work. He exchanged glances with Caitlyn after crisscrossing another segment of land without finding the entrance to the bunker.

As if reading his mind, she said, "I could use a cold beer about now." She mopped the sweat from her forehead and adjusted her protective sun hat. He smiled.

To the east, a wooded area had sprung up, perhaps over an underground spring or broken culvert. Several unfamiliar dark green bushes grew there—maybe once they'd been part of a park or a garden. He recalled Elsa's account of the Davis bunker, and how it had been in an overgrown rock and shrub garden.

Mason made for the greenery and the shade, Caitlyn beside him.

He was about to suggest they move farther south, when Caitlyn pointed to a shape hidden in the fringe of gigantic half-dead evergreen bushes that rose taller than a house. The shadows and the lower branches obscured the building—excellent camouflage.

"How the hell did you spot that?" Mason was impressed. "About damn time."

"Solar panels." She grinned as one of the iridescent panels winked in the midday sun.

They strode closer and peeled back the thick bushes to find the door jamb marked with a leaf. This time, the entrance wasn't a small stone hut, but more like a fancy garden house. The porch had fallen down and pokey weeds had grown between the flat paving stones, obscuring the way to the metal door. Up close, Mason recognized the style of construction as matching the Aberdeen bunker.

Before unlocking the door, he climbed the side of the house and stood on the edge of the roof, scanning the area back toward Riverside. Best to be safe. With the thick shrubs behind him, he felt protected from that side and he only needed to check the other directions. The people in the distance, searching in pairs, were all his rebels. Still no sign of GreenCorps. He let out a breath, hoping it was going as well at the other locations. He squinted at the sun and checked his borrowed timepiece. It should be safe to open the bunker door.

He slipped back to the ground, sparing just a second to consider Elsa at the Davis bunker and Kurt at Aberdeen. They were all scheduled to enter today, barring problems.

"Nobody else around," he said. "Time to use the whistle."

Caitlyn smiled, removed a whistle on a lanyard from beneath her shirt, and gave two quick blasts—the signal they'd found the door. Within five minutes, the breathless team assembled, ready to enter.

Mason debated with himself for a moment. Everyone wanted to check out the bunker, and a few guards would be a waste if a large contingent of GreenCorps soldiers came upon them. They all needed to enter, close the door to avoid surprises, and retrieve as many seeds as they could carry. The four people chosen to return to Utah with most of the seeds would leave from Riverside station on the first northbound train tomorrow. The rest would redistribute food and head to Long Beach, then Texas.

He smiled at their first success, though he had a feeling not everything would be as smooth. He'd take this first win and carry on until things went south.

CHAPTER 20: JANNA

The rebels sat in a low-windowless box-like room of metal situated beside the railroad tracks. Janna sighed, breathing in the stuffy warm air. She'd spent a week with Elsa in Utah, relieved beyond measure her friend had also gotten out of SoCal and landed on her feet. Though their lives had taken parallel courses at first, they'd deviated when Elsa escaped the whorehouse before she'd been violated. At least they were free of that life now.

Elsa had downplayed her importance in what was happening with the rebels now, but Janna had seen the respect Elsa was given when she spoke. Her friend had become a vital part of the rebellion—it made Janna proud to see a girl from SoCal become a leader.

When she wasn't assigned a rebel group with either Elsa or Caitlyn, Janna was surprised and disappointed. She didn't know anyone in this group and sat alone, empty chairs separating her from the others. She wasn't great at making friends and kept to herself, meaning the last three days had been quiet. With this group, she was new and not yet trusted, so she hadn't been privy to any of the important conversations, leaving her out of sorts and confused. She missed Clark and missed feeling useful, like she had with the Saints.

Janna wiped her damp hands on her pants, fanned her face with her hand, and lifted her sticky shirt away from her skin in an attempt to find relief from the oppressive heat. She didn't know why she'd been included with this team. Perhaps because Grady wanted to learn what she brought to the rebels. Butterflies flew through her stomach and wouldn't settle. She craned her neck to look around the chair-filled room filled with sweaty, restless strangers.

An undercurrent of tension circulated through the group. Were they all as clueless as she felt? Grady and Darren had remained outside upon arrival but should return any minute.

The leader had been nothing like she'd assumed before meeting him. He was slim, thoughtful, and reserved, with steely eyes that seemed to see to the heart of things. After hearing his whispered name for years, she'd pictured someone powerful and tall, more forceful, and larger than life. Instead, he spoke with a quiet voice and was nondescript except for the mark on his forehead.

Grady had become mythic, avoiding capture by GreenCorps for almost his entire life and few pictures of him existed. Not only were his Wanted posters old and faded, but they could have described half the men she'd met since leaving SoCal. Not one included his identifiable ax-shaped birthmark. That he'd lived as a fugitive for his whole life spoke to his popularity. Nobody was willing to turn him over to GreenCorps, even for a fortune.

Janna fidgeted in her hard, uncomfortable chair, while sweltering in the heat. Right now, part of her wished she'd stayed with the Saints. This trip didn't seem so important and she didn't understand why she was here. Why were any of them here, in the middle of nowhere?

There were few clues in the drafty room with blank walls. They'd taken the train for an hour past the city of Boise and it had stopped at this building, one that wasn't an actual train station. They'd disembarked the almost empty train and for the last half hour, they'd been idle, sitting. Why were they waiting? Or for whom? The suspense kept her on edge.

Her gaze lifted as Darren and Grady slipped into the room.

Darren gave her a nod, and he smiled at the other dozen rebels in their group. "They're on their way. Should be here any minute. Get ready."

Several people sat up straighter in their seats while Darren and Grady stood at the front near a long table. A skinny man in a fancy navy blue suit fussed over the placement of everything on the table, shifting sheets of paper by less than an inch, at least twice. He'd been here when they'd arrived. Fussing.

Outside, the sound of approaching vehicles made the hair on her neck rise. The rumble grew closer, then stopped. The sound of several doors opening and slamming followed, then many sets of footsteps tapped along the outside walkway. Janna shifted once more, her eyes cutting to the main door at the back. Who had arrived? Grady and the others looked more excited than nervous. She should take her cues from them. The steps thumped on the stairs leading to the door.

Four serious young men and two women entered, wearing unfamiliar matching uniforms with scarlet coats, black pants, and funny brown hats with a wide flat brim all the way around—not the black and green of GreenCorps. They took up positions along the aisle leading from the entrance to the table, staring straight ahead.

The next person through the door was a woman of about fifty, with long black and gray hair braided and pinned like a crown and golden-brown skin. Her attire consisted of brilliant orange and hot pink with gold accents. Her loose clothing differed from anything Janna had ever seen before. It should have been garish, but it was stunning. She found it difficult not to stare at the woman's exotic beauty. Behind her, overshadowed by her presence, walked four more uniformed guards, their guns in leather holsters on their black belts. Together, they were an impressive sight.

This beautiful woman must be someone important. Janna held her breath, waiting to see what would happen next. Grady approached the woman and inclined his head slightly when he stood in front of her.

"Prime Minister Singh. Thank you for meeting with me today." Grady extended his hand.

The woman smiled a radiant smile, clasping his hand between both of hers. "Please, call me Malinda. The pleasure is all mine, Ryan Grady. You're a challenging man to find. I've hoped for many years that we would have a chance to meet. There's much to discuss and limited time. My security detail will intervene and cut the meeting short if we are about to be interrupted. Shall we begin?" She gestured to the table.

The man in a suit stepped back to the corner.

Janna sucked in her breath. The beautiful woman was the leader of Western Canada. Janna didn't understand everything, but a meeting between the prime minister and the rebel leader might mean the other country was prepared to be an open ally, and not just a covert one. The Canadians had chosen the rebels over GreenCorps. Historic. Her throat tightened. This made Grady's claim to speak for the people believable. Janna had never considered that winning the rebellion might not just be fighting and raids, but might include politics and friendships.

A feeling of pride swept over her, and hot tears pricked her eyes. This was an important time to be alive. A powerful urge to write to Clark and tell him about this insight surged through her. There was no one else she wanted to tell, no one else she wanted to explain the significance of this moment to. Hell, she wouldn't need to explain. He would understand. Clark was smarter than just about anyone she'd ever known. Angry with him or not, she felt compelled to put some of her thoughts on paper. Sometimes committing them to paper made them clearer. She would write him a letter. She shifted in her chair. Would that be allowed? After all, this meeting must be secret.

She returned her attention to the discussion at the front. Grady and the prime minister spoke in voices too quiet for her to hear more than half of what they said, but it didn't matter. She watched their facial expressions and listened to their tone. They laughed twice for all the hushed, serious talk. Their conversation seemed to be going well.

The meeting had been in progress for less than an hour when someone in a red and black uniform flung open the door and dashed in from outside. They held a strange black object in their hand. "Prime Minister, GreenCorps has sent a cavalry troop headed this way. The satellite image shows them less than ten miles out. We need to leave."

Janna didn't understand the talk about satellites or cameras but caught the part about GreenCorps troops moving in.

Grady and the Prime Minister stood and shook hands again, still smiling despite their entourages' sudden hum of activity. She glided up the aisle, past Janna, and out the door, her original guards now trailing. The man in the suit gathered the papers from the table and followed—leaving no sign the Canadians had been there. The sound of engines returned. Doors slammed and the Canadian vehicles left, their noise fading as they drove away across the empty land.

"Time for us to go too," said Darren, his voice booming in the sudden silence. "Everyone back on the train. Now. We pull out in five. GreenCorps must have gotten a tip about the meeting. Some of the railway workers could be spies."

Everyone scrambled and hurried out the door, loading onto the strange train composed of an engine facing in each direction with two passenger cars between them. They boarded within the prescribed time and the train got underway. Now the reason for the second engine made sense. They couldn't turn the train around on this dead-end spur of a track, instead, they headed in the opposite direction, back toward Boise.

Once underway, Darren strolled through the passenger car, talking to many of those sitting while he checked in with everyone. Janna watched him instead of the drab brown early spring landscape rolling by outside. He seemed to know just what to say to each person and to be well-liked. As he passed her seat near the back, Janna swallowed, working up her nerve.

"Excuse me." Her voice was hoarse. She hadn't spoken since they'd left Salt Lake City three days ago. Darren stopped and raised his eyebrows, perhaps surprised she'd broken her silence. "Would I be able to write a letter to my friend at the Saints settlement?"

His friendly eyes grew serious. "The Dawson boy who ran out of the dining hall?"

She nodded, feeling her emotions threaten to embarrass her. "Clark would appreciate not all wars are fought with knives and guns." She blinked several times to keep her emotions in check. What was wrong with her?

"Because of the sensitive nature of our mission, I'd like to see your letters before we find someone to take them. Will you let us read them?" His tone was even. We must mean Grady.

She nodded. Of course. Her thoughts wouldn't be private just, personal—there was a difference. She missed having someone to tell her thoughts. She missed her friend.

With permission granted, Janna took some folded paper from her pocket, now used to keeping a pencil and paper handy. Lowering a folding tray attached to the seat in front of her, she took a breath and wrote.

Dear Clark,

I don't know if you'll read this or how long my letter will take to get to you, but I wanted you to know how sorry I am that we parted in anger. I'm not apologizing for leaving, just that our last words were harsh—too harsh to leave between us.

I saw someone unexpected today, and it has made me rethink something important. You are too hard on yourself about not wanting to fight the corporation bullies that have tormented you for your whole life. However, you might be correct that weapons aren't always the answer. Please don't say, "I told you so." Even if you must be thinking it.

Sometimes connecting with the right people, at the perfect time and place is more important than anything else. Don't ask me who I saw, or what happened, just know that I recognized the significance of this meeting. I might have undervalued words as a way of seizing opportunities. I feel like you believe in the power of words and would understand.

I'd love it if we could write to each other again. I miss our friendship.

Yours,

Janna

Chapter 21: Elsa

Elsa glanced across at Walker and back at the rebel team accompanying them on the trek through the knee-deep golden grass of the plains. Fluffy white clouds floated like bits of Styrofoam packing in the clear blue sky, reminding her of last spring, when she and Walker had made this trip for the first time.

They hopped off the train and left Sacramento without going into town. As they traveled, she monitored their backtrail to ensure they weren't followed. Hiking along beside the discontinued railway berm made her feel exposed from that side; too out in the open, making her shoulder blades twitch. Still, this was the best route to the Davis bunker.

When daylight waned, the group stayed in the same campsite with fresh water where she and Walker had stayed last year. As it was only March, the cottonwood trees stood bare, like sentinels guarding the abandoned former community. She couldn't shake the feeling the rebels weren't alone and organized a rotation to take watch—she and Walker took the first shift.

The night passed with little sleep and no problems. She rose early and the last watch reported that it had been quiet, except for distant coyote yips. After a quick breakfast, they broke camp and continued their journey.

Several times Elsa turned and scanned the horizons, but they remained empty. The memories of the previous year came to her with each step—a perfect distraction from the sensation of hostile eyes that made her skin crawl. Checking out the Davis bunker for the first time had been an adventure and a chance to get to know Walker. Now the return was an integral part of the rebel plan. A lot had happened in less than a year.

The rebels moved into position around the small stone hut within the university ruins in Davis, still astonishingly intact, including a roof with solar panels. Even after all this time, when the university had crumbled around the building, the panels collected energy to run underground lights, circulate air, and maintain an even cold temperature for the seeds below. The rock garden around them was filled with an overgrown tangle of dead bushes and weeds, with a few new green shoots poking up through the pale dirt and crumbled buildings.

This was the closest she'd been to home for over a year. If Jaxon and GreenCorps had access to the bunker maps, as she suspected, this was the bunker he would most likely stake out waiting for her. After she didn't appear in SoCal, this was the next logical place for them to try. She had a feeling she still had unfinished business with the McCoys.

The surrounding countryside remained empty despite her watchfulness. Still, anyone could be hidden, monitoring the bunker from afar, especially if equipped with binoculars or a scope. The rubble of the university buildings provided ample cover. Maybe the rebels should scout more before entering.

Elsa glanced back at Walker. "Is it time yet?" Despite her misgivings, this felt too easy.

He consulted the borrowed timepiece and nodded. "Mid-morning. Any time now."

"I wonder if Mason's team found the bunker at Riverside. That one was so close to home, but when I'd never hopped a train, it seemed impossibly far." They'd never returned in that direction.

When she'd left Long Beach, she and Walker had been intent on escaping. The Davis bunker had been a side trip to kill time.

In the shade of the bunker hut, she lowered her UVee goggles. How would her life have turned out if she'd escaped Long Beach to search for the Riverside bunker on foot instead of working at Ginny's? Her forehead tightened. She wouldn't have known how to hop trains safely, and probably would have been caught by the corporation and deported to Texas—an unpleasant thought. She could have ended up like Janna. Or worse.

"No way to know yet," said Walker. "But probably. Kurt and his team should be ready too at Aberdeen, since we're all supposed to enter at the same time." He nodded. "Let's go. We want to get everything on the train tomorrow or we'll fall behind."

Elsa looked at the anxious faces around her. "It'll feel cool and dark inside at first, even before we're on the stairs." She swallowed. "If the door still opens."

Her hand trembled as she unlocked the outer door. She held her breath, hoping the duplicate key worked. It would be horrible to be stuck outside after coming all this way. She smiled when the familiar green light above the lock flashed and the lock clicked, loud in the silence of anticipation. Someone let out a noisy exhale. Everything about the bunkers was foreign and unknown to the others, despite the briefing in Salt Lake City.

As far as they'd been able to determine, Elsa and Walker had been the first people to venture into the seed bunkers in almost two hundred years. Judging by newspapers they'd found in the Aberdeen bunker, the last entry had been at about the same time as the Collapse in 2025.

She shifted again and searched their surroundings, a frown tugging at her face. Though she hadn't discovered the source, they weren't alone.

"Don't worry," Walker said, resting a large hand on her shoulder, its warmth settling her nerves. "I'll get the satellite link and screens on as soon as we're underground. We won't come out unless we know the path is clear."

"Thank you." Elsa shot him a partial smile, which was the best she could muster right now. She pushed on the door. Like the first time they'd been here, the door wouldn't budge. Several others on the team exchanged glances. She ignored their mutters, though her hands grew moist.

"It's still broken." A frustrated edge crept into her voice. She'd never been patient.

Walker lifted and strained, grinding the door forward an inch, creating a narrow gap. He pointed to two of the men. "Can you help? The hinges are bent. We've got to lift the door while we push inward."

The men stepped forward, almost tripping in their haste. Walker lifted the handle while the others gripped the edge of the door. All three of them shoved, their shoulders against the cool metal door.

With their continued effort, the outer door scraped forward. When the space between the door and the leaf-marked frame grew wide enough for entry, they stopped. Cold, stale air wafted out from inside. One by one, the rebels slipped into the dark opening and crowded into the dim cobwebby room inside. Without windows, the only light came from the partially open door.

Elsa spun, trying to notice details she may not have noticed before. There wasn't much to see. The dust-filled room seemed undisturbed since her last visit, with no new marks on the floor, just the same dirt and litter of bug carcasses. After the second interior door, there would be nothing but fine dust.

"Candle lanterns out, just in case." She kept her tone brisk. "The lights on the stairs will be faint, just enough to see the steps." She crossed to the second door on the far side and inserted her key. Once more, the green light signaled the door unlocking.

Half the team held their lanterns aloft, the steady yellow glow accenting the swooping cobwebs covered in dust that criss-crossed the windowless room. Elsa held the door for the new rebels. She motioned to the outer door to the last one in line. "Brad, can you get that? Or do you need help?"

Brad grunted.

Before she followed up, the others departed. She glanced down the dim stairwell as Walker led the group down the first flight of stairs, his boots clanging on the metal treads. Like the previous times they'd been on the bunker stairs, pale lights flicked on with a snap, making Elsa jump. They illuminated the treads, but little else.

A chill ran through her despite the clear weather outside and the trouble-free entry. Had Brad closed the door? She hadn't heard a clang. A glance over her shoulder revealed his negligence. What a rookie mistake. She grit her teeth. Somebody was out there. Jaxon would have ensured it, even if he wasn't here. She needed to slow down and take precautions.

"Just a second," she called down the stairs. Walker turned and raised one eyebrow, and she waved him forward. "Brad, come back and help close the doors so we can avoid surprises."

"Need more help?" Walker said.

She shook her head. "Easier to push from inside. We'll be fine."

Soon, she and Brad stood alone in the entry room. "We can't leave this open. If someone outside checks the location regularly, the door being left ajar is damning evidence of our presence." She tried to be firm but keep her irritation in check. Plus, the rebels needed to keep GreenCorps out—the corporation would confiscate all the seeds for their exclusive use. No food or crops for regular people.

She shoved on the door with her back, using her legs as leverage. Brad joined her, straining as it scraped across the concrete floor with a grinding sound, leaving a cleared swath on the dusty floor. Beads of sweat dotted her forehead.

When the door closed, a red light flashed where the green had been.

"You go ahead. I'll see you downstairs." She shook the handle to ensure it was latched while Brad ducked his head and left. She rotated her neck and shoulders to ease her tension and breathed a sigh of relief. The bunker could be opened from the inside without the key, but it was once again locked from the outside. There still might be someone outside, but GreenCorps couldn't get in. Some of the others might think her foolish when the area seemed deserted, but she'd learned to pay attention to her instincts.

Elsa crossed the gritty floor and stopped inside, just before the top stair. She shut the second door before following the others deep into the cold underground, her steps clanging as she descended. From the sounds below, they were several flights ahead. The stairs turned several sharp corners; each couple of flights went in different directions from the previous. She lost track of the original direction as she wound down several more flights.

At the bottom of the metal stairs, by the third door, everyone gathered, waiting. Elsa forged ahead and unlocked the third and final door into the seed bunker.

With their entry, motion-triggered lights snapped on with popping sounds as the overhead lights turned on. Inside appeared the same as before. A regular door led into the main seed vault beyond, which was separated from the entryway by a long wall of windows. Boxes full of labeled, foil-wrapped seed packets filled the vault room from floor to ceiling. They were here to collect a selection of seed packets to take back for distribution.

She turned to Walker. "Please get the satellite camera operating first. I can't shake the feeling someone else was out there."

He nodded, slipped off his pack, and left down the hallway toward the living quarters and satellite relay room. He'd figured out how to use the equipment when they'd been trapped underground in Aberdeen for just over a week, thanks to Jaxon.

The others looked to her for orders.

"Let's collect clothes and gear for the refugees first," said Elsa, motioning to the gear on the nearby shelves. "We can load some containers to pull with ropes, like sleds. They should slide on the slippery grass without too much trouble. The hard part will be lugging everything back up the stairs, but that won't slow us down too much. The seeds can go in our packs."

She assigned several people to gather items and took a few others aside. "We need to gather only a few dozen large packets of each type. A lot of the seeds at this location are for trees that will have to grow and develop for years before they'll produce nuts and fruit to eat." She'd never had most of these fruits but was excited to think that one day she might.

Elsa and the second team entered the cold vault with the packed seeds. She made a list of what they took: almonds, apricots, cherries, figs, grapes, kiwi fruit, nectarines, olives, peaches, persimmons, pistachios, plums, pomegranates, several varieties of tomatoes, and walnuts. She'd only seen two types of tomatoes in the past, ones with large fruit or clusters of small tomatoes, like berries. On two occasions, she had eaten grapes and once peaches, all as gifts. Under GreenCorps domination, she'd never been able to afford either. Her mouth watered at the possibilities. If everything worked, someday everyone could afford these varieties of fruit.

The rebels had traveled light, with few personal belongings, knowing they would need space to carry the precious seeds. The foil seed packets were almost the size of a book, though flatter and lighter. She glanced back through the windows at the rest of the retrieval team. They'd made quick work of the clothes and sleeping bags from the shelves. A couple were now trying on new boots. Maybe they should take a backpack full of dehydrated rations, too. It wouldn't hurt to carry easy food for some of their travels. Other than the four returning to Salt Lake with the seeds, this was just their first stop.

Walker returned and beckoned from outside the window. Elsa stopped working and left the cold storage room. He didn't speak, instead tossing his head toward the hall, but he didn't need to—his face said it all. She followed him to the satellite link room like the one in Aberdeen where they could speak in private.

He didn't wait to fill her in once they were alone. "Entered the coordinates for this location from the front of the guide like last time and played with the focus. Looks like your gut was right, as usual." He pointed to the view on the screen furthest to the left.

Outside, two young men in GreenCorps uniforms stood near the stone wall across from the small entry building. They appeared to be having a discussion.

"Flaming hell." Her Granny's favorite curse slipped from her lips. "I could feel them out there, even if we couldn't see them. Do you think they know we're here? Or is it a coincidence that they're here right now?" She bit her lip, considering what action she needed to take.

Walker didn't answer at first, his eyes locked on the screen.

Her heart sank when one of the men crossed to the door and banged on the outside. Then he tried pulling the handle. Thankfully, she'd locked the door.

"They know." Walker crossed his arms. "Fuck."

"We were careful. They were just sneaky." She couldn't look away from the screen. "We can't stay here long. Too many other things we were sent to do are time-dependent. It's important that GreenCorps spreads its troops out searching for all the teams at once. If we try to wait those two out, we're trapped. If they leave, we have to chase them down. We can't let them report we were here. Jaxon would kill for that key, especially if he thinks we have the only one. Besides, we don't want anyone in GreenCorps suspecting that we're already planting seeds this year, or they'll seek them out and destroy them."

"We could capture those two," said Walker. "See what they know."

"Let's finish up right away. Maybe we could race them back to the train in Sacramento." The two GreenCorps soldiers could travel light and the rebels would have loads. Even saying it wasn't realistic. Elsa sighed. They couldn't afford to have GreenCorps know they had more seeds.

Walker shrugged. "We can't get out if they're waiting at the exit. We need them to move back far enough so that we can leave safely and not get picked off, one by one."

"It'll take another hour or two before we can get everything up the stairs," she said, still biting her lip and staring at the screen.

As they discussed what to do, the two men left the close-up view, so Walker adjusted a knob, scrolling back to give them a wider view. They watched as the men picked up small daypacks and turned, striding through the grass, east toward Sacramento.

"Looks like that decision is made." Walker's jaw set and his face paled.

"We'll have to go after them," she said, the words feeling strange on her tongue. Her stomach churned.

Walker shook his head. "We aren't done packing, so a few of us will go outside and chase them down. You finish here, gather the gear, and move it upstairs as soon as you're ready. In a couple of hours, you can meet us up top, just check the screens before to make sure the way is clear. We don't know if they're alone, though I scanned the area and didn't find anyone else."

She swallowed. He was right. "Let's go."

They returned to the other room and explained the situation with as few words as possible to the rest of the team, as time was limited. Then she and Walker ran up the stairs with three others they'd chosen to accompany him outside. Everyone carried a light load, so the trip wasn't wasted.

At the top, they stacked the loaded containers by the wall for now and the rebels opened the difficult door to outside. Elsa's hands shook as she let them out. She didn't like the idea of splitting up the team, but it couldn't be helped—she especially disliked being separated from Walker. She didn't feel like they had a choice. If those GreenCorps men got word back to Jaxon, he might return with reinforcements and take not only the key, but everything they'd retrieved from the bunker. They needed to be stopped.

Before he stepped outside, Walker kissed her with an unnerving fierceness.

"Be careful," she said, her lips still tingling.

He winked and took off at a jog, his long strides eating up the distance, the others trailing behind, moving swiftly, being unencumbered. This might not take too long. Instead of going back downstairs right away, she considered her options, the taste of bile filling her mouth.

Elsa didn't watch for long; she didn't want to chance additional trouble with the door unlocked. There could be additional soldiers lurking in the area, hoping for a mistake. She took a breath, a last quick peek toward the empty expanse where Walker had disappeared, and shoved the door closed once more. Grinding it across the floor was a little smoother this time. She made sure the door was locked, and shivering, she returned underground.

CHAPTER 22: MASON

Mason squinted into the dark and adjusted his hat. The night air remained warm due to heat soaked into the rock by the merciless daytime sun on the parched SoCal countryside. The stench had faded to a background reek, no longer making his eyes water. Caitlyn waited beside him while the rest of the team had hidden nearby. They'd been in position for over an hour. Every breath seemed too loud. Every rustle and creak gave their location away. He grit his teeth. Rookies. He ran through the plan again while they waited.

A low hum filled the air, and he strained to hear it better. It could be distant planes, headed here for the first airdrop. He glanced at Caitlyn, her eyes gleaming in the moonlight, and his pulse raced. They had ferried the goods from the bunker to the train station after dark, leaving three rebel guards to supplement the turned railway guards on their side. The rest of the rebels had returned to the twisted tree to wait. Finally, they could take care of the second part of their job.

Mason looked around, searching the dark for signs of movement. This seemed like it was taking too long. They needed to lug everything back to Riverside, find a place to camp, and be back aboard the train in twenty-four hours. They might end up even shorter on sleep.

His sense of unease grew when the plane passed overhead without lights—a noisy moving shadow. His team murmured as it flew. Few of them would have seen such a sight before. It seemed far-fetched that the pilots would spot the glint tape from so far above, but he had to trust their experience. If they said it was possible, it must be. The aircraft was also noisier than he'd expected. He hoped they'd marked the ground well enough. The buzzing overhead grew louder again as the plane returned, this time closer, moving east to west. The plane passed, banked, and dropped the crates.

Light-colored parachutes opened over dark shadowy boxes floating in the night sky, barely discernible to his naked eye. A dozen large crates descended, the first coming to rest at the edge of the staked circle—the wooden platform on the bottom shattering on impact. The other crates landed behind them in a clump. Bull's eye.

Several crates landed with splintering sounds, despite the floating parachutes, now draped over the boxes. This was far enough from town that he didn't think the corporation forces would have seen or heard. Hopefully, this site would work again. He scanned down the dry field. A few from his team were too far out in the open and talking amongst themselves. Would their lack of training show on more dangerous missions? He'd have to speak to them about the need for quiet.

Mason glanced up. The plane was almost out of sight already, a charcoal shadow flying through the inky night. Its faint rumble headed north and faded from earshot. The pilots would return to Portland, reload, and return two nights from now for a drop in Long Beach. Then, his team would move on to Texas and hopefully, additional air drops would continue. There was no sign that GreenCorps had spotted the plane or knew what their presence meant.

Mason signaled, and the rebels ran forward, disentangled the parachutes, unclipped them, and stuffed them into bags. They ripped into the crates and formed a human chain, passing the contents from person to person—smaller boxes from inside filled with dried goods— toward the town and the back of the station where they'd be hidden like ordinary freight. They'd move things in relay, relocating the pile each time. Several team members attached ropes to the broken shoulder-height crates and towed them away to dispose of the evidence. Once finished, this group would join the relay line, passing boxes of food.

The team would have to make several short trips, each one increasing the risk of detection as they moved toward town and the railway station. The railway workers might have defected to the rebel cause, but the soldiers hadn't. This was going to be a long night—and everything needed to be stowed before the sun rose or it would be confiscated.

At the station, the workers would know the best method to distribute the contents without causing suspicion. It might be different in each town, so he'd leave that to the experts. Only when they'd squared everything away would Mason and the others search for a place to crash outside town. Close enough they could sneak back to the train when they needed to hop to Long Beach.

* * *

Other than the lack of sleep, the Riverside operation went well, including getting back on the train as it moved closer to the coast at Long Beach. Mason yawned, trying to focus as the train neared the next stop under smoky skies. They hadn't even arrived in Long Beach, but it all felt a little off to him. He examined every detail with a critical eye, trying to determine the source of his discomfort.

This was Elsa's hometown. It wasn't special, just another corporation town, but a strict one—like many others across the south where GreenCorps controlled not only jobs and food, but water. Of course, GreenCorps might guess Elsa would be sentimental and want to help Long Beach.

The city and the flattened countryside around it were bleak and ugly, coated in an oily patina of gray dust. He rubbed the greasy coating of the railing of the shuttle train between his fingers. People shouldn't have to live in an environment like this, especially with all the open land further north that was much more pleasant. Maybe one day soon that would change and people could move, build new settlements and better lives.

The rebels jumped off the train in pairs again, their feet crunching in the rough gravel as they landed. As always, Caitlyn was his partner. As soon as they were on the ground, they sprinted away from the train and the station.

"Hey. We got hoppers," called a voice on the other side of the train.

Damn. Security. Boots pounded across the platform in the distance as reinforcements headed toward the train.

He and Caitlyn hadn't gone far yet when another closer yell came. His stomach sank; someone else had been seen. Perhaps they hadn't been fast enough, or it had just been bad luck as they'd been hopping off in broad daylight. Maybe they'd been complacent because so far, riding the trains had been easy.

"Get back here," shouted a bull with a deep voice.

"I got the left. You take the right," said another nearby voice. Hadn't these railroad workers changed sides? Perhaps security hadn't, as Long Beach was the most secure work camp, so it was possible they always had heightened security. Or did it mean higher-up GreenCorps officials were here to be impressed by their efficiency? Perhaps Jaxon McCoy himself?

Mason put on another burst of speed and leaped to the top of the rusted metal sheeting that made up the high fence. The metal bent and twanged as he climbed. He scraped his hands on the rough top edge as his feet scrambled for purchase. Ignoring the discomfort with Caitlyn beside him, he landed on the hard-packed dirt on the other side. Not stealthy, but it got them away quicker.

He peeked above the fence surrounding the station as several team members launched themselves up and over, making the fence bow as it bent. Many of the new people joined them, winded and gasping for breath from their sprint—too much soft living over the winter. They would improve. This wouldn't be the last time they ran from the authorities. Caitlyn's cheeks were rosy, but her breathing wasn't ragged like the others. He loved that his wife was fit and tough.

"We lost Chelsea and Dawn," said Vee, one of the more experienced rebels. "They got off on the wrong side of the train." She pointed to the station platform, where they were just in time to see two of the newer rebels escorted inside, flanked by muscular GreenCorps soldiers. Bad fucking luck.

"The creep on the left might be Jaxon's second," said Caitlyn, whispering into his ear. "I recognize that overgrown beard and his nasty scowl, even at this distance. Not a lot of guys are also that broad." She sighed. "That might mean Jaxon is still in town, too. At least if he's here, he won't be on Elsa. We'll have to watch our step, especially if he thinks Elsa is here; he'll do anything to stop us. It would explain the heightened security."

"Yeah. I remember his sergeant from outside the bunker at Aberdeen. Elsa said he grew up with her. Wade, one of her neighbors. He was the reason Tatsuda and Ginger left SoCal with Avery when they did." Mason spoke slowly, staring at the door that had swallowed his people. "Chelsea and Dawn might talk." There went the plan and their chance at surprise. What did it mean for tonight's airdrop?

Caitlyn shook her blonde head. "I doubt GreenCorps will ask them much." She shot him a sidelong glance. "They'll just ship them to Texas. They're still short on women to replace those we freed last fall."

He nodded, feeling his grimace fade away. "Unless we bust them out tonight before we leave town. After the plane has gone."

She gave him a sharp look. "There's that. Or we take our chances without the airdrop." She wouldn't let him jeopardize the mission for two individual rebels, but if there was a way to break them loose without risking the rest, she'd be the first to help. "Maybe we should concentrate on getting them back and bail on the airplane." As always, she was reasonable.

Mason clenched his jaw and shook his head. "These people need the food more than anywhere else I've seen. I want to try." He pointed to the mouth of a nearby alley. "Let's move our discussion and choose a drop site for tonight."

"It stinks here," said one of the rebels, holding his nose as they moved further from the station. "I don't see why people have to live in this kind of filth."

The speaker, a man named Gary, wore manufactured clothes that came from back East. He may not have experienced much personal hardship, his rebellion being idealistic. He said he'd joined the rebels because it was the right thing to do. Here in SoCal, he was about to get an eyeful. While Mason didn't doubt the man's loyalty, some recent converts couldn't be trusted to stick around.

"Yes, Long Beach has its own special stench from the Heap," said Mason. "That is why we are doing this. People here still have rights and need to eat. Even when GreenCorps allows them, there's not much here that will grow. We're trying to make sure the people here are strong enough to join our fight."

Gary dropped his gaze to the ground and stopped yammering.

The rebels moved deeper into the town, winding through a network of quiet streets and alleys. They didn't see any residents, though twice they interrupted skinny feral cats who slunk away. Taking Walker and Tatsuda's previous advice, Mason led his group south of town, past the massive steaming Heap of refuse that dominated that whole side of the city. They split into twos and threes along the way, finding hidey holes in the rubble that lined the path. The plan was to wait until dusk to choose a place for the drop, somewhere farther away from the garrison and the town built amidst the rubble of long ago.

Mason's eyes drifted upward, noticing several teams of plastic poncho-clad women and ragged, bone-thin children winding their way down the narrow trails from the top of the mound.

Heapsters, like Elsa and her Granny had been. He couldn't imagine his friend here; she had too much attitude and fire. He'd sometimes thought his life unfair with just a mother. For all they'd been poor, his father had sent money when he could. At least Mason had grown up in Utah, not a dreary work camp like this. He'd seen some rotten places in his years as a rebel, so he wasn't shocked, but the state of the weary children made his heart ache for something better for everyone. Nobody should have to grow up in a place like this with limited options for their future.

While he waited for the townspeople to move along, the sun sat just above the horizon, its color obscured by the yellowish-gray haze that clung to SoCal like an extra layer of filth—this one airborne.

"We don't blend in very well here," said Caitlyn softly. "I hadn't realized how different we'd look. We should move further out." Her blue eyes looked haunted. The hungry children would have hit her hard—it was different to see starvation in person.

"Just keep walking," said Mason, taking her hand and leading her back to the main track as it wound past the distant end of the Heap, headed toward the ocean.

They passed several paths leading up the mountain of garbage from this side and several scrapyards. Men in plastic coveralls or ponchos with black and rust-colored streaks on their expressionless faces trudged past, exiting the gates in singles or pairs. Their gruff voices contrasted with the shrill overhead cries of the seagulls. These grunt workers might just be able to afford a beer or two before going home to eat and sleep just to do it all again tomorrow. This wasn't living; it was simply surviving.

Nobody paid them any attention as he and Caitlyn continued, trying to act like they had a purpose, taking long strides. The laborers' lack of curiosity surprised him as he and the other rebels stuck out. Maybe their disinterest rose from being too hungry and weary to care about much else. This was as rough a life as Mason had seen, even after years of Texas campaigns. How had Elsa not just survived here, but thrived and escaped? Hard to believe her great-grandmother had lived in this work camp for over fifty years in exile. After seeing this shithole, their story was that much more impressive.

Ahead, a pair of armed soldiers blocked the road that wound around the back of the Heap. Mason pivoted into a junkyard, pretending that had been his destination all along. Once he was deep among the rusted remains of old vehicles and scavenged building materials, he ducked down and crouched, Caitlyn following. They used the largest scattered pieces and piles of bulky metal to keep out of sight, winding their way through the scrap, and climbing over rust-spotted dividers between junkyard sections, all while maintaining vigilance.

There could be laborers, supervisors, or soldiers anywhere. From what Elsa had said, he didn't think guard dogs would be an issue, except maybe up at the rich houses on the hill. It would be difficult to keep pets, even working ones, when food and water were regulated and expensive.

Moving this way, they worked their way far enough along that they should be past the guards and their line of sight. He looked both ways and climbed the outer fence, Caitlyn dropping down beside him. They crossed the partially overgrown dusty track well beyond the soldiers, staying low to the ground, and scooted toward the beach. They scrambled down the sandy bank and hid. There was no sign that they'd been seen or followed. He sat down to wait for the sun to set.

"What do you think of a beach drop?" Caitlyn shaded her eyes as they swept north to south along the coast. "It's a long flat stretch we could mark."

"Will have to be the beach. Everywhere else is too patrolled," Mason said, his gaze looking up the long expanse of beach with its brownish-gray foaming water breaking in massive, curled waves up the plastic-littered shoreline. Jagged chunks of pale plastic floated and bobbed just beyond the breakers, waiting to make landfall with the next swell or with high tide. This position might be too exposed, but there was nowhere else to try.

"GreenCorps claims they're reclaiming the beaches," said Caitlyn, her voice almost too quiet for him to make out. "Liars." As usual, she was right. What a mess.

Mason closed his eyes, tugged his hat lower to reduce the glare, and settled in for a brief nap, trying to ignore the feel of rounded stones under his back. He awoke about an hour later, the light dim, the sound of the waves lapping closer than before. The harsh cries of seagulls were gone. He sat up. The waves had reached the regular high-tide line, based on the yard-wide swath of broken plastic bits and dingy seaweed scattered along the rocks and sand. As long as they stayed above this line, the airdrop should be fine.

He didn't like the spot they'd chosen, but he didn't see an alternative. He had a bad feeling about the whole situation. The sensation intensified while they waited, but there was no way to call off the plane.

He and Caitlyn picked their way through the refuse to the waterline and looked back toward the flat town of brick GreenCorps buildings and falling-down shacks. A few lights glowed, showing where the bar and brothel district lay. Wasting no more time, he passed half the stakes to Caitlyn, wrapped them with glint tape, and pounded them into the sand and rocks to wait for night and the plane.

* * *

Mason's sense of unease wouldn't pass, even once they'd placed the stakes. Maybe Caitlyn was right and they should wait for Texas for another airdrop. Perhaps he was being stubborn. He brooded while Caitlyn rounded up the other rebels who'd also made their way to the beach. The two rebels who'd been pinched weighed on his mind, but that wasn't going to stop him from collecting the airdropped food.

Though it was dark, tonight wasn't black like the previous nights. An almost full moon shone through a break in the persistent clouds, illuminating the beach and the edge of town beyond in a swath of moonlight. It was too bright for his comfort. Darkness provided an illusion of cover and tonight, they wouldn't have even that pretense. He stared out at the ocean; the waves crashing as hard as before, covering not just the sounds the rebels might make, but masking the sounds others nearby might. Something was wrong.

A heavy quiet settled on the beach—the muffled silence niggling at him as he tried to listen beyond the surf. He strained, waiting for the distant sound of the plane's engine. When at last he discerned the humming sound, the plane was already directly overhead, probably zeroing in on the marked circle on the beach. Mason closed his eyes, visualizing the crates dropping from the sky. This was a mistake.

In a place like this, it would be impossible to miss the crates and parachutes. He didn't blink, staring into the night until his eyes watered, holding his breath, waiting for the drop. The plane released the crates, just like before.

A dozen parachutes drifted toward the sand.

Mason was about to dart forward when his stomach clenched. This was something he shared with Elsa, a sense of imminent danger. A well-honed tool he was used to listening to and probably responsible for his long-term survival as a rebel.

"Hold up," he said, his loud whisper carrying to most of the team. "I'm not sure we're alone." Two rebels nearby gave him odd looks but remained crouched near the bank. Mason waited, hoping something would indicate what was wrong or for GreenCorps to make a move and prove his feeling correct.

Those farther up the line must not have heard or grew impatient because Gary raced into the circle and gathered up a tangled parachute, tugging it away from the crate. He managed a second before glancing back, perhaps wondering why he was alone.

Gary froze as all hell broke loose.

Several bright lights flashed on with a snapping sound, shining onto the beach and the dozen large crates, illuminating them brighter than noon in the desert. A siren wailed further down the beach, past where the crates had dropped, a blood-red light flashing and swirling. Two dozen GreenCorps soldiers flooded the beach from the north and south. The rebels scattered, unable to collect anything from the food drop.

Jaxon McCoy was the first to reach the crates. "Catch everyone you can." He spun in a circle, scanning the shoreline. "Elsa, if you're here, my father has signed an execution order. You're as good as dead. You hear me? Dead."

Mason didn't need to hear anymore. He bolted toward town and the darkness, only running three steps before checking on Caitlyn. She grabbed his elbow and propelled him toward the Heap.

"That asshole," she said under her breath. "He has such a hard-on for Elsa, it never occurred to him she wouldn't return."

Mason couldn't tell where anyone else was, but he and Caitlyn stumbled and ran, climbing boulders and scrambling up the rocky bank separating the main beach from the near edge of the landfill. He hesitated at the brink, but she tugged him forward.

"We need to make for the train," he said. "That's where the team will gather." He grimaced. As soon as he said it, he wished he hadn't. Returning to the rails is what GreenCorps would expect.

"We need to hide where they won't search or we won't be getting on a train unless we're in chains." Caitlyn's common sense won and he followed.

Soon, they slowed, their steps careful on the uneven terrain as they fought their way up the mountain of trash in the dark.

They traversed the slope, angling away from town as they slid and lurched in the loose garbage on the surface, making their way to the side of the Heap farthest from the lights of the city and away from the patrolled beach.

Caitlyn stopped when they came to a flat spot about two-thirds of the way up. "Let's dig in and wait it out." She kicked several cracked plastic containers aside and sat on a chunk of concrete sticking out of the Heap. Mason settled beside her, still scanning the scene of the disturbance below on the beach. There was enough light remaining to take in the view of GreenCorps soldiers dragging the crates away. Shit. The airdrops would only work if they appeared to be random. Plus, it was Elsa's hometown. They never should have agreed to it here. He sighed. Catching Chelsea and Dawn may have tipped off the authorities about the rebel presence if the plane hadn't. What a mess.

Caitlyn said, "Unless the soldiers shine their fucking lights up here we should be safe. For now. I hope the others were as lucky." Her mouth remained flat and unimpressed.

Only then did the significance of him and Caitlyn being alone sink in. His throat tightened. What had happened to most of his team? Had they been apprehended? He was responsible for this group and the GreenCorps ambush was a major setback. Not only had the rebels lost the food drop, but they were also going to approach the train hopping from a different location. The SoCal station's level of security would be at its peak for days. Maybe weeks, or until Jaxon McCoy left town.

Mason would have to improvise or they'd be caught. Even if the rebels ran the trains, the local GreenCorps patrol would be on alert and a factor. Texas could be too. They would have to be extra cautious. He also couldn't allow everyone to be deported.

He stared up the railroad tracks. Whatever he and Caitlyn decided, GreenCorps couldn't see it coming. Part of the multi-prong rebel strategy should spread out the GreenCorps retaliation and keep them guessing. He would just have to get a step ahead.

CHAPTER 23: CLARK

Spring arrived in the Utah mountains in the last week of March with warmer temperatures, leaving bare muddy patches in the sun and icy piles of dirty snow in the shade. Clark was sick of the cold and winter, and without Janna to keep him company, was more than ready for the change. Thankfully, April showers melted the remaining snow. Like last year, the warmth of the sun and longer daylight hours brought grueling days, where Clark exhausted himself by planting and laboring in the fields. He worked alongside the Saints as they planted their usual crops, with seeds liberated from GreenCorps warehouses and sold on the black market.

In the middle section of each field, they planted the seeds Caitlyn had delivered last fall—ones from a vault deep underground that had been saved from before the Collapse. The idea of these seeds surviving so long to be planted now gave him hope for the first time he could recall. The rebel cause was actually making a genuine change. With the rows marked, the Saints had devised a plan to harvest them in a unique way, ensuring the preservation of the crop for next year's seed. If they were truly viable, it could mean actual self-sufficiency.

Earlier this week, the farming supervisors had asked them to prep an area to be an orchard. Since most of the level ground in the valley was already under cultivation, they chose a south-facing slope with decent soil, one not too far from the settlement. Tree seedlings had been started in the greenhouse through the winter and were almost ready to plant now that it was no longer freezing overnight. More varieties were expected soon. He hoped they took and grew strong and healthy. Long-term access to fruit and nuts would be incredible. His mouth watered at the idea.

Clark volunteered to be part of the orchard crew, even if it would be back-breaking work, picking heavy stones out of the rough ground and working fertilizer into the sun-baked hillside. This job was more than just exertion—it was a chance to be part of the future. He grabbed a few fist-sized chunks and tossed them into the wheelbarrow where they thunked on the others of various sizes and bashed against the metal side with a twang—almost a full load.

He spared a thought for Janna, wondering if she would deliver the next batch of seeds. To avoid disappointment, he managed his hopes, making sure they didn't get out of control. Somehow, despite her words, he doubted she would be back. The thought made his chest ache. He'd never told her he wanted to be more than friends.

He hefted the handles and drove the wheelbarrow across the hard-packed ground on the perimeter to the edge where the crew was depositing the rocks. Even more than other years, Clark welcomed the hard work outside in the fresh air, hoping fatigue would allow him to sleep without nightmares—which still plagued the majority of his nights. Sometimes he was successful.

Clark dumped his wheelbarrow, causing the stones to crash into the growing pile. Volunteers would use them to build the base of a wall to enclose the new trees to keep out the wild deer and wandering goats. They would wind rolls of chicken wire from back East along the fence to extend its height. He would try to be part of that group too; it could keep his mind occupied.

Taking a breath, he mopped his brow and stretched, his back cracking. He leaned one way, then the other, to ease his cramped muscles before he took a long pull of refreshing water from his canteen. The muscles in his lower back screamed in protest. He was going to be sore tomorrow.

He glanced toward the community buildings that looked like toys from this distance. Soon, he would stop and return for dinner. Meals were the hardest time, when he missed Janna's companionship the most. He didn't bring them to dinner, but his conversation papers from the winter were creased and soft from repeated nighttime reading.

Every day, Clark regretted his shutdown and how he'd fled the scene when Janna had decided to leave. Most of all, he wished he'd had the courage to do something like she had when she'd joined the rebels. Or told her how much she meant to him. He wasn't just concerned for a friend. He tamped down on that thought, not wanting to let his mind go there during waking hours.

It had become too dark to see the stones by the time he finished picking and carting chunks from the new orchard area. He leaned the empty wheelbarrow upside down over the growing mound of dusty orange and gray rocks and sighed. Cataloging his aches, he trudged back to his cabin to drop off his work gear before heading for the shower in one of the communal wash stations. He'd love to soak his aching body, but sitting in one of the bathtubs would be too quiet and allow him too much time to think. Plus, he didn't want to nod off there. Instead, he sluiced off the dirt using homemade soap, changed into clean clothes, and grabbed his writing before heading to the dining hall.

He hadn't written much this morning, so he'd try to write tonight instead. Staring at the notebook, he wished he could share the latest completed story with Janna, the one finished in the notebook she'd left. He'd enjoyed writing more again, knowing someone else might read what he produced. He hadn't had that feeling since the old days with Mathew.

Clark had only just sat down with his dinner of potato bacon soup and cheese bread, when a shadow fell across his plate. He glanced up when the person remained beside the table. Brother Campbell and

Sister Hope stood next to him. A pit emerged in Clark's stomach. Had he done something wrong? Why else would the community leaders want to speak with him?

"You're eating even later than usual tonight, Clark," said the leader. "While you were working, the next shipment of seeds arrived." He paused. "And a letter came for you."

Clark dropped his spoon, splashing himself with the hot soup. "A letter?" He'd been here almost four years and never received mail.

Sister Hope handed him a light brown envelope with his name written on one side in Janna's familiar handwriting. All the air in the room evaporated. He bit his lip and his stomach fluttered, from more than a woman expecting him to converse. This meant that sometime since Janna had left, she'd been safe. His hand shook as he stretched to take the envelope. Had they noticed the tremor? "Thanks."

He set the paper on the table, picked up his spoon, and continued eating.

"Aren't you going to read it?" Sister Hope tilted her head, a quizzical expression on her face.

She must wonder why he wasn't tearing into the letter. He would, but he feared what Janna might have written, especially with how their final conversation had gone. He didn't think he could take more of her anger and even kind words might make him emotional. She had a way of seeing things he often tried to leave unsaid.

"I think it's from Janna," Sister Hope said. "It's the first you've heard from her since she left, isn't it?" Her expression remained hopeful.

Brother Campbell crossed his arms and frowned at Sister Hope.

Clark nodded. "I'd rather read it in private." He kept his eyes trained on Brother Campbell. Even this much attention from Sister Hope made his tongue feel thick.

The leader nodded. "I understand. We'll leave you to it." He leaned closer and lowered his voice as Sister Hope left. "One more thing, Clark. It has come to my attention that you've returned to your solitary ways and I'm concerned. I don't think you've spoken in weeks. If there is something I can help you with, or if you'd like to speak to someone about the things on your mind, please let me know. I feel the heaviness of your heart and wish I could lighten your burden." He rested his hand on Clark's shoulder briefly before walking away.

The rest of the meal passed without Clark noticing. He ate mechanically, without paying attention or tasting his food, his brain stuck on the contents of the letter. As soon as he finished, he grabbed his mail and headed back to the bunkhouse. His roommates were seldom around until late, often after eleven at night. Many had girlfriends or friendship groups they hung out with in the evening, so he should have time to read with some privacy.

As he'd hoped, the cabin was empty. He lit a lamp and sat on his bed, staring at the envelope. With trembling hands, he slit the top, cutting the side of his finger. He stuffed his bleeding finger into his mouth, removed it, took a breath, and extracted the letter. There were two pages with different dates. It looked like she'd written on two separate occasions, one over a month previous and another less than two weeks ago.

He grabbed the oldest one first and devoured its lines. The letter had few details about where she was or what she'd been doing, but her personality still infused the page. Reading her observations and thoughts was almost like hearing her voice. By the end, he felt like she'd forgiven him, even if all was not forgotten. She understood him better than anyone. He closed his eyes and savored her words before setting the page aside and turning to the second letter.

Dear Clark,

I found it therapeutic to write to you last time, even if I didn't get a chance to send it along yet. We've been on the move, with a new town every day or two, and I didn't find anyone going up the canyon. I've been traveling, so security is tight. I'm sick of sleeping somewhere different each night. I miss having anything constant and familiar, like a certain table near the kitchen with a person I can count on to be there—simple pleasures.

We're on a train and will pass through Salt Lake later today. I will leave this at headquarters to be carried up the canyon at the next opportunity. By the time you read this, we'll be somewhere else. I also wanted to reassure you that though we are busy, we are cautious and safe.

Because I'm writing on my own instead of side-by-side, I feel brave enough to ask you something again, something that caused you to become upset. What happened with your mom? You avoided answering me whenever we went near the subject. If whatever happened didn't affect you so much, I wouldn't keep wondering, but the topic still makes you shut down. When you're forced to think about her, it's like you become a different person, one tormented and trapped in the past. Your pain relates to your mother and a promise. I've figured out that much.

Did you promise her you wouldn't join the rebels? I suspect that's part of it, but I have a hunch there's more. If it will lighten your heart to share it with me, please do. I want to understand.

I realize talking about painful memories is hard. Like you, I have also been hurt and betrayed. Hell, for six months I was forced to allow strangers to violate me. If it wasn't for the rebels, I would still be in Texas. Alone and miserable. I'll probably have issues with physical contact for years. Trust me, I understand being hurt by people you love.

I'm not trying to judge you for anything in your past, and I suspect whatever happened wasn't of your choosing. Whatever it was, it rips you up inside and it hurts me to see it. Many people can unearth strength within and not let the past define them. Something I'm working on. I think you can find this too. Think about it. Our friendship helped me to see that I wanted to be better. I won't forgive my brother. Ever. But I have to get past what Wade did, for myself, or I'll never be happy.

I'm here, listening if you need to talk. If you send mail to headquarters, it will reach me, eventually.

Take care,

Janna

Clark closed his eyes as if he could press his tears back inside, to prevent them from leaking onto the paper. He set the letter aside to prevent blotching Janna's words. Hers was the second offer of help today. Maybe the universe was trying to force the issue. Maybe he'd wallowed long enough and needed to excise his misery. Easier said than done. Still, the idea of letting Janna in was better than Brother Campbell's kind offer. As well-meaning as the older man was, Janna was correct. She might relate.

Clark collected a couple of sheets of loose homemade paper and wrote.

Dear Janna,

I loved receiving your letters. I'll add them to my stash to read when I have nightmares and can't sleep. Thinking of you and rereading our conversations keeps me sane and reminds me I'm not alone. Traveling every day sounds busy and annoying. I enjoy getting to know a place when I go somewhere new.

We've been planting crops and getting a new field ready for others on the hillside.

She would understand it was for the new seeds, so he didn't spell that out.

I'm embarrassed about my outburst and how I treated you on your last night here. I'm so sorry. I could give you several excuses, but none of them are a proper reason. I can't believe I let you leave without another hug and my best wishes. You were a friend when I have so few and you deserved better. Please forgive me.

I hope you're being careful and that Grady isn't doing anything too risky. If anything happens to you, I couldn't stand it. What I should have said before you left was that I was proud of you for doing your part in something so important. I admire your strength.

Take care of yourself. Don't forget about us in the mountains. If you're looking for a place to rest when this is done. Come find me, I'll be here. Waiting for you.

—Your Clark

Clark didn't think he was ready to commit everything she'd asked about to paper—it would make what had happened all too real again. Not that those events were ever far from his troubled thoughts. However, the promise to his mother weighed him down like plodding through thick spring mud, each step heavier than his last. His throat closed picturing his last day with his mother. He would try anything to get unstuck.

He leaned back against the headboard, closed his eyes, and let his mind drift to that summer four years ago. It had been after John's overdose and the body blow of his father's unexpected death, but more than two years before Mathew had been killed in action. Clark and his mother were the last Dawsons on the farm and it had seemed too quiet without his father's hearty laugh and his brothers bickering.

Clark watched his mother's ashen face and stooped form as she hobbled from the table to the sink with the remains of her lunch. She set it on the counter and stared out past the line of windbreak trees Mathew had planted a couple of years earlier. They were a spot of shade in the otherwise furnace-like heat of a yard at the height of summer, where average daytime temperatures were often a scorching 110 degrees in the shade.

Her gaze wandered where it always did, toward Salt Lake City, though Mathew could be anywhere. Seeing his mother so weak and devastated broke Clark's heart, leaving him feeling helpless. He wished there was something he could do to help. Their loss was significant, and he was also hurting. When had she gotten so frail?

Clark knew, though it was still a shock. When John had overdosed, she'd slowed down and been prone to forgetfulness. Over time, she'd regained some of her energy, but not all. Then, his father had been killed three weeks ago in a freak accident on what should have been a routine trade run. His mother shrank, as though part of her had also died.

Her condition preyed on Clark's mind, and this morning he'd woken with a feeling of dread. His parents had been so close and without his father, she seemed lost, adrift in an ocean of grief. He swallowed. He hadn't seen her eat more than a few meager bites in days. Was he going to lose her, too?

"Hey Mom, let me help," he said, hustling across the room to take care of the still half-full bowl of soup. "Want me to warm it up?"

She shook her head. "Will you come for a walk with me?" Before he answered, she at last turned from the window, grabbed his forearm, and squeezed. Her nails dug into his skin—enough to drive home her intensity, though it didn't hurt much. She fixed her gaze on his face. "There's somewhere I want to go, and I need your help."

"Sure. Anywhere in particular?" It was a hopeful sign that she wanted to be outside in the fresh air. Wasn't it? Even if it must be well over a hundred degrees.

"Up the canyon to the lookout. I haven't been there in a while and will need some assistance." She shuffled toward her bedroom. "I'll get dressed."

He exhaled, the ache in his chest loosening. That would also be a first in recent days. Maybe it was a step on the road to recovery.

Fifteen minutes later, they left the house wearing wide-brimmed hats and headed toward the mouth of the canyon. His mom strode across the dry field with more vigor than she'd had in days. She must be feeling better out of doors, even if the air was so hot it sucked his breath away.

Several times as they hiked the canyon, his mother took his outstretched hand to clamber over jagged orange rocks as they climbed the steep path toward the viewpoint that looked out over the flat bench land where their farm was situated. A wave of nostalgia washed over him as they worked their way upward. He hadn't been up here in years, not since the three brothers had come to say their goodbyes to each other before Mathew and Mason had left to join the damn rebellion. That trip must have been ten or eleven years ago, unless Clark had also come with John before he left a couple of years later. It bothered Clark that he couldn't remember.

Whenever it had been, it had been a struggle for his shorter legs, but he'd always strived to keep up with his older brothers, so he'd scrambled and hauled himself upward using tree roots and bushes. Now it was easy to reach the next stable foothold. The blistering heat of the August afternoon lessened in the deep shadows of the canyon walls on either side, and the dark green shrubbery by the water seemed to give off an aura of refreshing coolness. A sense of peace came to him as the gurgle of water in the narrow, but deep, creek provided the backdrop for their hike.

When at last they reached the top, his mom sported rosy patches on each cheek as she gasped for air. Stopping at the head of the trail, she bent over and rested her hands on her knees while she caught her breath. He hoped she was okay; he was winded himself and moved slower than usual. She waved him onward to the lookout rock, a solid piece jutting out from the cliff face facing the plains.

With a quick check over his shoulder for his mom, he moved to the edge, staying far enough from the lip that he wouldn't accidentally fall. A patchwork of land stretched below, the farm buildings resembling miniatures. The green squares were gardens or irrigated pasture lands. The yellow-browns that predominated the landscape were the dry land between farms, now burnt to a crisp after the season-long drought.

His father had told him that there'd been a city here once, before the Collapse, but now the land was sparsely settled, with only eight farms in view, even from this vantage. Staring down at the scattered farms, it occurred to him that growing up here in Utah had been wonderful and free, especially if the stories he'd heard from Mat about other places were true. It shouldn't be that way. GreenCorps had a lot to answer for. Even if Clark's way of being a rebel would differ from his brothers, he could write articles for the paper or help rally others to their cause. Maybe he could help the ordinary people understand what they could do to help.

"Mom, I was thinking I might wait to travel to the city until next year." He turned as his mother approached. There was a lot to do with just the two of them and two farmhands, especially right now. He would postpone joining the rebels for now.

At first, she didn't speak, as she, too, surveyed the lands far below. "This is where your father proposed." Her voice was soft and dreamy, her eyes misty as she relived that time long ago. "In the spring, when the land was pale green below, criss-crossed by water flowing in both rivers. I'd never seen the sky so blue. I thought it stretched forever to meet the horizon."

A cloudless sky not unlike today. Clark hadn't known this place had been special to his mom. She'd never shared that before. What other secrets had she kept hidden? It was odd to see his parents as regular people, not just as mom and dad.

"When your father was young, he still dabbled in the rebellion, and he would leave for a few months most summers, at least until we had all three of you boys. Once a summer, I'd ask Mason's mom to watch Mat and John so I could sneak away and climb up here to feel close to your dad." A tear escaped from her right eye, but she didn't seem to notice. Then another trickled down her cheek. "When you came along, your father decided to stay home. Until this year, when leaving got him killed."

Clark swallowed. He hated to see his mother cry.

"Will you do something for me, Clark?" The intensity in her hazel eyes bored into him as she faced him, once more clutching his arm.

"Of course." It didn't occur to him to say anything else.

"Promise me you won't join the rebels. Not ever. They were the reason John turned to drugs. They're the reason your father died, and I'm waiting for the day they'll take Mathew, too. It's just a matter of time. You're my last son. Promise me." Her anguished eyes pinned him in place.

Clark couldn't breathe. He hadn't thought much about his distant future, not beyond farming and writing for the rebels. He'd thought perhaps he could find someone going to town and send in a couple of articles he'd written for the rebels. They might use them. He could offer his support to them that way, even from the farm. Most of the time, he enjoyed the solitary life in the country. Even joining the rebels wasn't about fighting. For him, it was about meeting Grady and writing about things that mattered for a change.

"I'm not planning to leave, mom." His voice sounded scratchy and strange. "Just for a few weeks. Nothing permanent."

"Promise," she said again.

His forehead tightened. Her insistence was scaring him. "I promise not to join the rebels."

"It's my final wish," his mother said.

"Final?" He wouldn't let her waste away. Tears pricked behind his eyes and he blinked, turning away. He would have to try harder to get her to eat. She wasn't allowed to give up.

She nodded. "Swear on your life, Clark."

His chest seized under her intense gaze, but he did as she requested. "I swear on my life never to join the rebels." He tried to turn it into a joke. "My writing idea was silly and I doubt they'd want me, anyway. I've never been brave like Mat or John."

She ignored his lame attempt at humor and smiled, a strange one he'd never seen her wear before. "Thank you. Now I can be at peace."

Suddenly, Clark didn't want to stay up here anymore. She wasn't acting like herself. "I'm heading home. I have a lot of chores to do this evening. You ready to go?"

He'd taken half a dozen steps before he realized his mother hadn't followed. He turned, only to see her close her eyes.

Then, she stepped off the cliff.

His muscles froze and he couldn't breathe. It was as though time stopped for him, while she moved double-time, disappearing in an instant. He ran to the edge, somehow hoping to grab her, or see that she'd caught herself just below the lookout.

It was too late.

He covered his mouth with a shaking hand. All he could do was stare in horror as she plummeted without sound toward the distant ground.

His mom landed amid the boulders at the bottom of the canyon. He stared, unbelieving at first, but as the dust settled, she lay motionless. A stain at the foot of the cliff. He should have saved her, but he hadn't seen it coming.

Blinded by tears, he hurtled down the trail, leaving the viewpoint forever.

Tears returned Clark to the present, as they scorched a path down his cheeks. How could he tell Janna that he relived that afternoon almost every time he closed his eyes to sleep? He had yet to save his mother. In his dreams, sometimes she changed her mind, but it was always too late. She always fell.

Taking a deep breath and swiping the tears from his eyes, Clark picked up his pencil with sweaty fingers, struggling to get a solid grip. He would tell Janna, after all. Maybe he could unburden his soul to someone who would understand. He wasn't just sad about losing his mother; he was angry about how she'd left him, leaving him to pick up her body and mourn all of them, alone.

He wrote until his fingers were sore and he'd filled three sheets of paper, front and back, in small, neat writing. Before he changed his mind about sending his letter, he stuffed it in an envelope and slipped it under Brother Campbell's door. The leader would see that his letter was delivered to rebel headquarters.

That night and the several others that followed, Clark slept without dreams.

CHAPTER 24: ELSA

Elsa and the remaining rebels on her team transported their boxes and backpacks up the metal stairs, each making more than one trip before they moved everything outside into the daylight. By the end of the third trip, her calves burned. She squinted at the afternoon sun before raising her UVee goggles to cut the glare. Hopefully, Walker and the others would return soon because the team needed to get moving, or they'd be caught by dusk without the well to replenish their water.

She scanned the empty countryside and decided not to wait. With a little luck, they could meet him partway back to the campsite. The sooner her team was underway, the better.

"Let's go. We should find Walker and the others on the way back." She turned to address the group.

"How do you know where to find him? Shouldn't we just wait?" One of the younger rebels asked to nods from a few others.

Elsa stared into the ruins. "All of us should use the most direct route back to the trains along the old rail line. Even the GreenCorps soldiers." She adjusted her pack and stepped into a loop of rope to pull a container on a sheet of cardboard fastened underneath to help it slide.

There was no argument as the rebels headed out, walking through the knee-deep grass leftover from last year's growth. Scattered throughout the brown were paler green shoots poking through the mass of dead roots as new life stretched toward the sun. Seeing things growing, even here in the wild, gave her a feeling of hope.

Elsa hadn't gone far when she spotted Walker returning; she recognized his gait and his size from a distance. There were six figures in total. She let out a deep breath. He'd caught up to the GreenCorps men. She wasn't sure what she would have done if they'd escaped.

Less than ten minutes later, when they were close enough for Elsa to see Walker's grim expression, her feeling of relief vanished. Had something gone wrong? She scanned him for obvious wounds, but he seemed uninjured, as did his flanking group of rebels who surrounded the prisoners.

Walker stopped in front of her, his mouth flat and his gray eyes stormy and dark. "They saw everything. They've been following us since this morning, before we entered the bunker. Jaxon left them here with instructions to watch for us. For you. I got that much out of the older one before he clammed up."

She turned to the two prisoners in black and green uniforms. Their hands were tied and their feet had been hobbled, giving them enough slack to walk, but no more. Both sported reddish-purple patches on their faces. She glanced at Walker's hands. Bruised knuckles.

"What else did they share?" Her gaze shifted from one to the other.

"They won't say anything else." His jaw flared and he flexed his right hand. "We stopped them from reporting us to Jaxon, but we can't let them go." His eyes snagged hers again and what he wasn't saying sunk in.

She'd said to stop them at all costs. He'd caught them, and now he wanted to know who was going to pay the final tally. A sinkhole formed in her stomach.

He would take care of it for her. But she couldn't ask.

She'd killed Jace, but that had been in the heat of battle, a kill-or-be-killed situation. Goosebumps broke out on her arms and she shivered. This was cold and calculated. She played other options in her mind. Maybe they could tie the soldiers up and leave them out here? Death by starvation, exposure, or wild animals might take care of the problem, but that was even crueler than a quick death. She bit her lip and stared at their captives. Whatever decision she made, it needed to be done soon. Time was ticking. They needed to be back in Sacramento with their burdens by late afternoon tomorrow. They had no time to waste.

She gave the captive men another hard look. One soldier was older than she and Walker were, probably in his early thirties. The other couldn't be over sixteen or seventeen. Not much more than Tatsuda's age. This one met her eyes with a youthful defiance as he raised his chin and stared. She didn't want to kill anyone. How was ordering their death going to help the rebel cause? Was it worth being a rebel if she were responsible for taking someone's life?

Her chest tightened. Decisions like this came with the burden of leadership. Was killing someone ever the right thing to do? Should she ask one of the other rebels to shoot the prisoners? Her stomach clenched.

Elsa couldn't give that order.

She would have to pull the trigger herself. Her stomach churned and bile rose in her throat. How would she be able to live with herself afterward? The nightmares after Jace's death had haunted her for months. She didn't want to be a killer.

"What exactly were your orders?" Her voice was so icy she didn't recognize its sound.

"Watch and report. Capture you if possible. Captain McCoy wants to execute you himself." The more experienced soldier spoke. "Another pair of us will be out here the day after tomorrow. If you let us go free, we could promise to tell them nothing." He hesitated, then spoke fast, his words tumbling from his split lips. "You need to get back on that train before they find you, and it won't be easy. We have people stationed everywhere watching for you." Maybe he hadn't spoken to Walker, but the soldier was spilling everything now. "Leave us here unharmed and we won't tell anyone that we saw you."

Words burst from the younger man's trembling lips too. "I won't say a thing either. It's like you were never here." His eyes shone with hope. "I promise."

Elsa wished she could walk away and pretend she hadn't seen the captives. Their words ripped her inside. Even if she believed them, she couldn't leave them; there was too much at stake. She didn't want to have to make this decision, but there was only one way this encounter could end.

The soldiers were correct about one thing. The rebels needed to leave so they could hop the train tomorrow. They needed to keep to the schedule to support the other raids if the larger campaign were to succeed. This was the biggest push Grady had made in his lifetime. He needed GreenCorps to send troops all over at the same time and keep them guessing—his strategy for spreading out their forces. This was the best chance that rebels had to take the fight to GreenCorps. More things were in their favor than ever before with the takeover of the railway, general discontent, and the seeds that gave regular people hope they could change the world. If this was to succeed in her lifetime, she had to do her part.

Fighting tears of her own, Elsa stared at each of the prisoners. She glanced at Walker one more time and took strength from him. He met her gaze and nodded. This wasn't about her, it was about all of them. She had a job, and she'd promised to keep her end of the bargain.

"On your knees," she said, taking out the pistol Grady had supplied and Darren had taught her to shoot. She hadn't expected to use it for something like this. The soldiers' eyes opened wider, but they didn't move.

The younger man glared. "You're a fucking coward and a thief. I won't go along with that." He glanced at his partner. "Besides, she doesn't have the guts to kill us."

"Elsa," said Walker, stepping up beside her. His voice was tight. "Let me."

"You did your part in capturing them," she said. "Grady put me in charge. This has to be me." She couldn't look at anyone else. She couldn't bear to see their judgment or fear. "Knees. Now," she snapped.

The older man sank to his knees first. "Just make it quick." At least he understood.

The younger one refused. "You won't do it." He stood straighter and stared at her, perhaps trying to break her resolve.

"I don't want to kill anyone, but I don't have a choice," Elsa said. "I can't bring you. I can't leave you and I can't trust you. You'll never change sides." She took a deep breath as she steeled herself inside. "I'm sorry." She gestured to Walker to force the young man to his knees. Walker kicked the side of his leg and the youth collapsed to the ground.

The young soldier's lip trembled as he stared at the gun in Elsa's hand. "I'm not scared to die." Tears welled up in his dark eyes. This was worse than anything she'd imagined.

"I'm sorry," she said. It wouldn't get easier or change a hard decision to deliberate longer. There was only one conclusion. Steeling herself, she walked behind the men, raised the gun, and shot first one, then the other, in the back of the head. Quick.

In two seconds, they both lay slumped on the ground with the echo of the gun reverberating in the air. The smell of gunpowder and something metallic hung in the air. She broke out in a sweat and it was all she could do not to vomit. She lowered the gun and, arm trembling, she shoved the gun back in its holster.

"We should go," Elsa spoke aloud, struggling to maintain an even tone.

At first, no one spoke or moved toward the loot from the bunker.

"I'll move the bodies off the path." Walker touched her arm on the way past—a comforting zing at the contact. "I'll catch up."

She nodded, wishing she could hug him now and cry. She didn't want to be a murderer, but this campaign was about much more than her and the soldiers had worked for the enemy.

"Aren't we going to bury them?" said Amanda, staring at the fallen GreenCorps soldiers.

"No," said Elsa. Let them think she was heartless. There could be other tough decisions ahead, and they needed to trust that she would make them. "We have a train to catch. Let's go."

Everyone scrambled for the packs and the container sleds without meeting her gaze. She glanced at the motionless soldiers one more time and swallowed. She would fall apart and take comfort in Walker's arms later, but not until the comfort of darkness arrived. For now, she had to be tough and keep moving. Adjusting her backpack, she grabbed the rope attached to a container filled with boots and started the journey back to Sacramento and the true fight for freedom.

CHAPTER 25: MASON

Mason checked on his shrunken rebel group one more time where they crouched, hidden trackside outside SoCal. He had four remaining members of his original group, plus Caitlyn. They'd gotten information about the trains from one of the railroad workers last night and they were ready to hop. GreenCorps had snagged the rest of his team and was sending them to Texas by boxcar transport. The usual. Or, so they thought.

As far as the young railwayman had determined, the prisoners had divulged little when questioned. As planned, his people had claimed Grady had sent the airdropped food, leaving the Canadians from their account. GreenCorps could wonder where the rebels had gotten planes. He hoped it made them squirm. Their ally was to remain secret as long as possible. It would tip Grady's hand if GreenCorps learned of the scale of the campaign and of outside involvement.

Mason clenched his jaw. He wouldn't let his team be deported. They had planned to free more of the deportees along the railway route in Texas as the next part of their mission. Now they were starting early, if only by a matter of hours.

Caitlyn had been part of liberating several boxcars full of people in her last year with Mathew—men and women alike. Attacking a moving train was riskier, and a move the rebels hadn't used since—

not for the two years since the ambush that had killed Mathew and a dozen others. Mason spared a glance for Caitlyn, but she seemed to take everything in stride, even if this could bring up tough memories.

The hardest part of the last couple of days had been hiding in Long Beach without being discovered. Nowhere had felt safe despite the disinterest of the majority of the heapsters. Mason had spent the time sweating bullets, with more time covered in garbage than he wanted. He couldn't wait to get somewhere he could wash away the stench. It might be a while until they had water for such a luxury.

Scouting for a workable hopping location, he and Caitlyn had returned to the rails yesterday and hiked along the tracks toward Sacramento. They'd hidden in the dust-covered bushes and tangled brambles, giving a wide berth to the wide-ranging GreenCorps patrols, which were probably searching for them. Luckily, the GreenCorps recruits hadn't been stealthy, so he and Caitlyn had no trouble avoiding them.

A few miles outside town, they'd found a sharp bend in the tracks where they turned beside a long-dry gorge of a former riverbed. The train would be quick coming along this part of the track, but would slow for the turn. Hopefully, it wouldn't be so fast the rebels couldn't hop onboard. It was their best shot of leaving on the same transport. He couldn't take the remaining few members closer to the station without serious risk of being caught.

Mason focused. They had eight team members to rescue and several other deportees on board. At least two dozen folks in total who needed their help.

"Everyone clear?" He wanted to double-check before they separated into smaller groups to hop. As usual, they'd go in pairs.

"Yes, sir," said Gary, one of the remaining rebels, probably safe because he'd run at the first sign of trouble on the beach. He excelled at self-preservation. "We get on the last three train cars of the first half, 'cause that's just behind where the boxcars are attached. We wait until the appointed time, then work our way forward into position." He frowned.

Gary was probably worried about moving between cars, something most of the rookies had never attempted. That move was dangerous, but they were desperate. One advantage was that they'd be hopping on gondolas, making them lower and easier to move between. Taking inexperienced hoppers along the roofs between covered hoppers would have been too risky.

Mason nodded. "This train's a two-day express to the first stops in Texas. We strike on the last day, so stay in position on your original gondola for the first thirty-six hours. Then we move forward and free the captives. We'll check in with each other then, if necessary. Who has the blowtorch?" He smiled. This part of the plan had been Caitlyn's. His wife was brilliant.

Nate raised his hand. "I'm all set to burn everyone out of the boxcar tomorrow afternoon." He seemed relaxed and confident about his part with the torch.

"We'll also need people to be ready to help relocate those from inside the boxcar, away from the transport car. Footing is unstable and limited between the cars, so we'll form a chain and send those we rescue along. There's just one transport car this time," said Caitlyn. "We need everyone to help."

In the distance, the roar of the approaching train grew louder.

Mason shoved in his earplugs. "Positions everyone." The nose grew too loud for further instructions. The reminder would have to suffice. He turned to check the group but remained crouched until the lead engine roared past, the fast-moving wheels screeching on the metal rails. He was close enough to the train that vibrations traveled through his boots into him and the air quivered, even inside his lungs. Damn. The train and its wind moved fast.

The front section consisted of two passenger cars, three water tankers, and half a dozen boxcars, before more than a dozen gondolas, where they aimed to hop aboard. This might be a foolish idea. But it was too late to change their minds now.

Once the boxcars passed, Mason jumped to his feet and jogged beside the train. Most places were chosen for level footing. This wasn't a regular spot for hopping and was more uneven. Once he stumbled in a hole but regained his footing. Despite slowing for the corner ahead, the train still traveled faster than any of the others he'd hopped before. He increased his pace, his arms and legs pumping as he tried to match the train's speed.

Grimacing, he lost ground with every step despite his effort. He wouldn't get onto the lead gondolas. Only he and Caitlyn had kept pace with the train. He glanced back. Everyone was struggling. Any gondola would have to suffice.

The next ladder passed, and he grabbed high with first one hand, then the other, before taking a quick step and hop to leap onboard. He swung out of the way and climbed as Caitlyn clutched the same ladder and hauled herself aboard.

Reaching the top, and gasping for breath, Mason swiveled from the ladder, getting out of the way. Water streamed from his eyes caused by the rushing air. He blinked, trying to determine if everyone had gotten onto the speeding train. Two figures had climbed onto the next gondola back, but only one on the following. Kaylee was waving and may have been shouting, though Mason couldn't make out her words. A chill ran through him. Remaining astride the top of the thick metal box, he sat straighter, trying to see more.

Kaylee's partner, Jason, seemed to flounder, his hands on the metal ladder and legs dangling too low to reach the rungs. Mason watched helplessly as she reached down, trying to hold her partner. Was she going to lose her grip? Was Jason going to fall? At this speed, that would mean certain death.

Caitlyn passed Mason and jumped into the bottom of the rectangular car while he watched the action behind, still holding his breath. The train swooped through the corner and accelerated once more, the wheels on the cars ahead now a blur of speed. It seemed to take far too long, but at last Jason and Kaylee swung aboard and disappeared into their gondola. Only then, did Mason draw a full breath and drop down beside Caitlyn. That had been close.

They cleared a space on the floor of the gondola by rearranging chunks of scrap metal. Plunking down next to Caitlyn, he leaned back against the front wall and closed his eyes. Enough had gone wrong on this leg of the trip already. He didn't want to report to Grady that he'd lost more than half his group by the fourth day.

* * *

The blowtorch hissed as Nate melted a small opening to speak through. Mason and Caitlyn stood nearby, and he huffed out a large breath as he watched the blue flame. He wanted to warn the occupants of the boxcar to move out of the way before they created a bigger hole. Mason grimaced. He didn't want anyone else to get injured.

He surveyed his motley group of rebels. Kaylee, Jason, Nate, Gary, Caitlyn, and himself.

Mason hoped this move would restore the rest of the group. He had no way of knowing if everyone else was aboard this train, even if they'd seen Chelsea, Dawn, and Clayton being shoved aboard the transport by soldiers in Long Beach. He hadn't dared move closer or watch for longer.

The torch turned off and Nate banged the piece of painted metal through, where it hit the floor inside with a small metallic crash.

"Hallo," Mason called, cupping his hand to his mouth near the hole. "Anyone inside?"

He waited a beat and tried again. "Hello?"

"Mason, is that you?" said a faint voice. Clayton?

"The rest of the team is here," said Mason, unable to stop a grin from forming. He loved this part of his job. From inside the car, the speaker must have shared the news because a loud cheer erupted. "We're going to get you all out. Stand back, we're using a blowtorch."

He moved out of the way and signaled for Nate to resume.

Nate nodded, tugged on his UVee goggles, and turned his torch on with a hiss. He held the blue flame to the rear boxcar wall around the double-fist size speaking hole. He dragged the torch across the metal, which glowed bright orange as it melted through the wall. After about two feet, he switched directions, dragging the torch downward in a straight line. Mason waited while the perimeter of the new opening grew. In a couple of minutes, they had the outline of an opening two feet wide and slightly taller.

Nate turned off his torch again, and then punched the metal piece attached by two small tabs at the top through to the inside, creating a rough-edged hatch. The chunk landed with a bang on the floor of the boxcar. From inside, the sounds of people talking and gathering their belongings became clearer, though it remained dim inside.

Mason and Nate positioned themselves on either side of the hole and helped pull people through. Caitlyn and Gary stood on the next car to help everyone across the knuckle, while Kaylee and Jason waited at the top of the next gondola.

Chelsea emerged first from the boxcar, then Dawn, followed by several other rebels in a line—most decorated with cuts and bruises. GreenCorps hadn't gone easy on them. Each came out blinking at the brightness after a day and a half shut inside the dim boxcar. Mason and Nate helped them across the joint between cars, passing them along to Caitlyn and Gary, where Kaylee and Jason hauled them over the lip of the gondola to safety.

Eighteen thin young women filed past next, many with no possessions. They'd probably been gathered in a SoCal roundup, a disgusting GreenCorps practice. Mason was glad they'd prevented this group from being forced into the sex trade.

Next came ten strange young men. Most looked strong and fit, if a little scrawny. They'd probably been new to SoCal, perhaps wanderers or hoppers. Future rebels perhaps. He would take anyone willing to help. The last two at the opening, about to come through, were the familiar faces of Vee and Clayton, rebels who must have stayed to be the last to exit.

"That's it, boss," said Clayton with a nod as he pulled himself up. "Car's empty."

Mason tallied the group that had moved across to the next gondola. The tight feeling in his chest lessened. Every rebel on his team was accounted for, plus the deportees they'd planned to free. He was back on schedule and had reunited his crew.

As they steadied Clayton moving from one car to the next, the boxcar shifted sideways as the train changed direction at speed. It wasn't much, just a bump, but it was enough to send him sliding onto the joining knuckle between the two railroad cars. The gondola shifted and jolted again. Clayton screamed as his foot was smashed between the jostling pieces. He grabbed the gondola, his face pale and sweaty, his eyes wide and panicked.

"Fuck that hurts." His eyes rolled back and he bit down on his lower lip. "My foot's stuck."

Without waiting for anyone else, Mason climbed down, avoiding the knuckle itself, standing on a narrow lip of metal that held the joint. He waited for the next shift as the train turned again and he tugged Clayton's foot free from where it had been crushed inside the knuckle. His boot was split and a steady stream of dark red blood dripped out. Mason hoped Caitlyn could save his foot. He sucked in a breath. The bleeding might be the worst problem.

With the release, Clayton screamed, a shrill sound at first that turned guttural as Mason shoved him upward, where Caitlyn and Nate caught the injured man under the arms and heaved him over the edge. Mason turned and hauled himself up, hoping there would be no further movement until he was over the lip and into the next car.

Inside the gondola, Caitlyn put pressure on the mangled foot while she used her other hand to pull supplies from her medic kit. Clayton's eyes rolled back, and he mercifully passed out, probably a combination of shock and pain. Caitlyn met Mason's eyes. She hesitated, then shrugged and nodded, answering his silent question. She thought she might save Clayton. Caitlyn chewed on her lower lip. She might think it possible, but she had doubts.

"What can I do?" Mason moved to her side and took over holding a large gauze pad while she worked, now using two hands. The gauze turned bright red. His chest tightened. Damn. This was a lot of blood.

It was easy to forget how dangerous the trains were and how quickly things could change from successful to disaster. Caitlyn's quick hands inspected the damage, and she did her best to reset the bones of his foot and staunch the bleeding. One side continued to bleed, and thick red blood oozed despite bandages and pressure. Caitlyn's frown deepened as her efforts to stop the bleeding had limited success.

Once she'd done everything she could, including wrapping his mangled foot, Mason scanned the serious faces of his new entourage.

"Everyone sit at the back of the car. Give Clayton space. We've slowed the bleeding." Mason kept his tone brisk and business-like, though he wasn't sure he was telling the truth. "Kaylee, why don't you pass around some food." They could use a distraction.

"Is he going to be okay?" said Vee, a deep crevasse in her forehead. "He won't be able to keep up on his own. There's no way he can walk or hop trains with his injury."

"If his foot doesn't get infected, and the bleeding stops, he should be okay. Clayton will need a couple of helpers to help him off in El Paso and onto a northbound train with the newcomers. The rest of us will stick to the original plan. When we arrive in El Paso, the rest of us will bolt and lie low. The next train to Dallas should be through tomorrow night and we'll be on it.

An hour later, Caitlyn stood up and came to Mason, weariness lining every limb and motion. She shook her head and sat at his side. Dark shadows ringed her eyes like she'd been sleepless for days.

She took a deep breath and hung her head for a moment before saying, "I couldn't stop the bleeding. He didn't make it." She leaned into him.

Clayton was popular and well-liked, and his death would be a massive blow to their team's morale. The newer recruits on the team may not have been this close to death before and the dangerous nature of their mission had just become real.

Mason concentrated on Caitlyn. "I'm sorry. You did everything you could." He could do nothing else but give his wife a shoulder to cry on, though she would wait for tears until they had some privacy. No medic likes to lose a patient, plus Clayton's death had to bring back memories of when she'd lost Mat. She would feel like she should have done more.

"It wasn't your fault," Mason whispered. "It was just an accident." He wrapped his arm around her shoulders and pulled her close. She nodded and closed her eyes, leaning into him with a deep breath.

When they left the train in El Paso, they had to leave Clayton's body aboard. No sign he was anything more than just some hopper riding the rails. What would GreenCorps make of a dead body and an empty boxcar with a hole?

CHAPTER 26: TATSUDA

Tatsuda leaned back in the worn leather of the swivel chair as he hung up the telephone in Grady's office. The space was uncluttered now because Darren had locked everything important away before he'd left. Tatsuda had picked the lock once and checked through the files, but there was little to hold his interest, though GreenCorps would have been keen to learn some of the information he'd found.

He and Ginger took turns monitoring the phone line, making notes on rebel progress when groups checked in and relaying messages to Grady through Darren when he called twice a week from different stations. The leaders liked to be kept up to date while on the move. Turned railroad executives also called every day to keep the information current about their stations and which trains had arrived or departed.

Tatsuda had two more on the schedule to hear from today before he finished—Salt Lake and Denver. He was proud he'd been entrusted with this important job, even if he suspected Elsa had recommended them for the job to keep him out of trouble. She would have guessed that Salt Lake City was the safest place. He frowned. Considering the trouble some teams had encountered, it was also correct.

A month into the train-hopping campaign, their victories had been encouraging, if not the resounding success they'd hoped.

Sporadic, random-seeming raids had been promising throughout the West. They'd liberated hundreds, if not thousands of GreenCorps prisoners and seemed to have growing overt support from communities throughout the West. Small temporary communities had sprung up along the train routes and away from GreenCorps control. The rebels often threw food items off the train to augment their food supply. The harder GreenCorps clamped down on the population, the more disillusioned regular people became—that part going according to plan.

However, the rebels had to do something about the military soon. Maybe someone would think of a way to sway more of the soldiers to the rebel cause. Though, competing with steady wages would be difficult. Still, getting them to defect would be the real victory. The corporation would crumple without their army.

So far, GreenCorps seemed to remain ignorant that the railroad and its workers had been compromised, a condition Tatsuda hoped was permanent, though unlikely. GreenCorps still dictated the train schedules, unaware of the extent the rebels used them. They also seemed oblivious of the swing in political support of their workers, who now ignored rebel hoppers, even when they threw foodstuff from the trains. He was convinced GreenCorps would figure it out and strike back. Hopefully not for a few more months, when it might be too late.

He jumped when the phone rang—Darren calling to say that Grady was headed back to Salt Lake City. The leader had spoken in most cities throughout the West, calling for revolution and elections as he worked his way back toward Utah. Hopefully, he'd swayed public opinion to the importance of doing something now. Tatsuda sighed. Darren and Grady should be back in the next few days to take control again. Tatsuda couldn't wait.

Darren was always careful not to be specific about their location or their exact arrival time. Since they'd spoken last, Grady had met with Kurt's group in Idaho, taking possession of another batch of seeds from the Aberdeen bunker. They'd also collected everything sent on by Elsa's and Mason's groups. Those seeds had been safely distributed, including a large batch for the canyon settlements.

At five o'clock, when Tatsuda still hadn't heard from the station across town, he decided to save them a call. He would walk over for the report in person because he was sick of staying inside and wanted to stretch his legs.

He strolled through the bustling streets, watching for faces he recognized in town, nodding at several as he passed. Many of the shopkeepers, market workers, and regular-seeming townspeople had passed through the public rebel headquarters on more than one occasion. Not the hidden bar, but a cafe facing the market that Grady's people ran as a decoy. Once he did a double-take of a slim young man standing outside a general store, waiting for him to turn for a better view of his face. Was it Hayden? As there was no sign of recognition, Tatsuda was probably mistaken.

He passed the Saint's Temple in the middle of town and continued on, toward the train station. Seeing the large structure at this time of day reminded him of that afternoon a year ago when he'd recovered Elsa's tube from Jace and led the man on a chase through the city. Hard to believe that had only been a year ago, before he'd even met Ginger.

Thinking of her gave him an idea. He would stop and collect Ginger too, since he was in the neighborhood where she was volunteering. While staying at the same place, he rarely saw her until dinner, as they tended the phone on opposite shifts. He would enjoy the walk back with her, after all, she must be almost finished for the day. She'd been helping at an elementary school during her afternoons off and learning how to teach. Working with the children gave her joy, especially since she missed her nieces. Plus, it made her feel useful.

Gray shadows lengthened in the city, though it was still warm as daytime temperatures turned more summer-like. It hadn't rained in months, which was common in Utah, or so Tatsuda had been told several times. Everyone was prepared for another summer of drought. Since the city had been built in a desert, it made sense that everyone here was preoccupied with water. At least they had their own deep reservoirs in the canyons, monitored by the Saints and other farmers, so they weren't dependent on GreenCorps.

Tatsuda neared the station and a couple of trains pulled into the depot, cars crashing their way up the line as they braked. He cocked his head, listening. Long trains from the sound of echoes fading up the tracks. What trains were these? The last ones scheduled should have arrived already. He stopped while the noise continued, much longer than it should. He furrowed his brow, feeling his forehead tighten. Something was off. He didn't remember another arrival this evening, let alone more than one. That must be why the station had delayed its report; perhaps they'd received word of additional trains.

Still, why hadn't anyone informed him? This unscheduled train was out of the ordinary. He resumed walking and increased his vigilance, scanning for other signs of abnormal activity. Suddenly, the possible Hayden sighting made sense. He was now sure it had been him, after all. He'd been a GreenCorps informant before, so he might act in that capacity again. Tatsuda's senses screamed that something was wrong, but he couldn't put his finger on what else was off. He almost discounted the sensation, but couldn't. He'd have to be careful.

Tatsuda had almost reached the station, when stuttering gunfire stopped him in his tracks, his heart pounding. He ducked into the shadow between two buildings and listened. There were four more shots from what sounded like the next block—at or near the station. He remained in hiding, listening for additional clues. He wiped his sweaty hands and peeked around the corner of the building.

A vibration came through the pavement, becoming stronger and clearer. There was a distinct rhythmic beat. He listened a few seconds longer as he identified the sound. Boots. Marching in unison. What the hell? The volume increased, sending shivers shooting down his spine.

Shouts rang out, and two additional gunshots echoed through the evening. His heart sank as suspicions clicked into place. The quiet city with Grady gone had been too good to be true. Tatsuda needed to get a look, but he'd bet a massive influx of GreenCorps soldiers had arrived on the unexpected trains and were marching into the city. That had to be why he hadn't heard from Salt Lake City and Denver. GreenCorps had compromised the rebel control. He tucked his tongue into his cheek as he decided what action to take.

Tatsuda slipped behind the brick building and scaled the back wall. He'd get a better vantage from the rooftops and was less likely to be seen. He slunk to the other side of the building and lay flat on the warehouse facing the troops, sliding forward until he had a view of the street below. People seldom looked up without a reason. He'd be sure to stay quiet.

A tight feeling centered in his chest and took up residency as he confirmed that hundreds of GreenCorps soldiers with rifles in hand spread throughout the neighborhood, advancing like an insect migration. Soldiers branched off into each cross street, leaving a pair behind to stand watch at the corners. Before long, they'd have the city under their control. Shit. Jaxon McCoy and that Wade were here too. Ginger would need to stay indoors from now on or risk being taken back to her old family.

Grady hadn't left a standing army. He'd taken almost all the able-bodied fighters remaining after the groups had left the city in March. Behind the GreenCorps soldiers, a group of men in fancy business suits followed, also armed with guns. What were they doing outside of Denver? Even the suits were invested in this takeover. Shit. More miserable luck.

Tatsuda glanced up the street again. The citizens of Salt Lake melted out of the way of the soldiers, leaving the streets bare. Smart. They avoided confrontation as they scattered to their homes. They could fight another day when they wouldn't be overpowered. He approved of choosing the right moment for stealth.

They needed to warn whoever he could reach by phone. Headquarters should remain safe if he followed protocol, but he wouldn't batten down the hatches until he had Ginger inside and she was safe.

Tatsuda crept along the edge of the building, crouching out of sight, hoping to overhear the men below before he left. Maybe they'd say something he could use. He couldn't stay for long, but they looked like the leaders of this operation. He didn't think there'd been a coup or invasion of Salt Lake before. The occupation happening on his watch disgusted him.

The fancy men stopped on the sidewalk below to talk. "Let me know when everyone is in position and the loud-speaker is in place," said a barrel-chested older man with close-cropped iron gray hair flecked with white. His mouth twisted. "Let's see what prize we've taken."

"Yes, sir, Mr. McCoy," said another man, bustling up the street behind a guard of half a dozen soldiers. "The first wave has taken over the Temple and is setting up our base of operations inside. They've readied the garrison for additional troops. The cultists don't like our presence on their precious holy ground."

"I don't give a damn if they like it or not," said Mr. McCoy with a sneer. "They brought it on themselves this time. That's what this city gets for harboring rebel criminals."

The hair on the back of Tatsuda's neck rose. Another McCoy? Stopping directly above the men, Tatsuda peeked over the edge again to take a better look. The leader wasn't Jaxon, but someone who resembled an older version of the man. This must be Malcolm McCoy, president and CEO of GreenCorps. Jaxon and Ginger's father.

Tatsuda clenched a fist at his side. He'd heard nothing favorable about the man. If Malcolm McCoy was here, this was a serious problem. It meant he had access to the full might of GreenCorps. They weren't here for a raid, but probably hoping to take control and stay. They'd never had a forceful presence in Utah and must want to change that.

Tatsuda needed to warn Grady and the others, so they didn't return and fall into a trap. He swallowed. Based on the earlier call, it might already be too late. He wouldn't be able to contact the leaders before they were supposed to arrive tomorrow or the next day.

The other suits left at a fast walk, following the remaining soldiers. Down the street, the elder Mr. McCoy stopped outside the Temple to bark orders, though Tatsuda was no longer close enough to hear more than his tone.

Tatsuda ran to the back of the building. This was too important not to share, and he'd gain nothing by waiting for additional information. He shimmied down a drainpipe into the alley and sprinted for Ginger. How would she react to the news that her father was in town?

His heart raced as he crept through the now empty streets, still a block or two ahead of the advancing wave of soldiers. He glanced over his shoulder and checked both ways every time he changed direction. Tatsuda reached the schoolhouse before soldiers arrived on that street. Without pausing for breath, he interrupted Ginger and the teacher in the empty classroom, where they were discussing lesson plans.

"Your father's here. We've got to go," he gasped.

Wide-eyed, Ginger jumped to her feet and gave him a searching look. "You're positive it's him?"

He nodded.

"I might not be back for a while," Ginger said as she grabbed her bag. She stuffed three books inside and followed him at a run. "I should have known he might have done something today, of all days."

"What's today?" Tatsuda said as he returned to the quiet street. He took her sweaty hand and looked both ways. Still clear.

"The anniversary of Jace's death. Here in Salt Lake City." Ginger squeezed his hand. "Let's hurry. We can't let him find me."

They wound their way deeper into the city, using alleys and side streets as they worked their way back toward headquarters, avoiding busier streets where GreenCorps soldiers now patrolled in number. It took three times longer than usual, but they made it without being seen.

Tatsuda would make damn sure Ginger stayed out of her father's clutches. They didn't know what Jaxon had told Malcolm McCoy, but it wouldn't favor Ginger because she'd thrown in with Elsa and the rebels.

* * *

For two days, Tatsuda, Ginger, and half a dozen rebel regulars kept to headquarters. The inner door disappeared as they extended a hidden section of wall to cover its existence. If anyone breached the green door from the alley, all they would find was a storage room connected to the small neighboring bar. The second bar, which was rebel headquarters with Grady's office and the telephone, remained secure and hidden.

Outside, GreenCorps clamped Salt Lake City down under martial law. Closing time was five p.m. for businesses, but most remained closed, their windows shuttered as if battening down for a storm. Curfew was five-thirty. The city's inhabitants hunkered down, most barely leaving their homes. The soldiers took those who caught outside after hours to jail. Nobody who'd gone in, came out. The cells must be crowded. Then, an unscheduled train departed for the south.

Twice daily, GreenCorps broadcast announcements through a system of speakers, demanding Grady be brought to justice. Each day, the incentive for his capture increased, but Grady's whereabouts remained unknown. GreenCorps would need to do more than ask the people of Utah to turn him in—this had been Grady's capital for all of his life. This was his home. They'd have to capture him on their own. Still, Tatsuda worried. They'd had no word from Grady, his location a mystery.

On the third night, Tatsuda snuck out after dark, just to get the lay of the land. He wanted to listen to rumors on the street because he didn't like not having enough information. He exited from a third-story window, sticking to the rooftops wherever possible—jumping from one to another. It was quiet, and he learned nothing. He returned a nervous wreck, but unscathed.

Neither Salt Lake nor Denver stations had ever checked in by telephone, but Tatsuda had spread the word to the railroad executives in other cities to avoid stopping at those stations, even if it meant rerouting trains. From the headquarters rooftop, he'd used binoculars, noting several additional trains arriving and spilling out hundreds more GreenCorps soldiers each day. His biggest concern was that he still hadn't heard from Grady.

Tatsuda cracked his knuckles. Had their leader been captured at the station? Wouldn't GreenCorps advertise if they had him in custody? Maybe. Maybe not. They continued to make demands for information about Grady, Mason, and Elsa, but it could be a bluff.

Too bad Elsa wasn't here; she and Walker would know what to do. Tatsuda had last heard from them somewhere near Vegas. Maybe she was on her way back? Now, he hoped not. He couldn't stand the thought of her being captured.

To the McCoys, she was the enemy. With her, it was personal.

He moved back through the cool building to the office and released Ginger from her telephone duties before he sat in the leather chair, waiting for the shrill ring of the phone. After sitting for another hour, he changed his mind. He was sick of doing nothing. Tonight, he would visit the garrison's jail and see what he could find. He needed better information and to take action.

CHAPTER 27: JANNA

Janna leaned back in her chilly cell and closed her eyes. The GreenCorps soldiers that had captured them when they'd arrived in Salt Lake had ignored her once she was secured, leaving her grateful to be left unscathed. They hadn't touched her, limiting their interactions to taunts. Her imprisonment could have been worse. Plus, Wade hadn't been one of her captors. From him, she would have expected a beating. He probably would have also dragged her back to the station, selling her south again. She refused to dwell on that possibility, instead focusing on staying alive.

Her stomach rumbled. It was well after midnight, but she couldn't sleep, no matter how motivated she was to rest, so she stared into the dark. Busy thoughts swirled through her head like water rushing down a drainpipe. She didn't know when someone would feed her next, but she didn't want to attract more attention by complaining about hunger. Enduring the uncertainty in solitude for the last two days had been long and excruciating.

Ever since they'd stepped off the Salt Lake train at sunset, only to be met by GreenCorps soldiers, things had gone wrong. They'd been escorted to the cell block. At first, they isolated her because she was the only female in their group, which seemed ominous. Now it seemed to be a gift.

The other rebels had disappeared deeper into the prison in pairs or small groups. Did GreenCorps know they'd captured the infamous Grady? They hadn't treated him any differently than the others—and nothing about the unassuming leader would give away his identity. Few people outside Utah knew what he looked like—one advantage of avoiding pictures his entire life.

One of the contingency plans in case of capture was for Darren to masquerade as Grady if the soldiers looked too closely, though it could get him killed if GreenCorps decided to execute the rebel leader to make an example. As far as she could determine, other than heavy security, the men had been treated much like her and no one had bothered to look deeper at who they had captured. Janna stifled another yawn and hung her head between her knees, feeling lightheaded. She remained that way for some time, conserving her energy and ignoring the growls of her empty stomach.

A jingle of keys at the outer door alerted her to someone returning—odd for this hour. Had she missed the buzzer for the shift change? Maybe it was almost morning. She sat up straighter.

In the dark, she couldn't make out the shadowy figure who unlocked the door and slipped inside, leaving it ajar. Whoever it was, wasn't carrying a light. Someone was sneaking around. Maybe it was another rebel—and since they were here, a daredevil.

"Did you at least bring me dinner?" Her whispered voice seemed loud in the quiet night.

The figure jumped. "I didn't expect anyone to be in here." The person moved closer. "Janna, right?"

"That's my name." She frowned. She didn't enjoy being at a disadvantage and peered at the darkness, trying to determine the stranger's identity. No luck.

"Where's… everyone you were with?" He was too far back to be seen, but it was obvious he knew who she was and that she'd been with Grady. He was also smart enough not to say that.

She hesitated, deciding to trust this person. "They took the men down the hall on the right. Deeper inside."

"Do you remember who I am?" He sounded closer, but his face remained cloaked in shadow.

She shook her head. He wouldn't have seen her response, either. Before the silence went on too long, she spoke. "No."

"I'm Tatsuda." He stepped up to the bars, revealing a face younger than she expected and vaguely familiar. "Who did you grow up with?"

It must be a test. "Elsa and Avery Lee," she said, keeping her voice low. That information in the wrong hands would also be dangerous.

Tatsuda's keys rattled as he tried one, then another, and then a third in the lock. The click of the correct one was audible.

She sighed. How had he gotten the keys? She pushed the barred door open. "You won't be able to get to him. They have round-the-clock guards in there." Her legs trembled as she stood.

"Are you alone?"

"I am. Let's get out of here. We can talk more when we're safe." Tatsuda relocked her cell and placed the keys across the room on an empty desk. She doubted they would notice her absence and raise an alarm.

They flitted through darkened hallways before slipping out a side door and into the alley behind the garrison. Though there was poor light, it was enough to make out details about her rescuer. She couldn't believe he'd broken into the GreenCorps stronghold alone. He couldn't be more than sixteen.

Tatsuda led her through the sleeping town, across the deserted market, and to a knotted rope dangling from above in a dark alley. He scampered up its length to a third-story window like a squirrel and motioned for her to follow. She grabbed the rope and climbed, knot by knot. It wasn't too difficult because she had help from above once he reached the top and hauled on the rope—which was necessary as she wasn't feeling her strongest.

Janna thumped to the wooden floor and looked up. She faced Tatsuda and a young woman with long red hair. Elsa had introduced her to several rebels back in early March, ones who had been Elsa's group of friends. "Thanks for getting me out." Her stomach gurgled.

"I don't suppose you have something I can eat? They might have forgotten about me while I was in lock-up. They picked us up two days ago, and I haven't eaten since.

"Of course. I'm Ginger. We'll get you some leftover dinner." She turned to Tatsuda. "Is Grady okay?"

He shrugged. "I found Janna on her own in the front row of cells, where they usually keep those they're deporting to SoCal or Texas."

Janna's stomach clenched as she fought not to be sick. Even without Wade, they'd planned to send her back to Texas. She refocused on what Tatsuda was saying.

"The others have twenty-four-hour guards close by. Without a major distraction, I don't think I can break Grady out. Even if we did, with all the rebels away from the city, we can't fight GreenCorps. There are too many soldiers here already. We have to wait. We need the teams to come, but they run the risk of being captured."

"I'll be right back," said Ginger. "I'll get that food." She slipped out the door and her footsteps disappeared downstairs.

Tatsuda sighed and ran a hand through his short hair, making it stand on end. "I don't want to be in charge of this mess. I'm not sure what to do, but the rebels will follow Elsa. We need to hurry, though; we don't want old Malcolm to decide to kill or interrogate the prisoners." He glanced out the window with a harder stare. "If they haven't already."

"I'm not sure GreenCorps realize they've taken Grady," said Janna. "GreenCorps planned to use us as bait to draw in the rebel leaders." She shrugged. "I heard them talking." Handy thing about being underestimated. It made her invisible. They hadn't even asked her questions.

Ginger returned with a few slices of bread on a plate, a knife, and a jar with red jam. She slathered jam on the bread and handed it to Janna.

"This tastes amazing," she said. "Thanks. What happens next? I need to help. Can you sneak me out of the city? I know the way to the Saints' settlement and have friends there. They might provide back-up." Clark might not be able to help but after the last few days in a cell, she wanted to be near him. Plus, Brother Campbell may have ideas about how to free Grady. His capture might be enough to shake the Saints from their complacency. It was worth a shot.

Tatsuda and Ginger turned toward her, their expressions becoming animated as they spoke over each other, both blurting their plans aloud. Their babble was fast, and it was challenging for Janna to discern anything that made sense. She gnashed her teeth. The Saints were far away on foot, but not an impossible distance. Two days, maybe three.

"Hey," she yelled.

Both faces swept back to hers. They'd forgotten her in their excitement.

Janna unclenched her jaw and took a deep breath. She tried to keep the exasperation from her voice. After all, Tatsuda had freed her from jail. She owed him that much respect, but talking wouldn't help her tonight.

"Thanks for the snack, but I need to be on the road before dawn, or GreenCorps will scoop me off the streets and throw me back in that stupid cell. To be deported."

Tatsuda nodded. "You're right. The Saints need to be told about what's happening. I hadn't thought of notifying them. Ginger, can you get three days' worth of travel rations, a backpack, a canteen, and some of those processed bars for Janna? Perhaps she can convince the Saints to send help because they know her. It would be outstanding if they'd take a stance and come out of isolation. We need them."

Ginger turned toward the door, stopping when he continued speaking. "I'm going to leave you in charge here. You'll have to monitor the phones for longer hours and relay messages."

"Where are you going?" Ginger narrowed her eyes, and a crease appeared between her brows. She must be worried.

"I'm going after Elsa. Will you please call New Vegas station first thing in the morning? Let Elsa know to wait there for me. She, Walker, and I can help figure out how to free Grady. If Mason checks in, tell them too. We need to retake Salt Lake City." Tatsuda shrugged like that battle wouldn't be a big deal.

They left the room, returning only minutes later. Tatsuda had gathered his backpack and Ginger returned soon after with one for Janna. At least they'd both been quick. She was itching to leave.

Ginger passed a pack to Janna and a handful of processed protein bars. She kept one in her hand and shoved the rest in her pocket. They tasted like sawdust, but she'd eaten hundreds the last few years so she would manage.

"Thanks for the gear." She no longer had possessions because the soldiers had confiscated everything when she had been captured. She'd owned little of value anyway, but there were a couple of items she'd miss. Her book and her sweater being her most important possessions.

Tatsuda said, "Do you remember how to locate the Saints' settlements? Brother Campbell is typically in the one farthest north, where you were before Darren picked you up."

Janna bit her lip. "If I have directions to the Dawson farm, I'll find it from there."

Tatsuda nodded. "I'll draw you a map." He reached inside his shirt. "This was downstairs in the office. It's for you." He handed her an envelope with her name written across the front in familiar handwriting.

Her heart skipped. Clark had answered.

* * *

Janna lowered herself using the rope from the window and dropped the last few feet to the dark cobblestone street. She didn't know her way around Salt Lake, but she had directions and her priority was avoiding patrols to get out of town. Under martial law, nobody was supposed to be outside between five-thirty p.m. and eight a.m. Her heart fluttered as she crept from shadow to shadow. Maybe she should have waited until morning to leave so she could have blended in with the townspeople going about their business. Except that every second counted. The longer Grady sat in jail, the more likely his identity was to be discovered.

At the end of the alley, she headed north. Tatsuda had said the quickest way out of town was in that direction. She checked her map, left the downtown and empty stores, and flitted through quieter outlying neighborhoods. The houses were all dark, though once a faint outline around one window showed someone awake inside. She glanced at the paler sky over the eastern mountains. It was almost morning.

Twice she froze, her heart in her mouth as pairs of soldiers wandered the street, their rifles on slings as they held them across their bodies. She pressed herself against a wall each time, hoping she wouldn't be noticed. When the soldiers moved on, she continued.

When at last Janna reached the outskirts of town, the north gate was blocked. She hadn't been given instructions on how to get through the gate, other than not to be seen. With freedom so close, she felt like bursting into tears. She had to get out and had to find Clark. He would know how to help. She touched the letter tucked inside her shirt. She still hadn't read it, but knowing he was close helped her deal with her fear.

In the end, she climbed a fence into a backyard. Inside the house, a dog barked and her heart skipped. Hurrying, she tiptoed to the end of the yard and scaled the second fence. She dropped onto the other side, pressing herself onto the hard ground.

"Did you hear that?" said one guard. He walked in her direction, his steps drawing closer; she squeezed herself closer to the fence, hoping to blend into the sagebrush lumps in the remaining darkness.

Another voice spoke to the first guard. "It's been dead quiet every night. The citizens have already been thoroughly cowed. We can do what we like here. I doubt anyone was brave enough to venture out before curfew's lifted. I'm not sure why our troops haven't had a stronger presence in Utah this whole time."

"I thought I heard something." The first voice was no longer so definite. Good.

She held her breath. Nothing to investigate. She willed him to return to the gate.

Time stretched as the soldier continued to stare in her direction. Her heart thumped so loud he surely would hear, but at last he turned away.

"You're right. Probably nothing." He yawned.

She stifled one of her own. It didn't matter if she hadn't slept. She had a job.

"Or a raccoon. They're all over the city."

The young soldier returned to the gate and at last Janna stole away, heading into the plains, following the wagon path that ran parallel to the mountains as she headed north toward the mouth of the canyon.

Janna hadn't gone far when the first rays of sunlight peeked over the mountains. She'd made it out of the city just in time.

* * *

Janna hurried along the rough trail through the canyon as the sun rose two days after she'd left the city. She scrambled over jagged rocks and grabbed bushes to haul herself up the steepest sections. She'd taken longer than expected coming across the plains and then hours locating the mouth of the canyon in the inky dark night, with only the faint starlight as a guide. In an area that was supposed to have few inhabitants, she hadn't wanted to risk using a light.

She hadn't expected trouble finding the path, even at night, but Darren had taken a different route down the mountains when they'd descended. Nothing looked the same as the time she'd climbed the trail with Caitlyn and Mason last November, when everything had been covered in several inches of snow.

Janna yawned, making her eyes water. She'd gotten this far on adrenaline and a few power naps along the way, but she wanted to crash. Her lungs labored in the high altitude and her calves burned as she trekked up the last of the narrow path before the canyon opened up and the ground leveled off.

Almost straight ahead, the morning sky filled with hues of pink and purple as they shaded into the true-blue sky of day. She looked around, taking in the valley and the water. This part of the route seemed familiar, with the dam and reservoir on her right and the lofty mountain peaks on the left. She spun, appreciating the beauty of her surroundings, so unlike SoCal. At times like this, it seemed a different world, and it was difficult to believe a place like her dismal hometown existed.

Birdsong filled the shallow valley nestled among the snow-tipped peaks jutting skyward. Pale green bushes and blanched-tree trunks lined an expanse of turquoise-blue water. The amount of water beside her took her breath away and she couldn't rip her gaze away at first. Would she ever get used to the incredible beauty in the world? The image of sitting and watching a sunrise with Clark flashed through her head. He would appreciate the magnificence of this location. Perhaps that was why he stayed in Canyon Country.

While taking a quick break, Janna took a long drink and wiped the sweat from her forehead. She'd love to rest longer, but the Saints settlement should only be a few miles farther. Her eyes burned, but she rose and pushed on; she closed her water jug and continued along the path beside the water, despite her shaking muscles and intense fatigue.

At the end of the trail was the potential for help, a hot meal, and Clark.

She'd read his letter when she'd stopped to eat well beyond the city and out of immediate danger. While she'd already guessed some of what he'd shared, his mother's suicide and his blazing well of anger had come as a surprise. He seemed so quiet. It was no wonder he hadn't spoken of what had happened. She wanted to wrap him up in a hug and tell him she understood his pain. He deserved so much better. No wonder he was afraid to break his word, even if the promise had been extracted under duress.

Black spots appeared in her vision and she paused for another quick drink, feeling more lightheaded than ever. She needed something else to eat, but she couldn't stop now. She was so close, and every minute mattered. She glanced at the reservoir on her right as the path widened, becoming more well-traveled.

Janna hiked for another two hours, forcing one foot in front of the other until she reached the edge of the Settlement by mid-morning. Her leg muscles spasmed and her steps faltered.

Stumbling alongside the edge of a cultivated field where a dozen Saints worked in their fields, she planted her tired feet while she gazed at the long rows of plants—every shade of green was represented and some had blossoms of white and yellow. The nearest ones were dark green leafy plants in mounded hills. Potatoes? Further over were pale green y-shaped spears that rustled. Maybe corn? She didn't recognize most of the others. In the winter, the scope of the Saints' farming had been hidden. An impressive patchwork of fields and crops spread toward the distant buildings of the settlement. No wonder they ate well here. Her mouth watered. Tonight, she could eat proper food.

"Is Brother Campbell here?" she called. Her throat ached and her voice was hoarse and scratchy. A trio of workers ambled in her direction and she repeated her question.

"I'm looking for Brother Campbell. Or Clark Dawson." Her exhaustion caught up to her and her voice cracked. "Please find Clark." The world spun, turning blurry, then dark. She collapsed as her mind went blank and everything disappeared.

CHAPTER 28: ELSA

Elsa hung up the phone and stared out the grimy window of the cramped, dingy office of the New Vegas station. She took a deep breath. What was she going to do? Her team of rebels had staged raids and liberated people for almost four months now. They'd chosen a dozen sites for air-dropped food and taken the crates to several safe locations for distribution. She'd done a thousand small things, hoping to make a difference and better everyday life for people, and their ranks had swelled. She hoped it wasn't for nothing.

It was almost July, and her team had been on the move every day since March. She was bone weary and wanted a break. Part of her wanted to disappear into the mountains, head to Walker's cabin on Lake Tahoe with him, and stay there. She sighed. That would have to wait.

This morning, she'd received an urgent message and hustled down to return Ginger's call. From the moment she'd answered the door to the messenger and her stomach clenched, she'd prepared herself for the emergency. Her gut was never wrong. The news from Utah had been terrible. Salt Lake City had been taken and Grady along with it. She wasn't sure Tatsuda's faith in her problem-solving was justified, but she was going to try. Utah was too important to lose.

Elsa exhaled and stared at the ceiling. GreenCorps must have gotten sick of fighting the rebels on a dozen fronts and changed their strategy. She'd known something would happen as retaliation; still, she hadn't guessed this was the direction they would take. She was grateful that Avery had guessed and insisted on leaving Salt Lake with her family. They should be safe in the mountains. Elsa's blood chilled. Maybe.

Potential plans raced through Elsa's mind. If they didn't rescue Grady, was this the end of the rebellion? She clenched her jaw. She wouldn't let GreenCorps win after all this hard work. Granny Lee had been the rebel leader, and the movement hadn't died when she'd been captured and exiled. It had taken another fifty years to rebuild to where they might win. They were still fighting the same battles.

Elsa squared her shoulders. Inheriting the struggle from Granny made the old lady seem close again. Elsa would always miss her tough grandmother; she wouldn't have let GreenCorps get away with this latest maneuver.

"So, what happened? Why did Ginger call, not Tatsuda?" Walker's voice startled her as he leaned in the doorway. He'd accompanied her to the train station when she'd come to return Ginger's call.

"Come in and close the door." She kept her voice low. Even though this station remained in friendly territory, she wanted to keep the information between them. Once alone, she said, "Grady was captured and Salt Lake City taken. Instead of a token force, Malcolm McCoy himself brought thousands of troops. Tatsuda is on the way here to fill us in and plot how to get the city back."

"No pressure," said Walker with a lopsided grin. Despite his expression, his gray eyes darkened with concern.

"We're to sit tight and figure out a plan with Mason and Caitlyn, who are headed this way too. We're keeping the information about Grady to ourselves. It seems GreenCorps doesn't realize they have him."

"We'll have to use that." Walker took her icy hand in his warm one and squeezed.

She and Walker could do this together. There had to be a way.

With a nod to the stationmaster, they headed to the safehouse where their team would stay for the next few days. They strode through the dirty, sprawling town, ignoring the signs of poverty everywhere. The buildings were more solid and the jobs more varied than in SoCal, but the lives of the people were much the same—everyone scraped to make a living. Life was a success if you had food, water, and shelter, but shouldn't there be room for more than just survival? If she let herself notice that there was still so much left to accomplish, like making these people's lives better, it might break her heart.

Vowing to keep scheming, she kept her head tucked, her hat low; she wasn't about to be picked up by random authorities at this stage by being careless. Her Wanted posters still adorned the window of every corporation store, as did increasingly accurate pictures of Caitlyn, Mason, Walker, Kurt, and half a dozen others—rewards varying from three gold to the whopping thirty GreenCorps would pay for Elsa's capture.

She replayed the phone conversation with Ginger as she walked. Ginger had sent Caitlyn and Mason to Vegas today, so they'd be here in two days. Tatsuda should arrive this afternoon. Elsa quickened her pace. The prospect of having her most trusted friends and family together again made her believe they could rescue Grady and take back his city. She didn't have to do this alone. They'd all played a part in getting this far and events were rushing toward a long-awaited conclusion. She wanted to play a part in the victory.

* * *

The train station in Salt Lake City was lit up like Portland at night when the train slowed on arrival, bumping and crashing. Nothing stealthy about arriving on the rails. Beyond the station, the city was darker than usual, an inky smudge in front of the shadow of the looming mountains in the east. From the final train car where Elsa stood, security remained far ahead, probably waiting for groups of rebels.

Instead of bringing a team, Elsa, Walker, and Tatsuda had come on their own. If they got caught, Mason and Caitlyn could make another attempt. For now, those two had traveled to Idaho Falls. Mason was going to declare war against GreenCorps and pretend that he was Grady. If that didn't make a large contingent of soldiers leave Salt Lake, nothing would.

Elsa's small group planned to take advantage of his diversion to free Grady. She chewed her lower lip as the train lurched to a halt. They snuck off the train like the old days. This station was once more controlled by the enemy. Walker climbed down first, not making a single sound. She descended the ladder next. He lifted her off and set her on the ground so she wouldn't make noise with the final drop. Tatsuda came last, landing as lightly as a cat. Their minute sounds should have been covered by the bangs as the train came to a rest down the line.

She removed her earplugs, and they slunk backward on the tracks, using a second train as cover as they made their way into the darkness. Arriving by train in such a heavily occupied station was as risky as it could get, but it was time to make a bold move or they would lose their progress from the entire year. Well, not the seeds, but Grady's execution would set them back. Plus, her personal loss of yet more family would be devastating. She hoped they weren't too late.

Two hundred yards down the track, the night still seemed quiet and her chest loosened as the prospect of discovery lessened a little. This late in June, the ground radiated heat soaked in from the scorching daytime, though it was almost midnight. They crossed into the warehouse district and slipped between buildings, taking a long route into town that should allow them to avoid contact with soldiers. Because the city was under martial law, the night was abnormally silent, almost as though it had been deserted.

Twice Elsa jumped, heart racing when they encountered corporation patrols moving through the streets. Without fail, Tatsuda led them in a new direction without discovery. It was lucky that only the three of them made their way through the night. It took several hours of tense, careful sneaking before they reached headquarters from the north by circling the city. Elsa's neck and shoulders ached from constant tension.

"Ginger was supposed to throw the rope back down tonight after dark." Tatsuda motioned to the alley, his eyes gleaming in the faint light of the moon and stars. "We'll have a good vantage from the rooftop to see if they take the bait tomorrow." He reached into a gap between the brick buildings and tugged a heavy, knotted rope into the open. Its length disappeared in the shadows above. He scampered upward, reached a window on the third floor, and tapped with his knuckle. From above came the sound of scraping as the window was raised.

Elsa winced at the noise—her nerves already frayed.

Ginger helped Tatsuda inside, her fire-red hair glinting when it caught a stray beam of light from within.

"You next," said Walker, holding the bottom of the rope steady. Elsa glanced over her shoulder, took a deep breath, and climbed, the rope rough under her hands. Tatsuda helped her inside at the top, and she helped Walker. Squeezing him through the window was more difficult and awkward because of his size, but they managed. The room they were in wasn't much larger than a closet, with bunk beds on one side. Tatsuda's and Ginger's packs sat on the floor at the foot of the beds.

Tatsuda hauled the rope inside and shut the window. "This is my room. Let's get some sleep. We can send out the misinformation about Idaho Falls first thing tomorrow." He showed them to the next room down the hall—this one with a dresser and a bed with two pillows. Ginger carried a basin of water down the hall and set it on the dresser.

"Thanks," said Elsa. She and Walker washed away the dirt of their travels and fell into bed in record time. Walker drifted off to sleep almost right away, while Elsa tossed and turned—her nightmares since the executions haunting her thoughts and stealing sleep. At last, she nodded off, before sunrise, for a few hours of fitful rest.

* * *

Ginger sat down in the chair in Grady's office and looked up at Elsa, her expression one of confidence. "This is the message you'd like me to send?" She picked up the piece of paper, scanning it again. She grinned, showing her white teeth, accompanied by a wicked gleam in her eyes. "This oughta get them moving."

Elsa nodded. "I hope you're right." She'd written the message over breakfast, though the idea had been racing through her mind for days as they'd refined the scheme.

Ginger punched the buttons on the phone, double-checking her list, leaving her connection to Salt Lake station open to ensure they would "overhear" her conversation.

The telephone rang three times on the other end before someone answered. "Idaho Falls Station." The sound came through the speaker and they all listened.

Ginger leaned forward. "This is a message for Kurt from headquarters. Make sure Grady is in position outside Idaho Falls in three days. The plan to take the Snake River reservoir is to proceed at dawn."

From the other end came three endless seconds of silence. "Message received Headquarters." Then the phone clicked and the line went dead. There was a second click on the line. Probably Salt Lake Station hanging up.

"Hope they took the bait."

Ginger hung up and turned, facing Elsa, Tatsuda, and Walker, who'd crowded in behind her. "How soon until we know?"

Elsa chewed on her lower lip. "If there's no troop movement by tomorrow, we'll have to think of something else. For now, we wait."

CHAPTER 29: MASON

Mason hadn't returned to Idaho Falls since the incident last summer, when his arm had been slashed in a knife fight. He wasn't wild about returning now, though he hadn't argued with Elsa's logic when she'd suggested this scheme. He stared at the flat countryside, already buff-colored for the season, except for the pale bluish-green of the scattered sagebrush. While he watched, a trio of pronghorn antelope dashed away from the slowing train, their pale haunches bouncing with their escape.

His mind returned to the task at hand while the rebels prepared to hop off the train. The problem last summer seemed more distant than only a year with all that had happened since, but other than arriving at the station, he wasn't staying in town. One speech, then he was gone. It was only to create a diversion.

They'd chosen Idaho Falls for several reasons, including how close it was to Salt Lake, a simple five-hour train ride—close enough GreenCorps shouldn't hesitate to dispatch soldiers from Salt Lake, far enough they wouldn't be able to stop Grady's rescue. Tatsuda would have Elsa and Walker in and out before anyone was the wiser. It also helped that Kurt had used this town as a base of operations all spring and summer, adding his rebel group from Boise to the current sympathizers in the area.

Freeing Grady wouldn't be enough to retake Salt Lake, but it would give the city's inhabitants a boost. If it became common knowledge that Grady had been captured, their morale would sink to a new low. However, this setback wouldn't mean the end for the rebels. Once free, his father would probably move his headquarters to one of the more difficult-to-reach canyons and rebuild. Unless the rebels also removed GreenCorps' leadership—the McCoys.

Once they had all cleared the station, Mason tipped his hat to Nate and the other rebels before he and Caitlyn headed off on their own, keeping a low profile by avoiding the station. He would spread the word of "Grady's" speech the day after tomorrow because he had a network of contacts in town. Nate would ensure the crowd included as many of his contacts as possible, plus he would connect with Kurt. Nate and the medic knew each other from Kurt's previous rebel work.

Besides Ginger leaking the false information about Grady over the phone, corporation lackeys might also inform GreenCorps they'd confirmed Grady's arrival in Idaho Falls, so Mason wasn't sure of his reception.

Mason, Caitlyn, and the others strolled into town in inconspicuous groups of two or three, being sure to give each other space. Mason felt every eye, convinced there must be a target on his back. Because of the still numerous Wanted posters plastered on the store windows, he and Caitlyn slipped away first, choosing not to spend time in town. Most of the others planned to shop, buy something to eat, and take their time. Although this was a job, it was also their first slow day in months and they wanted to enjoy it as much as possible.

Everyone would meet across the bridge after dark tonight. Once everyone was accounted for, they planned to camp in the plains along the river far enough from Idaho Falls they could chance a fire and a hot meal.

Too bad he didn't have a gift with words like Clark Dawson or a fiery personality like Elsa. Still, he was the best choice to play Grady, especially if it could help the others rescue their leader. Mason hadn't ever been someone who spoke in front of crowds, but he would do his bit to make sure Malcolm and Jaxon McCoy paid attention and split the GreenCorps army.

Mason turned to his wife. "Want to help me practice my speech?"

* * *

Mason looked out over the massive crowd of assembled farmers, railroad workers, and people of Idaho Falls. His throat closed. There must be more than a thousand people assembled here to listen to the rebel leader—a terrific turnout. How could he speak to a group this size? He hadn't expected so many people to gather in the middle of a workday. A few shopkeepers dotted the crowd, but corporation soldiers didn't seem to be present. The majority of townspeople seemed, if not supportive of the rebels, at least sympathetic and willing to listen. Mason swallowed. Nate had done his job well, perhaps too well.

Mason wiped his damp palms on his pants before stepping up to the makeshift podium set up on the bridge over the river. He forced himself to face forward and not to check over his shoulder at his escape route. They'd chosen a town where they expected a positive reception, but he couldn't help being cautious and prepared. They'd set one up just in case things went south and the crowd turned ugly or soldiers surprised them.

"Many of you know who I am and why I'm here today. I'm compelled to speak and tell you the truth." His voice cracked on the last word.

"Grady, Grady, Grady," people in the front chanted.

Their loud cheers interrupted his flow. Mason cleared his throat, letting them die down before he continued.

"Under GreenCorps management, we never get ahead. We work for a pittance and rely on the corporation. They set up the rules in their favor to keep us dependent. We need them for seeds, water, food, and for most jobs. This has to change."

This was nothing new, but it wasn't often spoken of so publicly. Encouraged by the nodding of heads before him, he spoke again, his voice gaining power and volume.

"Our children will be trapped by the same circumstances, as were our parents. Under the current regime, we have no hope of improving our lives."

"Fuck GreenCorps."

"Down with the corporation." Heads nodded with each statement.

Mason took a deep breath. This was going better than expected.

"You've all seen the Wanted posters for my niece, Elsa Lee. GreenCorps will pay thirty gold to have her killed. Have you ever asked why?" Including her relationship was a gamble, but if anything happened to Grady, their group had appointed Elsa as interim leader, if only to infuriate the McCoys. If enraged, Jaxon and GreenCorps might make mistakes.

"Cause she's a thief," someone shouted.

"Trumped-up charges that mean nothing," said another loud voice.

"Tell us, Grady," yelled another member of the crowd.

This part might blow their minds. Mason took a deep breath. "Last spring, Elsa found a key and maps to six pre-Collapse seed vaults located deep underground. GreenCorps wants to keep this quiet and take everything for themselves, but this time, they can't cover up the truth. We've recovered the seeds and have been distributing them in havens throughout the West, like here and in Utah. They're not only viable but produce new ones for the next year's crop, as plants are supposed to. You wouldn't have to beggar yourselves to plant the following spring. You wouldn't have to. farm only designated corporation fields. Your children and future generations could move to unoccupied lands and live productive lives. Lives free of GreenCorps."

Loud mutters swept the crowd.

"How do we get these special seeds?" said the loud voice from near the front.

"What does it matter if they don't allow us to keep our crops?" Angry voices spread through the ranks of people, the change in mood palpable. This felt like striking a match to tinder and fanning the flames.

Mason grounded himself with another breath.

"Won't GreenCorps just take them from us?" Nate said from halfway back.

Mason met his eyes. "We need to stand together and resist. The rebels want to call an election, allowing everyone sixteen and older to vote. We want everyone to have a voice and the freedom to choose their own lives."

"Isn't that what led to the Collapse?" Someone in the front row frowned after asking his question. His arms crossed while he waited for an answer.

Mason directed his answer toward him at first, then forced his gaze to sweep the crowd. They all needed to hear this.

"That's what GreenCorps would have you believe. The world used to have billions of people and it's true they polluted the world with their carelessness and greed. They caused catastrophic climate change, with extreme weather and drought—much like we still struggle with today. Civilizations across the world were on the brink of disaster, worried about lack of water and food. They might have figured out how to solve their problems, but in the end, it was an asteroid that accelerated the Collapse and decimated the population."

"GreenCorps claims to be our savior. I say they are our slave masters. Insist on the right to make choices and better your lives. Take up arms, free the water supply, and allow access to viable seeds. Grow your own food. We need to take back the West. We want an election and a new leader, a person, not some corporation who only cares about money."

"Hell ya."

"Down with GreenCorps."

"Grady for President." These chants swept the crowd, with more voices taking up the last.

Mason's heart pounded in time to their words. Maybe he was better at making speeches than he'd guessed. Or perhaps people were ready for action. His throat ached from projecting his voice and his heart thumped hard enough it might escape his chest. He hoped this speech did the trick.

He held up his hands and the voices eventually quieted. Caitlyn stepped to his side and spoke in a loud, clear voice. "GreenCorps troops are coming here tomorrow. They want to arrest Grady. Are you going to allow them to take us prisoner and deny these truths? Or will you help end this domination? Will you fight, not just for us, but for yourselves? Will you fight for our future?"

A roar issued from every throat.

Mason stepped back to the podium. Hands shaking, he grabbed both sides while the tumult died down. "We need everyone. Troops will arrive at the station tomorrow. They think I'm to attack the Snake River Reservoir. That was a ploy to get them here. Take the fight to GreenCorps. The future needs you."

A tremendous roar rose from hundreds of throats. Fists shot skyward as the citizens of Idaho Falls worked themselves into a frenzy. The air trembled, and the ground shook, the vibrations filling Mason's chest. Holy shit. He glanced at Caitlyn.

"Well done," she said with a breathtaking smile.

Tomorrow, GreenCorps was in for a surprise.

CHAPTER 30: CLARK

Clark slathered a liberal amount of mortar onto the section of rock wall he was constructing. This section was back to ground level after starting the foundation in a foot-deep trench. He positioned the three flattish stones he had ready, one at a time, adjusting each to sit better before adding the next. He glanced up at the azure sky—not a cloud in sight. Today was going to be another scorcher. Though only mid-morning, sweat ran down his forehead and back, making his shirt stick to his frame. To rest, he stretched and made his way to the shade of the new garden hut at the base of the slope.

He'd only just grabbed his canteen when sound carried from across the field, where he swiveled to squint in that direction. His expression turned into a frown. It sounded like someone had called his name. He took several steps forward and peered at the cloud of dust stretching in his direction.

"Clark Dawson." The call came again, from a fast-approaching runner.

Clark's heart thumped harder. Why was he wanted? News about Caitlyn? Mason? His blood ran cold. Janna? He trotted toward the runner.

"I'm over here." His mouth was parched but fear sat in his gut and he no longer wanted water, so he slung it across his chest.

The teenage boy dropped to his knees in the dirt and gasped. "A woman ran up the mountain from Salt Lake with news. She asked for Brother Campbell and you. Then she keeled over."

Clark's heart stuttered. It must be Janna. Everyone knew Caitlyn, so they'd probably use her name. After all, she was known to many. He hauled the teen to his feet and turned toward his supervisor. He needed to find out about Janna.

The lead stonemason called to Clark. "You go. We got this."

With an apple-sized lump lodged in his throat, he grabbed his bag and raced toward the cluster of people at the far side of the fields, closest to the canyon trail. He dropped to a walk when he reached the crowd. He slid through the gathered workers and knelt beside Janna, assessing her condition. Her skin was pale, with purple shadows in the hollows of her eyes, bruises all over her arms, and scratches on her legs. She looked thinner, too. He lifted her hand. It was cold and clammy.

"Did someone send for a medic?" He said to the assembled bystanders.

"We did," said one farmer. "You just beat them here."

Janna's chest rose and fell as she breathed. There was no sign of major injuries or open wounds. Clark ran through other possibilities for her condition. Probably dehydration or extreme fatigue. "She asked for Brother Campbell and myself. Did she say anything else?"

"She asked, then dropped like a stone. Maybe she's exhausted."

Clark agreed, but his worries still swirled, unable to settle. He glanced toward the canyon and the path she'd taken. If she was that tired, what news had she brought? It must be important.

Clark didn't say this aloud, but he caught several looks between the others. They too must be wondering. "I'll stay. You can go back to work." She probably needed space. If she awoke still surrounded by watchers, she'd be embarrassed.

The foreman pursed his lips and nodded. "You heard him. Back to work. We'll find out the news after she's awake and the leaders talk."

The others shuffled away, back to weeding the rows of potatoes and thinning the young lettuce plants.

Clark settled more comfortably on the ground beside Janna, still holding her hand. She must have urgent news. Otherwise, why push herself so hard? He clenched his jaw. Where was the blasted medic?

Janna's eyelids fluttered. "Clark." Her voice was weak.

He breathed a sigh of relief. "I'm here," he said, his voice thick.

"I need to talk to Brother Campbell." She struggled to sit up, swaying even with his support. "Will you come with me?"

"Just rest." Clark rested his hand against her back. "Are you thirsty?" He unstoppered his canteen and held it steady enough for her to drink.

She took a few sips of water. "I'll be fine," she said, glancing around. "I feel foolish about fainting."

"A medic should be here soon. Let them decide if you're okay. You frightened everyone when you collapsed." He hesitated; his voice quiet. "You scared me."

Her brown eyes met his. "This is the most I've ever heard you speak."

"Special pass for scaring me," he said with a smile as he ducked his head. He hadn't even thought, he'd just acted. He peered at her face. She was still pale like milk. "I can go back to writing messages tomorrow if you'd prefer."

She laughed, a glorious sound. He loved how her face lit up when she was happy.

Clark grinned in response. He couldn't believe she was here, even if the reason might be unpleasant. He'd have to learn how to handle his feelings when she left again. Until then, he was going to enjoy her company as much as she'd let him.

At footsteps behind him on the main trail, Clark turned. Brother Campbell, Sister Hope, and one of the medics hurried toward them together, carrying a stretcher board.

"I don't need that. I can walk," said Janna, her attention shifting to them.

"Janna," said Brother Campbell with a nod.

The medic crouched beside her to check her condition. "What happened?"

Janna looked around, her gaze alternating between the three newcomers and Clark.

He squeezed her hand in encouragement, his thumb rubbing the back of her hand.

Her voice dropped. "Did news get through that GreenCorps invaded Salt Lake City and have it under martial law? Soldiers took control of the railroad station and the city almost a week ago."

Clark clenched his hand and regulated his breathing. She must be devastated. What a disaster.

Brother Campbell shook his head, his expression becoming indecipherable. "Go on."

"Most of the leaders were out of the city working on the summer campaign. Tatsuda was left in charge of communication in the city, but he could only talk to the other railroad stations. Five days ago, thousands of GreenCorps troops arrived and overwhelmed the city. Before he could warn us, we arrived. I was with Grady and we hopped into Salt Lake, not expecting trouble, and our team was captured and thrown in the garrison cells."

Sister Hope gasped and covered her mouth.

Janna shook her head. "They didn't recognize Grady. They locked me up separately. Tatsuda found me when he was poking around for information and he snuck me out. We decided to get the news out about Grady to those on our side, so I ran straight here. By now, Tatsuda will have told Elsa, Mason, and the other rebel leaders who were out of town. They're going to bust Grady out." Her voice faded as she seemed to run out of energy. "I hope."

The medic held his hands up. "This young woman is exhausted. She needs food, water, and sleep. Keep your questions to a minimum. There's nothing you can do about anything today. I want her to rest in the infirmary at least until tomorrow morning." The medic looked at Brother Campbell. "If there's nothing else you need to say right now, we should go. Staying out in the sun is bad for my patient." He reached for the stretcher.

"I can walk," Janna said, pushing to her feet.

The medic raised his eyebrows but didn't argue.

At her first shaky-kneed, wobbly step, Clark wrapped his arm around her and tucked her against his side to give her support. "Let's go." He'd almost never touched her before, knowing how she felt about being touched. Right now, she didn't seem to care.

He ignored the small fleeting smile that flashed across Brother Campbell's serious face. It was gone so fast Clark might have imagined it. Her news was grave. Would the Saints be willing to get involved now? Would he?

The group walked at Janna's snail's pace, Brother Campbell and Sister Hope splitting off to return to their work, or to discuss the news further. As much as Clark wondered what they would do, his place was with Janna.

* * *

Clark sat in the packed dining hall across from Janna at their table, his eyes still feasting on her. Her color was better this morning, and she wore clean clothes. He was grateful she was here and recovering. Clark hadn't let her out of his sight since yesterday. She hadn't seemed to mind, falling asleep almost as soon as she'd eaten a few bites and had more water. He'd insisted on staying overnight in the infirmary at her side.

For breakfast, she ate three bites of scrambled eggs and a few chunks of bacon, then nudged the rest around her plate without eating while they waited for Brother Campbell. The leader had sent word that he wished to speak further with Janna.

Clark said, "Are you okay? Usually, you love the food."

Tears filled her eyes, and she shook her head. Her silent suffering hit him harder than any words. His Janna didn't cry. He slid closer and wrapped her into a quick hug. She leaned in for a moment before pulling back with a sigh.

Swiping the tears from her cheeks, she said, "Grady's in jail. Salt Lake City is in the hands of the enemy. Everything we did this spring feels like it will have been for nothing. GreenCorps always wins."

Clark understood how this was difficult for her to handle. She'd put a lot of faith in the rebellion. "Brother Campbell said he'll meet with you after breakfast. Maybe there's something you can say to nudge him into action."

She ate another minuscule bite.

Clark wanted to offer more reassurance, but without a solution, it would be empty. He didn't know what the Saints could do, or if there was anything that would push them into openly taking a side. What could he do without breaking his shackling promise? He'd promised his mother, but if his father had lived, his mother would be the first to tell him to fight. Should his promise still hold?

He stared at Janna and she shrugged, her shoulders remaining slumped.

She spoke aloud in a rough voice as she fought further tears. "There has to be something we can do to help." Her chin trembled. She didn't look or sound like she believed her words.

He hated her defeated tone and bleak expression.

Clark closed his eyes. If he was different, more courageous, he'd do his part. A wild idea that had come to him at three a.m. returned. Their future was more important than the promise made to his sick mother. What if he rallied support for the city from among the Saints? Maybe he could convince them to leave the mountains and get involved. Caitlyn and Mason had tried both times when they were here, but they'd never lived among the Saints. Clark knew them better than anyone, having lived in their community and on the outside, giving him a unique perspective. Better than many here, he understood what would happen in Utah under GreenCorps' rule and how it would change.

He inhaled, filling his chest with air, opened his eyes, and stepped onto first the bench, then the table.

"Clark, what are you doing?" Janna's voice came as though from far away.

He couldn't believe he was brave enough to speak, but he needed to try. He couldn't focus on any of the curious faces nearby. Instead, his gaze traveled around the room filled with acquaintances and strangers.

"Excuse me." No one even turned his way. He must not be loud enough. He cleared his throat and tried again. "Excuse me." His voice shook and his knees wobbled. Conversations ground to a halt and the scrape of cutlery stopped. A giant lump filled his throat, as this time, people stopped walking and stared. Even the kitchen staff froze, watching. He forged ahead, unwilling to stop. He needed to speak.

"Some of you know me. Some of you don't. I'm Clark Dawson, and I've lived among the Saints for three years. I have valued the community and the peace I've found here. However, this is no longer a time for peace. I'm sure most of you have heard that for the first time since the Collapse, GreenCorps has taken control of Salt Lake City, the heart of Utah." He took another breath. "The rebels are on their heels and we need to help take back the city."

Clark's words were met with grumbles and head shaking, and he despaired at being unable to rouse them into action. Hope surged within when Sister Hope stepped forward, but it was dashed with her first words.

"It's none of our business," said Sister Hope, her arms crossed. "We help in other ways, like providing refuge for those in need." Several heads nodded in her vicinity. "We can live here, in the canyons. We don't need the city."

"That might be true for a while," Clark said, searching the crowd for signs of support. "But with Salt Lake in the hands of the corporation, how long until the soldiers extend their reach into our settlements? How long until they crush us, one by one?"

"We'll work together," said one of Clark's roommates from by the door.

Clark shook his head. "If they bring their troops here, it'll be too late. We need to fight now, before Salt Lake City is firmly in their grasp. I say we march on our city and take it back."

The room remained silent, the air almost humming with an eerie quality. No one would meet his eyes and several people shifted in place. Was this going to work? The hair on the back of his neck rose, while the odd quiet almost caused his heart to stutter to a stop. Would the people listen to reason? Would they remain "safe" and neutral?

Janna stepped beside him and took his icy hand in her warm one, lacing her slender fingers through his. Relief shot through him at her touch. At least one person believed.

"Rebels and Saints," she proclaimed, her clear voice ringing through the room. Her eyes shone as she met Clark's gaze. "Together."

Her words broke the spell on the dining hall.

"Rebels and Saints." Voices rang out throughout the room, accompanied by fists pounding the tables. "Rebels and Saints."

"We're headed to Salt Lake City tomorrow," said Clark. "Who's with us?"

The room erupted as everyone shot to their feet. "We are."

Clark couldn't believe they'd fired up this crowd. He'd found a way to help the rebels using his strength with words. He turned to Janna, and she kissed him, in front of everyone. Her lips were soft, but her kiss was eager. He was grateful to her for waking up his heart and his passion once more. His face flamed as another cheer went up.

"You were amazing," Janna said as they climbed off the table. "I can't believe you spoke to everyone and convinced them."

It hadn't sunk in yet for Clark.

Several minutes later, when the chaos died down, though the excited buzz of chatter remained all around them, Brother Campbell joined them, sitting beside Clark, who once more sat in front of his breakfast. "I hope you know what you're doing."

"It's time to join the cause," said Clark, his hands still shaking. He laid them flat on the table to keep them steady. "For all of us."

"For what it's worth," said Brother Campbell. "I agree, and I'll march with you. I can't let GreenCorps destroy our life's work, one settlement at a time." He stood and winked. "Rebels and Saints."

CHAPTER 31: ELSA

Elsa stared out the window at the dark city below—a thrill zinging through her veins despite her bone-deep fatigue. She, Walker, and Tatsuda were dressed in dark clothing, prepared to sneak into the garrison prison to free Grady. She turned her attention to her fellow conspirators. They were ready to make their move. It was risky putting so many of them in such direct danger, but they needed to make this happen. She bit her lip as she turned to Ginger, who stood in the crowded bedroom gathering the thick, knotted rope they used to enter and exit the building.

Elsa had considered backing out, convincing the others to stand down. She'd never forgive herself if something happened to Tatsuda and Walker. If this plan didn't work, they risked capture and possible execution. She didn't doubt her instincts, but she couldn't help but worry for her family. It must be the pressure of leadership affecting her decision-making.

But she had faith in her friends, herself, and believed in their cause, so they were going to battle.

They had to at least try to free Grady and his inner circle. Though everyone had agreed to appoint her as the interim leader, she didn't think her whole life could be this intense. She didn't want to be in charge of everyone and their lives. She wanted to be free to enjoy the new life once this was over.

Without Grady, the rebels would be leaderless unless someone like Kurt, Caitlyn, or Mason rallied them in the future. Kurt was the more likely candidate because Mason and Caitlyn would like to retire to the Dawson farm and be farmers. They'd lived this strenuous life for at least fifteen years already. They deserved a life of peace and a chance to have a family.

Ginger tossed the rope out the window after checking it was still anchored to the metal ring on the wall below the window. She gave Tatsuda a quick hug before she spoke. "You're good to go. Be careful. If you can't get in and get Grady, you're better off trying again tomorrow night than forcing it." She seemed unruffled on the surface, but she'd picked the edges of her thumbs raw. She'd probably make them bleed before the night was over—whether or not she and the others were successful. It wouldn't be easy to stay behind and wait.

Tatsuda scooted out the window first while Elsa monitored the alley below for movement, which remained still. When he reached the bottom, she turned and lowered herself out the window, descending from knot to knot with ease despite the swaying. Walker waited until her feet touched the ground before climbing down. The rope held his bulk without trouble, and soon they were ready. He grabbed the rope and tucked it out of sight in the gap between buildings, fumbling for the hook Tatsuda had installed.

"There will be patrols everywhere." Tatsuda kept his voice to a whisper. He'd run through this inside, but this was how he showed his nerves—concern over the details for others. "I don't know how long this will take. When I freed Janna, it took us a couple of hours to return."

Elsa nodded, and Walker squeezed Tatsuda's shoulder.

He turned and slunk along the left-hand wall, stepping without any noise. Elsa and Walker followed. Though she was as careful as possible, something gritty made noise or crunched underfoot. Each time she winced, but continued, her tension increasing until her neck ached.

They skirted the empty market along the surrounding buildings and turned south toward the train station and garrison using the winding alleys and side streets—staying off the main streets where there would be lights and more frequent patrols.

Curfew was five o'clock, even in the bar district. The only patrons were those who stayed overnight, which meant that everyone abroad was at risk or working for GreenCorps.

Twice Tatsuda motioned them to a halt and Elsa held her breath as the sound of booted feet marched past the alley where they crouched. Sweat trickled down her face and neck, pooling between her breasts. Tatsuda was an excellent thief and Walker had spent years being sneaky to avoid security. She swallowed, hoping they were successful tonight, so they didn't have to try again. Her ragged nerves remained on a knife edge as they worked their way across the muted city.

A disquieting sense crept over her as twice she caught an echo of her soft footsteps. Neither Walker nor Tatsuda seemed to notice. Perhaps it was her imagination, but her gut told her they were being followed. Her forehead tightened. Ginger wouldn't have been that foolhardy. If she'd wanted to come, she would've insisted from the beginning. Elsa's stomach tied in ever-tightening knots as they flitted from shadow to shadow while she strained to hear anything behind. The hair rose on the back of her neck at the faint patter of steps from behind.

At last, they came to the rear of the warehouses near the train station and the garrison.

"Someone's following," Elsa whispered. Walker frowned.

Tatsuda nodded. "Good catch. I heard them too. If it was a guard, I'm sure they would have raised the alarm by now. Hopefully, they're just curious about where we're going. I'm not waiting to find out what they want." He pointed upward next to a ladder he'd found last time, fastened onto the building beside the one they needed. He scampered up the rusty ladder. Elsa went next. It wiggled as she climbed, with an intermittent squeak that grated on her frayed nerves. The sound grew louder as Walker joined them, but they remained undisturbed. The three of them crouched and dashed across the roof for the edge of the building overlooking a section of the main security building. Above a gap of pitch black, the gutters appeared as fainter shadows.

"The short jump," whispered Tatsuda. He'd prepped them before departure. With only a whisper of sound as he launched and landed, he disappeared into the darkness. He'd said the gap was only two feet wide. At night it seemed further—a yawning gulf.

Elsa backed up to get a running start. She'd better not stumble. With a deep breath, she jumped, Walker on her heels. She landed but rolled her right ankle, a stabbing pain shooting through her foot. She took a couple of exploratory steps. Not a serious injury, or at least not enough to slow her down unless she had to run a long way.

Tatsuda led them to a rooftop door where he got to work with his pick and shear, opening the metal door without trouble. They entered and Tatsuda left the door ajar. He lived by his motto—you never knew when you'd need to make a quick escape. They descended a pitch-black, narrow set of stairs by groping with one hand along the wall and feeling for the next tread with their feet until they reached the top floor of the building.

They crossed a dark, empty room, a faint glow seeping into the darkness as they came to the top of the flight of steep stairs. One by one they filed downward, every rattle of the rickety treads making Elsa's heart race. She wasn't built for a life of crime. This amount of sneaking made her stomach hurt. A sound came from above once, and she stopped. Walker halted directly behind her, his hand resting on her shoulder.

"I heard something again," she whispered. "Upstairs."

Tatsuda turned. "I did too, but whoever it is, it isn't GreenCorps. There's no reason for soldiers to be stealthy. We're going to wait for them to get closer. You good?"

She trusted him, but it was difficult to let go of her fear. With a piece of her inner cheek tucked into her teeth to gnaw, she nodded. "Let's go."

At the bottom of the stairs, they crept along a long hall, with a single light bulb burning at the far end, where another staircase headed down into the heart of the building. "This part is used for storage and was empty last time. Once we're downstairs, we'll be on occupied levels." Tatsuda's whisper was barely audible.

She and Walker nodded at the reminder. It helped reduce the tension, but now they needed utter silence.

For this staircase, Tatsuda walked right beside the wall and they followed suit. They descended two more levels until they reached the ground floor. Here Tatsuda led them through a darkened dining hall where even their quiet footsteps echoed. Next was a kitchen large enough to cook for the entire garrison. At this time of night, the lights were off and it was deserted. This must be the back way to the holding cells.

They'd almost reached the far side of the kitchen when the overhead light flicked on. They dropped down, hovering over the scuffed boards of the dirty floor. Elsa blinked at the sudden light and her heart raced at the possibility they'd be discovered. With a lump in her throat, she waited, hidden behind an island where stacked pots and pans rested on shelves. Walker released the snap on his sheath, set to draw his blade if necessary. A glint from Tatsuda's hand showed his knife was also ready.

Footsteps trudged toward the large chiller and some yanked it open with a sucking sound. Someone rummaged around in its interior, causing rustling noises and glass clinking. Was this just one of the soldiers getting a midnight snack? Maybe an officer. Or worse, Jaxon? She bit her lip at the absurdity of being found by accident, praying they remained undiscovered.

The chiller closed and then the steps receded out of the swinging door with a hush. Once more, the kitchen became silent enough that her heartbeat seemed too loud.

Time stretched to an eternity before Elsa breathed. The three of them stood and Tatsuda eased another door open a crack, peering into the hall beyond. Closing the gap, he held up two fingers to indicate two guards on the other side.

There would be a shift change soon. When the first pair left, Tatsuda, Walker, and Elsa would have five minutes. She inhaled. There could be additional guards inside near the cells, but Tatsuda hadn't explored that far before. After this, they were entering the unknown.

Elsa and Walker nodded. She bit her lip, hoping everything went according to plan. They settled in to wait. It shouldn't be too long.

She shivered in the cool building, overhead fans moving the air with a faint whir. Once a different clunking sound made her head jerk upward. She turned her head, listening back the way they'd come, feeling her forehead bunch. Had their shadow followed them into the building and down the stairs? If so, whoever it was must have stopped. She couldn't sense their follower anymore. The kitchen remained empty.

A loud buzzer sounded in the far reaches of the building.

"Midnight. That's the watch change signal," said Tatsuda. "Get ready."

Almost immediately, a door opened with a bang down the hall, and footsteps hurried in their direction.

"Even the prisoners get more sleep than I do," complained someone who walked past the kitchen where they waited. From several yards past their position, keys jangled. "They'll have us out on patrol in the streets eight hours from now. Then we'll pull another double. I can't take much more. I need more sleep. Martial law sucks. I wish we'd never come to Utah."

"I pity the graveyard watch because they have to patrol half the day after their first shift before they can sleep," said his partner. "I'm ready to fall into my bunk. After this, I could sleep for a week."

Interesting that even regular GreenCorps troops were unhappy with the current situation.

Another door closed with a bang. Their words and footsteps became faint.

"I think we're alone," Elsa said. "No follower anymore."

Tatsuda sprang into action, pulling the kitchen door open. He checked both directions and then nodded. Elsa and Walker followed him through.

"This is the hall behind the cells. Last time, I went right and found Janna. We exited through an exterior door on this level, saving us the return trip through the building." He pointed. "We'll try the left for Grady, then the same outer door." Tatsuda indicated the two doors at the end.

Elsa nodded to show she understood, and they continued, leaving the kitchen door behind them closed but not latched. In the low light conditions, to a casual observer, it should appear undisturbed.

Tatsuda tried the first knob on the left. The door was unlocked. It opened into a security office where a guard sat behind a desk, his head nodding. At their entrance, his head jerked up and his eyes widened.

With a quick bound, Walker knocked him unconscious with his fist before the guard could shout a warning. Though they didn't have much time, they secured the guard before they moved on. Tatsuda slit open a cushion from the chair, grabbed a handful of stuffing, and shoved it into the guard's mouth. He tied it in place as a gag. That should buy them time. The man made quiet muffled sounds as he returned to consciousness.

Walker tied the man's hands, Tatsuda secured his feet, and then they belted him to his chair, all while Elsa guarded the door. It wouldn't hold the guard for long, but if it got them through the next several minutes, it would be enough.

Tatsuda snagged a ring of keys off the man's belt with a wicked grin. He twirled the keys around a finger, making them jingle, the sound loud in the otherwise quiet office. "Let's go. Time's ticking." He turned the lock on the way out.

The second door on the left opened into the main jail with several bar-lined cells. A window at the far end near the ceiling provided some gray light from outside. Though they couldn't see far into the interior, several snores filled the stuffy room. No guards; new ones would be here soon.

"Who's there?" came a whisper from the far end. Not everyone was asleep.

"Friends," said Elsa.

Tatsuda jammed a key into the lock of the nearest cell. It turned, and he opened the gate with minimal noise. Elsa slipped inside to wake the sleeping prisoners. Walker stood ready in case the guards returned sooner than expected.

Shuffling sounds moved closer as Tatsuda worked on the second lock with the same key. Elsa scanned the prisoners in the first cell. Darren gave a crooked grin as he swung his feet to the floor and into his boots. He took over waking the remaining sleepers.

"Where's Grady?" asked Elsa.

"Third cell," said Darren, tossing his head to the left. "He's probably awake."

"That you, Elsa?" said Grady, his voice the one she'd heard at the start.

"Yes. With Walker and Tatsuda."

"You shouldn't have risked this," said Grady. "But I'm glad you did. We kept waiting for them to figure out I was already in jail."

Elsa entered the second cell while Tatsuda moved onto the third lock. All the prisoners were already awake and moving. They must have only a minute or two remaining.

Grady took over with the rebels. "Everyone get in line and grab a backpack." He grabbed several from across the room on a long table, tossing them to his people at random. "We'll sort out who's got whose when we're back at headquarters." He grabbed two, his own and a spare.

Tatsuda left the room, the others stretching in a long train behind, with Walker at the rear. Elsa's heart pounded. Surely that had taken at least five minutes. They must be out of time. The guards could return any second.

The rebels made it as far as around the corner and out of the main cell block before the replacement guards arrived.

Someone behind them dropped something with a crash. Then came a loud shout. In the distance, two sets of hard-soled boots pounded on the hard floor. They must have discovered the empty cells or the tied-up guard.

"Run," shouted Grady. The rebels took off, following Tatsuda down the hall.

A shot rang out, hitting the wall behind them. Probably a warning. The soldiers were gaining, but weren't close enough yet to fire with any accuracy.

The rebels skidded around the final corner, a crowd forming around the door labeled "EXIT."

"Last door, then we're out," said Tatsuda. "Even from inside, they keep this one locked."

An ear-splitting alarm sounded from deeper within the building. Elsa threw her hands over her ears. It made little difference to the piercing sound.

"Shit," hissed Tatsuda, working faster, sweat beading his forehead. His pick jammed, and he struggled to tug it free. His hands fumbled as he started again.

Two guards in black and green skidded to a stop, their weapons drawn. One was Hayden. Walker's brother. Elsa's heart plummeted into her boots. She hadn't seen him since he'd stormed away from Caitlyn's farm a year ago when he'd informed Jaxon and GreenCorps where to find them. When had he joined GreenCorps?

Walker stood in front of the other rebels, his arms outstretched. "Hayden. It isn't too late to join us instead." Walker's voice remained calm and steady.

Elsa's sweaty clothes clung to her skin.

Hayden's eyes darted past Walker, stopping on Elsa. They narrowed. Fuck.

"Not only are you mixed up with the rebels, you're still with *her*. I told you that bitch was trouble. Look where you've landed." Hayden's voice had the same grating whine as before.

Hayden's companion shook his head. He glanced over his shoulder. Probably waiting for reinforcements. He eyed Walker's size and shifted backward. What expression was on his face that made the guard look so nervous?

Walker advanced another three cautious steps toward his brother. "You still don't understand. This is for all of us."

The second guard clenched his weapon, his knuckles turning white. His hand shook. "Don't come any closer."

At last, Tatsuda unlocked the door and flung it wide, letting in a waft of cool night air.

"Stop," said the second guard, his eyes flicking to Hayden. "What's going on?"

Taking advantage of the guard's hesitation and Hayden's distraction, Darren, Grady, and the other rebels slipped into the night. Elsa hung back. She couldn't leave without Walker. Tatsuda stepped outside, but stayed nearby, his head swiveling as he searched both directions.

"Decide which side you can live with," said Walker. "Can you stomach being part of GreenCorps long term? After everything they are responsible for and the lives they've ruined?"

The second guard answered instead of Hayden. He shook his head, handed his gun to Walker, and bolted outside, disappearing into the darkness.

Hayden glanced from Walker to Elsa, his weapon forgotten. Tears gathered in his eyes. "You left me behind."

"You tried to turn us in." Walker stepped closer to Hayden.

"Only her. Never you," said Hayden. His voice cracked. "You were my brother."

"I never stopped being your brother. Even when you're a dumbass." Walker took Hayden's gun and handed both weapons to Elsa. She took them and resumed her position in the open doorway.

They needed to go. Her stomach clenched. Footsteps pounded in a nearby hall and the alarm continued to wail in the distance.

"The prisoners are gone," came a shout.

Walker grabbed Hayden's shoulder. "Come with us."

Hayden gave a single nod and ran for the open door.

With Elsa, they shot into the night, slamming the door with a bang.

The back lane was empty. Everyone except Tatsuda was gone. The deserting soldier was either with the others or alone. Tatsuda led them to the nearest alley at a sprint.

CHAPTER 32: CLARK

The Saints marched in several large clusters as they made their way toward Salt Lake City. Looking back, Clark couldn't even see the end of their line. He hadn't imagined this magnitude of response when he'd stepped onto the table to speak. A feeling of pride filled him. He felt free.

It took two days on foot to reach the outlying area of the city, camping together overnight. Clark spent the nights tossing, turning, and staring at Janna, who slept peacefully nearby. When this was over, would he have the courage to tell her how he felt? He didn't want her to leave again.

They rose before first light on the third day as they made their final approach while the city slept. Clark shivered, not dressed warm enough for the chilly predawn temperatures. The sky remained dark without a moon, plus there were fewer lights in town than he'd ever seen—maybe because of the GreenCorps occupying force. Clark hiked with Janna near the front of the Saints, carrying shielded lanterns to keep their presence secret.

They traveled along the railroad tracks to enter city limits—a crowd several thousand strong as they came from the north. Runners had gone from the main Saints settlement to the others, so the throng had grown as they neared Salt Lake.

They weren't far from the train station and garrison when a piercing wail split the early morning. Clark's heart pounded. An alarm? Had the Saints been discovered already? He swallowed. Soon they'd be in the thick of the action, and he wasn't sure he was ready. He glanced at Janna and tightened his grip on his wooden club. Was there a way to keep her safe? He'd been ecstatic to have her at his side once more, but he was terrified that he still might lose her. They hadn't spoken about the future, but he didn't think he was alone in being overjoyed at their reunion. Sometimes he caught her studying him and blushed. Plus, she hadn't asked him to give her space.

"What's that noise?" Janna turned to Clark, who shrugged.

He wished he knew. "Hopefully it isn't because of us. It's too soon." His forehead tightened and his chest constricted, making it difficult to take a normal breath. He tried counting to five, then ten, while concentrating on his ragged breathing. It helped a little.

Behind them, the tracks vibrated, and a train roared up the track honking, its light shining forward, casting shadows onto the ground before the Saints. The group surged off the rails in either direction as the train rushed through, splitting the marching Saints in half. Crashes and bangs indicated the train was decelerating as it came into Salt Lake Station.

Was it carrying rebel reinforcements or additional GreenCorps troops? It was too dark for Clark to discern what the distant forms wore as they disembarked. He strained for a better look. It might be the black and green of GreenCorps. Or not.

Clark looked around, and though a few people seemed upset at the train ahead, everyone returned to the tracks and continued forward, still resolved to meet GreenCorps and take back the city. Hopefully, the townspeople would pitch in when they saw they had help from the Saints. Otherwise, this march might be a short-lived disaster.

"Stop right there," shouted someone from in front of the garrison, where the grating alarm originated. "The escaped rebels are on the tracks."

Clark whipped his head around, searching for escapees. Oh. The soldiers hadn't figured out it was the Saints.

Escaped? Maybe Grady had been freed. That was excellent news. It meant the Saints didn't have to worry about what would happen to him if he was still held prisoner while they attacked. Clark's heart rate soared. It also meant it was time to charge the GreenCorps troops.

"Let's go," shouted Clark, breaking into first a jog, then a run as he found more solid footing further from the gravel surrounding the railroad tracks. He held his staff in front of him like an old-fashioned knight from a storybook. At least he wasn't alone. All around him, the Saints advanced. Janna's face was set in a determined glare. His lungs labored as they ran, still picking up speed as the Saints surged into the trainyard as dawn broke.

Before the GreenCorps troops could react, the Saints bowled over several soldiers. The Saints fought with clubs, staves, and slingshots. They hadn't wanted to bring the few guns the settlement owned. Hunting rifles were for shooting game, not for killing people. Clark couldn't believe that the GreenCorps troops hadn't fired in retaliation, but the surprised soldiers didn't put up much fight. They ran in every direction in their confusion without cohesive orders from their officers.

"Saints, forward," roared Brother Campbell. He waved a club overhead as he picked up speed. Clark wouldn't have believed the older man could be so fierce.

Clark swung his long wooden staff, connecting with a shadowy form with a thud, the reverberation jarring his arm. The soldier dropped with an oomph. Clark's momentum carried him forward, away from his group of Saints. He lost track of who was around him as he thrust and swung, connecting several times. Though dawn, the light was poor, and the shrieks, yells, and continued blaring of the garrison alarm became overwhelming. His chest ached as he looked around, unable to make out friends from foes.

Shouldn't he be able to identify those in uniform? His breathing grew ragged as he struggled for control. Bracing himself, he continued to flail, knocking weapons away from himself. Was he going to hurt someone he shouldn't? The chaos left him disoriented. He seemed to be alone in a pocket of fighting as his gaze searched for Janna, lost in the commotion. Where was she?

A cry picked up from the soldiers between him and the garrison. "It's not just the rebels. It's the Saints."

From in front of the newest train came a different call. "Rebels, form up. Hold the line." The familiar voice helped ground him.

Clark squinted. In the pale morning, he made out Mason's tall slim form with the same battered hat he always wore. He stood on the stairs of a passenger car as he directed rebel fighters into the fray. The rebels turned and charged the garrison together, plowing through the line of soldiers who struggled to maintain organization. Screams of pain filled the air. A few fired shots, but their aim seemed wild in their panic.

Clark surged forward again, adrenaline kicking in once more as he bashed two more soldiers in the dim morning light. A shaft of golden sunlight slipped over the mountain and bathed the station yard, illuminating the troops from both sides. The soldiers faced overwhelming odds. Hope filled Clark's veins as he stepped forward again, following several other Saints as they pushed forward to join the rebel forces.

"We're surrounded." Several loud, panicked voices cried from in front of the garrison. The soldiers found themselves hemmed in between the buildings and the occupied tracks.

Several dozen GreenCorps troops broke free, scattering. Some followed the southbound tracks, while others fled into the city. Another group splintered, the troops scrambling over the high chain-link fences on either side of the train yard. Soon only a few dozen confused GreenCorps soldiers remained.

A burly bearded man dressed all in black held their center. "Back to the garrison. We're outnumbered." His crisp voice rang with authority. Everyone in black and green ran, following his order. In minutes, they'd disappeared into the garrison through the main entrance and lowered a solid grate over the double doors.

Mason's voice crackled over a loudspeaker. "GreenCorps soldiers, throw down your weapons. Surrender and you won't be harmed."

The remaining soldiers, those stranded on the fringes by the retreat and the deserters, stopped and threw down their guns, knives, and batons. The closest ones sunk to their knees and stared at the ground. Clark's sweaty hands shook as he picked up extra weapons from the hard-packed ground.

"What's going on?" said Janna, returning to his side. The tension he'd held since losing sight of her reduced somewhat. She didn't seem to have serious injuries, though her face sported a large purpling bruise across her cheek.

"Are you okay?" He touched her cheek.

She nodded. "You're unhurt too?" Her gaze raked him from head to toe. Standing on tiptoes, she grabbed him and kissed him again, her lips claiming his.

All the tension left him as they broke apart and smiled. For a moment no one else existed, the world reduced to Janna and himself. Finally, the surrounding hubbub returned, diverting her attention. As she turned toward the train, he spotted a bloody patch on her sleeve coming from a cut on her shoulder. His forehead tightened with a frown.

A medic should check it, just to be safe. Clark swiveled, searching for one. He spotted Caitlyn, grabbed Janna's hand, and towed her toward Mason and Caitlyn a couple hundred yards away. "Let's get something for that cut."

Janna followed without argument.

They passed Brother Campbell, who said, "Let Caitlyn know I'm setting up a perimeter around the garrison. The Saints will keep it contained." The fire in his eyes and determined jaw made him look years younger than before.

Clark nodded and continued. He hoped Mason and Caitlyn had a plan for dealing with the remaining soldiers, including those that had fled.

When he caught up to his friends, he said, "I'm surprised to see you two here."

Mason nodded. "Great to see you here, too." His eyes flicked to Janna and smiled, giving Clark a small nod. "Our business in Idaho Falls concluded much faster than anticipated. We expected to be back next week, sneak out of town, and join Grady elsewhere. The rebels of Idaho had things in hand and sent us back with reinforcements. Too bad I don't have a way to let the others know. After we find Grady, we're going after the McCoys."

CHAPTER 33: ELSA

Elsa's group didn't stand a chance of making it back to headquarters without a confrontation. The plan was to hide overnight at headquarters with Grady, then head for the mountains. From the time they left the garrison, GreenCorps troops swarmed the streets searching for the escapees—the claxon continuing to blast its alert. Everything was chaos. The entire city must be awake after that din. The blaring sound faded only slightly as her group made their way into different sections of town.

Walker, Hayden, Tatsuda, and Elsa dodged soldiers several times, evading capture, but made little progress. It was a frustrating night of constant detours and doubling back. At some point, the alarm sounds had died. Soon it would be light and their slight advantage would disappear. They needed to get off the streets, as there was nowhere to hide. They'd wanted to leave the city with Grady, hoping Mason, Caitlyn, and Kurt would make it back to the city before the troops that had departed, in a few days. Grady might need to leave without them.

They turned down a new street and Elsa strode through the quiet neighborhood, watching for early risers and soldiers. Dozens of small brick houses that looked almost the same stood on either side. At this time of early morning, the houses were peaceful. This wouldn't have been such an awful place to grow up. From a nearby street came the sound of marching. She clenched her jaw. If this level of GreenCorps forces remained in the city, the quiet community would be ruined and all these lives would be worse off. They'd gotten Grady out, but they still needed to free Salt Lake City.

"I'm not sure where else we can hide, since we can't get back right now," said Walker, breaking the silence. "Ideas?"

The group stopped to catch their breath again near a playground, keeping their voices to a minimum. Elsa's forehead tightened, matching frowns on both Walker and Tatsuda. A sinking feeling filled her stomach. It was already light enough to read the others' expressions. The night was gone, and they'd spent hours creeping through the streets and headquarters remained halfway across the city. Hopefully, Grady and the others had better luck and had reached safety. After all, they'd lived in this city for years and might know a better route.

If they'd made it back to headquarters though, they wouldn't know about the rope. They would probably try to enter the building downstairs from the green door entrance in the alley, only to discover that it had been bricked over. Unless Ginger spotted them. Elsa's thoughts continued to whirl.

Still, if the escaped rebels made it that far, they should be safe until nightfall, when they could sneak out of town and into the canyons. Maybe Grady and the others could regroup when Mason and Caitlyn arrived in a few days.

"I have an idea," said Hayden.

Elsa's eyebrows shot up. Since when was he helpful? It shouldn't be a surprise since he'd come with them, but still, she hadn't expected him to get involved.

"What're you thinking?" Walker turned to his brother when nobody else asked.

"I hold you at gunpoint as if I captured you, and march you straight down the street," said Hayden. "None of the other soldiers will interfere. I'm in uniform, after all."

She didn't like this plan. Hayden wouldn't meet Elsa's eyes.

"We'd be going in the wrong direction," said Elsa. "We'd get caught." She pictured Hayden betraying them a third time. "No way."

Hayden's gaze shifted, and he spoke to her for the first time. "It's chaos. No one will stop me. Trust me."

She shook her head. Did he think she was stupid? Even if he was telling the truth, she needed time to adjust her view of him. Maybe he had changed.

"I know I haven't given you any reason to trust me, but can you believe I wouldn't hurt Walker? Not on purpose." He didn't look away while she considered.

The image of Walker lying at the bottom of a slope of scree, his head bloody, flashed into her mind. Their frantic late-night escape from Caitlyn's farm when Hayden had turned over her location to Jaxon.

She bit her lip. Hayden might turn them in. She hadn't seen him in months and they'd never gotten along. Still, he seemed less twitchy than in the past. There was no one she trusted less, but she didn't see an alternative.

"It could work," said Tatsuda, his eyes still scanning for options. "We can't stay here much longer. It's almost daylight."

"You're up for it?" said Walker, turning to his former travel companion.

Hayden nodded.

Walker faced Elsa. "It's our best shot. What do you think?"

Still, she hesitated. She didn't like putting her faith in Hayden. Plus, there was still a price on her head. What if he decided to collect? Tatsuda had mentioned Jaxon and Malcolm McCoy were in town. She wouldn't live to see deportation if Hayden turned her over to the McCoys.

"Why would you help us? Help me?" She sounded ungrateful, so she took a breath and tried again. "You don't like me. A few hours ago, you held us at gunpoint."

"I could've turned you in long before that." Hayden's voice was calm as he met Walker's eyes, then Elsa's. She raised an eyebrow. "I was out for a stroll before my shift when I saw you sneak past. I followed you onto the roof and into the garrison. When it got close to time for the shift change, I left you hiding in the kitchen and reported for duty. I took an assignment near where I'd seen you. I was curious what you were up to." He shrugged, still pleading his case. "I knew they had Grady locked up, and I didn't tell my superiors. Does that count for something?"

Damn. It did.

The soldiers from the next street grew closer, their footsteps in sync. Probably half a dozen men. They would be here soon.

Elsa needed to decide. "Remove the bullets from his gun," she said to Walker.

Walker did as requested, pocketing the ammunition and checking the second gun was loaded before hiding it under his untucked shirt.

Hayden nodded, motioning with the empty gun. "Let's go. Walk in front of me. Take the direct route. Everybody else can keep your weapons, but hide them."

Tatsuda changed direction, taking quick steps. Elsa's shoulder blades twitched with Hayden behind her, holding the gun, loaded or not. Still, unlikely as it was, her gut told her that she could trust him this time. It was their history that made her chest ache and her breath tight.

They made their way toward headquarters as the city residents joined them on the street. It wasn't clear where people were going, but the people of Salt Lake added to the general confusion. Several soldiers ran past alone or in pairs, paying them no attention. Hayden's ruse was working. So far. Elsa's stomach clenched. Something was going on. Something big. They'd been out of touch with the other rebels all night. Anything could have happened.

With only a few blocks remaining, a GreenCorps officer with a dozen troops stopped in the middle of the street. They fanned out and watched as Elsa, Walker, and Tatsuda approached.

Elsa's heart stuttered as they neared. She recognized the leader's stance. She'd know Wade anywhere. Hayden's plan might be well meant, but in this situation, it wouldn't work.

"That's Wade," she said over her shoulder. "We can't bluff our way past him. He's known me my whole life. It also means Jaxon is nearby."

"Let me try," said Hayden.

She ground down on her teeth. He didn't know Wade like she did. He was capricious and cruel.

"Well, well, well. If it isn't Elsa," said Wade as they approached. "I had a feeling you were related to the fuck up last night with the prisoners. What did you do with them?" He didn't wait as he stepped forward. "I'll take over from here, Private," he said to Hayden. "Nice working capturing this one. Jaxon McCoy will make sure we get a cut of the reward." His eyes glittered. "I'll be sure you get your share."

His hard eyes showed Hayden's cut would be insignificant.

"Reward?" said Hayden, his eyes widening. "Who's worth a reward? How much do I get?"

Ah. Playing dumb. That wouldn't throw Wade off. Her poster was everywhere.

"That bird is worth thirty gold. To me. If you hand her over now and watch her companions for a few minutes while she and I go back there," Wade tossed his head toward a shadowy alley. "I'll see you get at least a gold outta this."

"These are my prisoners and I'm turning them in. If anyone gets the reward, it's me and I wasn't planning to share." Hayden didn't back down.

Bile rose in Elsa's throat. Wade was the same. Even working for Jaxon and with a city to occupy, he would take time out to enjoy a little rape.

"Fuck off," she said. "You'll never get to touch me. I'd sooner die."

"Listen to the mouth on you, bitch," said Wade, almost smiling. "I've always wanted to take you for a ride."

"You disgust me." Elsa reached for the concealed haft of her knife.

"You don't get to lay a hand on her," said Walker, stepping in front of her. She rested her hand on his rock-solid shoulder. Though she could fight her own battles, she loved she didn't always need to do it alone. Walker had her back.

"Hey, big guy. You don't make the rules." Wade's mouth flattened and his hard eyes narrowed. His hand dropped to his holster. Was he going to shoot her in cold blood?

"You can't talk like that," said Hayden, waving his gun. It was unclear if he was speaking to Elsa or Wade.

"I don't think you'll get through the Saints," said one of Wade's men, his gaze flicking back toward the garrison. "They've got the garrison surrounded."

Hope surged through Elsa. The rebels weren't alone if the peaceful Saints had weighed in. This could turn the tide of the rebellion.

"What's going on?" said Hayden. "Why are the Saints here? Don't they live in the mountains and stay out of politics?"

"The Saints have risen and joined the rebels," said the same soldier. He edged away from the other GreenCorps troops. He seemed on the verge of bolting, his gaze switching between Hayden and Wade.

"Private. Where do you think you're going?" Wade turned to face his men while the talkative soldier froze. "GreenCorps will rally and you need to be on the right side of this mess. Stick with me." He stepped forward and lunged toward Hayden's gun.

Though much smaller, Hayden kicked Wade's knee and then dodged as Wade swung his fist. He stumbled and missed.

"Who the hell do you think you are trying to mess with my prisoners?" Hayden stepped forward and shoved Wade's chest while he was still off-balance.

Wade stared, an odd expression on his ugly face. Hayden was like a puppy trying to fight a wolf. Still, this was his idea.

Elsa's muscles tensed as she waited for an opportunity to escape. She edged further away from Hayden and Wade.

"You must be the dumbest recruit I've met." The burly man grappled with Hayden, pulling him into a headlock. "Face it. The prisoners are mine."

"Go," Hayden shouted.

Elsa and the others took off at a sprint, their feet pounding the cobblestone street. The blood pounded in her ears and she gasped for breath.

"Stop. Get off of me," said Hayden, behind them.

"They're getting away."

Elsa glanced over her shoulder. The remaining soldiers scattered while Hayden and Wade wrestled. She spared the energy for an inward cheer while she ran. The remainder of Wade's soldiers were deserting. Hayden's loud curses followed Elsa as they rounded the corner and lost sight of the altercation.

Hayden was providing the diversion they needed to get away. For once, he'd done the right thing. If she saw him again, she owed him a thank you. For now, she ran. Headquarters wasn't much further.

A shot pinged off the wall beside her as they turned the final corner. Wade must have managed to get loose and taken a shot. With Tatsuda in the lead, they headed straight for the alley and the hidden rope. They just needed to cross the square. Maybe downstairs and a locked door were the better bet.

They reached the edge of the market, skidding to a stop. A massive crowd blocked their way—the entire square was full of people. Elsa's eyes widened. How had she missed the sound of this gathering? A shaft of red-golden light fell on a platform across the square, bathing it in the day's first sunlight.

Grady stood on the raised central platform, the area before him packed shoulder to shoulder. The crowd wasn't quiet as the market square boiled with voices. With all the commotion of the escape, she hadn't heard anything other than troop movement and the search her group had caused after they'd freed Grady. Somehow, while they were on the run tonight, word must have spread about this meeting.

Townspeople, rebels, and Saints had gathered to hear the rebel leader speak. Scattered throughout the crowd were several men in GreenCorps uniforms. Perhaps they'd changed sides. The crowd around the soldiers ignored their presence.

Elsa stood on her tiptoes to see better. Darren, Mason, Caitlyn, Janna, and a slim young man with shaggy dark hair stood behind Grady.

Her breath whooshed out. She looked around at the assembled people. If they worked together, this might be enough to take the fight to GreenCorps—not just get Grady to safety. Walker, Tatsuda, and Elsa looked at each other as they waited near the edge of the crowd. Maybe there was actual hope.

"GreenCorps is on the ropes right now." Grady's voice resonated through the morning air. "They thought they could take our city and silence our voices. We need to take it back, not just for today, but for all time."

The people cheered, including many of the GreenCorps men interspersed among those assembled.

Elsa slipped through the congested bodies and jumped up to join the leaders. Walker and Tatsuda followed.

Grady gave her a wink before continuing. She'd never seen him so animated as he pointed to Mason, who turned pink and coughed into his elbow, hiding his face.

"My son says the GreenCorps leaders have barricaded themselves in the garrison." The crowd cheered. Grady waited until the noise stopped before speaking again. "We need to draw them out and capture their leaders."

Elsa met Caitlyn's shining eyes. Grady had acknowledged Mason publicly; his pride in his son clear. Had someone told him what Mason had done in Idaho Falls? His speech and timely diversion must have been perfect. Hundreds of troops had pulled out yesterday and somehow Mason, Caitlyn, and their group had returned here in the nick of time, ahead of schedule. Their quick return and the arrival of the Saints explained the rout of the GreenCorps soldiers.

"If we capture Malcolm and Jaxon McCoy, with their troops scattered, we can free our city. House by house, street by street, let's take it back." Grady leaned forward as he spoke.

"Rebels and Saints," the crowd chanted. It seemed the perfect combination as they moved out en masse.

CHAPTER 34: MASON

Mason strode through the empty halls of the garrison, his footsteps and that of his companions echoing through the building. The front gate had crumbled, his people searching room to room and hall by hall. They intended to root out all the GreenCorps officers and suits while they had a chance. He glanced over at Caitlyn on his left. Her hair had come loose from its braid during the previous fight and she'd gathered it into a ponytail that swung as she walked. What a partner to have by his side.

He focused his attention on the task at hand. So far, they hadn't come across many higher-ups from GreenCorps, just several dozen young soldiers, most of whom threw down their weapons rather than fight hand-to-hand. Many swore to join the rebels and declared they were leaving GreenCorps. Today must set a record for the greatest number of deserters. Ever. He checked over his shoulder, pleased to see the large group of rebels with him as well as two dozen Saints as he jogged up another flight of stairs.

At the end of another hall, he came to a door. He tried the knob, but it was locked. He pressed his ear against it. A grating sound of sliding furniture and muffled voices came from within, but a raised voice could be heard above the rest. Though Mason couldn't make out the shouted words, he had a feeling this was where he'd find

GreenCorps' leadership. Not just the McCoys, but at least a dozen other suits from Denver that Tatsuda had identified. They'd been in Salt Lake City all week. Their mistake had been listening to the McCoys.

Mason waited for his entourage to gather. Nate joined him at the front with his blowtorch, turning it on with a hiss. The blue flame made quick work of the lock. Without waiting for anyone inside to make a move, Mason kicked the door in and the rebels surged through.

A shot rang out from inside the room but went wild, striking the wall. Before anyone could fire a second shot, Mason had his gun drawn on the man who appeared to be the leader. "You shoot. He dies." He kept his weapon on the older man in the rumpled blue suit.

Like other rooms throughout the building, the junior officers dropped to the floor. "I quit," yelled one. "I surrender," called several more from underneath the window. The rest kept their hands up and their eyes down.

A dozen older men in suits huddled in the corner. "I'm not a fighter," said one with shaking hands and wide eyes. "I'm only here because of him." He pointed to the red-faced man in the middle of the room, facing the door. Thankfully, he was smart enough not to fire another round, not with Mason's pistol aimed at him.

Some of Mason's men burst in through another door on the right, Jaxon McCoy in their grasp. Mason's gaze narrowed.

"We caught him trying to slip up to the roof," said Kurt. The big medic pinned Jaxon's arm in a firm grip, twisted behind his back.

"You can't do this," said Jaxon. "Dad, tell them who you are."

The angry man in the middle of the room came to life. "I'm Malcolm McCoy, president and CEO of GreenCorps." He brandished his name like a weapon.

So, this was Ginger's father? Mason crossed the room, relieved the heavy-set man of his gun, and grabbed him by the lapels of his jacket. Caitlyn was only a second behind. She patted Malcolm down, searching for additional weapons. When she didn't find any, she tossed her head, and the team scattered through the room, scooping up the weapons dropped by the GreenCorps soldiers in their haste to surrender.

"By the power invested in me by Ryan Grady, I hereby take control of this garrison," said Mason. "We're relieving you of duty and placing you under arrest."

"You can't do this," said Jaxon, struggling in Kurt's grasp, but unable to pull free.

Malcolm's eyes bulged and the veins in his temple pounded. He was probably used to getting his way. "I'll pay you a hundred gold to put me on a train to Denver. You'll never have to work again."

"You don't have a hundred gold on you," said Mason, tipping back his hat.

"Back in Denver, I have ten times that amount," said Malcolm. "All you have to do is let me go."

"I can't be bought." Mason looked around the room where the rebels and Saints had secured the GreenCorps leaders and their remaining soldiers. "It doesn't seem you're in a position to negotiate, either. GreenCorps is done."

He looked around the room. "Anyone here own the railroad?"

Three of the suits who'd been cowering in the corner raised their hands. They glanced at each other and a man in dark-rimmed glasses cleared his throat. "Between us and the investors we represent, we control seventy-five percent of the railroad."

The two men beside him nodded, one wringing his hands.

"Grady would like to buy your shares. Figure out a fair price. You're selling." Mason's voice brooked no argument.

The three men whispered in the corner, reminding Mason of snakes sliding through tall grass. He didn't trust them, but for enough money, they could be useful.

The rebels, starting with Elsa's great-grandmother and Grady's grandfather, had been setting aside a fund to buy the railroad for as long as there had been an underground movement. They had a substantial amount of coin saved.

"You can't buy the railroad," Malcolm shouted, his attention diverted. Foam appeared at the sound of his mouth as he turned back to Mason. "You could never afford it."

Jaxon lunged for the far door, once more coming up short as Kurt slammed him into a wall, rotating Jaxon's shoulder to an impossible angle.

Jaxon screeched, his cheek pressed flat. "I'll still find some way to make Elsa pay."

Mason watched, his lip twitching. The bastard deserved a little pain for all the pain he'd caused with his greed and his lies. Elsa wouldn't have to watch her back anymore. Mason was glad they'd intercepted these two at last. They wouldn't be causing trouble for much longer. Not if Grady did what was necessary.

CHAPTER 35: ELSA

It was almost sundown and the bright red orb blazed above the western horizon as it dropped like a coin through a slot into a bank of bright pink and gray clouds. Elsa had never seen such a stunning display. The entire population of Salt Lake, including the rebels, the railroad workers, hundreds of former GreenCorps soldiers, and the Saints, had stormed the garrison and hauled out Malcolm and Jaxon McCoy. They were going to be held accountable for many of the GreenCorps' atrocities.

Most of the crowd waited for the last troops to emerge with the captured leaders.

Tatsuda and Ginger held hands beside Janna and her boyfriend, Clark. Grady and Darren stepped forward as a group emerged from the captured garrison. Walker wrapped his arm around Elsa's shoulder, squeezing, as Caitlyn and Mason returned. A dozen Saints and an equal number of rebels escorting a group of important prisoners accompanied them. Reaching the waiting rebel leaders, Caitlyn and Mason remained beside their prisoners, which included three lesser GreenCorps officers, a dozen cowed men in suits, and Malcolm and Jaxon McCoy.

Father and son stood in chains near the train platform while Grady spoke. "We have some conditions you must agree to before we put most of you on a train and escort you back to Denver."

Elsa's feet shifted. Exile was too good for the McCoys. She hoped Grady had another plan for them.

Neither of the McCoys said anything as Grady continued. "Any remaining GreenCorps troops need to withdraw from Salt Lake City and pull out of Utah. Permanently. Word will go out that we've disbanded their army. None of you are welcome outside of Denver. Go home and don't come back." Grady's steel-like voice left no room for doubt. He turned to the McCoys. "You two are facing more serious charges for your crimes and inhumane acts."

Elsa held her breath, waiting for their sentence.

"I don't recognize your authority!" screamed Malcolm McCoy. "This city is full of worthless, murdering criminals. They killed my Jace. We came here to bring back the law. How dare you send me away when the bitch that murdered my son walks free?" His face grew redder, an unhealthy florid color as he ranted. He directed most of his tirade at Grady and Elsa, but turned to yell at Ginger at the end. Though handcuffed, he pointed a knobby finger in her direction.

"You're my daughter. You can't let them do this to me. Convince them to let me go, and I'll let you work for any publishing company you want."

Ginger shook her head. "It's too late, Father. This is my home now." She buried her face in Tatsuda's shoulder. It didn't matter where they went, those two were staunch friends. They'd be fine together wherever they lived.

Elsa smiled. Much like herself and Walker, Caitlyn and Mason, and she suspected, the Clark guy who was with Janna. Clark looked at Janna like the sun rose and fell with her, and she returned his look. Elsa was happy for her long-time friend. Janna had been through a lot this year and deserved to find happiness. Satisfaction filled Elsa with how the fight for Salt Lake City had turned out to be the final fight for freedom. The rebels had worked so hard and the reward had been

GreenCorps crumbling like a sandcastle when their leadership was challenged.

"You're all cowards. I want a trial back in Denver. My son and I deserve better."

Elsa's attention returned to Malcolm, tuning out his rant. Foam sprayed from his mouth and he turned an unhealthy shade of grayish-red. His voice cut off mid-sentence. He clutched his left arm. He staggered to the side, his leg chains clanking. His mouth moved again, but made no sound. That couldn't be good.

"Oh no," said Ginger, her face turning pale. "His heart." She rushed forward, but her father collapsed to the pavement, grabbing his arm. He let out a deep groan and slumped flat, mouthing something to his daughter.

Caitlyn dashed forward too—always the medic. Crouching by McCoy senior's side, she checked his pulse and shook her head, saying something quiet to Ginger.

Elsa had been too far away to hear Malcolm McCoy's last words but was close enough she'd seen when he died, his body becoming still and his gaze vacant.

Ginger closed her father's eyes. She looked up with red-rimmed eyes, tears streaming down her cheeks. He was her father, after all, even if he'd been controlling and unkind. "He couldn't get past Jace dying here. It's almost fitting that this is where the great Malcolm McCoy died, too." She glanced up at her brother, who avoided her gaze. He hadn't said anything yet. Perhaps Jaxon was in shock.

Grady strode past them while Ginger ran back to Tatsuda, who pulled her into a friendly hug.

Grady held up his hands and the waiting crowd hushed. "Without Malcolm McCoy, GreenCorps is done. We have time to rebuild and hold an election. To bring back democracy."

"Grady for President," called Mason. Everyone on the platform joined the chant, and then the crowd picked it up, roaring it into the dimming light as twilight fell on a once more, free Salt Lake City.

Grady and Darren stood apart, strange smiles on their faces. They'd worked for this for a long time.

From out of nowhere, Jaxon launched himself at Elsa with a snarl. He'd gotten his hands free, though his feet remained shackled. "You weren't happy killing my brother. Now you're responsible for my father's death, too." His lunge must have surprised his guards because he got past them.

Elsa stood her ground and slipped her knife from its sheath. Her eyes narrowed as she focused, blocking out everything else but the advancing Jaxon McCoy. This had started with him. Maybe that's how it also had to end. "Those were accidents, but if you insist, I'll fight you. I'm sick of being pushed around and I'm not running anymore." It was freeing that he no longer had power over her. With her sister and the kids free, Jaxon McCoy didn't matter.

Before Jaxon reached her, Walker tackled him, driving Jaxon into the hard ground, a poof of dust rising in a cloud.

She winced. That would have hurt. "He doesn't deserve a life in exile in Denver. He'll cause more trouble." She appealed to Grady, who nodded.

Walker stood up and dusted off his pants. "Lock him up and keep watch. He's slippery."

"For his crimes on behalf of GreenCorps, I sentence Jaxon McCoy to life in prison," said Grady. "Take him away."

"You can't do this," Jaxon repeated this several times as Darren and half a dozen others forced him back toward the jail and the overrun garrison, now controlled by the people of the West.

Elsa stepped back, and Walker's arms wrapped around her, holding her close. Somehow, they'd won, the rebels and the Saints. They'd won the right to rebuild and to make a society where everyday people had a voice. They would have fair access to food and water. Grady wouldn't allow anyone to be sold south ever again. She couldn't ask for more, even if Wade had disappeared, escaping justice. Reports said someone matching his description had hopped a train south. He might cause trouble yet, but they'd track him down if possible with rebel contacts.

She leaned back against Walker, and his arms tightened. With Grady sentencing the GreenCorps executives, it was sinking in. They'd won. Not a bad year's work for a heapster and a train hopper. She glanced around at the surrounding group. She couldn't have dreamed of this sense of family and belonging when she'd been shoveling guck in her reeking tunnels of the Heap with Granny.

The image of the tube and the tingling sensation of the first moment she'd held it flashed through her mind. The metal tube had been a treasure beyond value and had changed her life, opening a whole new world.

Elsa grinned, knowing exactly where she wanted to go next. She and Walker would have to add on to the cabin, so they had a place for all their friends and family to stay whenever they visited.

She wanted to go home.

CHAPTER 36:
HOMECOMING

Despite their victory, Elsa and her friends agreed to stay in Salt Lake City for the rest of the summer. Grady needed people he could trust to start the slow process of changing their society. Three months after their victory, Elsa looked back from trackside to the cluster of people approaching on the nearby train platform. They were here to say farewell. The few trees beyond the fence had a smattering of yellow leaves and the early morning air contained a chill. She zipped her jacket higher and adjusted her gloves.

This time, she and Walker were the ones leaving. For the first time since she'd left SoCal a year and a half ago, they would ride in a passenger car on the train instead of hopping. With Grady in charge, anyone could ride the rails for a nominal fee. The cost of moving people was insignificant compared to the wealth generated by the movement and sale of goods. Plus, without GreenCorps taking the harvests, thousands of farmers had money for themselves to spend on items they ordered from the East, all delivered by train. Grady's people and the railroad officials worked together to keep prices fair.

Elsa glanced at Walker and smiled, twirling the plain silver band on her left hand.

He grinned, her favorite lopsided one. "We'll be back. It isn't goodbye forever." He kissed her temple. "Us hoppers won't stay in one place forever, even if we have a home now."

"President Grady will do a great job," Elsa said. They'd stayed in the city until the first election of West America had concluded. As expected, Grady had been elected by the masses, receiving votes from SoCal, Texas, Utah, Denver, and from all over the scattered West. The people chose freedom.

Tatsuda was the first of their friends to reach them. He squeezed Elsa in a crushing hug. "No need to look so glum about leaving me behind. I'll follow the map Walker made and visit in the spring."

"Me too," said Ginger. She held Rose by one hand and Charlie by the other.

Elsa knelt to give her nieces gentle hugs, grateful for the last few months when she'd gotten to know them. Charlie gave her a messy kiss on the cheek. Elsa looked up. "We should have the addition on the cabin ready by then. You're always welcome." A lump formed in her throat.

"Don't forget, you promised to come this way next summer," said Avery. She handed little Aki to Darren. As soon as the city was secured, he'd retrieved Avery and her girls from the mountains. She and Darren spent a lot of time together. There had been no discussion about their status, but Elsa found it comforting that her sister had someone kind looking out for her. Tatsuda and Ginger were staying in the city too and after their time in SoCal, they remained close to Avery.

Elsa held her sister tight, tears pricking her eyes. At least this time when Elsa left, she got to say goodbye and could trust that her sister would be safe.

Darren winked and smiled his friendly, toothy smile. "I'll take good care of your family."

Elsa swallowed. Saying goodbye was harder than anticipated.

Yesterday she'd seen Janna and Clark off. They'd left with a group returning to the Saints. She was happy those two had found each other amidst all the trouble. She'd been surprised to learn that Clark was Caitlyn's brother-in-law. For all the world had opened up, it was still small in some ways.

The last two to step forward to say goodbye were Caitlyn and Mason. Caitlyn hugged them both and kissed Walker. His eyes widened, and Elsa chuckled at his expression. Mason shot his wife a glare, but nobody believed he was annoyed. Turning to Elsa, he smiled, an uncommon expression for his usually impassive face. He surprised Elsa with a tight hug and another for Walker.

"Don't be strangers," Mason said. "We're leaving for the farm next week, but if you drag yourself as far as Salt Lake City, what's another day to our farm?"

"I'm glad Caitlyn gets to have new chickens and to see her cat," said Elsa. "We'll come to check everything out and catch-up next summer."

"We might get a dog too," said Mason, putting his arm around his wife.

Hayden hovered on the fringes apart from the others. Elsa gave him a nod. He'd taken a beating to keep them free; she wouldn't forget he'd helped when they needed it. He and Walker had spoken several times this summer. While they'd never be as close as their traveling days, they seemed at peace with their current relationship.

A railwayman stopped nearby. "All aboard. Anyone headed south to Reno, Sacramento, or Long Beach. Time to go." He bounded up the stairs to the passenger car and disappeared inside.

Elsa took a deep breath. With a last glance over her shoulder at their family, she and Walker climbed the steps and hurried inside, taking a bench seat beside the window.

As the train lurched forward, tears filled Elsa's eyes. For once, she let them fall. Walker took her hand and squeezed as they left Salt Lake City, the buildings, then the flat countryside rolling by in a blur.

She would miss everyone, but couldn't wait to start her next adventure.

* * *

Mason stole a glance at Caitlyn in the seat of the borrowed wagon as it bumped along the dusty road. Though it was late in the season, they'd bought a couple of pigs, a new goat, a dozen hens, and a rooster. They'd also bought feed for the animals and supplies to get them through another long winter on their own.

He smiled, the skin by his eyes crinkled as he held back a laugh. Caitlyn kept sneaking peeks into the back where her new creatures were traveling. Once they were settled, they planned to try for children too. Caitlyn loved having young ones to take care of and he liked the idea. After all these years as a wandering rebel, it was time to be a farmer.

* * *

By mid-afternoon, Elsa and Walker emerged from the forest above the lake. He took her hand at the last viewpoint overlooking Lake Tahoe. They were on the land where he always said he felt most at home. Where he belonged. She breathed in the fresh air, filling her lungs. They'd camped once on the way from Reno but were almost there. The expanse of turquoise water below still took her breath away.

"Do you think the cabin cat will still be there?" Elsa adjusted her loaded backpack.

"Probably," said Walker. "She's got a good thing, though she's going to have to learn to share the place again." His gaze returned to the lake below, where it lay surrounded by a forest of evergreens interspersed with patches of yellow, orange, and red. The fall colors were in all their glory, a riot of brilliance that seemed welcoming after their journey.

Excitement raced through her veins at the possibilities for the next stage in her life. She and Walker could stay here and live a self-sufficient life—one they'd help to earn. They wouldn't need to leave for a long time, other than the promised visits next summer. Tucked in Elsa's pack were seeds for several kinds of fruit and nut trees and others for a vegetable garden. This place was the reward for all the hardships they'd endured—all the stress, pain, and hard work of the last year and a half.

"Let's go home," said Walker, turning for the cabin, his gray eyes alight.

Elsa smiled. "Let's catch some fish for dinner. It's going to be a perfect evening for the canoe." The tingly feeling she'd always associated with treasure came to her as they scrambled down one last steep trail. Reaching the bottom, a sandy beach stretched in both directions, with their cabin nestled against the face of a cliff.

Her heart was full. She was home.

The Edge of Life

Love and Survival During the Apocalypse

CHAPTER 1: KAT

Today would be a carbon copy of hundreds that had preceded it. Once, every day had seemed new and fresh, now each was another obstacle to overcome. Kat smothered the intrusive thoughts as she stress-bit the inside of her lower lip, a distraction while she searched the radio for something cheerful to get her through her Friday morning commute. Yesterday, she'd forgotten her phone at work and already she missed her music.

"As asteroid 2025 NR hurtles toward Earth, scientists forecast…" Kat changed the radio station. Nope. Not cheerful.

"Forest fires rage throughout the Pacific Northwest and into Canada, ahead of the summer forest fire season…" She pushed a different button.

"April temperatures break the one hundred eighty-year record…" She stabbed another button, searching for something less depressing.

"Climate change…"

"No," she said, pushing yet another.

"Riots last night in Portland and LA mirror…"

"Flooding along the Columbia…"

"Reduced snowpack and high temperatures combine…"

"The mass shooting at Snake River Elementary was the fourth shooting this…"

She wanted to scream, but fought the impulse and took a deep breath. "Last chance," she said with a final stab.

"Near miss forecasted for asteroid…"

"The umpteenth 'near miss' this year, blah blah blah," said Kat as she snapped off the radio. She forced her clenched jaw to relax. "How many million miles away is this one?" Rolling her eyes as she took in the now ominous morning sunshine. "Why can't one station play music?"

Tulips, daffodils, and heather blooms provided splashes of much-needed color as she passed the nearby houses and townhouses. Maybe flowers could help her be more positive. Spring had arrived and with it the promise of the upcoming summer vacation. Another six weeks of school until she was free. Though, with all the doom and gloom predicted, there'd be nowhere left to go. The last few summers had been similar. Climate change, protests, and misery. Before that, the pandemic. She wished there was something to look forward to besides staying home.

Kat used to love her job, but now she couldn't wait for the holidays, for time away from work. She kept the radio off and drove the rest of the way in silence. Arriving at the three-story stone building outside Seattle that housed the private school where she taught, she parked in the staff lot. Her sport model crimson hybrid Camry stuck out like a sore thumb in the expanse of black and white SUVs. It had been her only major purchase since Mark died two years ago. He wouldn't have liked her flashy car, but for her, its vibrant color had been the draw.

Her eyes swam with tears at the thought of her late husband. "Get a hold of yourself, Mrs. Davies. Time to be a teacher," she muttered. Collecting her book and lunch bag from the passenger seat, Kat blinked and checked her mascara in the overhead mirror. She pasted on a smile. Fake it till you make it. She might not be the same person she used to be, but she could pretend.

It didn't matter how difficult the rest of her life was, this was the one place she needed to be friendly and pleasant, at least to the students. Her starring role was as her old self, the version that hadn't been widowed at twenty-eight. The parking lot filled as her colleagues arrived. Not wanting to walk in with anyone and be forced to chitchat, Kat hurried, glad that her sensible shoes made it easy to escape into the cool hallway inside.

She signed in and kept moving, not making eye contact with anyone. She bypassed the staff room and hustled up the stairs, taking them two at a time to the second floor where her classroom was located. Entering, she unpacked her tea, found the forgotten phone, and turned on her favorite playlist to block the incessant hum of the fluorescent lights.

She shifted into teacher mode and opened the window to reduce the ever-present underlying scents of dust, whiteboard marker, and stale lunches. She straightened desks, posted the schedule, and checked her email to ensure no last-minute changes were required to the day's plan.

When the students shuffled in, she greeted each by name and with a smile. Kat poured energy into her performance, making sure to hear from each student at least twice that day, keeping a mental tally in her head. She called on the quiet students to ensure they were included and checked in on the few who needed extra help. She'd done this for so long, her friendly teacher role had become automatic.

She also made side deals with two students to reduce their required homework, knowing it was a struggle. The last thing was a verbal "ticket out the door" math question. She personalized each question, making sure it was challenging enough to be interesting, but not too difficult for the student to answer. Correct answers got a high five and a goodbye with their name that let each student know they were valued. The routine also kept the kids from giving her unwanted hugs.

Kat had sorted the numerous crises for the ten-year-olds in their Kelly green and crisp white uniforms, pretending she was doing more than going through the motions. Her performance mattered. It wasn't the students' fault that her heart was numb and encased in ice.

Sipping tea, she marked the work needed for Monday and prepped her day plans for next week. She preferred to be a week ahead, rather than the one day required by the school. You never knew when things wouldn't go according to plan. She'd learned that the hard way.

Just before five, Kat scurried out to her car with a vague wave toward the other fifth-grade teacher from across the hall, who was also on her way out.

"TGIF," said Tracy. "That sounded like a great lesson on the rock cycle. Maybe I could borrow some samples next week. You have any weekend plans?"

Kat smiled on cue, the last toothy one until Monday. Her cheek muscles ached from over-use. "Not really. See you Monday." She headed in the opposite direction.

Getting in her car, Kat relaxed her face, massaging the tight muscles along her jaw. Once the tension eased a bit, she turned on the radio to check the traffic for the route home. Seattle and the outlying area were gridlocked at the best of times, let alone during Friday afternoon rush hour. She had to make it home; then the weekend was hers, hers to do with as she pleased. Her hands shook as she drove. All week she'd been anticipating peace and oblivion.

One nagging doubt plagued her as she drove. She couldn't shake the idea that she'd promised someone something, but she couldn't recall what. Her brow furrowed. It wasn't a birthday or her parents' anniversary. She hadn't spoken to them in months, so that wasn't it. The sense that she'd forgotten something persisted.

She parked outside her townhouse and hurried upstairs. Kicking off her shoes with a sigh of sheer pleasure, she threw her bag inside by the door and headed straight for the cabinet over the stove with the alcohol. She needed a drink.

Kat opened the fresh sapphire-colored bottle of Bombay gin, took down a large glass from the cupboard, and free-poured a generous measure into the bottom. She sliced a lime from the fridge into wedges and rinsed the knife and cutting board. The tonic, pre-chilled in the fridge, fizzed when opened, the sound making her mouth water. She swallowed in anticipation. She filled the glass three-quarters full and squeezed in two lime chunks, licking the excess from her fingers because she loved the tang. Adding four ice cubes, her drink was perfect.

Taking it in both hands, she breathed deep, inhaling the bubbling citrus scent. Without thought, Kat tipped it back and gulped down half. The bite of alcohol was strong and delicious. Her hands shook as she let the rest wash down her throat. Setting her empty glass down, she sighed. With a deep breath, she made a second, stronger drink, ignoring the nagging voice inside that told her to go slow. The ritual was calming and her hands no longer trembled as she carried it to the couch and sat, putting up her feet. It was easier not to think when she drank.

Kat didn't bother with the TV, but instead stared out the window, though she didn't pay attention to the view. She sipped, savoring her drink, noticing how each swallow slid down her throat. She didn't touch a drop Monday to Thursday, but from Friday to Sunday she could do what she liked, beholden to nobody.

Three drinks later, Kat wobbled to the fridge to see if she'd bother with food. Many Fridays, she preferred to drink her dinner because cooking seemed like too much work. Each week on the way home, she told herself to order something if she didn't want to cook, but more often than not, she didn't. The first drink wasn't a problem, but by the time she had a second, it was never worth the effort to do more than make another drink, despite the twinge of guilt about wasting her life. She shouldn't be this way, but she didn't have a reason to change.

Her phone rang, but she let it go to voicemail. Three minutes later, it started again, the ringtone piercing and setting her teeth on edge. She glanced at the phone where it was charging and exhaled a mouthful of air in disgust before muting the sound. Nick knew better than to call on a Friday. What the hell did he want? After a hectic week, she didn't feel like talking.

Her phone chimed with a text moments later. God, he was persistent tonight. She squinted, trying to make out the jumble of words on the screen, but they were difficult to read.

"Shit," she said, deciphering enough to get the idea.

"Be there in ten with pizza."

"Shit, shit, shit."

She unlocked her front door, staggered back to the couch, and sat while she waited for her best friend to arrive with dinner and a lecture. She sat up straight, trying to look sober.

Nick didn't bother ringing the bell, knowing she hated the loud noise. He entered, two large pizzas in hand. The rich scent of cheese, tomatoes, and basil filled her living room. It smelled better than anything in her fridge. Maybe this could work.

He took one look at her and put the pizzas down. His shoulders slumped.

"I'm already too late." He flipped open the top box and grabbed a slice.

"Too late?" she said, trying to focus on him while the room spun. Feeling proud for covering her inebriation so well, she lurched to her feet and tripped over her shoes lying on the floor. She crawled a few steps and got to her feet, her cheeks burning.

"Kat, you promised, remember?" said Nick, his mouth full. "One drink to relax, then we'd have pizza and watch a movie."

"Just had one," she said, concentrating on walking in a straight line. The floor buckled and swam as she made her way toward the pizza. She'd been stupid to think he wouldn't notice.

"Three drinks or four?" he said, lifting the bottle of gin. "Kat, what are we going to do with you?" His tone was concerned. "Can I help?"

"Can't do nothing," she said as she chose a wedge of pizza with ham, pineapple, and bacon, her usual favorite. Her words might be flippant, but she was disappointed in herself. Nick was a good friend and deserved better. She wished she'd remembered their plans.

"I'm starting to think that's true. You won't come to our place. You won't meet us anywhere and you never answer your phone. As far as I can tell, all you do is work and drink."

She shrugged and took a big bite. She chewed while thinking of a reply, her brain functioning slower than usual. "I don't drink all week. I just need to blow off a little steam."

She scowled, feeling resentful. He had no idea.

"Kat, I'm worried about you. The only time you aren't alone is when I inflict myself upon you. You don't see anyone else. Do you?"

"Don't want to," she mumbled around another bite of pizza. The sauce was tangy, still hot, and oh so delicious. A niggling voice in her head called her a liar, but she squashed it and focused on the pizza.

"Are you looking forward to time off work, your summer holiday? What have you got planned?" He grabbed a slice and sat.

"Nothing much," she said with a shrug. She hadn't wanted to make plans because she didn't know what would help her feel more connected again. The look in his eyes made her cringe inside. He was up to something.

"We should plan something. We used to hike all the time."

The pizza stuck in her throat and she glanced at her empty glass with longing.

"We should pick a day for hiking every weekend. Every Sunday? Start right away. No need to wait for summer. Jake can join when he's free. I have another friend who needs to get out, too. We should all go."

She didn't feel well. The pizza in her stomach had become a greasy lump. She set her half-eaten slice down in the box and walked on unsteady legs back to the couch, the room spinning.

Nick's eyes held concern as he put two slices of pizza on his plate and her partial piece on another. He carried them to the coffee table as he sat at the opposite end of the couch. At least she hadn't driven him away. Even in her foggy state, she recognized she needed to meet his efforts part way. She didn't want him to give up or think she was hopeless.

"Who else for hiking?" She didn't want to go, but it might be easier to agree. She could always not show up or cancel. Or hike and get out of this place with all its terrible memories.

"A friend. You might have met him years ago in university."

"Ugh, this isn't a set-up, is it?" She wasn't ready to consider the idea.

"No way. I wouldn't do that without permission, and you don't like surprises. I just want to spend time with both of you, and I don't have a lot of spare time. If I double up, I can see you twice as often." He nudged the plate in her direction.

He seemed sincere. She picked up the pizza and nibbled. "Lucky us."

"That's a resounding yes, then?" He perked up, his tone hopeful.

"I guess."

"Last week you freaked me out."

"What happened last week?" She wracked her brain but came up empty.

"You don't remember, do you?" He slumped back on the couch.

She shrugged and shook her head. She took another bite of pizza, humoring her friend. Dinner was a good idea.

"You didn't answer your phone or your doorbell even though that morning you said you'd be here, and your car was parked out front. I wanted to tell you about my big discovery at work. You used to love to hear about comets and meteors and space dust."

"I would still like to hear." She eyed her drink where she'd left it on the counter.

"Kat, your door wasn't locked, and I came in and found you on the floor. I found you on the floor, unconscious, and passed out cold. I put you to bed and came back early on Sunday. We made this plan for tonight."

"I don't remember." She swallowed, her food tasting like cardboard as she touched her forehead, remembering the goose egg.

"You sobered up some on Sunday and we talked. You admitted that you blackout every weekend. You agreed to try not to this weekend. I don't want to babysit you, but if I can help be a distraction until you break the habit, I will."

Tears leaked down her face at his words. She seemed to have no control. What was wrong with her? Maybe not remembering what she'd done was better. She was such a mess.

Nick took her hand in his. "Mark wouldn't want you to mourn him this way."

"Mark isn't here." It came out sharper than she expected. The usual filter had fallen off her mouth and emotions. "He doesn't get a vote."

"You're acting like you're dead, too." Nick squeezed her hand and let go. "I want to tell you about my cool discovery. If you forget, I'll tell you again on Sunday. I want to share it with you like I used to."

"I don't want your pity time," mumbled Kat as she stared at the floor. She needed to clean. Crumbs and dusty balls of hair floated along the edge of the baseboards and she couldn't remember the last time she'd swept or washed anything other than a dish. Afraid she might have offended him, she forced herself to make eye contact and saw he was smiling. Why was he being so kind? She didn't deserve it.

"It isn't pity," said Nick. "I'm looking to get my friend back. This is purely selfish."

She didn't believe him, but got up to collect her drink. She could sip while she listened.

Nick followed her to the counter, his hands jammed in his front pockets. His eyes looked sad, and she wished she could stop hurting him. She stopped with the glass halfway to her mouth and handed it to him. He gave her a tremulous smile and emptied her gin and tonic down the sink; the ice clinking on the stainless steel.

She didn't say a word, but the drink being gone came as a relief. She picked up the bottle and handed it to him with shaking hands.

He took the remainder of the gin and dumped it with a gurgling sound, the ice cubes bumping into each other, clinking as they swirled around the drain. She closed her eyes, concentrating on her breathing. It would be okay.

"You might be angry, but you need help."

Nick's voice brought her back to the moment. She looked at him and nodded. How did she explain she was empty inside?

"Can I have a hug?" Stabbing pains in her chest accompanied her request. From her, it was an unusual request. Most of the time, she preferred not to be touched. It shouldn't hurt to let herself feel.

Nick held out his arms and gave her a squeeze that loosened some of her pent-up angst and loneliness. She rested her head on his shoulder for a minute before stepping away. She needed to try harder to get her life back.

She took a deep breath and swiped the tears from her cheeks with her hands. "Let's hear about your space dust."

Chapter 2: Ryan

Ryan glanced at the clock. It was late enough that Nick should be awake. Dreading the task, he called his friend, who answered on the second ring.

"Hey, Ryan. What's up? You running late?"

"Nick, sorry. I have to cancel. I like the idea of a hike, but not this week. I just arrived at the office." Ryan ran his fingers through his hair, standing it on end. He didn't like to disappoint his closest friend.

On the other end of the line, Nick paused. "Again?"

Even though his friend sounded understanding, it still didn't make Ryan feel any less like a flake.

"Yeah, sorry. I'm up for a promotion soon. I'm on track to make partner in six years, so I need to keep up my hours. If you're available, we could do lunch this week, say on Tuesday. My treat." He hated canceling, but he'd woken up at four and hadn't dared to wait around for a nine o'clock hike. He needed to keep his mind occupied.

"I'd like that," said Nick. "There's something I want to talk to you about. In-person, if that's okay. Something I found at work."

His discovery couldn't be that awesome because Nick's excitement level seemed more muted than usual.

"Sure. We can text on Monday to set up a place. Enjoy the hike."

Ryan hung up and swiveled his black leather office chair to take in his cramped office. At least there was a window, as this was just about the only view he saw nowadays. More downtown office towers filled the skyline, but it was better than the cubbyhole he'd used as a junior associate his first two years at Goodrich, Singh, and Hardcastle.

Though it was Sunday, he put his head down and worked, concentrating on writing the brief a partner wanted later this week.

He went over it a dozen times before he could no longer ignore his stomach rumbling, reminding him he hadn't eaten yet. He'd finished, ahead of schedule. Ryan prided himself on getting everything done early. He checked his phone for the first time since lunch. Nine thirty. He'd been here for fourteen hours with only a sandwich, but he'd come in because it was easier to avoid distractions here than at home. Writing his hours on his timesheet, he stood as he gathered his laptop. He'd grab a bite on the way home. He couldn't remember his last home-cooked meal. Or rather, he could, but he didn't want to. It always led to him feeling foolish, rejected, and ended with crushing regret.

Ryan drove home, the streets dark and quiet this time of night, making it an easier commute than weekday Seattle traffic. He collected his mail from the lobby on the way up to his seventh-floor apartment, his bag of chicken tacos in hand. The apartment was quiet and smelled of unwashed laundry with a hint of garbage. He hated coming home to an empty apartment night after night. He dragged one of his two kitchen chairs into position and flicked on the TV, wishing for a comfy chair instead of the rigid remnants that had been left behind.

The wall-mounted wide-screen TV and the surround-sound speakers were the only things in the otherwise barren living room. When Heather had annihilated him last year, she'd taken the couch and loveseat, lamps, coffee table, and end tables when she moved out. She'd taken the artwork from the walls and every symbol of their life together. Including the other chairs, the table, and… his heart; leaving him as empty and hollow as his apartment.

He hadn't gotten around to replacing anything. Thankfully, he wasn't here often enough. Of course, she'd left the bed, the last thing he wanted. He slept on it because it was softer than the floor, but he should have it replaced.

When he finished dinner, he sat for half an hour, letting his food digest before he changed into workout clothes and did four reps of his exercises, each with a dozen weighted arm curls and lifts, twenty-five each of sit-ups, push-ups, and squats. After a quick shower, he set an alarm for four forty-five a.m. as Monday was a run day. He had to go early in order to clean up and be at work by seven a.m. He'd have to keep the pace up to get in his eight miles.

Before he fell asleep, he remembered Nick had mentioned a discovery at the observatory. He made a mental note to be sure to ask for details on Tuesday.

* * *

When Tuesday morning rolled around and Ryan's alarm woke him for work, he was covered in sweat and his heart pounded against his ribs. He'd been dreaming about Heather again. This time when he'd proposed, he was naked and in front of all their watching friends. When she'd said "no" she'd pointed and laughed, joined by everyone he knew. Their cruel laughter echoed through the room. His mom had shaken her head and turned away, her lip curling in disgust. The alarm had been a game show buzzer for the wrong answer.

Despite the venue changing, the dream wasn't much different from the nightmare reality. No one else had witnessed his humiliation, but he'd caught Heather cheating. In the subsequent fight, she'd laughed and said she would have refused his proposal. She'd lived with him for two years, but it turned out she'd never loved him. He hadn't expected the words that followed and tore through his soul. "Are you kidding me? I'd never marry an unfeeling bastard like you." It had shocked him to his core. He'd worked hard to make a better life for the two of them, but she'd only felt neglected.

He hadn't trusted himself since. His perception of reality and where he fit in relation to others must not be what he thought.

Shouldn't he have seen it coming instead of being blindsided? Perhaps that was why he worked so hard now. It wasn't enough to think he was working long hours; they had to be excessive to impress the partners.

He hopped in the shower, determined not to think about Heather anymore or to allow lingering thoughts of her to ruin his morning. It worked because his day went as they typically did, spent writing briefs that those above him on the food chain would take credit for until he left work at eleven fifty to meet Nick, as promised. They'd agreed to meet before the downtown lunch rush.

Nick was seated when he arrived at the hole-in-the-wall sushi spot they favored. His friend looked stressed; his forehead creased more than it should be at thirty-one years of age. Did he also look that weary?

"What's up?" Ryan slid into his seat after placing his order at the counter.

"I might need new friends," said Nick. "Ones willing to spend time with me."

"We can't all be that bad," said Ryan as he sipped his ice water.

"Between you and Kat, it's a tie." Nick held his hands up as though he surrendered.

"Kat, the bubbly elementary school teacher you tried to set me up with right after university? Didn't she marry some uptight guy named Matt or Mark or something? You haven't mentioned her in years. I assumed you'd lost touch. What's she doing wrong? Working too hard, like me?" He threw that out there, knowing that was why Nick worried. Broken-hearted Ryan, who lived at the office and had no life.

"Her Mark died two years ago. A heart attack at work. A heart condition that nobody knew about. He keeled over one day. They'd been married less than a year." Nick frowned and looked out the window.

Ryan felt like shit for not remembering. He recalled hearing about the tragedy. He hadn't meant to shove his foot in his mouth. "That's horrible. How does that make her a rotten friend?" He didn't see the connection, but his heart went out to the poor girl. They might have something in common now, even if he hadn't thought so in the past. She'd seemed like someone whose life had always been perfect.

"She was devastated and wanted to be alone, so I gave her space. I tried to reconnect a few times, but kept getting the brush off. I asked around and nobody had seen her in ages. I hadn't heard from her in forever and thought she might need someone to talk to or hang out with, so I tried again." Nick's voice sounded strained, and he poured himself another steaming cup of green tea.

Ryan sat up straight. Nick seldom showed this much emotion. Perhaps he needed a friend to talk to if something was troubling him.

"What happened?"

Nick hesitated before speaking. "A couple of weeks ago, I got pushy and Kat and I made plans. When she blew me off, I checked on her and found her passed out dead drunk on the floor. She'd smashed her head. Had a lump the size of an egg on her head." He swallowed and looked out the window, his eyes moist.

Ryan pretended not to notice. Finding a friend in that condition would be difficult.

"That doesn't sound like the person you tried to get me to date," said Ryan with a frown. He hoped it wasn't a setup now. She sounded like a real mess. At least he was productive in his heartache. He'd never been in better shape and had billed an extra four hundred hours last year. "If I recall, you warned me she was almost too happy and positive, if that's a thing."

"Not the case now. It wasn't then either. I just figured that would be your first impression because that's the face she shows to the world. The thing is, that isn't even the worst."

Ryan waited.

"I went back a couple of mornings later, and we talked. What I'd seen was the tip of the iceberg. I read between the lines and was horrified. It's like she's a different person. She drinks until she blacks out every night every weekend. For two years. How could I not have noticed?"

"You have your own life," said Ryan. "We're all busy. She probably didn't want you to know. If she hid it from you, maybe she hid it from everyone." She sounded like a disaster. He grimaced to himself; to be honest, he wasn't much better.

"She hasn't lost her job because nobody knows or cares what she does on weekends and holidays. She's kept it secret because she holds it together during the week."

"It could be worse. She might have lost her job."

Nick shrugged. "It's bad enough. We made plans for last Friday night. She forgot and was smashed by the time I got to her place, barely an hour after she got home from work. She didn't remember talking to me the previous weekend. I have to do something."

"You aren't her babysitter. It's been like two years. Isn't it time she pulled up her big-girl pants and moved on with her life?" Was that advice intended for himself too, to get over it and move on? Ryan flattened his mouth into a frown.

"Easier said than done. Kat needs help, but it kinda sucks trying to help when she doesn't want me to interfere. She's trying to drink herself to death. She didn't use to drink more than the odd hard lemonade at a barbeque."

"Maybe you just saw her on a bad day?" said Ryan.

"Every Friday, Saturday, and Sunday? That's a lot of bad days."

"I can't picture that," said Ryan. "Thanks," he said to the server who dropped off their orders. He poured soy sauce into a dish and separated his chopsticks.

"Will you help me?" Nick dipped his sashimi in soy. "I was hoping you would come hiking with us, make it a group thing. Jake will come too when he's free. There's twice I'm busy on Sunday with work commitments and I need to know that someone will get her out of her house, whether she wants to or not."

"Maybe she wants to wallow," said Ryan as he ate. He didn't mean to sound unsympathetic.

"It's been two years. I don't know where the hell her family has gone, but they aren't helping. She's isolated and alone. That isn't good for anyone."

"Okay." Ryan's heart wasn't in it, but he owed Nick. Nick was awesome and had taken care of everyone at one time or another. Back in their university days, they used to joke, "Nick's your buddy, Nick's your pal, Nick won't make you clean it up if you puke in his car." Nick helped people, and it appeared Kat was his new project, and Ryan owed him for kicking his ass into gear when Heather left.

"Thanks," said Nick as he popped another chunk of California roll into his mouth.

"So, let's hear about this discovery," said Ryan, switching to a happier topic. He wanted to show that he was a decent friend.

"It's that asteroid they're talking about on the news. Did you notice its name?"

Ryan shook his head. "Haven't there been like six already this year?"

Nick laughed. "Nope. Three. But the recent one, the one they're talking about this week, it's my discovery. Its name is the year, cause that's when I discovered it, and my initials. It isn't too far away, but nobody had seen it before because the Sun was in the way. It's called 2025 NR. I discovered it and I've been assigned to observe it. I have to figure out its final trajectory, where it will go after it passes by Earth, and if it will be back."

"Is it one that will make that Sentry list you mentioned, the one that ranks potential threats?" Ryan leaned back to listen to his friend.

Nick shifted forward with a smile. "It's over 800 meters…"

* * *

Findings by Nick Rhodes as of April 15, 2025

2025 NR was discovered on April 12, 2025, by a camera mounted on a telescope.

<u>Preliminary Findings:</u>

Estimated diameter: 825 m +/- 100 m or 0.825 km +/- 0.100 km

Estimated speed: 23.95 km/s +/- 5.0 km/s

Initial threat assessment: Should be added to the Sentry Table as a precaution.

<u>Recommended Action</u>: Further monitoring to increase data.

Conditions affecting visibility: weather, position relative to the Sun, phase of the Moon

1. Assess asteroid orbit for a minimum of fourteen days.

2. Follow-up observations after the initial window to increase the accuracy of orbit determination.

3. Calculate if, when, and where the orbital may intersect with Earth in the future (as defined by within the next 200 years).

Conclusion: At this time, there is too little data to make an estimate of the probability of an impact event on Earth.

Acknowledgments

It seems incredible that I was sitting on close to 700 agent rejections for my first five stories combined before I pivoted and submitted what was my newest at the time, *The Edge of Life*, to Black Rose Writing. A year and a half later, I have three books published, and another three written with release dates in 2024 and 2025. By the time this book is released, it will be my sixth, and I hope to have another in preorder. Strangely, I want to acknowledge… me.

That's an odd thing, but what if I hadn't persevered? What if I didn't have grit? I'd have given up and I wouldn't have six books. I also wouldn't have a working relationship with BRW that could lead to more books in years to come. I'm proud that I kept writing. It isn't meant to sound boastful. I'm just proud of what I've accomplished.

Publishing books can be difficult, with lots of stages. It isn't just writing, but so many rounds of editing, beta-reading, finding ARC readers, reviewing for others, and promoting, all while writing something new. Having published books has changed how I approach reading. I no longer give 1 or 2-star reviews to books, even ones I don't like. Someone worked hard writing that story and even if I am not its ideal reader, it is important to someone. I now take the approach I was taught as a child. If I don't have anything nice to say, I say nothing.

Again, I want to thank everyone at Black Rose Writing for taking a chance on me. They've allowed me to release my books out into the world and promoted them. Thank you as well to so many fellow Black Rose authors for reading and reviewing so many of my books. Six in less than two years is a lot to ask of anyone. Special thanks to Cam Torrens, Dave Buzan, Diane Hawley Nagatomo, Gary Gerlacher, and Karen K. Brees for reading everything I've asked at the drop of a hat. Your reviews are gold. I owe you all.

I also want to acknowledge more Black Rose authors who volunteered to read my *Train Hoppers* series when I needed blurbs for the third, A.J. McCarthy, Bill Schweitzer, Carla diFulco Seyler, and Terrill Sullivan. Though not Black Rose authors, I also wanted to acknowledge a few Creative Academy writers for their help and support, in particular Bonnie Jacoby, Eileen Cook, Keay Francis, Leslie Wibberley, Michele Amitrani, and Stacy Sakai.

As always, after writing a book, I wish to thank my critique partner, friend, and editor, Tracy Thillmann. She's the best luck I've had along my writing journey. I couldn't do this without her and I hope I never have to. Thank you also to my other critique partner Ben Brockway, who figured out what was missing with *Rebels and Saints*, allowing me to make it better.

I also wish to acknowledge my family who support me by buying books, talking me up to friends, and giving me the time and space to write daily—special thanks to my husband Rob, who understands that I have to write for me.

About the Author

Award-winning author Lena Gibson is a storyteller as an elementary school teacher and keeper of the family lore. She holds a First Class Honors degree in Archaeology, with minors in History, Biology, Geography, and Environmental Education from Simon Fraser University.

A voracious reader since childhood, Lena seeks wonderful books in which to escape. Because of her passion for different genres, she combines elements of many in her writing. As an adult newly recognized with autism, she often creates characters that reflect this experience.

When Lena isn't writing, she reads, practices karate, and drinks a ton of tea. She resides in New Westminster, Canada, with her family and their fuzzy overlord, Ash, the fluffiest of gray cats.

Learn more at lenagibsonauthor.ca.

Other Titles by Lena Gibson

NOTE FROM LENA GIBSON

Word-of-mouth is crucial for any author to succeed. If you enjoyed *Rebels and Saints*, please leave a review online—anywhere you are able. Even if it's just a sentence or two. It would make all the difference and would be very much appreciated.

Thanks!
Lena Gibson

We hope you enjoyed reading this title from:

www.blackrosewriting.com

Subscribe to our mailing list – *The Rosevine* – and receive **FREE** books, daily deals, and stay current with news about upcoming releases and our hottest authors.
Scan the QR code below to sign up.

Already a subscriber? Please accept a sincere thank you for being a fan of Black Rose Writing authors.

View other Black Rose Writing titles at www.blackrosewriting.com/books and use promo code **PRINT** to receive a **20% discount** when purchasing.